Rachel Heard the Crying Baby and
Followed the Sound down the Corridor,
to the Torn Walls of the Vanity—
and Heard a Scuttling Sound . . .

The baby, wherever he was, was whimpering, and the
sound seemed to be coming down the stairs. Rachel
gingerly stepped around the shards of broken glass,
over the fallen bricks, leaving footprints in the dust.
The floor was cold, the room itself was cold, colder
than it had been outside.

The baby seemed to be crying down those dark stone
steps—where did they lead?

The house now *did* seem evil and Rachel knew that if
it were anything other than just before sunrise she
would not be so terrified.

Rachel felt fear trickle down her spine. She was
suddenly overcome with dread.

Something was scratching on the stairs, like an animal
raking its claws across the stones . . .

Books by Douglas Clegg

Breeder
Goat Dance

Published by POCKET BOOKS

BREEDER

DOUGLAS CLEGG

POCKET BOOKS

New York   London   Toronto   Sydney   Tokyo   Singapore

An *Original* Publication of POCKET BOOKS

 POCKET BOOKS, a division of Simon & Schuster Inc.
1230 Avenue of the Americas, New York, NY 10020

ISBN: 0-671-67277-0

First Pocket Books printing July 1990

10 9 8 7 6 5 4 3 2 1

POCKET and colophon are registered trademarks of
Simon & Schuster Inc.

Printed in the U.S.A.

**FOR LISA SEIDMAN,
A GOOD FRIEND AND A GREAT WRITER.**

With thanks to various people who were there at the conception and the delivery: Linda Marrow, who is more than an editor; Dana Isaacson; John Scognamiglio; John Scoleri; my publisher Irwyn Applebaum; Margaret Ruley, the agent of choice; Tom, Jill, Paul, Kirsten, John, Andy, Nancy and Fritz, all of whom have opened their houses in Washington for my inspection and none of whom are depicted in this novel.

Is You Is Or Is You Ain't My Baby?

(B. Austin, L. Jourdan)
Leeds Music, Ltd.

THE SCREAMING HOUSE

1.

April 1968

The girl could still taste the kerosene on her lips.

Her name was Nadine and she had been feverish for the past four nights. The decision had not been made by her, but by her lover. She hadn't wanted to go through with it; she had no energy to resist. Just the throbbing pain, the leaking blood. If she'd been coherent, this seventeen-year-old girl would've told them that her baby was going to be all right, that she knew the baby would be all right, even if she herself died. She was not afraid of death if it meant her baby would breathe and grow.

She lay down in something cool and hard like stone, a large basin. The room smelled of rubbing alcohol and soap; the odor of kerosene and vinegar still lingered. *The perfume of death or of birth?* Above her were the most beautiful dark eyes she'd ever seen, so warm and cool at the same time; eyes that looked *into* her to find the root of this pain, this illness. Her own vision wavered, and the world around her became transparent, empty, as she tried to look beyond this shadowy room, through these beautiful eyes into another existence, into a dream where there was no pain. She saw no faces in the room, only eyes, only hands, only lips curling in smiles and anger.

Someone above her, a white hand, wiped her brow with a cold, wet hand towel. Nadine shivered; it was like ice on her forehead. These people surrounding her in this small room were no more substantial than the dreams she had at night: she thought she could pass her hand through them like

1

ghosts. Who was here with her? Who would help with the birth of her child?

A man, her lover she thought, said, "The whole fucking block's going up. What the hell's this going to do to property values?"

But the man to whom the beautiful eyes belonged, the man who watched over her as the spasms hit, grasped her hand as she tried to pass her fingers through him. "Have faith, your child shall be born." His large black hand seemed to swallow hers alive like a hawk devouring a fish. She felt his pulse—a pounding drum. It beat steadily, hopefully against the ever weakening sound of her own heart.

Where was her mother? Her mother had promised to stay with her. To hold her hand the way this man held her hand. Her mother's hand was warmer than this man's, warmer and softer, open, unfolding. Her mother was there among the smoky shadows, but why wasn't she beside Nadine now? Why would a mother hide from her daughter?

Her lover, out in that misty darkness of the room, muttered, "Jesus, do you think this could go a little faster?"

"Baron Samedi," Nadine gasped. It was a plea; the pain was clutching the baby inside her, the room was dislodging itself from the earth and running away, her womb would burst with overripe, fermented fruit. "Baron Samedi, I pray . . ."

Her lover whispered, "I'm not going to wait around here for some lunatic to shoot out the window!"

"Please," Nadine gasped to the woman she could not see who stood above her. Her ribs were chafing against her skin as if they longed to break free of her.

She knew then that she was going to die. She wasn't scared, not with the man with the dark eyes holding her, leaning toward her. They called him Baron Samedi, guardian of the graveyards and the dead. She did not believe, not like her mother believed, but if it saved her baby, Nadine would, if *he* could save her baby . . .

The man above her grinned. His teeth seemed huge, but that was her fever. His teeth seemed to be coming down for her, down for her baby, down to find the place inside her where her baby's heart beat.

Her lover screamed, "Fucking animals is what you are!"

Then her mother *(She's here! She's with me! She will protect me!)* screamed, "My baby, what you doin' to my baby girl?"

Then Nadine felt and heard nothing.

Her breathing stopped and what little life there was in her empty body ran out in a warm, red pool from between her legs.

2.

April 1989

"Maybe it's a blessing in disguise," Hugh whispered. "Maybe it's just as well, Scout."

Rachel knew that he wasn't about to do his *Let's Pretend* line: *Let's Pretend, Scout, that you're the mommy and I'm the daddy and we have a whole mess of kiddos, an acre of kiddos, and I'm coming home from work at the end of a hard day and you're exhausted and we sit up and read them bedtime stories 'til they fall asleep . . .* Nope, *Let's Pretend* went out the window when you got a miscarriage in the family. *A blessing in disguise.* She'd cried for three weeks over this particular blessing, soon followed by a therapist, two group sessions a day for three weeks, a psychiatrist, a brief (and less than heavenly) flirtation with antidepressants. She still kept the leftover pills in a shoe box beneath the bathroom sink on the off chance that she might get the urge to jump out a window again. It had been great fun, if useless, getting all the medical attention over what she basically felt was a fact of Normal Life *(lots of nice folks have miscarriages, although Rachel herself didn't seem to know any of them).* And even if she did start crying every time she saw babies, or when she accidentally wandered into the baby supply area of Dart Drug and caught herself buying Pampers, or in Safeway picking up Gerber's baby chicken. Only her work seemed to keep her from forgetting what Hugh had called "a minor glitch."

"It's just as well," Hugh said (had said, would *continue* to say).

Rachel hated him for that and also loved him for that; he even promised he would make it up to her, that he would kiss it and make it better, that this was a blow, certainly, no one would deny how tragic it was, but couldn't they turn it around? Couldn't they try to see it as a momentary setback, but in the long run an advantage? Wouldn't there be things to compensate?

She didn't really hear him say all this. She heard the words the way she would listen to the radio while ironing or eating breakfast. Instead she wondered if she really wanted to be married at all, *except* to have children; how she could've just *lived* with Hugh and that would've been enough, except she'd been pregnant, except she'd wanted a child, and now for some reason that child had chosen not to be born of her.

"Nature took care of it, Scout, it must be for the better. You have to try and see it that way," Hugh droned on, and no doubt her doctor had prepped him on the sorts of lines to feed her, and she loved him for it, and she despised him for these spineless rationalizations, but she loved him, too.

She loved him because when she didn't love him she hated herself and remembered the other woman, the one who was dead. Hugh's first wife.

Hugh always emphasized that they weren't financially ready for a baby, not yet, his feet weren't on the ground, he still had to try the bar for one more go 'round, his job as a consultant in a tax lawyer's office was only for six months and would be over soon, and how could *she* really afford to leave her firm so soon, anyway? Just a year or so at the outside and then, *yes, a whole litter of babies if you want, so you see it's just as well.* Although Hugh wouldn't say *babies,* because it was a word they both avoided.

He would blanket her with hugs and kisses while she turned her face into the pillow. *It's not a baby, it's just a little sphere, a little subdividing sphere, a glitch in the system.*

Rachel loved her husband then and hated him more than she'd ever hated anyone; and she hated her body for betraying her like that.

* * *

Later, when she was feeling less tired and Hugh brought in a large bowl of ice cream, he told her about the house his father was giving them as a late wedding present.

Rachel sniffed at the ice cream as if smelling it might make her feel better. *What I really want is a cigarette, but I guess I'll just get healthy and fat.*

She was purposefully trying not to act too excited about getting the house. That would kill it if she acted too excited; perhaps her excitement had killed her little sphere, too. Hugh didn't like it when she was enthusiastic; he didn't trust liking anything *too* much. She said, "See, your dad's coming around, I knew he would."

Hugh didn't respond. He pretended to read the paper; chocolate ice cream on his upper lip. She knew that he had only accepted the gift as a means of compensating for the miscarriage. This was part of Hugh Adair's sense of fair play, and which Rachel knew was the underlying reason he had trouble with the concept of being a lawyer: fair play was rarely involved. He thrived on frustrating himself. He wanted very little to do with his father, but he would accept the house for Rachel's sake, and then get numerous headaches concerning how miserable he was knowing he'd let the Old Man, as he called his father, buy them this way.

For a split second Rachel considered that she could avoid a lot of trouble about this wonderful if tardy wedding gift by simply saying, *"Oh, Hugh, let's wait until we can really afford a house on our own terms. Let's not have the Old Man lording it over us, let's not compromise our* integrity.

But it was only a split second, and then Rachel came to her senses.

She put the bowl of ice cream aside. "Our very first house. Is it in a good neighborhood?"

PART ONE

WHERE
THE HEART IS

JUNE

ONE

FIRST IMPRESSIONS

1.

She walked ahead of Hugh, through the alley, stepping over broken glass, around a trash heap. This side of the house was in constant shadow, this wall looked more like old plaster than stone, and the only window onto the alley was small and bricked over. *Well, who wants to look out their window and see an alley full of trash and the wall of the next building over, anyway?* When she reached the Hammer Street side of the house, facing the park, she waited for Hugh. In the park she saw a little boy and girl playing what seemed to be a game of freeze tag. Where was their mother? How could a woman let her children run through a city park like that all by themselves? This wasn't the worst or the best neighborhood in Washington, D.C., but it was getting better; even so, how could anyone take a chance like that?

The oaks had burst with heavy green branches, and there was a breeze; the heat hadn't exploded yet as it would in just a week or two. It was a quiet street. That was good. Just after rush hour and the sound of traffic from two streets over was just white noise. A jogger went by and waved, and Hugh came up behind her and said, "I saw a rat in the alley."

"Good. If he stays outside the house we'll all get along fine."

She hadn't looked at the house yet.

Our house.

She wanted Hugh to be with her, she wanted to see it clearly, she wanted it to be as if she had closed her eyes and then opened them to see *our house.* They'd driven by it three times before, she'd jogged by it once, but more to gauge the neighborhood, get a feel for the potholes and what parking was like along Hammer Street. When she'd glanced at the house before she'd just thought of it as a house, not as *our house*.

Rachel Adair turned with her husband and faced the house that was now theirs.

2.

Rachel's first sight of the front of the house in Northwest Washington was not a pleasant one: a middle-aged black woman, a bag lady from the park with her grocery cart full of trash, was squatting down near the stone steps urinating on the sidewalk. The woman was fat and moved like a Jell-O mold, wiggling down on her haunches—she pissed a stream that would apparently flow right to Rachel's Reeboks. Rachel and Hugh both looked away—up to the turret, across to the park, to the taxi pulled over on the other side of the street. When Rachel glanced back to the house, the bag lady was gone, vanished, and all that remained of her was the drying urine on the sidewalk.

City living. Rachel forgot about the bag lady and looked at her new home.

It was a simple nineteenth-century stone house— resembling every other townhouse on that side of Hammer Street, just off Winthrop Park with Kalorama and its embassies on the opposite side of Connecticut Avenue; on the other side, a shady avenue of shabby redbrick buildings that seemed to have been bombed out all the way back to Eighteenth Street. This block was the border between a good neighborhood and a bad one, the shade from the park marking the line between them. The house was gray and tall and thin, with a beard of ivy along its edge; three stories high, the bottom one, almost a basement, a separate apartment. It looked like it had once been a longer house but was sliced at the side just along the turret; the house attached to one side of it was a plain, white box-shaped house, obviously new—someone had torn down part of Rachel's house *(our house)* on one side, someone had been dissatisfied with their half of the old stone house and decided to build that ugly white thing instead with the chain-link fence in front and that threatening face of a doberman just behind the side glass of the front door.

"I always dreamed I'd live in a house like this," Rachel said, turning her attention back to her new home. Hugh led the way up the stone steps. Rachel touched the thick carved stone post beside the door: it was cold, and felt good.

Beside the front door, the brass plaque which her father-in-law had finagled out of the city government: HISTORIC HOUSES COMMISSION. DRAPER HOUSE WAS BUILT BY THE ARCHITECT JULIAN MARLOWE IN 1822. EDGAR ALLAN POE WROTE HIS FAMOUS STORY, "PREMATURE BURIAL" IN THE TURRET ROOM WHILE RESIDING AS A GUEST.

"One of the Old Man's vanities," Hugh pointed out. "Poe did stay here when it was a hotel or something, for a weekend, but it's doubtful he wrote any stories while he was here. He probably played some all-night poker games and recovered from hangovers the rest of the time. But the Old Man has always been an ace at perpetrating lies."

"A house with a *name.*"

"A full name, too. The Rose Truthful Draper House, the architect's mistress. I've heard old Rosie was a wild one."

"In what way?" Rachel asked, but at that point Hugh lifted the heavy door knocker and let it fall. It sounded like a hammer coming down on a bullet—Rachel winced at the noise, covering her ears. *"Je*sus."

"Sorry, Scout, just testing." Hugh reached in the pockets of his khakis for the front-door key. "How many keys can this place have, you may well ask." He held up a large key ring with several keys dangling from it. He pointed them out: "This one's for the front door, the downstairs hall door, this is for . . . I think the patio, and this one—I don't know, maybe the back gate. I guess we'll find that out. And this little piggy," he jangled a small key, "goes wee-wee-wee all the way home."

Rachel wasn't listening to him. "Did you hear that?"

"Huh?"

"Nothing."

11

"Was it a cat? The woman who rents the downstairs apartment has cats, I think. She's either a psych*o* or a psych*ic*, I get those two confused."

Yes, Rachel thought, *cats mewling for milk, kittens searching for their mother. I'm not going crazy after all. It's not babies. Just because I lost a baby—a sphere—doesn't mean I'm going to hallucinate about it. Cats, yep, sounds good to me.*

Then she heard it again, the sound, and for just a second she thought she saw Hugh blink twice having heard the baby crying. But she'd been thinking of babies since the humidity had risen, babies at her breasts, babies at her ankles, babies floating among the clouds. Babies were everywhere she looked. *Why does it surprise me that I think I hear them? This is what the doctor said: "You'll notice that everyone has babies except you, you'll think that somehow you're built differently from other women, that you're unnatural, but don't believe it. Miscarriages are as natural as deliveries. Rachel, you lose this one, well, somewhere down the road you'll have another." Yep, Doctor, you play the Let's Pretend game just like my husband does.*

Hugh opened the door to the inner hall. "To the dark tower, Scout."

But the baby crying: it sounded like it came from beneath the stones of the porch, right beneath her feet.

TWO

INTERIOR

1.

They met the downstairs tenant, Mrs. Deerfield, briefly—
Rachel barely got a glimpse of her when the older woman
opened her door, leaving the chain on. All Rachel caught of
her were blue eyes, pale wrinkled skin, and a shock of blond
hair the color and texture of dry hay. And a strong whiff of
either cleaning fluid or alcohol. Paint was peeling on the
apartment door. *We've got our work cut out for us.*

"Just got out of the bath, dears," Mrs. Deerfield said.
"Come round to the patio." Rachel shook the damp hand
before it slipped back behind the closing door.

"Veddy British," Rachel said low enough so as not to be
overheard.

Hugh raised his eyebrows. "Like Mary Poppins gone to
seed." He unlocked the inner door that led to the upstairs.
"Voilà," he said, flinging the door open.

Rachel went quickly through the house assessing the
damage; the dark blue wallpaper in the bathroom which
should come down, the track lighting that didn't comple-
ment the wonderful nineteenth-century flavor of the house,
the layer of grease on the stove and oven. Two bedrooms on
the top floor, one bath on each floor, the bannister was a
little rickety—would need repair but not right away—the
living room was long and with a high ceiling, and that
wonderfully large manor house fireplace set like a cave into
the wall, the kitchen *was* small, not much room to turn
around in, but the dining room was large, and there was the
patio for summer entertaining. She ran up and down the

stairs, shouting out to Hugh to come up and see this small room that would be perfect for a den. At the living room, the house twisted in an L, and Rachel clutched Hugh's hand as they went down the narrow hallway.

"Secret passages," Hugh said.

"Don't you think this is a weird layout? From the alley it didn't look like it went this way at all."

"I'm not sure, but I think when the block was divided into separate residences the divisions made their own geometric messes of things."

"So dark," she said, "when you can just see this place was made for light—they've practically boarded it up." She went and pulled a heavy curtain back from one of the second-floor hall windows. She wrote her initials in the dust on the pane.

"It's so stuffy—Hugh, come see if you can open this one."

Leaving Hugh to struggle with the windowpane, Rachel walked towards the room at the end of the hall. The door was shut; Rachel played with the doorknob until it came off in her hand. She set it on the floor. "This must be . . ." She pressed her shoulder up against the door and shoved.

"Yes!" The door swung open, slamming against the wall. "My favorite: the turret room."

The room was a semicircle, dark and cold even in the hot summer. It reminded her of a dungeon, its airless darkness conjuring up images of torture chamber paraphernalia: thumbscrews, iron maidens, bone-stretching devices, steel fetters. On the other hand, it also reminded her of the basement apartment she and Hugh lived in but without the tacky gold wallpaper. Instead, the room was plastered with tacky *dark* wallpaper—a design that was supposed to be peacock tail feathers in a paisley swirl, but which looked more like a thousand eyes staring out of a coal mine. The curtains blocking the sunlight were a dusky shade of purple, ragged and moth-eaten, dragging across the dirty floor. She shivered just looking at the room, but her mind was already working: with some white drapes, strip the wallpaper, a paint job, some good old-fashioned scrubbing, it would be the friendliest room in the house. *But who the hell wants to do all that work?*

The window was convex and enormous, like a curved screen around the turret; with the curtains drawn back it must take in a panoramic view of the park. Rachel pictured a window seat with cushions—a place to read books and sip tea on Sunday afternoons. Yes, this would be her favorite room.

"This will be the nursery," Rachel said mostly to herself, thinking Hugh was out of earshot; she said it like a prayer, like she knew it would never come true. She swept stale dusty air back with her left hand; she felt a sneeze coming on. Her wedding ring, loosening with the summer humidity, slid off her finger and clanked to the floor, reminding her again of thumbscrews and chains. She squatted down, balancing herself with one hand on the floor, the other reaching for the ring. She picked it up, but felt a stinging in her thumb: not from an imaginary thumbscrew, however, but from a splinter fresh from the floorboards. She nursed her thumb before plucking the offending bit of wood out from between her thumbnail and skin. A small period of red appeared there, just under the nail. She pressed her thumb against her lips to stop the flow of blood.

"Oh, Scout," Hugh sighed, sounding defeated; he must've heard her little prayer, her mention of the word *nursery*, which was innocent enough as words went. Hugh would go and think she was making herself sad again, thinking about the child she hadn't been able to carry. He didn't seem to understand about hope. She wanted to tell him then that she wasn't going to start crying just because she'd thought of a baby-related term. *You don't mourn the death of something that's barely eight weeks conceived do you? It's not even a baby, it's just a little sphere.*

Hugh gave up the struggle to open the hall window and came down into the turret room to her.

Since her miscarriage in the spring, he'd kept emphasizing *how right and natural* it had been to lose the baby, and *how we're not prepared for parenthood,* and *when it's right we'll know.* There were subjects they didn't talk about anymore, jokes they didn't make. Life was becoming a serious business in which spheres did not subdivide into babies.

Hugh came up to her and drew her to him, enveloped her. She liked that feeling of being inside his arms. It made her think he desired her, and she could momentarily forget that he had ever been in love with anyone else, had begun to raise a family with that other woman—that other woman who was able to give him more than Rachel had been able to. That other woman, four months pregnant, who was dead and buried.

The other woman *(wife, damn it, his first wife—why can't you even admit it?)* to whom Rachel was constantly comparing herself. *There was Joanna, beautiful, pure, and obviously fertile. And then there's* me: *making plans to steal her husband away even as Joanna's Volvo was being demolished by a drunken driver. Always, always we pay for our sins— even the not-so-nice Catholic girls who don't really believe in sin, only in stupid decisions.*

Hugh went over to the turret window, his loafers clicking like angry beetles against the echoing floor. He pulled the drapes apart; Rachel heard some of the material rip. Light flooded the room through the snowstorm of dust that blew off the curtains. The sunlight was almost too bright. Rachel squinted for an instant—she'd gotten used to the heavy darkness of the house as they'd been going through it, room to room. "These windows haven't been washed in years. You know how much work we're going to have to put into this house? It's not going to be like the apartment."

"Good thing. It'll be nice to have something that's ours."

"Famous last words." Hugh twisted his head around and arched his eyebrows. Hugh Adair could do things like that and it would *mean* something to her—it was the one thing they'd developed over the past two years, that sort of ESP that came from living with someone. Rachel often wondered if Hugh and his first wife ever had that.

"Well, it *is* ours. A gift is a gift." She didn't want her chin to look so set and determined. She didn't mean it as the challenge that Hugh might understand it to be: but there it was, in her chin, in the steady gaze of her brown eyes. Her chestnut brown bangs needed a trim, but she was happy she hadn't gotten one yet. Rachel felt her hair suitably hid her eyebrows which were forming this statement into a question: *It is ours, isn't it? You're a lawyer, you know how to be assertive, if you can do it in court you can do it at home.*

Rachel was hoping he wouldn't go off into one of his

despairing moods about accepting the wedding gift from his father again. She was glad her father-in-law was going out of his way to prove to them that he *did* finally approve of the marriage. Rachel kept trying to drum it into her husband's skull that someday he would reconcile himself with his father, and the less he had to regret about his behavior to the Old Man, the better.

There was a momentary silence in the house as they stood there; silence filtered through dust. Behind the silence and the dust, Rachel wondered what other people thought, what other couples *meant* when they weren't speaking. *"I want to scream." That must be what other couples thought when they had nothing to say,* Rachel thought as she watched Hugh's face: the lines that hadn't been there two minutes ago. *He's thinking about the sphere, too, but he's not thinking about it the way I am. He's thinking about it with relief. I want to scream but I won't scream because you won't love me if I scream.* Someone was honking their car horn in the alley, breaking through the brief silence. She smiled because she didn't want this to be a depressing repeat of the past year. "Do you think that Mrs. Deerfield will still rent downstairs when we move in?"

"We can't really ask her to move, can we? We'd be doing the kind of thing the Old Man does when he thinks a neighborhood, like this one I might add, is ripe for gentrification. Kick the poor people out and bring on the yuppies." He tended to snap whenever he talked about anyone in his family. The front of Hugh's red T-shirt was blotched with sweat; his sandy blond hair was swept back in a shiny wave across his forehead, softening his aquiline features.

"You are a yuppie, previously a preppie. The enemy is us. But I think it'll be nice to have someone living beneath us."

Hugh went back to tugging at the window. "How. Comfortable. Will. You," Hugh grunted in between his attempts, "feel . . . having a woman living in the basement who in her last life was a princess in the lost city of Atlantis?" Again, he gave up his fight with the window.

"Just great—if she likes the vibes here, and she pays the rent on the first of the month. It won't hurt the budget, will it? And I won't mind the company, either."

"But," Hugh said jokingly, "I thought you were going to be too busy fixing this place up, and then let's not even mention your conventional seventy-hour workweek."

"Oh, I know, I know, but there *are* those coffee breaks. Mom told me that her first few years of marriage she just had lunch with the girls and went shopping," Rachel sighed.

"Recherche du temps perdu," Hugh chuckled. "This is what law school did for you, it made you want things you can't have."

For a second, Rachel thought: *you asshole, Hugh.*

2.

She'd thought that when she first met him—*you asshole,* back when she was still Rachel Brennan and trying not to flunk out of law school. Although they had not exactly met, formally. She was working on the law review and Hugh edited it. Her father was dying of lung cancer, so she was taking most weekends and going home. This left little time for her law review duties, which included refiling material she used, and the editor, Hugh Adair, sent her a memo:

> Ms. Brennan,
> It seems that some of the staff have not been attending to their more clerical duties with regards to the review. Among the neglected dead are filing, returning office supplies to the supply room, and a veritable graveyard of notes which have not been trashed. (Are they valuable? Should we start an archives for your research?) Perhaps if your office skills need sharpening, we can provide a refresher course in orderliness.
> I hope this memo is sufficient.
> Thank you,
> Hugh Adair, Editor-in-Chief

The words that had formed in her mind were not just *you asshole,* but *prick* as well.

Rachel had seen Hugh in a few of her classes, but did not know the handsome man with the winning smile was the same geek who wrote the officious memo. She wrote back to him:

Dear Mr. Editor,

Thank you for the delightful reading. It really made my life, honest. How kind of you to fire such knowing bullets my way. How compassionate of you to take into account the extenuating circumstances of my having to return home on the weekends and some weekdays for my father's last hours on this earth, to say nothing of the fact that a few of us have to work our way through law school while others sit on their asses while daddy pays off all those nasty credit card bills. If you want a secretary, I would be happy to apply for the position assuming, unlike the work many of us do on the review, secretarial work is PAID.

Again, thank you for such a COMPASSIONATE and MOTIVATING memo. I promise to be a good Girl Scout from here on in.

Warmly,
Ms. Brennan

The next day, Rachel received this brief note:

Scout,
Well, I guess this means lunch is out.
The Big Bad Editor

This struck her as funny—Rachel had a horrible time bearing a grudge, particularly when in the back of her mind she knew he was right. She had sloppy work habits. She was sure that her only salvation would come in a job where she had her own secretary to handle filing and neatness, because she was a mess. And then a good healthy dose of Catholic guilt had gotten the better of her. She'd been calling Hugh an asshole to everyone within earshot, and she felt bad about it.

So one Sunday, she returned early from seeing her father, walked right up to Hugh and said: "Lunch would be great."

"And you are? . . ."

"A good Girl Scout."

She immediately saw his wedding ring. That was one of the first things she looked for in a man, that or a tan line where he'd removed the ring. For some reason married men had always been attracted to her, and single men were not interested. Rachel rarely dated. "You're married," she said.

"It's just lunch," he told her. "I'm not only married, I'm, wonder of wonders, *happily* married. Can't an editor ask one of his staffers to lunch? I promise not to seduce you."

Too bad, she'd thought.

3.

"Penny for your thoughts," Hugh said. He stood in silhouette against the blinding sunlight that filtered through the dust-streaked window.

Rachel kissed him. *I want to scream,* she was thinking, but she knew this was not exactly the thought he wanted to hear.

He held her tightly, and she looked out the dirty window, down on the park where a woman played catch with her three children while their father opened a picnic basket.

"It's so damn humid." Hugh sounded as annoyed as Rachel now felt.

Rachel tugged herself free from him. She went over to the other window in the hall. She pulled upwards on the sill, and managed to open the window. "There," she said, looking out over the patio and the alley behind the house, "get some fresh air in here. Hello down there!" she shouted in a singsong friendly voice, and then turning to Hugh, said, "Mrs. Deerfield looks so lonely, let's go down to the patio and be neighborly."

THREE

MRS. DEERFIELD

"You believe in omens?" Mrs. Deerfield asked. Her British accent was like thick clotted cream. Rachel noticed she had trouble pronouncing her *l*'s; it sounded like she'd said *"beweev."*

"Good or bad?" Rachel produced a grin which made her feel uncomfortably phony. She had succeeded in dragging Hugh downstairs and outside to examine the split-level patio. Half of the patio was for the benefit of the lower apartment, and was defined by a neat brick rectangle under the wrought-iron staircase. Mrs. Deerfield was sitting at a small table beneath the shade of the stairs, drinking what Rachel thought was tea, but which Mrs. Deerfield assured her was a mug of Kahlua and milk. She offered a mug to Rachel as she came down the stairs ahead of Hugh. Rachel checked her watch: yes, it was only ten A.M. She shook her head to the offer of the liqueur.

"Well," Mrs. Deerfield said, "this omen is particularly good. My Ramona vomited a hairball."

The real estate woman had warned them that Penelope Deerfield was an odd bird who had been living in the basement apartment since before First Properties had begun handling it.

Mrs. Deerfield must've been in her early sixties, and her hair was dyed a golden yellow, worn long to her shoulders as if she were still a young girl. Hugh said later, rather cruelly Rachel thought, "She looks like a drag queen waiting to happen." Her heavily mascaraed eyes were of that clear translucent blue that always seemed to be looking over your shoulder, or through you. She wore a silk dressing gown with a red gold Oriental print, its darted edges revealing a pink calf-length slip beneath.

Mrs. Deerfield was so short that she appeared to be clinging to the table to keep from shrinking any further, and her hands were small like a child's.

Rachel pretended to be examining the perimeter of the patio, testing the gray wooden gate for sturdiness. She was afraid if she stared too long at Mrs. Deerfield it would be rude, and yet she was fascinated by the diminutive woman.

At the mention of the name *Ramona,* Hugh called down from the iron landing at the top of the stairs, "You have a daughter, then, Mrs. Deerfield?"

Mrs. Deerfield, ignoring his comment, continued. "Ramona is a Himalayan of distinct breeding, and she rarely has hairballs, but it is a good sign I think that this should happen on the day you will be moving in. I have a talent for the interpretation of such events. Omens, dreams, portents, new landlords. We have a ghost, you know. That's right, one of the early occupants of the house. She's harmless, of course, makes some noise now and again. Rose Draper, it seems, is *still* waiting for her lover to return home. But ghosts are attention getters, aren't they? Like little children, they just want someone to watch them, to know they exist."

Rachel nodded pleasantly not understanding what in God's name she was talking about; but just the idleness of the monologue was a delight, nothing about torts, briefs, or depositions. Just pure talk for talk's sake.

"May I inquire as to my . . . status, in this present situation, Mrs. Adair?" Mrs. Deerfield's voice acquired a curious drop as she spoke, as if she were embarrassed to even be asking such a common question.

"Call me Rachel, I still have trouble with the 'Mrs. Adair.'" Rachel, feeling odd standing by the back gate, walked over to the small white table that Mrs. Deerfield draped herself across as she poured out more Kahlua in her mug. Rachel sat down uncertainly in a wobbly wire chair.

"You sure you won't have a cup? It's just like a milkshake. A grown-up milkshake." Mrs. Deerfield lifted her mug.

"No thanks." Rachel heard Hugh *ahem* from above.

"Well, Rachel, then, the apartment—"

"Well, I think it would be great if you were able to stay on in your place."

"About the rent increase . . ." Again that embarrassed dive to the voice, like a child confessing to having wet herself.

Rachel looked up; she could not see Hugh standing above them, although she saw a bit of his hand clutching the dark, thin bannister. His knuckles were white. "Hugh? There's no increase, is there?"

Another throat clearing, and Rachel was worried that he might spit. Finally: "No, no, Scout, there's no rent increase. We're all status quo here."

Mrs. Deerfield reached across the table, patting Rachel on the wrist, "Thank—" but both of them felt it: a shock. Rachel brought her hand away; Mrs. Deerfield kept her arm outstretched. "You're a sensitive."

"Sometimes *too* sensitive."

"No, dear, I mean *a sensitive.* You're open, to the influence. A small percentage of the world's population is and always has been. Have you ever had any kind of psychic experience?"

Rachel heard Hugh whisper under his breath, "Sounds like a job interview." She hoped that their tenant didn't hear him. Sitting down on the steps, not bothering to be polite and come join them, he said, "Tell that story your mom always tells."

"Oh, that's just silly, and anyway I don't think it ever really happened."

Hugh began speaking for her. "When she was six, in church, she told her mother that the—Scout, you can tell this better than I can."

Rachel sighed, grinning as if she were embarrassed. "Well, I—oh, this is stupid." But Mrs. Deerfield gazed at her attentively, fascinated. "Well, I wasn't raised really Catholic, but we went to mass at Christmas and Easter, and during one of these Christmas services, I apparently went up to the altar. There was this figure of Mary and the baby Jesus, and I started petting the baby's head and told it not to cry. 'Don't cry, baby Jesus, don't cry.' Something like that. I wouldn't classify that as anything *occult*."

Mrs. Deerfield's face became pinched; she nodded her head as if thinking of something else. "When we're in the right place at the right time, and when we are the right person, *sensitive* to these things, it can happen. I'm of the opinion that these things are perfectly normal phenomena that simply haven't yet been explained."

Rachel was barely listening to her—she was thinking of that other time. "And then with daddy."

"Oh, Scout," she heard Hugh's voice as if from a great distance.

"After he died—two years ago—I was still in law school. I didn't know he was dead; mom didn't even know. I went back to our apartment between classes and this sounds really dumb, but the lazy susan in the pantry started spinning, just a little. And then I saw him—just for a second. Like an afterimage. Like the second before someone leaves a room, and you blink, and they're gone and you're not sure if you saw them or not. I heard him say something, in my head—you know how you know someone so well that your mind can even reproduce their voice? All he said was, 'It's done, sweetie, but mom'll need your help.' I knew he was dead. And then ten minutes later, mom called in tears." Rachel was thinking how much she wouldn't mind lighting a cigarette up right then. What little breeze there had been wafting between the alleyways had died, and she smelled something bad, something decomposing. It must've come from the dumpster out back by the car. The odor of rotting meat. *I am not going to start crying. If I start crying, Hugh's going to think I am losing it again the way I lost it over the miscarriage, and I am not losing it. If I keep talking, I will lose it, but if I just shut up like a good Girl Scout . . .*

Mrs. Deerfield perked up suddenly, as if injected with vitality. "You *are* special, dear, I'm sure of it."

"I've always thought so," Hugh said from the stairs. Rachel looked back to Mrs. Deerfield and felt such compassion emanating from the woman that she felt okay. The moment had passed. *Just don't start talking about hearing babies crying anywhere close by or you will be certifiable.*

Mrs. Deerfield smiled, revealing an impossibly crooked overbite and an enormous gap between her front teeth. Her blue eyes became devilish slits as she said, "You are a nice young couple, aren't you?"

"What were the former tenants like?"

"Ooh!" She shivered as if recalling the taste of a particularly sour medicine. "Horrible, unnatural persons, sexual perversions night and day, loud music, parties. It tested me, it certainly did, their friends tramping across my little garden, their foul language, the orgies, and worst of all, Rachel," and at this, she leaned over the table almost knocking the mug and bottle over, clutching Rachel's hand in her own tiny Deerfield fingers, "worst of all, most ob*scene,"* Mrs. Deerfield's eyes widened like a television tube warming up from a pinpoint to a nineteen-inch screen, "they hated *cats."*

FOUR

THE OLD MAN

If you glanced over at the sleek cherry-red Jaguar stuck like every other car in the middle of a traffic jam on the Fourteenth Street Bridge—and everyone caught in the tar pit of rush-hour traffic heading across the Potomac *was* rubbernecking to catch a glimpse of the Jaguar and *what was going on inside the car*—you would see a fiery flash of red hair whisking up and down like a dust mop just behind the steering wheel while the man who was driving kept a grimace of pain, or embarrassment, or pleasure spread across his fat face like Nero fiddling.

Gradually, the motions of the red hair slowed, and once, it rose up completely from the steering wheel. It was attached at the scalp to a pale girl with dark circles under her eyes, high cheekbones, sparklingly wet ruby-red lips and spidery false eyelashes. She looked less like a whore from the streets of Washington than a very tired girl of thirty-six who did not appreciate the car's air conditioner blowing cold air directly on her face as she went about her work.

"I'm not paying you to stop," the man said. The skin on his face seemed to have been pulled back tight, as if he'd once had a botched face lift. His hair—white, sparse, and blue in parts—began in a neat ridge at the very peak of his head, combed greasily back. Buttressing jowls supported the gothic arches of his various chins, and you might wonder if you could guess his age by counting those chins, like the rings of a tree. His cheeks and upper lip were spotted with sweat, which he wiped at with his fingers. His small, dark eyes were pushed by the puffy bags beneath them into eternal squints. He'd apparently been sewn right into the dark suit he wore—it looked like it could never come off without undoing the sleeves, the pants legs, and then piece by piece, the rest of the material. It was his exoskeletal armor.

The girl coughed, clutching her throat. "Something's caught in my throat, I think it's a hair." Her voice hit notes that most baritones would be proud of—it was far huskier than her small, fine-boned china doll face, powdered dead white, would suggest. She shook her wispy mane of red hair, with curls as large as malt liquor cans, and pursed her lips as if tasting something sour. The coughing continued.

"I don't know how the fuck you'd get a hair with this *thing* on," the man said disgustedly. He glanced down briefly at his crotch. Laying like a fat wobbly slug from between folds of blue pin stripe: his rubber-enshrouded penis.

Between coughs, the girl gasped, "These days you got to be careful."

"I'm not paying you to be *careful.*"

The redheaded girl began rubbing up and down on her throat—the man noted that it was similar to her hand-job technique. Her voice became garbled with hawking phlegm and intermittent coughs. "Sorry," she said. Tears were coming to her eyes. She began chanting the word *ahem,* over and over as if it were some mantra to cure throat problems.

"Shit," was all the man said.

Someone honked their horn from the car in back. Traffic was again moving across the bridge; the old man pressed his foot gently down on the accelerator. The girl had risen completely up in her seat, and was now leaning against her door, the side of her face pressed against the window as she continued to hack away. Her dress was sheer, lollipop red, covered with tiny fairy sparkles. The man would later find sparkles in his underwear and worry if this was a sign of some venereal disease.

His name was Winston Adair, and he worried constantly about the state of his penis—it was the center of his being, and it was one of the few parts of his body that had not become elephantine and bloated over the years. While procreation had never been his goal (although he had sired two sons and countless bastards that may or may not have survived birth), he enjoyed putting his member in whatever female orifice was for hire and available. Winston Adair had gone to fat in the past twenty years, but it only added to his imposing presence: he looked like a man who carried the excess luggage on his body like an arsenal. People who saw him wondered if he was as wide as he was tall. The streetwalkers who saw what he liked to call his Washington Monument tended to view it more as the part of the balloon where you blow.

And the redheaded streetwalker coughing next to him in his Jaguar was not inflating the balloon at all. As they crossed the Fourteenth Street Bridge to the George Washington Parkway, he reached across the seat and grabbed her by the wrist, keeping his left hand on the steering wheel.

She looked like she wanted to say something along the lines of "you're hurting me," but the coughing stopped her. She was trying to hold the coughs in, trying to swallow them, but they burst through her nose when she kept her mouth shut.

"Goddamn you, cocksucker, I paid you twenty-five bucks for those lips, and you're not getting out of it." Winston was always surprised by his voice in situations like this—in court he could sound like Clarence Darrow, but with a hooker he always sounded like a young naive boy. He turned the car in the direction of the Iwo Jima Memorial.

When he was twenty-one, he'd been with a whore who seemed as tall as the bridge they were standing under, and she had a face that could stop a truck. She was less black than a coffee yellow, as if she'd been sick for months and had just recovered. She'd had a slight dark mustache on her upper lip, but he was so horny at that point he would've fucked a hole in the ground. And fucking her had been like sticking his dick in a muddy hole. He imagined he was doing that when he humped the whore, his penis sliding in and out of a dark hole, loose pebbles tumbling against his sensitive skin—they screwed on the muddy bank, and he felt the ooze sliding like exploring fingers beneath his testicles, her yellow brown rump slapping noisily into the suction cup of earth and water.

And then, it had happened.

Just as he was coming, trying to yank his penis out of that whore because he'd been told you didn't catch the clap if you didn't come inside them, he felt something other than her fingers, and her damp receptacle, something other than the cool mud of spring beneath his scrotum.

Something small and hairy and ticklish. Tiny. Crawling. Up his balls. And then several of them. Perhaps a dozen.

Before he saw them and screamed, he saw the look on the whore's face, the thick-lipped smile, the eyes turned inward on themselves exposing the whites to him.

The fucking whore knew.

She knew.

She'd met him under the bridge because she knew this would happen. Winston, aged twenty-one, glanced down at his shriveling penis.

They covered his penis, his testicles, his thighs.

Mud dauber wasps.

"Fucking bitch!" he screamed, slapping the redheaded girl with all his energy. The back of her head hit the window with a sharp crack. The girl's eyes, bogged with tears, didn't even seem to register pain from this. She was still coughing.

They were parked along the drive up the Iwo Jima Memorial. The girl's hands were scraping skin off her throat; she began inhaling deeply, but Winston didn't hear any air coming out.

The whore knew, the fucking whore knew.

Winston Adair grabbed the girl by her hair, twisting his fingers into the ringlets.

He pulled her face over his penis.

"Maybe if you get to work it'll help." He pressed her lips against the tip of the wagging condom, and miraculously, her lips parted, and the redheaded whore from Fourteenth Street began sucking.

They looked like small jewels at first, parts of a necklace come loose. They were a sapphire blue in the twilight shade beneath the bridge, and he'd really thought that maybe they were the whore's, that they'd fallen off when they were rocking back and forth in the cool mud.

But then he saw their small legs, and their long slender wings.

And the pincers extending from their diamond-shaped heads.

Mandibles opening and closing, opening and closing.

Antennae touching his shriveling penis.

And then the pain had begun, somewhere in the back of his head at first, which he thought was awfully funny considering where the wasps were hanging out—a pain like a long sharp needle being thrust in his ear, poking around, twisting.

It took a few seconds before the pain localized to his crotch.

His fist was tight in the girl's hair as he remembered, but he felt a sharp pain, and looked down. The girl kept her head in his lap, her eyes wide with terror, gasping, sucking in air, breathing in, breathing in, breathing in.

But not breathing out.

She gazed up at him as if she had never seen a human being before. She looked like a Polaroid of a whore, not the living, breathing thing.

Winston noticed that his penis was a pinkish red color from her strenuous sucking. It felt sore. *But not as bad as when he was in his twenties.*

Winston noticed that the condom was no longer covering his penis.

When the girl stopped breathing in, she stopped breathing altogether.

Panic hit him in the gut like a tank of bad chili—he felt imprisoned in his tight suit—a spoonful of urine leapt out of his penis before he could bring it under conscious control. "You bitch, don't you die!" He pulled her jaw back—it wanted to bite down on his fingers—he reached back into her mouth. *It felt like dripping jelly, it felt like the inside of a rat's belly, it felt like a fucking mud dauber's nest.* He could feel the slippery edge of the condom that she'd sucked down her throat. *Lady, if you could figure out a way to live and keep this thing implanted down there permanently, you could revolutionize safe sex.*

Twice, the condom slipped through his fingers.

And then, praying for a miracle—*who the hell are you praying to?*—the third try, he managed to catch the rubber on the edge of his ragged middle fingernail. He hoisted it up. When it came as far as her tongue, he yanked the condom out and tossed it onto the dashboard.

He shook her, holding her indelicately by the shoulders.

But it wasn't so bad, those wasps biting him, really chowing down on his gonads—it hurt like an atom bomb, but that wasn't the worst of it. You forget pain as you get older, you forget the feeling that you've just stuck your Washington Monument into a garbage disposal when you screw enough women. You forget it in the face of other things. Worse things.

But at twenty-one, the worst of it was the whore's laughing.

The worst of it was looking down between her legs, and seeing where those wasps came from.

The worst of it was seeing that the mud dauber wasps were coming out of the woman's vagina.

The redheaded girl coughed, opening her eyes. Her eyelashes dripped with tears. Mucus flowed in a thick stream out of her nostrils. She wiped at her face. She sniffed. When she breathed in, she breathed out.

She was alive.

And she spoke.

She spoke with a man's voice, a man with a thick French accent.

A man with whom he'd done business once upon a time.

Before Winston Adair could get the fuck out of his cherry-red Jaguar, away from the whore with the man's voice, she whispered to him: *"Breeder."*

FIVE

CAUSE FOR CELEBRATION

1.

"I would've given anything to see the look on her face."
Hugh was laughing so hard he had to put his fork down.

They decided to celebrate off their usual budget, and so
they went into Georgetown for an Italian dinner. Hugh wore
the blue seersucker jacket he always felt uncomfortable in;
this was for Rachel's benefit—she loved the way he looked
in that jacket with his faded khakis, blue shirt and bow tie.
"You just might be the only man in America who doesn't
look goofy in a bow tie," she told him as she adjusted it
against his neck earlier in the evening. Hugh felt he looked
too conspicuously "yup." Rachel thought he looked disarm-
ingly handsome.

"You're so attractive with linguini on your chin, here—"
Rachel reached across the red-checkered tablecloth with her
napkin and wiped away the bit of food beneath her husband's lower lip. She'd already spilled tomato sauce rain-
drops down the front of her blouse, and in trying to daub
them away had turned the droplets into a crimson smudge.
("You can dress me up," she'd said, half joking, half
despairing, "but you can't take me out.")

Hugh shook his head from side to side. *"Most obscene,"*
he bit down on the words in his imitation of Mrs. Deerfield.
"They hated cats."

"Everyone's watching, now will you stop it?" But Rachel
could not help laughing herself. "Imagine, Kahlua and milk
at ten in the morning." She glanced towards the waiter for a
minute because she realized what she had just said and

could not bring herself to meet Hugh's brief glare. Hadn't she seen Hugh downing Bloody Marys that last year he was in law school, always before his eight o'clock class? But she mustn't think about that: it had been her one condition that before they got married he would stop drinking. And he had stopped, or at least cut down considerably which was the next best thing. *The same way I've cut out smoking,* Rachel thought, guiltily remembering the single cigarette she kept in her purse for life's little emotional emergencies. She'd given up her pack-a-day habit with her pregnancy and had stayed off them even after the miscarriage. "She really is something, though. In this world but not *of* it, as daddy would say."

"I'm willing to bet the former tenants really did give her a good scare."

"Who were they?" Rachel's eyes returned to him. She looked like a child ready for a particularly good bedtime story. Sometimes, not always, but sometimes she felt as comfortable and safe with Hugh as she had as a girl with her father.

"Oh, a nice gay couple—it was really they who were responsible for cleaning that place out, getting rid of the garbage. The place was practically empty for nearly twenty years—every vagrant in Washington must've slept there at one time or another. So when the Old Man decides that folks are returning to the city, he kicks out whoever's squatting there, has a team go in and do some superficial cleaning, but it was really those two young men who deserve all the credit. They're the ones who did the bookshelves. And the ornate bannister—as shaky as it is. *And* the fireplace. Did you notice how well the ceiling was restored? Them, too. I'm a little surprised by the grimy kitchen and the filth in the turret room, but you can't have everything."

"And they just left? They buy their own place or something?"

"Who knows? I think they moved out to the suburbs themselves. Too many breeders moving in to D.C."

"You know, Hugh, that's one of your less attractive qualities, saying that word *breeders* like people are cattle." Rachel wanted to add, *and I wouldn't mind breeding a little in the next year or two, either,* but decided that wouldn't be subtle enough for Hugh. "Or when you call your father 'the Old Man' like he's not even worth considering."

"I'm not about to call him 'daddy' like some debutante from Potomac." Hugh raised his palms as if to ward off a curse. "Just joking, Scout, you're not even *from* Potomac. Jeez, Scout, is the honeymoon really over?"

She felt his shoe scuffing against her ankle beneath the table. "I'm sorry, I guess I'm not in the best of humors. Daddy's sort of my sacred cow, and I know if he were alive, the two of you would get along really well. I guess when I hear you, you know, talk about your father like that . . . well, I'm just tired right now."

"All right, I'll lay off the lousy jokes for a few minutes anyway. So how did you like the stuff about the ghost?" Hugh asked.

"I think it's romantic," Rachel said. "I think it's neat that old Rose Draper still walks the halls waiting for Julian Marlowe to return."

"Ah, yeah," Hugh wrinkled his nose, "except for one little detail, Scout."

Rachel raised her eyebrows inquiringly.

Hugh grinned that perfect orthodontic grin of his.

"Really romantic, if it weren't for the fact that Rosie Draper was a notorious whore. They say she was the Typhoid Mary of syphilis cases this side of the Potomac. They called her The Clapper as a term of endearment."

2.

As she got ready for bed that night, Rachel looked not so fondly at their tiny one-bedroom basement for what she hoped was one of the last times. "Sassy and I can move the stuff that fits into the car on Thursday—I'm not going in to the office—and you've got an interview in the morning, right? But if you could be home by, say, *two,*" she called out from the bathroom to Hugh who didn't respond. "Hugh?" Rachel glanced out the door to the square bedroom. Hugh had fallen asleep on top of the covers in his khakis and pale blue button-down shirt. He looked adorable with his hair all mussed, the way his chest expanded and deflated while he snored lightly.

It all comes out in the wash, right? Between you and me, Hugh, I don't think we were fit to be parents yet. It was a silly thing, and maybe you were right, maybe it was a blessing in disguise. You'll get a job, and then in a few years when we have put away a little nest egg, we'll have some kiddos and I'll just be a mommy for a while. But first, first over everything else, we'll make a home together.

"Thank you for letting us take the house," she whispered quietly.

Her husband snarfled a reply as he sleepily turned over on his stomach. Rachel went over to the edge of the bed and sat down. She reached out and stroked Hugh's back. She felt the breaths he was taking, anticipated the snores, wondered what he was dreaming. They'd had their problems in the past year, but things seemed to be working out. Rachel was positive that the new home would help. In a larger place they would at least avoid the arguments that cramped quarters seemed to encourage.

And maybe on Thursday he would come back from the job interview, into their new home, with good news.

SIX

AFTER THE INTERVIEW

1.

Hugh walked up Connecticut Avenue in the rain. The streets steamed. Noontime traffic was awash with honkings and skiddings and brake slammings. Hugh was not crossing at the crosswalk, he was not waiting for the light, he was not looking both ways.

"Fucking asshole!" a cabbie shouted as Hugh passed in front of the taxi on his way to DuPont Circle.

Exactly, Hugh considered: *fucking asshole.*

It was the phrase in his mouth when he'd gone up to the tenth floor of the building at McPherson Square, waited at the receptionist's desk for fifteen minutes, and then was given an audience of another quarter hour with his old fraternity brother, Raymond "Bufu" Thompson.

"Hey, Bufu," *Hugh had said, extending his hand.*

Thompson caught his hand but didn't shake it; he just took it and dropped it. "I'm afraid my associates call me Raymond these days, Hugh." Thompson looked like every young Washington lawyer: well groomed, eager, shallow and possessing that pathological trait of always seeing the world as a movie in which he is the star. The power tie and blue pin-stripe suit didn't tarnish that image one bit. Bufu Thompson, his old roomie, his frat-rat brother, the only guy who could turn in a term paper two weeks late and still act stunned when he flunked the course—this man looked like every other man in every other office in downtown Washington.

Hugh walked across DuPont Circle, and then up to

KramerBooks. It was a bookstore with a cafe called Afterwords, and Hugh found during his recent days of unemployment that he could sift through the stacks of books and then sit and have some coffee and a sandwich, and watch all of Washington go by before the end of the day.

"I'm looking for a book," he told the clerk. "I know you guys don't have it because I've been looking all week. It's called *Diaries of An Innocent Age,* by Verena Standish. Can I maybe get you all to order it?" At least Hugh could accomplish this: ordering the book. When Rachel heard that Verena Standish, wife to the diplomat, had written about Draper House in her published diary, she seemed interested in reading it.

After Hugh ordered the book, he grabbed a copy of *City Paper* at the entrance, and then went back to the tables that lined the long window in the back. A pretty blond girl who looked like she was about ten years younger than him—maybe twenty, twenty-one—was sitting, waiting for someone. She glanced over at him and smiled.

He smiled back.

She raised her cup of coffee in a silent toast. He kept smiling; he couldn't help it. When was the last time a pretty young girl had smiled at him? Was she a student at GW? At American U.? At Catholic?

But it had gone too far—she stood up and came over to his table. "Hi," she said.

Hugh was startled; he could feel his heartbeat under his tongue. He was soaked from the rain; his tan suit felt like a moist towelette wrapped around him. He combed his fingers through his hair, squeezing water out. He bit his lower lip but he couldn't bring himself to look at her face. He was trying to look down into his own coffee. He nodded his head and said a slight "hello." He made sure she noticed his wedding band by tapping on the table nervously with his left hand.

"My name's Isabel."

Hugh and Isabel exchanged a few pleasantries. The whole time Hugh was wondering how to get rid of her: the wedding ring hadn't done the trick. Then he remembered the one thing that most women seemed to find absolutely resistible.

"Yeah, well, I've been looking for work. Haven't had a job in a while."

Within seconds, Isabel excused herself; the rain seemed to be letting up, she had places to go, friends to meet, oh, and her boyfriend, who by the way has a job, was picking her up across the street at the Metro.

How had Bufu Thompson put it? Oh, yeah. "I guess of all people in this town, you don't need me telling you what it's like. Your dad's got the biggest firm around, and you're coming to me for work? We're part of this machine, you and me, Hugh. We all get stamped out like gingerbread men— and we're all after the same jobs. I can maybe throw some paralegal garbage your way, but you don't want that, do you? Now, if you'd take the bar again, maybe pass it this time— and I know you've got it in you—hey, if a guy with your background is coming to me, a junior shitkicker—" And Hugh had thought then: good, Bufu, they say the unexamined life is not worth living and you've only just taken the hint that if you had to examine yours it would take a team of highly-trained proctologists. "—with your connections—I even think Rachel could probably bail you out of this more than someone like—oh, man, don't look at me like that, Adair, I'm giving you some sincere advice here—"

Without realizing what he was doing, Hugh ordered a glass of white zinfandel. The rain had not let up as the blond Isabel had claimed when she abandoned him; it seemed to be coming down harder. The glass of wine was suddenly there before him.

Just a glass of wine. He had never been an alcoholic—that was something Rachel had dreamed up. She was from a family of teetotalers, never saw a bottle of anything in the house when she was growing up. So to her, one or two (or three or four) drinks meant a disease. Wine wasn't all that bad, and anyway—he missed the taste of it. That was the worst thing about giving up alcohol for Rachel: the taste of wine. It was such a hassle to put people out at parties and have to drink soda, especially since wine, one glass anyway, didn't have all that much alcohol. Now, if he had ordered a carafe, *that* might be considered excessive at midday, but not a glass. Especially with the headache he was getting, just thinking about Bufu Thompson and the whole fucking legal profession. Sometimes Hugh wondered how Rachel could live with all that bullshit. He wondered how he could have been so goddamn starry-eyed in law school.

He also wondered why in hell he had allowed himself to fall in love with Rachel. Why had he done that to a nice girl like Rachel Brennan? He rarely thought about his late wife, Joanna—it was as if that marriage was a picture from someone else's scrapbook.

His father's scrapbook.

Unlike Rachel, Joanna had been the perfect debutante, someone his father absolutely approved of, a woman who, as the Old Man had put it, "has what it takes."

What it takes.

The waitress came by with another glass of wine.

"Did I order this?" he asked.

She nodded. "But if you don't want it—" She made a motion to take the glass away.

Hugh shook his head. "No, it's all right, I guess I did order it—rainy days always make me thirsty."

He thought about his father, in the Volvo with his pregnant wife Joanna, and he wondered why in hell the Old Man had been allowed to escape that accident alive.

2.

Let's Pretend, Scout. Hugh raised his glass to the people passing on the street. *Good Christ, Scout, Let's Pretend I haven't failed you in your search for the perfect daddy. Well, slap my face for thinking that!* And Hugh reached up with his free hand and slapped his own face. It didn't even sting. "I love my wife, you know." He didn't realize he was talking to anyone until the bartender replied, "Sure, buddy, I love mine, too. Tied one or two on this afternoon?"

One? Two? Hugh Adair had lost count of the number, seven, maybe? How many glasses had he drunk? If only he'd ordered by the bottle, he could look at it and say: all right, I've had two bottles. But ordering by the glass was so deceptive. He wasn't even sitting at a table at the bookstore cafe; he was leaning against the bar at Childe Harold's—at some point, he had crossed the street.

"You okay?" the bartender asked.

"At times," Hugh replied. He ordered coffee. "Hell, just bring the whole pot."

Hugh Adair had an epiphany right there at Childe Harold's, sipping black coffee. It came to him, probably because of the ratio of stimulant to depressant—just enough caffeine to get his neurons shooting around those dendrites, but not enough to override the deeply philosophical effects of the alcohol. He was thinking about his career which was no career. The work in the tax law firm had been little more than glorified paralegal work, all the more humiliating because his wife had a terrific job with one of the better firms in town and had passed the bar exam her first try. Hugh had yet to pass it, and he dreaded the next go around with it. He was sick of tests. Sick of job hunting. Sure, he'd begun the job search with enough confidence to launch a rocket, but within the space of a few months all the glitches in the system became apparent: he really disliked the company of lawyers, with the single exception of Rachel. Rachel who seemed so ill suited to the legal world, and yet there she was: *successful, damn her, and she didn't even want to be successful, she just wanted to work for a few years and then get out and turn Let's Pretend into reality. How the hell had she gotten through law school if she didn't really want to be a lawyer, anyway?* But he knew the answer to *that*, and stupidly enough it was the same answer he might've given, but in less complimentary terms: *Daddy. "He just wanted to make sure I could take care of myself, and I wanted to do that one thing for him, get a law degree, before he passed away,"* she'd told Hugh, and she'd fulfilled that obligation imagining that somehow it would keep her father alive a year or two longer. *Not like* me, *I was, ahem, kinda hoping my Old Man would bite the big one before I turned thirty.* Again, Hugh slapped his own face, or at least thought he did. *Well, hush my mouth, more wishful thinking.*

And there it was, the ultimate *Let's Pretend.*

Let's Pretend that if I clean my room up every day and put the toilet seat down and wash behind my ears and go to law school, Let's Pretend the Old Man will die before I'm thirty.

But Let's Pretend will always get you in the end, Scout, because they're just more words from a bullshit artist. You do things based on Let's Pretend and your whole damn life goes down the toilet with the lid left up. "It's not even a choice," he told the bartender.

"What's that?"

"This whole lawyer thing. Life. The pursuit of happiness." The barroom was spinning. Hugh tasted something sour at the back of his throat. He began hiccuping.

"Maybe I better call you a cab."

"Call me whatever you want . . ." Hugh shrugged.

SEVEN

MOVING

"Well, it always rains when you move," Sassy Parker said, and Rachel could practically hear Sassy's smoker's lungs vacuuming up the air in one terrific *whoosh* as they lifted the long cardboard box around the corner through the front door. Sassy's short afro-styled hair glistened with the rain as if it barely concealed diamonds among the black curls. Both women were soaked to the skin; when they were safely inside the downstairs hall, Rachel set down the large cardboard box and ran upstairs and into the townhouse.

She returned a few seconds later with towels.

"You didn't tell me you have a tenant." Sassy nodded towards 1201-B's mailbox.

"Penelope Deerfield, she's a nice lady," Rachel said, flopping a pink towel over Sassy's head. Rachel squeezed the water out of her hair and shook it out like a wet dog coming inside. "These summer storms." She had changed out of her business clothes after she'd left the office at ten, just stopping in there to drop off some papers. She had scrounged through their packed suitcases and come up with these painter's pants, and one of Hugh's smelly old basketball T-shirts; the rain seemed to coax the odor of the gymnasium right out from the armpits. Rachel combed her wet, squeaky hair back into a ponytail, tying it up with a rubber band. She felt more like a twenty-eight-year-old bobby soxer than a junior associate with the firm of Newton, Bancroft & Hamer.

"Remember Barbie's best friend Midge? That's who you

remind me of, Retch," Sassy said, laughing. Sassy was taller than Rachel by about five inches; Rachel had always figured her friend was pushing six feet. They'd been roommates as undergraduates, and Sassy seemed to be the only girlfriend of Rachel's who truly understood her. As well as her craving for nicotine. Sassy had been working at the *Washington Herald-Tribune,* the third-rated newspaper in the city, but had moved up quickly and now ran the "Home" section, which sponsored an annual house tour through the old neighborhoods of Washington. Rachel hoped that one day Draper House would be on that tour. *Once we get it fixed up.*

Normally, Sassy looked pretty glamorous, "as every big-city assistant editor of trash newspapers should," Sassy would herself have said, but right now, dressed in baggy chinos and a white cotton blouse ("Looks like something out of the *Victoria's Secret* catalog," she said, glancing down at the damp material which seemed to have molded to the shape of her breasts), Sassy looked simple and unassuming. She drew a damp cigarette out of her breast pocket. She snipped off the end between her long red fingernails and slid it into her mouth. The cigarette drooped. "I suppose this is as good a time as any to go cold turkey." Rachel envied Sassy's ability to ignore things like the surgeon general's warnings and continue to smoke; Rachel desired a cigarette even now when she knew she shouldn't have one. The image came up: *Daddy coughing, knowing his lungs were pock-marked with cancer.*

"So you have a nice setup, Mrs. Adair," Sassy laughed. "In the ghetto we used to call a place like this 'honky heaven.' You have a patio, a house, a renter, what more could a girl want?"

"A ghost."

"A what?"

"We have a ghost—really. It's supposed to be the original owner of the house, Rose Draper, a courtesan to the political world of the nineteenth century. Mrs. Deerfield says that she's heard her walking the halls."

"Maybe we can get your ghost to help us with all this junk." Sassy squatted down to try and lift her end of the box up. "I never thought records could be so bleeping heavy."

Rachel nodded. "Not just ordinary records, Hugh's collection of Big Band. He finally gave up trying to teach me the jitterbug in law school, so now he listens to them when I'm not around."

"You were always more of a disco kind of girl, weren't you?"

"Please," Rachel groaned with the suggestion and the weight of the box.

When they'd gone up the flight of stairs, Rachel leaned her end of the box on the new sofa that had been delivered on Tuesday. "Here, let's set this down for a minute."

"Amen to that."

"Gently, gently, these are his babies, remember, the only thing his mother left him that he treas— Now why are you looking at me like that?"

"I was just wondering what a nice white girl like you is doing in this neighborhood. Used to be, six, seven years ago, all the winos on the block hung out on this front stoop and tossed their cookies in the hallway."

"A sobering thought."

"When I was fourteen, my mom would bring me down here because there was some old doctor who lived down the end of the block, and he was real cheap, and then I'd sit in the park and wait for her. I was scared to death of this street—old men used to try to get me to go with them, winking at me and then spitting like it was going to make them irresistible. How times do change, Retch, how they change. The alley behind your place was called Dealer's Alley, and there was a string of red lights up in one of these apartment places, and they weren't on nobody's Christmas tree." Sassy looked out the French doors onto the alley—it was now a parking lot for the various occupants of Hammer Street. "Still looks like you could buy your drugs back there, I guess."

"I still have my supply of antidepressants," Rachel said. "I wonder how much any of those pills are worth on the street?"

Sassy glanced around the room. "You know, Retch, I'll bet we've even got something in research on this neighborhood—I've got so much shit in my files I wouldn't be surprised if Draper House is in there. God, my mind is a banquet of trivial facts from that job! And to think, I used to love reading newspapers."

"This alley is pretty depressing," Rachel said, grabbing her friend by the arm. "The best room is down the hall—it may be one of the best views in the city."

They went down the long hall to the turret room. Hugh had Windexed the windows to the point where Rachel noticed the paper towel streaks on the glass; the walls still needed painting, and there was Hugh's collection of Sherwin-Williams paints all ready for the job. The floor creaked as they walked, and Sassy went out of her way to find the locations of all the creaking boards. When they entered the turret room, Rachel was suddenly aware again of that dungeon look—it seemed dark, cold, and damp. The wallpaper was drab and full of swirling paisleylike designs, reminding her of an awful wide tie her father used to wear. Even with the convex window being so large, the light that came in from outside was like a fog. She switched on the overhead light.

"We still haven't gotten around to putting up drapes yet."

"You could have affairs up here and see Hugh coming a mile off," Sassy joked. "There's that park. I used to sit in there when I was little—scared to death that some druggie or psycho was going to grab me. Or a pervert—"

"Back then, I don't think I even saw D.C., my folks kept us safely in the 'burbs."

"Yeah, back then even us black folks used to roll up the window and lock the door when we drove through here. They call this park Winthrop Park—sounds pretty white bread doesn't it—but when I was in school it was still known as Needle Park, like every other park in the city. When I was a teenager, I'm telling you, I thought that as soon as I was old enough I was going to hightail it to the suburbs and become a white girl because I thought if this is what being black means, it's time for an *up*date, you know what I'm talking about? Now, look at this whole neighborhood: people pay as much for a parking space as I do for rent! If only I'd known back then, girl, I'd have become a real estate entrepreneur."

"But this block has been owned by Hugh's family for

years. I'm sure after all that time of losing money on it, it's a welcome change . . ."

"You're telling me Hugh's daddy has owned this street since when?"

Rachel shrugged. "Maybe the fifties or forties. Sometime after World War II."

"I'd rather have had a corner of Hell than this place." Sassy raised her eyebrows as she scanned the rain-swept park, and then nodded at the window. "Look at her."

Rachel came closer to the turret window; she felt an icy shiver run through her and she didn't know why—it had felt for a second like someone had stroked his fingers down the back of her neck. She put her hand to her shoulders, rubbing the nape of her neck; it was nothing—she'd been thinking it was going to be one of the gross cockroaches she'd seen in the kitchen.

Sassy said, "That's so sad; she doesn't even know to come in out of the rain."

Rachel followed Sassy's gaze down through the dripping trees and puddles of the park until she saw what Sassy was talking about.

An old black bag woman was muttering to herself, glancing occasionally up at them and shaking her fist, shouting something that could not be heard through the rain and the window.

"Jesus," Rachel gasped.

"You know her?"

"It looks like the same woman who peed on the sidewalk the first day I saw the house. I didn't think she'd be a *regular.*"

Sassy turned away from the window. "It's the mental hospitals; they're full, and so they release these people. It's positively criminal. You know it's like they're invisible people, that they're somehow not real. Like she was born like that, full grown, with her shopping cart and trash bags. But she's probably just like this neighborhood, you know, she's got a history. Everybody's got a history."

EIGHT

THE INVISIBLE WOMAN

1.

Few people passing her by, stopping to give a quarter or a dollar bill, would guess that Mattie Peru, as she called herself, had any history at all. Her face was broad, a flat, round plate, with small, steady dark eyes that seemed constantly vigilant. When she wasn't shouting, she kept her lips puckered like she was tasting something sour. Her hair grew wild and greasy; because she hadn't looked at herself in years, she didn't know that there was any gray in it. She hadn't taken off this dress in years either. It seemed to be as much a part of her skin as anything. And her bags: balloonish, dark green and black plastic bags molded to suit the occasion—hats and coats and galoshes.

Mattie was a bag woman, that was enough. To the people passing her on their way to their meetings, their warm homes, their subway trains, their bars and hair salons, she might have been every bag woman they'd ever seen, black or white, middle-aged or ancient.

Once, two other street people, men she'd seen around the park at Farragut Square, molested her, held her up against a sea-green lamppost and raped her in the early evening as rush hour was just beginning. They called themselves Willy and Pete, and Pete said, "We been watchin' you, sugar, and we been waitin', and now the watchin' and waitin's over." His breath smelled like dog shit as he kissed her; she kept her teeth clenched together, she tried to push him away, but the other one, Willy, held her arms back against the

47

lamppost. He chanted over and over, "Nooky, nooky, gonna get me some nooky."

Pete punched her in the stomach when he'd done slobbering all over her, and then it was Willy's turn.

Willy was less kind.

"Nooky, nooky," he said, biting her throat. Willy raked his fingers through her trash bags, beneath her dress, across her breasts. She tried calling up the wasps to protect her, but that magic was gone.

She looked up to the sky as he pushed into her. It was an empty sky that seemed to go on up into forever and she thought of the world as a great jar without a lid, and everything inside spilling out.

It hurt, what Willy was doing to her, but she sent her mind flying, one thing she could do, like her Magic Touch and her trash bags, she could send her mind flying somewhere else. To a cool spot beneath a bridge where she went sometimes to talk to her babygirl. She left her body there, *let 'em have it! Ain't got no need for no body,* and her mind flew away.

The people, the Mr. Big Men and Women passing through the park on their ways to the Metro, hailing cabs, strolling, messengers on bikes, none of them stopped. No one came to her aid. No one seemed to notice what the men were doing. No one noticed that she was really there and not just part of the scenery, like the pigeons, the bushes, the benches. If someone asked her, Mattie would probably tell them that her Hefty trash bags were a cloak of invisibility, and when she enshrouded herself with these raiments, people just could not see her at all. When she'd discovered this secret to remaining invisible to the naked eye, she decided it was safe to return again to Winthrop Park. To sit in her favorite bench, or stretch out beneath the scanty shade of the malodorous gingko tree, and do what she did best: watch for signs of life.

She didn't know for sure why she went there; her memory of the past was jumbled like the junk in her grocery cart. She knew they'd done something bad to her babygirl there, she knew it was the baron, she remembered her love and her fear of him.

And she remembered the one who watched and waited in the Screaming House. Like the two vagrants who'd raped her, the spirit in the house was through with watching and waiting.

And once again, there were signs of life in the house on Hammer Street. Two women, one black, one white, stared out of the turret room window as if they were looking straight at Mattie. Mattie covered her head with her trash bag of invisibility. She glanced out from beneath it.

She knew they could no longer see her.

Then, from the lowest window of the house, the one with the bars on the outside, she thought she saw the other gazing out at her.

Mattie shook her fist at the house. "Boshinus!" she screamed.

2.

The summer in Washington had been a living hell for Mattie Peru. People were moving back into the Screaming House, and she had done everything she could with her magic to keep them away. She had blessed the house three times the way she'd been taught by an old mambo when she was a young girl—she tried to appease the restless spirits who broke through the cracks in the earth. But none of them seemed to listen, and Mattie doubted that the old magic would work. There didn't seem to be any rules anymore—and the spirits of the dead ignored the old rituals the same way that young people no longer performed them.

And she could feel the breath of the baron, the guardian of the graveyards, warm against her face.

His rotting inspiration found her wherever she went. He crawled behind the skin of night.

Mattie Peru had slept a few nights in the Farragut West Metro station—of course, nobody saw her the night before when she'd stayed down low by the ticket machines—she'd wrapped herself in her trash bags of invisibility just before midnight as she saw the men in uniform closing the subway entrance off with a chain-link gate. Her scalp was itching something awful beneath the dark plastic, but with a little self-control she managed to resist scratching her hair out.

She needed some sleep—she'd been watching for *him,* and for *them,* ever since the Screaming House had come back to itself.

That night, after the rainstorm which she had raised in an effort to keep *them* out, after she had recited her curses at the Boshinus, she felt she was safest in the *down,* in the subway.

The subway was not the best place to spend the night in the summer: it was only slightly cooler than the air outside, in the *up.* The *down,* where the Metro was, choked itself sometimes with its stale, dusty air. She would've preferred a nice cool alleyway, or even a bench in the park, but when the baron was on the loose, she didn't feel safe in the *up.*

An old white wino crouched in the alcove behind the ticket machines. He was dressed in the urban uniform of the homeless: stained trousers and ragged shirt. A coating of filth ran across his face down to his burst shoes. Like the other bag people Mattie knew, his skin color was a moot point. They were all the color of city dirt, damp as an alleyway, smelly as the dumpster behind a fast-food restaurant.

He smiled at her, and Mattie was a little worried that he might try to rape her like Willy and Pete in the park. But his eyes seemed kind, the way her lover's eyes had once looked at her as if she was the most beautiful woman in the world. He offered her a drink from his bottle, so she went over and sat next to him. If there was evil in his eyes, she couldn't read it, and her need for a drink was powerfully strong. His name was Ken, he told her, and the people out there had fucked him something royal. Mattie asked him if he'd ever met the baron, and he snorted. "Don't know no dang baron," his voice like a rusty nail scraping on a chalkboard.

"He find you no matter where." She sucked at the bottle like a hungry baby. "He smell you like a hound, he go where he please. And when he get a hold of your collar, he yank on it, and he take-take-take."

The man grinned a four-tooth half-moon. His teeth and gums hung over the black chasm of his mouth like stalactites in a cavern. "Crazy bitch."

"You laugh, but he laugh louder."

"Those sonsofbitches stole my fuckin' money." He reached over for his bottle. His hand hung like a dangling spider in midair, waiting for her to let loose of it. It was a good bottle of Thunderbird.

"You see him 'round the eyes, he hide in the eyes like a speck of hell dust, but he come out from the teeth."

"Shut up, you crazy old bitch!" He grabbed the bottle and tore it loose from her clutching fingers. Raising it to his lips, he thrust it against his mouth and then howled in pain. Ken pulled the bottle away from his face—blood sluiced from his upper lip. He spat out a chip from one of his few remaining teeth, tonguing his uppers to make sure all four of them were still there and in place. Wiping his bloodied mouth with the back of his hand, he raised the bottle of Thunderbird once again to his lips—this time, gently.

"He got my baby, and he got my baby's baby. He come out through the teeth and get my babygirl and her child. He been 'round a long time." Mattie could not help herself—she began weeping, grasping her Hefty trash bags around her shoulders and poking small holes in them with her fingers. She felt her thick flesh beneath the plastic, and winced as she pinched herself. "I let him do it! I let him do it!"

"Get your ass away." Ken was looking at her from the corners of his eyes as he guzzled the wine. He shoved at her with his elbow.

"Gimme drink from." She motioned to the bottle.

"You gonna shut up?"

She nodded, her fingers still kneading and pinching her soft, flabby skin beneath the bags.

He passed her the bottle.

She chugged it long and deep.

"Save some for me, willya?"

"He got no place to come into, ya see? He look for a place, and *she* give him a place, she give him a place to come into. But she no mambo—I be a mambo, she just skin and spirit—she think she know it, but she don't—she got no power but what *he* give her."

"You shut up!"

"You got to believe, 'cause if you don't believe, you let him in."

The air brushed through the subway tunnel, up to where

they lay huddled together; she sniffed and smelled something rotten from down there in the dark tunnel. A three-day, lying in the heat, dead-animal rottenness.

"Oh, I believe you, whore," the man's voice changed, reminding her of another man, someone she'd once been in love with. His fingers clutched hers. "I believe you well enough, my little scum bucket, my love." The man screamed, cupping his hands over his mouth convulsively, pitching forward and backwards; foam bubbled from his lips across his gnarled fingers. He began pulling his last remaining teeth out of his mouth, digging into his diseased gums with his dirt-rimmed fingernails as if he were extracting splinters from his skin. His screams echoed throughout the subway.

"Samedi! Samedi!" Mattie screamed, pushing herself away from the man, crawling out into the light, trying to maneuver onto her haunches.

It was *him,* it was the baron. He was in that wino lying next to her and he was gone from him, swept like a summer wind down the long tunnel of the subway. Gone, leaving the man dead on the cold, red floor, frothy blood simmering on his chin, four teeth, torn out at the roots, in his right hand.

NINE

THE NEW OWNER

1.

Rachel could only stare at the newly painted walls for so long; but this activity took up some time between the seemingly endless phone calls that had been plaguing her since Sassy had left at three. First, the two teenagers that Hugh had hired to help move the bedroom furniture and the dining room table called at quarter to four wondering where Hugh was. They wondered if they would get paid even though they obviously weren't moving anything. Then her secretary called; messages were piling up for her at the office, and one of her clients was angry because he'd been arrested after his case had already been dismissed when the man bringing the charge had failed to show up for the preliminary hearing. Rachel then had to call him, then call the municipal court and act angry. Then Sassy called to see if she was all right. She lied and said that Hugh had gotten home about five minutes after Sassy had left.

Rachel did not even realize that she was watching a *pas de deux* between two large roaches. They skittered down the kitchen wall, disappearing behind the range. She had seen enough roaches to last her a lifetime that afternoon.

With some pathetic semblance of organization, Rachel Adair wandered around the house with the yellow Post-it Notes she'd pilfered from her office. At each door, each corner, along the refrigerator, above the stove, on the French doors, she stuck the paper with phrases like: WINDEX or GRBGE DSPSL? or ROACH!! or PAINT

PEELING. She stuck yellow papers all over the house with ROACH ALERT written across them. Then she saw what looked like mouse droppings in a faded rectangle of linoleum—every kind of vermin in the world seemed to use the kitchen as its dumping ground. The Post-it Note she left on the wall above it read simply, MOUSEDOODY, with an arrow pointing to the floor. The Post-it Note mania was on the advice of her mother who was perhaps the most organized person in the cosmos. "If you write notes to yourself, you don't have to overload your brain with minor details," mom had said. "You've never been good at getting your facts straight or your details right, Rachel, not when you were a little girl and not now, but if you just keep reminding yourself of these things . . ."

And if I don't remind myself, I know you will, mom. Would Rachel really say that to her mother? If she did say something snippy her mother would pause whether on the phone or sitting across the table from her or next to her in the car, and look away. Or Rachel imagined her mother would look away because it seemed like the Right Thing To Do, which mom was really, really good at.

Normally, I'd rebel against you on this, mom, but I want it to be right, I want it to be normal in this house. I don't want to start off on the wrong foot in my own house—our house—I want this to be a place we can start our family. Maybe only one baby, maybe six, maybe this year, maybe in three years. (But Dear God! before I turn thirty-five, please, please, please!)

She was again staring at the walls when the phone rang.

A woman's voice, "You hooked up your phone?"

"Mom." Rachel wanted to add: *Funny, I was just thinking about you.* Rachel always recognized her mother's voice by that sedimentary layer of Southernness that remained in the woman's voice all these years she'd been living outside of North Carolina: every sentence seemed to end in a question mark, so it was not just, *You hooked up your phone,* but, *You hooked up your phone?* If her mother were to mention the weather, Rachel knew she'd say in a slow, deliberate voice, *It's gonna be a sun-shiny day?* When Rachel had been younger, her mother constantly scolded her for talking back, while Rachel had always felt she was just answering her mother's questions.

"You don't sound thrilled." *You don't sound thrilled?*

"I was expecting Hugh."

"He's working?"

"He had an interview."

"You don't sound too hopeful. You went and had your blood sugar checked like I asked you, because when you sound like this—"

"When I sound like *what?*"

"You know, drained and edgy? I used to have bad periods, you know, it's not that unusual. But there's hypoglycemia and your brothers have it. Kelly has PMS. It's like having walking time bombs for children."

Rachel waited a beat, catching her breath. She was not going to argue with her mother over the phone; that would be playing into her hands. "Hugh was supposed to be home at two."

"Good lord, it's nearly seven. You don't think something happened?"

Sometimes I wish something would *happen.* "No. But I guess if he'd gotten the job he'd be home."

"Sometimes it takes a while. Your father had nearly a year when he left the navy before he got on with the beltway bandits."

"Let's drop it. Is something up?"

"I was just bored. I was playing grandma to Kelly's brood last week, and now the place seems empty. Are you all moved in?"

"There's a shitload of work to do."

"Since when do you use language like that with your mother?"

"When I get off the phone I'll wash my mouth out. Goodbye."

"Give me a call when you're feeling better, okay?"

"Right. Goodbye."

When she got off the phone from *that* call, Rachel felt like breaking something. Not because of her mother, although there was that little aside about "playing grandma" to Kelly's kids (she had four and she wasn't even thirty yet)—it was Hugh who was the object of her frustration. The thought *Hugh where are you?* was soon replaced with, *I could scream, I will just scream.* But she remembered the downstairs tenant. *So I can break something and it will be like screaming.* The plates and glasses were still packed away in boxes, so it would be difficult to break them. By the time she'd opened the boxes the anger would've dissipated. Rachel saw Hugh's record collection there by the fireplace. She went over.

This will really hurt him. She picked up his "Ella Fitzgerald Sings Duke Ellington" record, removing the disc from the sleeve. But instead, she looked at the shiny record kept in mint condition—"Take the A Train." She spent the next twenty minutes unpacking the stereo and connecting the speakers up. She put the record on. She sat on the sofa and gazed out at the patio and alley. The rain had stopped and in the sunless summer light, steam and mist glowed like morning dew.

Through the French doors she saw a man standing in the alley on the other side of the gate. For a second she thought it was Hugh finally home, but realized not only would he not be coming in the back way (it would make no sense) but also Hugh had lighter hair. Even from this distance she could tell that the skinny stranger was much better looking than Hugh (and she thought Hugh was pretty damn cute).

Rather than panic, as she was well aware any normal person would, Rachel thought: *This is one of the oddest neighborhoods, bag ladies in front of the house and thieves in back.* The tall, gangly man was attempting to climb over the back gate. He was the kind of skinny that reminded her of a skeleton, although his darkly tanned face seemed to have enough meat on it. His eyes looked like small coffee beans sunk above high cheekbones. Beneath the heavy eyebrows and the short-cropped light brown hair he was wearing a navy blazer and a yellow tie, hardly the uniform of the neighborhood thief. *Perhaps one of Mrs. Deerfield's friends.*

It was only when the stranger saw her and waved frantically that she realized who it was.

Ted Adair.

Hugh's brother.

Rachel rose from the couch, smiling.

2.

Rachel hadn't seen Ted since the wedding last fall, and then only briefly because naturally there was some argument between the two brothers. She was sure that if you put Hugh in a room with any member of his family, he would find something to argue about with them, whether it was the state of the world or a jar of peanut butter. Perhaps that's why they were a family of lawyers. At the reception, she'd pulled Hugh aside and said, "Can't you two get along for just five minutes?" But she'd felt it was Hugh's fault that Ted had not shown up for the reception. "What did you say to him?" she'd asked her husband.

Hugh had looked her square in the face and said: "I told him he wasn't welcome, Scout. He's just a messenger boy for the Old Man. He's only here to lay the family curse."

Because it was her wedding day and she had her own friends and family to contend with (particularly her drunken Uncle Paul who had begun flirting heavily with her bridesmaids), Rachel had decided not to reprimand Hugh for this kind of boorish behavior, although she would've liked to tell him, *"Hugh Adair, you're becoming more like your father every day."*

And now, as she went through the French doors and down the rain-puddled iron stairs in back, she was glad that Hugh wasn't home to drive Ted off.

"Rachel! Let me in or I'll blow your house down!" Ted banged hard on the gate; it creaked and shuddered as if it would fall apart at any moment. "I feel like a wet dog out here!" His voice rose and fell like a swing, and hearing it reminded her of Hugh before life had begun to bog him down.

She went to the gate and unlatched it from the inside. It swung open with an obnoxious squeal, threatening to slam against its side, but Ted caught the edge of it with his right hand. With his left hand, he reached over and clutched her shoulder as if he were off balance and about to fall forward.

"You should post a sign: Slippery When Wet." His dark

eyes drank in the whole scene: the patio, the house, Rachel with damp hair—and no Hugh. "I've caught you at a bad time."

"Of course not. Come inside and see the place."

"I hope I don't muddy my boots on the way from the carriage house. Quite a little manor you got here. Where's my baby brother?" He picked up his attaché case from the concrete and swung it from side to side. "Got something the two of you might be interested in."

"Oh, Ted, he's on an interview. But he's supposed to be back fairly soon."

"Who needs Hugh?" Ted patted the case. "You can handle this stuff yourself, I mean, it *is* in *your* name."

"What is?" She led the way up the staircase.

"Rachel," and when she turned around to face Ted on the stairs for just an instant she had a sense of something, something there on his face that was like Hugh but not like Hugh, and he grinned a broad uninhibited grin as if he had a terrific joke but if he told her it wouldn't seem so funny. But he could no longer keep it inside. Ted Adair said: "Didn't he tell you? The whole goddamn *house* is in your name."

3.

"My name?"

"I'm surprised Hugh didn't mention it, although, hey, maybe dad didn't even go over the details with Hughie—dad's not real good with his kids, but I guess you don't need me telling you that—" Ted spoke in gusts of conversation, still managing to take sips from the can of Diet Coke she'd brought him when they went inside. He slouched on the sofa in the living room, one leg looping through the other, his feet tap-tapping nervously against the hardwood floor. "Dad, in his own inimitable way, has his charming side, and he thinks the wife and kiddies—if any exist I don't know about, you tell me—should have some property. It's dad's soft side coming through. I think the way dad put it was: 'I don't want my grandchildren going homeless.'"

Rachel glanced through the papers. It all looked like just another batch of legalese to dump in her already overstuffed file cabinet, but there was her name on every page, and places for her signature. "I'm flattered he thought to—"

Ted interrupted: "Include you in the little grudge match he's got going with Hughie? It's an unenviable position. He treated Joanna—it's okay to say her name now, isn't it?—that way, too. He made sure everything was put in her name, what there *was,* anyway."

When Ted mentioned Hugh's first wife, Joanna, Rachel felt a jolt go through her that had nothing to do with all the caffeine she'd been drinking. She wasn't sure if Ted was joking or not; Hugh called his brother The Joker, and a tense moment arrived when she didn't know how to take this last comment. With Hugh, this would be a serious conversation because it concerned the Old Man and his late wife—and there was nothing to joke about there. Hugh always had that dead earnestness which she had admired in law school, a true-blue quality. *His fucking integrity. The same integrity that kept him from going to the Old Man's law firm for a job.*

Rachel watched Ted, trying to read his eyes.

They were dark brown, like hers, and unfathomable.

But Ted broke out laughing—it was a joke after all. "It gives one pause, as inappropriate as it is to bring such sacred cows as the dead, and the near dead—I mean pop, about being near dead. He believes that he's not going to be around much longer." But he was still chuckling as he spoke, and so, Rachel thought, *It's all a joke, he's not serious.*

His laughter was contagious; she, too, began laughing in spite of herself, in spite of her anger with Hugh for taking so long to get home, in spite of his dead first wife, and in spite of the Old Man and his deeds. "Oh, Ted, this is awful, making jokes about dead people."

"Don't forget the near dead, too," Ted giggled almost like a little boy. "I'm sorry, Rachel, I just couldn't resist. None of us in the family ever really liked Joanna—not that she ever let us near enough to know if she was likable. She was the most talented block of ice I've ever met." His words were punctuated with sniffling giggles.

Rachel crinkled the legal papers in her lap. *Maybe it was* Hugh *who never let you get near enough to her, the way he keeps his family away from his second wife, too.* She wondered how Hugh would react if he knew that his older brother had dropped by the house unannounced. But she felt giggly, silly, slightly dizzy—*probably just hungry*—her stomach was gurgling and she'd completely forgotten to buy any food. Ted continued talking, joking, saying hilarious things, and she felt like she'd been given a quick breath of pure oxygen. She was drunk from Diet Coke. "Ted, you're so *funny.*"

"What do you think Hughie would say if I was to tell him he's got the most beautiful and intelligent wife on the planet?"

"He'd say you were after something." Rachel heard her voice as if down a long hallway. *Watch what you say, Scout, this is a Greek bearing gifts, not your best old friend in college.*

But she'd said it: *He'd say you were after something.* She covered her mouth to keep other foolish things from pouring out.

Ted stared at her. His jaw seemed to drop to the floor, his eyes widening incredulously.

Then he was laughing even harder than before, gales of laughter. He slapped the sofa and his knees and his attaché case he was laughing so hard, clutching his stomach, kicking the floor with the heels of his loafers. Tears leapt from his eyes.

"No, no," she was laughing again, pointing to his shoes. "You'll scuff the floors," which caused both of them to laugh again because the wood floors were already mercilessly scratched like an ice rink after a hockey game.

But the laughing died inside both of them, Ted wiping his eyes and Rachel catching her breath, feeling like she'd just sprinted a mile.

"Families," Ted said, shaking his head wearily. It was as if he were coming down from a drug-induced high. The laughing moment was over and normal, steady life had caught up with them again. Ted stood up, stretching his long frame.

Rachel felt embarrassed as if they'd just shared something intimate. The camaraderie she'd just felt with Ted also felt like some kind of betrayal of Hugh. She sat there on the box that held Hugh's collection of novels, smiling up at Ted, wondering if she was betraying Hugh, and if Hugh knew she was betraying him. *A small betrayal, not a big one, just a normal betrayal. But what do you want me to do, Hugh? Tell him he's not allowed in the house? My house as it turns out. Well, Hugh, you may have been raised to be rude to people, but I wasn't. No grudge is worth nursing forever.* Rachel got up off the box. "I should show you around the place."

Ted reached over, touching her left shoulder, bearing down slightly. "No, you sit down and wait for Hughie. The grand tour can wait for a housewarming party—you're giving one, right?"

Rachel shrugged, sitting back down. "We've got so much to do to get this place up to a livable standard."

"Don't be stupid—that's what a housewarming party's for—everyone can bring a gift to keep your decorating overhead low."

"Look, Ted, Hugh should be back soon. Why don't you wait and join us for dinner?"

"Now, do you think Hughie would really want to have me sitting across the table from him?" Ted grinned. He went to the open door, about to leave, and then turned to face her again. "You're a mender, Rachel, that's nice. But no, I better skedaddle. And with those papers, no rush, just sign where you're supposed to, call if there's anything too weird in them, and then those at the end, well, it's all that household crap about how the furnace is set up and insurance bullshit about your tenant—also a blueprint—well, more of a sketch of the floor plan. It's a read-it-and-weep job, because I think a heck of a lot of work has been done in alterations on this place. I heard it was just a skeleton and a bunch of crumbling walls until about 1977. And Rachel, Rachel, Rachel, think housewarming party—I love a good blow-out and I always bring the best gifts, anyway."

He gave her a quick wink before descending the stairs to the patio.

Rachel went to shut the French doors behind him; the muggy, steamy day was almost over, Hugh wasn't home, *damn him,* and she watched Ted shut the back gate gently. He strode down the alley, looking back every few feet just to see if she was still standing there.

And what would Hugh think of this visit? Oh, Hugh—your brother dropped by today with some papers.

If the interview went well it might slide right off him. He might grin and say, "Oh?" and then tell her about this new job he might get.

But if the interview went badly, or if he hadn't made it to the interview (and that had happened twice in the past two months), what would he say? Would he give her his mad smile? The one that meant he was trying to maintain a pleasant exterior, but inside he was seething? He never mentioned his brother except to recall a particularly vicious moment from what Hugh termed "childhood's greatest hits."

Let's Pretend, Scout. Let's Pretend that you're me and you're standing at the top of the stairs and your big brother Ted pushes you down them and you're black and blue. But you don't want to upset your mom because she has problems of her own, big ones like the Old Man. And so you say that you fell down the stairs all by yourself. And Let's Pretend that this goes on, say, ten or twelve times one summer and you're black and blue to the point where mom, out of concern, takes you to several doctors, one being a kiddo psychiatrist, because she doesn't think an eight year old would normally be so clumsy. And Let's Pretend that your brother puts a rubber band around your pet cat's neck and he tells you, because you're younger and you want to believe your big brother, that it's a special, secret collar and not to tell mom or the housekeeper about it. And then you wake up one morning and the cat is dead on the balcony because this thing, this rubber band, has eaten into its neck and cut off its circulation. Let's Pretend that you take the blame for it because your older brother lies and calls you a killer.

It wouldn't matter that Rachel would argue that they were both kiddos themselves and that maybe it wasn't as black and white between the two brothers as Hugh made it out to be. *"You make it sound like the evil twins on those stupid TV shows,"* she would say if she had the nerve.

But as Rachel watched her brother-in-law Ted walk out of sight beyond the apartments next to theirs in the alley, she thought: *Okay, for marital harmony, Let's Pretend you never came by, Ted, and these papers arrived through the mail slot.*

She went over to the stereo to turn the Ella Fitzgerald record over. Then she lay down on the couch, wondering when Hugh—the bastard—would make it home, wondering when the sun would go down, wondering if it was a headache she was feeling coming on or if this was just normal life taking its toll. She closed her eyes for a few moments, then opened them again, then closed them. *Just for a few moments.*

Rachel Adair dreamed of babies, beautiful healthy babies coming out of her, all on schedule at nine months to the day, all little Adairs. And she was the mommy and Hugh was the daddy, and somewhere in the dream her healthy, beautiful father was saying, "I am so proud of you, sweetheart."

TEN

THE CLAMORING PLACE

1.

Rachel awoke on the couch feeling sticky and hungry. The summer light had not yet faded outside; it was almost nine P.M. *When is this day going to be over?* She turned off the stereo and went into the kitchen. The only things in the fridge were some Diet Cokes; she plucked an ice cube from the freezer and wiped it across her forehead. Rubbing the dwindling ice cube into her face, she walked down the hall towards the first-floor bathroom.

When she flicked on the light she saw something dart across the floor—even though the cockroach could not have been more than a half inch long it seemed to her to be a six-footer. She gasped when she saw it, then broke out laughing. *Join the club.* Pulling a Post-it Note from her pocket, she scrawled across it in magic marker: ROACH 17—CALL EXTERMINATOR/BUY RAID. She stuck this just under the light switch.

She turned on the shower, and the water came out in staccato bursts, rusty brown until she'd let it run for a few minutes. It smelled of rotten eggs. The pipes squealed and coughed, but finally ran clear water. Her clothes seemed to have attached themselves to her skin; peeling off the painter's pants was like skinning herself. The water was spraying out of the white tub—there was no shower curtain, another essential she had forgotten along with toilet paper. She hoped that she still had the small package of Kleenex in her purse.

Rachel stepped into the shower, and as she did this she

noticed the small window. It was above the toilet and across
the room from the tub and shower, but it had no shade and
she wondered if anyone could see in from the outside. The
cloud-filtered sunlight was flat and made the empty red
buildings across the alley look like cardboard cutouts. She
glanced down at her feet—the drain was clogged, and water
was backing up. She bent over and scraped her fingers across
the drain wondering if it was hair, but it was plaster dust,
and it seemed that no matter how much she scraped away,
there was more and the tub was filling up to her ankles. The
water was coughing out rust colored again, and her hands
went to the spigots. She turned off the water feeling dirtier
than when she'd stepped under the shower.

Of course, no towel. She shook herself off; it was warm
enough and she didn't mind the feeling of water on her skin.

She had the sense of someone in the doorway, someone
staring at her. When she turned, expecting Hugh, she saw
the cat.

It was a puffy Himalayan with a dark face but with a
streak of peach and orange across its nose. It looked up at
her with no curiosity, just empty blue orbs. Something dark
and shiny wriggled against the cat's whiskers just as it
registered on Rachel's brain what this thing was that the cat
was playing with. *A roach, gross!* The cat swallowed the
insect with a moist crackle, the kind of noise that Hugh
made when he ate bean sprouts.

Rachel gasped, and the cat darted off down the hall. *But,
on the practical side, as mom would say, just think of what
this animal could save on exterminator bills.*

Rachel knew this must be the infamous Ramona from
downstairs who vomited hairballs as omens. *How did she
get up here?* The first thought in her mind: *Hugh. Hugh was
home, finally, waiting in the living room with his bad news
and depressing apologies. He had accidentally left the downstairs door open, or the French doors to the patio. The cat got
past him.*

Stamping a wet foot pattern across the bleached wood
floor, Rachel went out to the living room. She realized at the
last second she was naked and would be crossing by those
French doors, but tried streaking through in case anyone
was watching. No one was.

There was also no Hugh in evidence, and Ramona was lying in front of the fireplace cleaning herself carefully. She rolled over onto her back, paws splayed in the air, gazing up at Rachel with patient eyes. Her belly was enormous.

"Even you can get pregnant." She reached over, petting the cat. "Now, if you'll excuse me a minute." Rachel sneezed, wiping her eyes—her allergy to cats always seemed to explode in her face like gunpowder in spite of the fact that she loved animals. "I've got to go put some clothes on."

Upstairs, Rachel rummaged through one of the boxes in the bedroom and found a summer dress her mother had given her years ago. She never liked what her mother gave her to wear, it was never anything she would've chosen for herself, but for some reason those gift clothes were always on hand in an emergency. They were dresses and skirts and blouses to be worn on moving days and when her other skirt was at the cleaners, or when she spilled ketchup on a blouse and needed another in a hurry. She felt like a little girl in them, and for some reason the clothes her mother bought her (like this dress she bunched up and pulled over her head getting lost in a sea of wildflower print) were always two sizes too large. Her mother no doubt expected her to gain twenty or thirty pounds, and perhaps one day she would. Yes, and then she'd have a complete wardrobe provided by mom. But right now she felt about twelve years old, which was probably right where her mother would've liked to keep her.

She came back downstairs expecting the cat to have run off somewhere, *however the hell it had gotten in,* but Ramona still lay in the same place, stretching lazily. Rachel bunched up the mumu around her waist and kneeled by the cat. Her sinuses were driving her crazy, but the cat was so adorable and furry. "You know you're cute, don't you? But don't expect a kiss after wolfing that roach down." She rubbed Ramona just beneath the chin and the cat let out an almost birdlike *mew* accompanied by a thrumming purr of satisfaction. A speck of dirt seemed to leap from the cat's fur onto Rachel's hand.

Not a speck, a *flea.*

"Shit." She pinched the flea between her thumbnails until it popped. "Let's get you back home before you contaminate the house. Roaches, fleas, mice, what other crawling things do we have around here?"

Gently, she lifted Ramona up, careful not to let the cat's belly sag. "Lots of little lumpkins in there."

2.

"You've found the beast!" Penelope Deerfield shouted as she opened her door. She seemed even shorter than she had when they'd first met. Her eyes were just about level with Rachel's chest. *Perhaps it's true that you shrink as you get older.* Her yellow hair was done up with gold plastic combs, reminding Rachel of haystacks in a damp field. She wore a more conservative outfit than the last time they'd met: almost a suit, although mismatched, probably from a thrift shop. The overall effect of the dress and light jacket was of someone who didn't care what anyone thought of her. Again, a momism, because Rachel herself found this aspect of Mrs. Deerfield's personality utterly charming.

Mrs. Deerfield's eyebrows curled prehensilely around her blue eyes as she grabbed the cat up beneath its front shoulders. "Naughty little Ramona running off from Nanny Deerfield!"

"I'm sorry to interrupt," Rachel said, peering around the open doorway without meaning to—there were two other women sitting at the day bed and the loveseat. They'd been speaking in whispers, and as soon as they saw Rachel their faces suddenly blossomed pleasant smiles as if Rachel were the last person on earth they expected to walk through that door *and wasn't this a nicer surprise than whomever they expected.*

"Not interrupting at all, dear, come in, come in, this must be moving day." Mrs. Deerfield flung the door open; it hit the back of the wall with a *thunking* shudder. Mrs. Deerfield was mildly drunk, Rachel guessed. "We've been gossiping and pickling."

Yes, Rachel thought, *and getting pickled.* The room was

redolent of vinegar and spices and the purest whiff of alcohol she'd smelled since she'd been in the hospital after the miscarriage. "Today seems to be lasting forever."

"As well it should, it's the summer solstice—this is the longest day of the year. Somewhere Druids are dancing." As she pulled Rachel in, tugging like an eager child at her arm, Mrs. Deerfield murmured an aside. "We won't even go into the *fertility* rites involved, at least not with this group." Her breath was laced with sherry. Then back to her stage voice: "My friends, this is my landlady, Rachel Adair, and Rachel, this is Betty Kellogg, and Annie Ralph—she runs the Ralph-Westford Gallery in Mount Pleasant."

Betty Kellogg and Annie Ralph were both in their mid-fifties to early sixties, and looked more uptown than Mrs. Deerfield. Betty looked as if she could be fascinated by the smallest mind, her eyes wide as if the lids were held back with tiny hooks, their pupils jiggling rapidly as if she were deep in REM sleep and wide awake. Her mouth was frozen in an apparently constant *O* of surprise and interest; her hair was dyed platinum and permed—it seemed an effervescent fizz above her slightly wrinkled, china-doll face. She was chubby—everything about her was round and getting rounder as she balanced her weight first on one hip and then on the other, creasing the royal blue fabric of her cocktail dress. "So young to own a house. Len and I were in our mid-thirties before we were owners."

"Your Len would've lived in a tent if you hadn't forced him to get that place in Chevy Chase." Annie Ralph cast the words out of her mouth like they tasted bad, and she snapped her fingers at Mrs. Deerfield (making Rachel feel suddenly protective of her tenant). "Honey, get Rachel a sherry, and honey," she added, the second *honey* intended for Rachel, "you sit down and make yourself comfy-cozy, 'cause moving day's always a bitch." Annie Ralph looked vaguely bohemian in a peach peasant blouse and wide gray skirt, although Rachel thought she'd seen this outfit in one of the more chic boutiques in Georgetown. It was what Hugh referred to as the artsy-fartsy look. Rachel had been in the Ralph-Westford Gallery once and its owner was a perfect enough match: the gallery was full of the kind of art that only interior decorators got excited about, lots of bright squiggly colors on plain white canvases. Annie Ralph herself looked like a squiggly smudge of a woman, stretched and framed and bearing an expensive price tag. She looked like she would go with any room, any sofa-loveseat combination, any color scheme. Although the ages were all roughly equivalent among the ladies, Rachel could not imagine what they were doing with poor Mrs. Deerfield—they looked like rich Georgetown women. *And if first impressions mean anything, I don't like them one bit.*

"No thanks on the sherry," Rachel said, stepping backwards to the doorway again. But Mrs. Deerfield's grasp was firm and she tugged her into the small living room.

"Penelope's told us such nice things about you," Betty cooed, sipping daintily from the sherry glass, not realizing she was dripping the liquid down the front of her dress.

"Don't believe a word of it, dear." Penelope went over to the kitchenette. "I grouse about everything in creation. I don't have a kind bone in my body. Are you hungry? Annie's brought a delightful cheesecake, only we're all complaining from diets."

"That's right," Annie said archly. "This is even diet sherry we're guzzling."

"No, I've got to get back, my husband might call."

Bringing a slice of cheesecake out to the living area, Mrs. Deerfield said, "She's got such a luvely 'usband, ladies, when these two have children we will have a clan of beauties above us."

"We can ask my Len if he knows." But as soon as Betty Kellogg said this, she acted as if she'd just wet her pants—she squirmed uncomfortably, tugging at the edges of her dress, her face turning red.

"She'll think we've all gone to the moon," Annie Ralph said, shooting Betty a nasty look. "And she may be right on that count." Then to Rachel: "Honey, Len is her husband."

"*Was* my husband."

Mrs. Deerfield studied Rachel's face for a reaction, but there was none. "He died in '78, dear. Heart attack—Betty had been dreaming for ten years that he would go that way."

"But," Annie added, "of course, Betty never told Len

about her dreams, probably because she was afraid he would take steps to prevent it. I believe she fed him a steady diet of butter, fatty red meat, and grease—"

"She's joking," Betty said, shaking her head from side to side.

Annie giggled almost charmingly and said, "Of course, Rachel, you don't know me, but I *am* joking."

"But not about communicating with his spirit through—"

"She'll think we're batty, Betty." Annie seemed to like this turn of phrase. She repeated it: "Batty-Betty, Batty-Betty, that's a good one."

"We *are* batty," Mrs. Deerfield said, and the steadiness of her voice momentarily silenced the other two women. She looked Rachel directly in the eyes, and her gaze was so pure and unclouded that Rachel had to resist flinching. But then the kind, overly made-up face of a retired nanny returned, softening her glance. Mrs. Deerfield said, "Rachel, we talk to dead people."

3.

Rachel helped Mrs. Deerfield with the card table. They unfolded its legs above a trap door. "This is the center of the house, you see."

"A cold spot," Betty Kellogg said as if she were translating a foreign phrase for Rachel. "The clamoring place."

Mrs. Deerfield tapped the trap door with the heel of her shoe. "In the old days, they called it a crib—I guess it kept the babies cool. I'm joking, dear, I imagine it was for perishables of various and sundry sorts. It's quite chilly down there, the house holds in the night. It's where I keep my jams and pickles, dear."

"And honey, you *must* try her pickles."

"Bread and butter."

"She's got jars this big full of jellies." Annie Ralph held her hands out as wide as her hips.

"Ladies, pull your chairs up."

"You called it the clamoring place?" Rachel felt like Alice in Wonderland; she wondered if they were all making fun of her, or if they really took this seriously. Right at that moment she was wishing that Sassy was there with her to witness this. She sat down with the ladies, setting the china plate with cheesecake in front of her on the table.

"It's a carrefour, dear, a crossroads of sorts. This is where the spirits cross on their journeys. You find it hard to swallow, I see." Mrs. Deerfield smiled pleasantly. "But Annie's cheesecake, on the other hand, is a bit easier to swallow. How is it?"

Rachel nodded as she took a bite, her mouth full.

"It's an old ladies' game, honey."

"Yes. When you see death up ahead, in the next ten, twenty years—" Betty let her voice die mid-sentence. "Len was taken when he was only fifty-one. They clamor here, can't you hear them?"

"We're giving her the creeps, really. They are just passing through, honey, like wind through an old house."

"Where are they going?" Rachel wished she hadn't asked; she wished she'd just gotten up from the table and gone back upstairs or gone out for a walk down to DuPont Circle for some ice cream or to see if Hugh was in one of the bars down there. *Where are you, Hugh? Don't you know that I love you even if you don't have a job right at the moment, don't you know that? Don't you know things like this make me mad, but I still love you anyway?* She felt slightly dizzy, but was getting a heady sugar rush from the cheesecake, which was not half bad.

"It's really only an old ladies' game, dear." Mrs. Deerfield seemed to sense her discomfort.

"We can't have all the answers. Even *they* don't have the answers. How is my cheesecake, honey?"

"It's delicious."

"I only use Philadelphia brand cream cheese. It's very simple to make."

"Don't give her the 'recipe,'" Betty said with a hint of sarcasm. "It's so hard to follow, and then it never comes out the way she does it because she always leaves something out."

"Betty Kellogg, you make it sound intentional. What I *do* is I forget to put something in."

"Recipe?" Mrs. Deerfield huffed. "My dear, she got it off the package of cream cheese."

"Bitch. Menopausal *bitch.*"

They were all momentarily silent. Rachel felt itchily uncomfortable, just as if she were surrounded by mosquitoes. Or those fleas of Ramona's. She made a slight move back in her fold-out chair; it scraped the floor and her knee hit the underside of the card table.

"I should be—"

"We're a rough pack of cards," Penelope Deerfield said, reaching over to squeeze Rachel's hand. "We're being rude—my goodness, dear, your hand is so warm. You're not running a fever are you?"

Rachel did feel warm suddenly, as if something had just been let into the room, some wild animal with its fur burning. She felt dizzy. She was sitting there with three versions of her own mother, at different ages: *when her mother was thirty, when she was forty-five, and then in her sixties. Her mother in her sixties pressed down on her hand and said, "Get her a cup of tea," and then it was no longer her mother, but a black man holding her hand. His skull seemed to be pressing outward against his coffee-colored skin, his large dark eyes sinking back into holes, becoming cracks, and then his eyes were sealed up completely—his lips dried like a riverbed. And emerging were ridged yellow teeth covered with a dripping scum, growing in size as they came towards her, his nose swimming in the dark flesh that gradually filled up her vision. The teeth parted, flying up, and she was looking down into his throat, his enormous purple tongue slapping just in front of her face, his pulpy uvula flapping like torn skin—and a blast of heat from his gut rising up through his throat—heat and something else, something sweet and sour, vinegary, reminding her of a biology class, of dissecting a frog when she was fifteen, and then she felt freezing cold and it was over.*

"How long does it take you to pour tea, Annie?" Mrs. Deerfield's face was turned away from Rachel's, but her hand was still clutching Rachel's wrist.

"She's coming down," Betty said.

Rachel coughed, wrenching her hand from Mrs. Deerfield's. "I'm sorry."

"Those who clamor," Annie Ralph said, balancing the tea cup as she came back from the kitchenette, "they've spoken through you, honey."

"It was the sugar shock," Penelope said. "That damn cheesecake of yours. You must be exhausted, dear. You'll run a fever if we don't get you upstairs for a rest."

4.

"Did they speak through me?" Rachel lay down on the sofa in her own living room. She felt drained and weak and wasn't sure if she was dreaming.

Mrs. Deerfield stood above her, gazing down at her with concern. "What?"

"Annie said it was those spirits. She said they spoke through me. You told me I was sensitive. Is that what it means?"

"Annie Ralph would believe anything. I say just because it happens doesn't make it real. You started saying some jumbled words, it was gibberish." Mrs. Deerfield felt Rachel's forehead. "You don't seem too feverish, but it's probably the humidity, too. Can I turn up the air conditioner?"

Rachel nodded dreamily. Mrs. Deerfield went over to the thermostat and switched it on, adjusting the temperature.

"Did I say something bad? They looked scared."

"Those old birds are frightened of their shadows. But Rachel, you see I knew it, you're *open* to spiritual influence."

"It doesn't frighten you? Jesus, I was terrified and I don't even believe in it."

"One never knows what to believe in this world. Nothing's really out there telling us what to believe, is it? But we all muddle through and sometimes the patterns reveal themselves to us. You obviously have a talent that way, dear, perhaps untapped, but still there. But who knows what to make of it all?"

"But you believe in ghosts."

"The child in me believes, dear, the child in me believes.

And the grown-up in me believes in letting that child out now and then, sometimes just to run amok in the garden and track mud across my quiet life. But one mustn't confuse things: a ghost is a remnant of a life, while a spirit is simply a life without flesh. I believe in spirits and their influence. But it is just a pastime for a little old lady like myself, nothing for a pretty young girl to worry about."

"You've been very sweet, Mrs. Deerfield—I'm sorry for wilting like that with your friends."

"It *was* the sugar, Rachel, the way your face went from peach to white and then red when you came to—it was only a second. What have you eaten today?" Mrs. Deerfield returned to the couch; Rachel scooted over a bit to allow her to sit on the edge.

"Oh. A Diet Coke and I guess that was it until the cheesecake."

"Sugar can do nasty things to you if you're not careful. I try not to use much in my jams and jellies—as we all get older we must watch what we put in our tummies. When I worked as a nanny I saw what sugar can do to children."

"You must've been a very good nanny."

"Not so good." She rose from beside the couch. "You sure you'll be all right? I can sit here awhile longer."

"No, thank you, though. I'm just sleepy."

"When Mr. Adair gets home have him make you a good dinner."

"When Mr. Adair gets home he'll be lucky if I'm still asleep."

Mrs. Deerfield wagged a finger at her. "Naughty girl."

5.

It was dark out when she felt a kiss on her forehead, waking her, and smelled a brewery pressed against her. She remembered the man's mouth in Mrs. Deerfield's Clamoring Place, and tried to scream, but the mouth sucked greedily at her lips. When Rachel opened her eyes, pushing the man away from her, screaming, he switched a light on and it was Hugh, his tan suit stained and filthy, his hair brushed in opposing directions, his eyes half lidded, his shirt opened almost to his navel.

"I didn't think you'd scream," he said, shaking his head aimlessly.

"Where the *fuck* have you been!" she barked.

PART TWO

INFESTATIONS

JULY

ELEVEN

PLAYING HOUSE

1.

"Washington is hell in summer," Penelope Deerfield said as she dug into her mulch pile with a small rusty trowel. The patio was hot as a broiler, and Rachel (standing over her, observing) kept switching from one foot to the other. She was barefoot and had only come downstairs to put the trash bags in the alley dumpster when Mrs. Deerfield called her over to the small mulch pile near her thin strip of garden.

Mrs. Deerfield explained to Rachel, "You see, even the rodentia go off on suicide missions." She tapped the dead rat that lay next to her. It was the size of her own fist; Mrs. Deerfield had discreetly turned the rat over on its stomach so that Rachel wouldn't lose her breakfast looking at the deep gash that the cat had made down the rat's stomach. Mrs. Deerfield wore a wide-brimmed straw sun hat, a stretched-to-the-limit pair of blue jeans, and a grass-stained blue chamois work shirt that made her look a little too "down on the farm" considering what she was doing— burying a dead rat into the mulch pile. "It's morbid, I suppose, to use the rat's carcass as part of the mulch, but of such things is fertilizer made, dear. I've often thought it a pity that we don't bury human beings in mulch piles—it would make them ever so much more useful, don't you agree?"

"I hope the mice in our house don't get as big as *that* thing," Rachel said. The soles of her feet felt like they were burning, and the cement of the patio was like a bed of hot coals. She'd awakened feeling fat and unattractive, found a pimple in the middle of her forehead, her car would probably not start (or if it did, it would make those funny noises), and now she had to look at a dead rat and be polite about it after having eaten runny fried eggs. *And it's my day off*. She clutched the sides of her bathrobe together. "You're sure it didn't come from inside somewhere?"

"Oh, no, dear, this is most certainly an alley rat who had the misfortune of crossing Ramona's path. Ramona is a warrior at heart, and although a pregnant lady, still a wanderer—I saw her bring it in from near the dumpster. She was quite proud, I assure you, and expected extra cream this morning."

"Makes me happy there's a cat around—even if she does make me sneeze."

"It's the easy season for felines." Mrs. Deerfield poked a hole in the mulch pile with her trowel, stabbing into the mound to make a wide berth for the dead rat. "When the humidity and heat explode like this—it's not even eleven and already we've got a drippy oven day on our hands—all a cat has to do is put her paws out to trip the rats." She pushed the rat into the hole with the back of her trowel and then began covering it up. "The rats get fat and stupid in this kind of weather and then start fighting with each other. Usually, they're at each other's throats before a mischievous cat like my Ramona even happens upon them."

2.

Rachel wondered if she and Hugh were as bad as the rats.

They had managed to survive the first few weeks in the house without being at each other's throats—this was Rachel's feeling, anyway. Unemployment, Rachel knew from only brief experience, was depressing enough without having someone hanging over you like a vulture reminding you of it. She'd wake up for work in the morning and see him lying there, still dreaming, snoring, for all the world like an innocent, while she bitched and moaned about her malfunctioning car, about the soaring humidity, about the slight weight gain she'd noticed from eating all those on-the-way-to-the-office bagels from the Chesapeake Bagel

Factory. She'd take her shower, still wary of the roaches darting beneath the tile where the grouting had come out *CALL EXTERMINATOR,* her yellow Post-it Notes scattered across the tiles, down the hallway, on the refrigerator), and look in the steamed bathroom mirror wondering who was the fairest of them all, knowing it was not her. She was tired even before the day began. One morning, she wrote across the steamed mirror: BREADWINNER.

She hoped that Hugh would see it. She could never commit these nasty messages to her Post-it Note mania—too permanent, not lighthearted enough. A Post-it Note he could slip in his pocket and confront her with; writing on a steamed mirror was somewhat whimsical, a joke to be rubbed away with a towel or two fingers. *Who wrote this? Oh, you and your little jokes!*

Then it became a habit, leaving messages on the mirror in steam: WORK, or CASHFLOW, or the worst one, THE BIG 3-0. All in hopes that he would see it, would laugh, think she was being cute. And still get the message. She imagined him pulling back the shower curtain, all set to shave, looking up in the mirror and seeing the magic mirror message appear. Shaking his head, *That Rachel,* he would think, *what will that little dickens think up next?*

But he never mentioned the messages which meant one of two things: either he was taking them too seriously or he didn't notice them at all.

Rachel couldn't complain about Hugh having nothing to do around the house. He managed to strip off most of the dingy old wallpaper in the halls. He'd regrouted the tiles in both the upstairs and downstairs bathrooms, completely replaced the downstairs bathroom sink. He acted like a kid at Christmas every time he got his tool kit out, his hammers, screwdrivers, planes, crowbar, and sledgehammer ("for when I need to take out my aggressions on the walls . . ."), and a series of wrenches of all sizes. If he was busy he seemed happy. Everything seemed to be costing an arm and a leg—some days Rachel would look at her paycheck and know that it was going to pay for refinishing the floors or repairing something or other. Paints and wallpapers ate up most of the money, with new drapes running a close third. But no matter how much work Hugh put into the house, it always looked half-finished, and Rachel was a little afraid that it would always be that way. She made enough money to cover all the household expenses, but she was saving practically nothing and it had never been their plan to only live on one income. Her car alone was eating up a lot of spare change—it made strange noises which were to her a mystery, and there were mornings when she had to take a cab to work because the car refused to start.

But Hugh seemed to be happy, just keeping busy—summer was a horrible time to look for a job, the fall would be better, and Hugh was going on at least three interviews a week as it was. She couldn't even begrudge him a few beers here and there.

Sometimes she thought about inviting people over—Sassy or Hugh's brother Ted, or her mother, but the house smelled of paint and nothing was quite the way she wanted it to be yet. She wanted the house to be perfect, or as close as it could get, before she undertook anything like a house-warming party.

3.

"Mouse shit!" Hugh cried out. "We've got mouse shit in our sink!" He stared intently at it as if it would move. "They're taking over."

Rachel turned away from the refrigerator. "I'm glad you can find some humor in it—are you going to scoop it up or what?"

"It's probably good fertilizer. Maybe Penny Dreadful would like it for her mulch pile." He had taken to calling their downstairs tenant Penny Dreadful, and her cat Baby Dreadful.

"Hugh, think about it: some mouse is climbing around our sink and stove and cutting board. Oh, gross, and I just made a sandwich over there. We've got to call the exterminator or something before we die of bubonic plague."

"You ate a mouse-shit sandwich?"

"Disgusting. Hold the mayo. I feel like we should call the health department to close us down. You're supposed to get some poison and traps. That's your job, right?"

"You don't really want to kill Mickey or Minnie, do you?"

"Even Gus-Gus and Mighty Mouse. The three blind mice, too. I don't care. This is getting sickening."

Hugh began squeaking. He wrinkled his nose and wiggled his ears. He stepped over to her, his chin pressed down against his neck making him look remarkably chinless, his eyes wide. *Squeak!*

"Oh, Hugh, really." Rachel clucked her tongue but could not help smiling.

"Hows about a mouse fuck?" His voice was a high-pitched falsetto.

"Hugh."

"Well, we haven't really, you know, had our inaugural . . . fuck."

"It's Tuesday afternoon and I have to be back in the office in twenty minutes."

"Squeak!"

"That is the least erotic sound I have ever heard a man or mouse make."

"You be Minnie and I'll be Mickey."

"And we'll both end up looking Goofy. Blasphemy."

"How do you think mice do it, anyway?"

"Something I can go my whole life without ever finding out. And I hope our mice don't do much of it around here. Now Hugh, stop that—I am not about to . . . right here."

"So don't."

She felt his hand climbing up the side of her thigh, tickling the light hair that she'd missed shaving, and then pulling aside her hose. "You'll run them, Hugh." But she let him continue and he did run them, tucking his fingers up between the elastic. Her breathing was getting heavy. Whenever they made love she always felt as if they were suddenly in some dark closet, two children naked together playing doctor. It made her feel happy and strong, to say nothing of the intense pleasure she felt and the thought that this was something so right and natural, a man making love to a woman, the two bodies becoming one monstrous but natural body, *normal life* . . . his lips, rough and heavy, never half as hungry as hers seemed—she was embarrassed by these sudden explosions of sexual heat. Her body would go out of control and she would do things with him that she would later feel were not things that *Rachel Adair, lawyer and daughter of Mike and Dorothy Brennan,* would normally be responsible for. Sometimes when they made love, in the dark closet of her mind, she imagined there were five of him, five Hughs stroking her, licking her, holding her, kissing her, pulling her against their moist, rutting bodies.

Rachel clutched the edge of her skirt up around her waist, as Hugh, kissing her, licking her neck, pressing his mouth up behind her ear lobe, inched her pantyhose down towards her knees. She reached with her hand towards his crotch and just as she touched the rough denim of his 501 Levi's, pressing her fingernails in between the buttons, about to pop them open, Hugh drew back. Away from her.

"God," he said.

Her eyes came back into focus. The heat brushed past both of them, dissipating into the atmosphere. "Mmm?"

"I just saw our mouse run behind the stove—it kind of unnerved me."

Rachel let the edges of her skirt fall back into place, and Hugh withdrew his hand from between her legs. He reached down and pulled her hose back up. He seemed very work-manlike about it. He reached up and kissed her nose, biting slightly. "Nose shark."

She looked at him, disoriented. "We've got to have our inaugural, um, you know . . ."

"Right now I think I should try to get that mouse out of here—do you know where the broom is, Scout?"

But she knew enough not to insist on returning to a potential fifteen minutes of animal lust—she didn't really want to work up a sweat, anyway, the humidity would take care of that.

Rachel also knew that Hugh had lost his erection.

And not when he'd seen the mouse.

He'd lost it when she'd touched him there.

You don't go around mentioning to the man you love that he can't get it up. Let's Pretend you saw the invader mouse, too, and make a thing of it, but don't make a big deal out of temporary impotence. She could count on her fingers the number of times they'd made love since Hugh had been unemployed. Maybe five times in five months. Only once in the past six weeks. Either she was too tired or he fell asleep early, or he was reading a really good book in bed, or she said something to make him angry, or there was a mouse running loose behind the stove. It had gotten to a point in the evenings when Rachel, coming home from a mountain of work and a full day in court, didn't even consider sex an option worth pursuing.

Hugh was bending over, trying to look behind the stove, when Rachel said, "When you find our mouse, be sure and ask him how mice do it. And take notes, okay?"

This is as bitchy as I get.

4.

People passed in and out of her office all day, but they might as well have been pigeons fluttering through one of the city's parks: Rachel felt isolated at work, isolated at home, and she found that she was losing her ability to concentrate on the things that had to get done. She'd been through something like this with the miscarriage. She'd gone to a therapist, who told her this inability to concentrate on the work at hand was a sign of depression, perhaps a very severe depression. The therapist suggested she see a doctor for a complete examination, and suddenly, when she was twenty-seven, Rachel Adair felt like she'd turned into Frances Farmer. She imagined that once she went to a psychiatrist, she'd be put in a hospital, they'd find out awful things about her mind, shave her head, force her into hot baths—followed, perhaps, by shock treatment and a tidy lobotomy. *Just stick that old ice pick up under the eyelids and everything will be hunky-dory. If only it were that easy.* Then one day, just as suddenly, this sort of anxiety was gone. The world seemed different to her. *You lose a baby—but not a baby, just a small subdividing sphere, a microscopic amoebalike thing, no heartbeat, something the size of a pea that was formed when one of those tadpole sperm collided with an ovum—you lose a baby and you get slightly depressed. Normal life, Scout, a blessing in disguise. You don't concentrate too well at work, so, hell, you take a few weeks off work (unstructured time, the therapist called it) and you maybe fall in love with the man you married—you try to concentrate on a little nurturing of*

*him because he really needs it—you help with his unemploy-
ment anxiety, with his "I didn't pass the D.C. bar" anxiety.
You listen to your mom's advice on How To Make A Man
Happy. 'Cause weren't mom and dad happy? Even when they
fought like tigers, weren't they happy? And wouldn't it make
daddy proud, if he were alive, to know she was working on her
marriage?*

*How come when Hugh and I fight I always feel like I'm the
bitch goddess of Northwest Washington, propelled on by one
of those delightful mood swings that the therapist had
mentioned way back in the spring?*

But now, in summer, the humidity, the monoxide-filtered
air of the Washington streets, the rush, the push, the phone
calls—zillions of phone calls to and from bitching clients—
Rachel felt herself slipping again. At least she was conscious
of slipping, and she couldn't blame it on a miscarriage,
nothing as understandable as that. According to her calen-
dar, she would be eight months pregnant if she hadn't lost
her little sphere.

Could she blame her bad feelings on Hugh?

Could she say *Let's Pretend* that it was Hugh's fault that
she was slipping into a lethargy, a depression, a deep
depression, a deep-shit depression?

Let's Pretend.

There is no Hugh Adair.

*I can't, I can't. I love Hugh. We've got our share of
problems and right now it seems awful. We've gotten up to our
necks in it—I hate my job, Hugh has no job, he's probably
ordering a drink right now, and I'm a witch to think that,
maybe he's in an interview right now, or dropping an
application off, or worrying about the next bar exam. But it's
a hot summer, and we have more than most couples our
age—we're healthy, we own our own home, I've got a
well-paying job.*

As mom would say, Normal Life.

As daddy would say, it all comes out in the wash.

She remembered—no, she *concentrated* on what she
loved about Hugh, and none of it had to do with his ability
to find work. She loved his smile, she loved the way she felt
when they cuddled together in bed at night, she even loved
him when he was down and sad, looking so much like a little

boy, the heavy shock of blond hair falling down across his forehead, his blue eyes becoming large and round.

Mom pushed daddy too hard. Rachel had seen it all the time she was growing up. *Why couldn't mom just have been satisfied with daddy the way he was? He provided well enough, and he made sure we all got good educations, and he was always there on weekends to do family things—he didn't have to be the most ambitious or wealthiest man in the world.*

Rachel was determined not to do the same thing with Hugh. He'd come around in his own time. Not all men had to have burning ambition. Not all men had to be ridiculously goal oriented. Hugh had a law degree and one day soon she might even be jealous of his success. And proud of him. She hadn't understood why she had passed the bar and he had not; he was bright, top of his class, she had faith in him most of the time, but he'd tied himself in knots over the exam—it was all a foreign language to him. One of the qualities that had attracted her to him during their courtship had been the fact that he seemed to take none of it seriously: *Let's Pretend, Scout,* he'd say, cradling her in his arms, *Let's Pretend, I'm the daddy and you're the mommy and I'm hammering loose nails back into the floor, I'm greasing the hinges on the doors, and you're telling the kiddos a bedtime story and we're all drinking hot cocoa.*

But it's time, Hugh, to take a few things seriously.

5.

At night, in bed, the heat rose in the house and seemed to linger in a cloud above her head; no matter how she adjusted the thermostat, it was warm in the bedroom. Hugh set up a small fan in the doorway, which seemed to do nothing more than make an annoying whirring noise. He'd set mousetraps up in the corners of the rooms, and every now and then, she'd hear the traps *clacking* and she'd imagine the dead gray mouse, its head smushed beneath the wire jaw of the trap. She could never recall the moment when sleep would come to her—she felt as if she lay awake half the night, listening to the clacking of the mousetraps, Hugh's breezy snores, and the whirring of the fan. Hugh would press up against her back in his sleep, and she would feel the damp fever of sweat along her back, tickling. The clacking mouse-traps reminding her of the supposed ghost of the house, the whore Rose Draper, The Clapper, who was supposed to wander the house clapping her hands together.

Somewhere, off where the sirens screamed down one street or another, out where the cats cried in sexual longing, she would hear a baby crying, too, and it would comfort her like nothing else and before she realized it, she would be asleep, dreaming.

6.

Rachel didn't even have to wake Hugh up—he was staring up at the ceiling. "I was dreaming of bombs exploding," he murmured.

Clack! A mousetrap from out in the hall.

She closed her eyes and thought about sleep again. *He'll take care of the mousetraps.*

"How many do you think we're catching?" His breath was like steam against her shoulders; she felt him move his head against the small of her back, his hair greasy against her skin.

She didn't answer.

"I'd guess in the hundreds. I better go downstairs and change the traps now that I'm up."

She sighed, realizing that she would not quickly get back to sleep. "I kind of feel bad for the mice."

"Yeah, they've probably been coming in here for genera-tions." Hugh chuckled and she felt his arm snake under her shoulder blades and curve around to stroke the skin cover-ing her ribs; she automatically pulled her stomach in. Then his arms slithered back away from her; the bed creaked, she felt his weight shift, he was standing up.

Clack!

She kept her eyes closed and tried to think about sleep, although every time she was falling (she imagined sleep as a downward drifting on a feather bed, like Dorothy in *The Wizard of Oz*, the house spinning through a cyclone while she slept) another trap would spring somewhere downstairs or in the hall.

She heard Hugh say, "I was sure the fan would make enough white noise to cover the sound of the traps."

She lay there, eyes pressed shut, a tension headache coming on, wondering what "white noise" meant—the phrase sounded foreign even though she knew in her heart of hearts what it meant, or at least she'd used that phrase before.

And then she was at her mother's house in Arlington, helping to can peaches—something her mother had never done in her life. If anything they'd be un-canning peaches. Her mother said, "All summer long they ripen."

Then her mother opened her mouth to speak and a *clack!* came out instead; Rachel grasped her heart, which was easy to do because she was standing there naked in her mother's kitchen. Naked and her mother didn't seem to care in the least.

But it wasn't her mother, it was Hugh, wearing her mother's housedress, and as he turned away from the jars of peaches, he said, "I think we just got Cubby, Karen, Bobby, *and* Annette."

But she was mistaken, her vision was going in and out of focus and it wasn't Hugh at all, but *daddy,* who smiled sweetly to her. His smile grew wider, a piano keyboard smile, until his teeth started bursting through his cheeks and stretching out, opening wide as he said, "Rachel, Let's Pretend I'm the daddy and you're the mommy and we have a whole mess of kiddos . . ."

Rachel heard a gurgling noise from inside her, and she looked down at her stomach: it was growing large as if she were being pumped up with water. Her breasts were rising like twin helium balloons to compete in the Macy's Thanksgiving Day Parade; her stomach was churning like a washing machine on a full cycle; she felt tiny feet kicking her from inside. She was getting fat and heavy, swollen. Beneath her enormous breasts, another pair of breasts sprouted, and below them, another, all the way to her navel which itself stretched from side to side of her puffing belly like a mouth opening and closing with each breath. She heard a *clack!*

from somewhere. She had the feeling that a kettle was about to boil over, and she remembered that she'd left eggs boiling in a saucepan and she had to go turn down the heat. Now the eggs were probably cracking from the soaring temperature. She realized that the boiling was going on in her stomach as her six breasts began leaking milk. Beneath the clacking and the bubbling, she heard her babies, inside her, crying—she was boiling her mess of kiddos before they even had a chance, her spheres were screaming beneath her flapping navel. Then her ears were ringing like an alarm going off, a kitchen timer, and she knew a *clack!* was coming, the biggest fucking *clack!* she was ever going to hear, a *clack!* to end all *clacks!*, like a time bomb, her fucking biological clock was going off, a *clack!* that would mean—

When Rachel's belly exploded into a shower of streaming spheres with tiny feet, and rivers of milk spurted from her breasts, and the scream was caught way down deep in her larynx which was now exposed because the skin had ripped from her vagina all the way up to her throat, she opened her eyes.

Hugh was standing, a silhouette in the hall light.

Her own body was whole and naked and she lay atop the sweat-soaked sheet of their bed.

"Nine are dead—nine mice," he said groggily. "I think Mouseketeer roll call is over for the night."

Rachel closed her eyes and pretended she was asleep because she knew if she could pretend she was asleep, maybe she would *be* asleep.

But she was awake most of the night, waiting for the next *clack!* to occur.

TWELVE

FEEDING THE DEAD

1.

Mattie Peru, her trash bags of invisibility wrapped around her face like a scarf, walked down the aisle of the grocery store—people were staring at her, someone's little girl was even pointing at her as she passed the frozen food section, but she didn't care. Her trash bags rustled like dead leaves underfoot, and as she lumbered down towards the L'il Ol' Baker's Pantry, she clutched them about her neck. She could not be invisible for this—that magic would have to be saved up now, saved for the big fight with Baron Samedi. Her thoughts were jumbled—language didn't come easy to her anymore, not since her baby died, and words came in strings like spit into her mouth—sometimes she couldn't control the way they leapt out, sometimes she managed to imprison them beneath her tongue.

He's gettin' through, he's crawling up and out, and this ain't his domain. The words wanted to fly from her mouth, but she reined them in. *You buy your yogurt and your frozen pizzas and your Trident Sugar Free Gum, but you don't keep him away, you don't got the magic inside you, you don't know what he comes for, you don't know the way he turn life and death inside out and upside down and take the baby before he cries and the mama before she gives milk, and he makes the house scream with the lost and the ones that don't know no better!* But some of the words spat out from between the gaps in her teeth without her being aware of it, and the nice middle-aged lady picking out the raspberry jelly doughnuts and the crullers for her breakfast was

91

treated to: "Getting! Crawlin'! Domain! Frozen pizzas don't keep him away! Inside out 'n upside down, take the baby! The house scream, no better!"

The teenage boy behind the counter, dressed in the L'il Ol' Baker's Pantry uniform of puffy chef's cap and large white apron, murmured, "You get all kinds in this neighborhood," but the nice middle-aged lady pretended that Mattie was invisible. *Joke's on you, lady! I know I ain't invisible without the trash bags over my face! You just trying to fool old Mattie, and you just don't go around foolin' no mambos!*

"Hey!" The boy behind the counter yelped like a dog whose tail has been stepped on. He reached across and slapped Mattie's hand—she was helping herself to the free sampling of pastries on the white paper doilies.

"Ain't these free?" Mattie growled; she hadn't even bothered to look up at him.

"Not for you," he said.

This didn't seem unfair to Mattie. She was accustomed to this kind of treatment. She refrained from laying a curse on the boy. She stared at the sliced bear claw and the neat square cuts of a cherry danish that remained on the doily. "Ain't for me, for my little girl."

The nice middle-aged woman pretended to be having trouble deciding if the raspberry-filled doughnuts were right, or if those coconut-covered ones were more suitable for the breakfast she had in mind. Her nose wrinkled slightly like a ripple across a pond.

She smells me. Mattie grinned.

Mattie knew how to make the boy give her the pastry samples.

She reached across the counter, her fingers grazing every crumb on the doily.

It was the Magic Touch that she possessed.

And the Magic Touch worked.

The teenager said, "Take all of them and get out of here—no one's going to want them now that your fat old hands got all over them."

Out on the street again, Mattie wrapped the pastries carefully in a newspaper and tucked it into her grocery cart; she found a safe space for it down beneath the empty cans she'd found behind the store, and her usual collection of blankets, newspapers, and bottles. The weather suited Mattie: the skies hung low like a sagging cushion—she felt she could reach up and touch them (she tried to, to push the stuffing of the clouds back up into the lining of sky)—and the humidity was itchy. The temperature matched the soaring fever in her soul, the sun was approaching midday, and the time was right to feed the dead.

I brung this for you, my baby. Mattie's words spun through the gallery of her head, although all that jumped out from between her lips was a bleating "My baby." *I done promised to keep him outta this world, and he ain't gonna come back. He ain't gonna use your little baby to come back, my baby.*

She pushed her cart down along Connecticut Avenue; the streets were desolate of pedestrians—a few people late for work, or an occasional bum hanging out on the stoop of Steve's Ice Cream, but the heat had sent lingerers inside buildings and shops. Mattie felt the plastic from the trash bags tickle her cheek. The wheels of the cart squealed and *pashucka*ed as she pushed it over the cracks in the sidewalk, negotiating the turn to the right around the DuPont Circle Metro entrance. The wind from the trains came up from the long downward fall of escalators, and she waited, tasting the wind for Baron Samedi—but he was not that strong. He had no power in this world. He ruled the dead. He could only breathe himself into those who were close to death. He had no life. *I don't fear no dead man.* She passed over the entrance, feeling that innocent train wind pass by her. Then at P Street, she turned right again.

I feed you, my baby, because I need your spirit strong to help your mama, I need your spirit strong. He's coming back again—they tried those girls, but none worked, but this one work because this one repayment, this one give for services due. He's tired, he's weary, but he sees his chance to come through, honeychild, and he's going to turn it inside out.

The sidewalks were hard on her: the grocery cart felt heavy, and she had to pivot and lift up on the wheels each time she went from the sidewalk to the street to the sidewalk crossing Twentieth, Twenty-first, Twenty-second Street, until she came to a wide green park affectionately named "P Street Beach" by DuPont Circle residents. There were even sunbathers down along the grass near the picnic tables—

just a few people in bathing suits, looking silly with the traffic speeding along Rock Creek Parkway just across the thin creek. When Mattie saw them she pointed and laughed.

But the laugh turned into a bleating cry as she remembered her duty. She set the cart parallel to the dirt path that led through the sparse bushes and trees to the right of the park, almost beneath the stone bridge of P Street as it ran over the Parkway into Georgetown.

Mattie reached down beneath the can for the pastries.

She walked down the path, into the woods.

She searched the area, trying to remember the spot—the summer with its hungry branches and thick green tresses of grass covering up the spot—everything was overgrown. Mattie slipped on a ridge along the path and came thudding down hard on her ass, pebbles scurrying towards the creek. The pastries wrapped in the paper bag leapt out from where she had been cradling them in the crook of her elbow, and scattered beside her. Methodically, she picked up the crumbs and the bits of bear claw one by one—placing them in the bag again. She looked down towards the cold running stream with the ragged grass growing along its banks, and beyond it, the deep purple of the road, the cars whizzing by.

Mattie prayed that she would find direction. She prayed for the place to be revealed.

The place where she'd buried her daughter.

She hunted with her fingers, crawling through the dry rough grass that scratched her like sandpaper—her fingers never let her down, not the way her eyes and her mind did. Mattie's Magic Touch still worked, and if she wiggled her fingers through the grass, it would begin talking to her, whisper the secret as to where the grave was. She sliced her finger across a shard of glass thrust upward in the dirt and cried out—but she was close, the glass seemed to sing to her, oh, she was close!

And then she found it.

Marked by a broken pitcher she had buried there in the earth. As she sat back to look at the grave she realized how obvious it would be if someone looked at the pattern of the grass: it had grown in a wavy pattern around the body of her daughter.

Nadine, she prayed, *for your strength. Help me, my baby, help me. Stop him, stop him. He can't be comin' through. Help, my baby.* But the words that leapt from her mouth were: "Help *her.*"

As if to answer her prayer, a tremendous droning hum seemed to swoop up from under the P Street Bridge, a noise that grew like cicadas on a summer's evening—only it wasn't yet evening and these weren't cicadas.

Wasps. The gray, tattered nest was thrust into the crotch of the bridge's underside; it shook as if by a breeze.

It was alive with hundreds of them.

Mattie knew what she must do, she must send a warning, the wasps must carry her warning.

Mattie Peru pressed her face close to the earth, gently scraping her lips against the singing grass above her daughter's grave.

2.

The sign on Roxanne Hastings' desk read: RECEPTIONIST, but everyone knew she had run the law offices of Adair, Long, Wilmot and Sanford almost single-handedly for the past thirty years. She prided herself on being a tough customer, a hard woman, someone who didn't put up with any guff, nonsense, or shenanigans. She could tell a wisenheimer as soon as he stepped off the elevator, and she could fix the company Xerox machine faster than anybody with just a kick of her heel. Roxanne had spent most of her adult life remaining unruffled by the scum bags who trekked to the sixth-floor suites—they were rich and sometimes famous, but scum bags nonetheless. The lawyers themselves—rude, overgrown babies who were quickly becoming old men— self-indulgent and so darn wealthy (Roxanne disliked strong language the way she disliked strong perfume) that they seemed to think they could buy anyone and everyone in their paths. And for thirty years she had been as sweet and hard as candy to them, had taken their messages, arranged their conferences and board meetings, their Christmas parties, even their trysts.

But in her thirty years with the law firm, she'd never

witnessed what came off the elevator on a lazy Friday afternoon in July.

Roxanne Hastings screamed, "Holy shit!"

She had never used that sort of language before in her life.

It might as well have been a giant sewer rat that had come up through the vents.

Make that a giant sewer rat with its guts dangling out.

But Roxanne could deal with rats.

But what got off the elevator Friday afternoon and stepped, or rather *shuffled,* across the pale blue plush carpet—it looked like the contents of a dumpster had come to life.

A large black woman whose smell preceded her stood in the hall between the four elevator doors. The smell was one with which Roxanne Hastings was well familiar: the smell of executive washroom stall number three which was always backing up. Roxanne knew about stall number three because one of the summer clerks had bet her that she wouldn't go into the men's room and check it out, and Roxanne was a sucker for a sure thing. And this *thing,* in her dark, rippling plastic bags and oversized, open-toed hiking boots, her partially covered face huge like a hydrocephalic baby's, round pop-eyes, broad lips split like twin slugs parting into a brown toothless grin—crying out, "Holy shit!" also as if the sight of Roxanne Hastings was enough to scare her, too.

"You—you can't be here," Roxanne gasped, pushing herself back from her desk, standing.

Vail Foster, a junior partner, was coming out of the Xerox room, a stack of papers under his arms. He shot a glance towards the creature (smelled her first, his nose wrinkling, he was wondering who farted); then he winked at Roxanne as he passed her desk. "One of Sanford's *pro bono*'s no doubt."

"You're on the wrong floor, lady," Roxanne said. She was regaining some authority. This was *her* office after all, and anyone who stepped off those elevators was trespassing on *her* territory.

The black woman's mouth opened wider. "Holy shit!" she shouted. Although it was beginning to sound more and more like "Hosheet," or "Horse shit," the more she repeated the phrase.

"I'm gonna have to call somebody if you don't get out of here." Roxanne was now in full blossom—*no crazy bag lady was gonna stink up her life.*

The black woman's chasmic mouth clamped shut. Her eyes crinkled into small silverfish, almost paper cuts of eyes, all white, and then they popped open again. "I come to see Mr. Big Man," she snarled, her upper lip curling back to her flaring nostrils, causing a ripple of tension across her round face that continued uninterrupted along the Hefty trash bags.

Before Roxanne Hastings could tell her again to leave— simultaneously reaching for the phone to dial the number for security—the black woman brought her arms into view. They'd been hidden beneath the folds of the torn, flapping bags. They were thick, flabby arms, but meaty like twin Virginia hams, and in her twisting, swollen fingers she brought out something. Something which Roxanne thought at first was some kind of ugly piñata. Or perhaps a gray papier mâché mask. For one terror-stricken moment she thought it was a bomb and that thought (*Shit! This is a bomb!*) after all the bomb scares the office building had sustained over the past twenty years, all those false alarms, now, today, this Friday in July, *it was for real.*

But then Roxanne heard the noise, saw the tiny particles floating out from the gray papery object.

Wasps.

This crazy woman was holding a *wasp's nest* in her hands.

The black woman held the nest up and shook it madly, the way you'd shake a snow globe to watch the tiny specks of plastic white snow fall down across a winter scene. But this snow, angry, buzzing, murmuring, flew in all directions, several towards Roxanne Hastings' desk, which is the reason she ran screaming back to the private offices of the senior partners of the law firm of Adair, Long, Wilmot and Sanford.

3.

Mr. Big Man! You come outta your office, you come out from behind your fat desk, and you see your children flying and singing, looking for you, they want to claim you, Mr. Big Man, they're gonna find you, too, and then you'll know you got to do something, something to stop the house from screaming, got to stop the babies from crying! You got to stop the abortionist from raising the knife! You got to stop the monsters from breeding!

All this Mattie Peru cried out in the hall, in her head, but when she opened her mouth she was crying, "Boshinus! Boshinus!"

4.

Winston Adair felt like he was sinking into the back of the plush leather chair. His office was dark, the only light stealing in like a coward from beneath the door and between the slats of the venetian blinds.

"I am a monster," he said to no one.

Beyond his door there was the clacking of his secretary's typewriter and a low murmur as if of whispering just on the other side of the door.

The headache he was having made his vision blur, and sometimes when they came on suddenly like this he hallucinated voices. When he heard the woman scream down the hall, when he heard a woman yelling some indecipherable word, when he heard the commotion of office doors opening and closing, he knew there was something.

He had stood at the window of his office, the blinds up, the afternoon light flooding in, not ten minutes before. He had no headache then. He was thinking about a case the firm was handling, thinking about a prostitute he was afraid he may have killed, thinking about what he would have for dinner, where he would go, who he would invite out with him.

Then he saw her.

Madeleine Perreau. Crossing K Street, narrowly avoiding being hit as she crossed against the light. It didn't matter that he hadn't seen her in over twenty years, and it didn't matter that he could barely see her through all the trash bags she wore.

It was her.

Not the Madeleine Perreau he'd remembered, not the woman with the smooth yellow brown skin and broad accommodating hips, the tantalizing walk, but the Madeleine he'd created: a grotesque sculpture, the Madeleine he thought he had buried in his memory of that night.

Thought *they* had buried that night.

All these years I thought she was dead. I thought . . . after what she'd done I thought she would've died.

I thought the housekeeper would've killed her.

The woman below on the street had walked up to the entrance to his building. Had gone inside.

Winston Adair felt a sudden throbbing in his temple; his stomach lurched and he tasted his lunch (pastrami on rye and two dill pickles) in the back of his throat; his knees trembled, and a muscle just to the right of his right eye began twitching.

The throbbing under the skin of his face seemed to explode, and he turned off the light in his office, closed the blinds.

He didn't notice the wasp that had crawled beneath the door of his office until it stung him on the back of the hand and he screamed just as Roxanne Hastings had done.

5.

Mattie Peru's fingers were numb, but fingers were nothing special. You had ten of them, anyway. Mattie licked each finger as she rode the elevator back down to the lobby of the building. She pressed her back against the coolness of the full-length mirror—the elevator was full of mirrors—and looked at her reflection for the first time in twenty years.

She saw nothing reflected there, because her trash bags of invisibility covered her.

He'll know it, he'll know it was me. He thinks he sits in his office all safe and sound. He don't have to see Mattie, he don't have to think nothing about Nadine, he don't have to think about my baby and my baby's baby, but he'll know it when he sees them bugs.

She took inventory on herself, glancing beneath her trash bags: *ten fingers, ten toes, two tits and all of 'em numb and scratchy from where the bugs took a bite or two or three or four.* "Ain't gonna breed no monsters!" she shouted uncontrollably as the elevator doors parted in the lobby.

A bewildered group of men in dark suits, coming back from late lunches, stood back as Mattie Peru invisibly stepped out of the elevator.

THIRTEEN

PLAYING HOUSE, II

1.

When Rachel Adair was not in her office, she came up with ways of staying away from the house when Hugh was around working on it—she and Hugh still had the occasional laugh, still began speaking at the same time saying the same thing, still had tender embraces when the day had been long and frustrating, but these were all becoming few and far between. *There are times to be close and times to be distant, and this was one of those times to be a little distant, to let Hugh work out his troubles on his own.* Rachel was afraid that if she were to sit down with Hugh and plan out his future, he would blame all his troubles on her. She did not intend to be used for an emotional punching bag, and didn't want to begin disliking Hugh.

"Well, I almost broke my sacred vow." Rachel was jogging with Sassy Parker on the bike path that ran alongside the Potomac River, with the Kennedy Center just across the parkway. The river smelled of dead fish, and the carbon monoxide from the traffic on the road to their right was equally as nauseating. Rachel sometimes wondered if jogging near heavy morning traffic was as bad for her lungs as her old cigarette habit.

"You running around on Hugh?" Sassy was her usual knock-out self in just an old T-shirt and baggy shorts. She wasn't even *sweating* half as much as Rachel. They jogged to Rachel's pace, which was very slow, almost a walk.

"Really, I don't have time to run around on Hugh."

"But you've got time to run around."

"No—I meant the vow about smoking. Hugh fell apart on me last Sunday and I ended up having the cigarette dream." Rachel's breathing was ragged and she had to slow down even further, until finally she *was* walking. "You know, the one where the cigarette is just *begging* you to suck it?"

Sassy gave her a nasty glance, but also began walking.

"Like a teenager horny for sex—you are a wicked girl, Retch. I never deny myself—in fact, I want to light up right now." Sassy withdrew something small, slender, and white from the pocket of her shorts. A cigarette. "I have another one in my pocket if you break down." Sassy brought a book of matches out. She paused, leaning against the railing of the walkway, and lit the cigarette. Sassy took a long fat drag, blowing the smoke over the Potomac River.

"No—believe me, if I could resist last Sunday I can easily turn down a cigarette—*not* that Hugh's been turning down his cherished booze."

"Enough!" Sassy covered her ears with her hands. "I am so tired of married women telling me their problems. Single people have more troubles, but we don't whine to everybody. Girl, go see a therapist."

Both of them said at the same moment: "I don't have *time* to see a therapist."

"Mmm—this Kool sure is good."

"Blow a little smoke my way."

"That would be cheating. How many miles do you think we ran?"

"Ten—twelve . . . maybe two."

"I'm sweating like I ran twelve. This river really stinks in the summer."

Rachel nodded, but fell silent for a while as they walked along the running path.

"All right, so tell me—what's going on with Hugh?"

"No, you're right, I shouldn't dump it on you. I should figure this out on my own. Or dump it right back on Hugh. And it's nothing really *bad.* In a way—a very sick way—it's kind of good. Hugh and I were bickering about something, I forget, and then he went racing out of the house, and then I didn't see him until midnight when he was throwing up on the stairs and crying."

"Whoa, now, slow down. He was crying?"

"It was about his first wife, something about her, but he kept pushing me away, and there was that vomit on the third step up. Not a pretty sight. Between that and the mice and roaches . . . His first wife, Joanna, is not one of my favorite topics, either."

"Chalk it up to life's ups and downs."

"I *wish*. Hugh is kind of—I know this sounds wimpy—sensitive and he's not a coward or anything, but he has that kind of poetic slouch to him. I always feel like I should protect him. But he's been sort of out of it lately, at least since we moved in. Maybe taking on a house this soon was a mistake—maybe we should've waited until he had some steady work, or at least passed the bar. I actually thought the house would *help* things. But I think he's . . ."

"Losing it?"

Rachel nodded. "One of us is, anyway."

"Maybe you two should start living a normal life—he doesn't get out much, does he?"

"Supposedly on job interviews, but I think mainly to grab a few drinks." Rachel almost laughed: her life with Hugh was beginning to sound funny to her, as if they were two sad sacks who had found each other.

Sassy's face was screwed up in the kind of intensity of thought that Rachel's mother was so good at when advice was forthcoming. "While I'm admittedly no expert on relationships, Retch, I think maybe you should cut back on your workload a little and try to do a few things together—maybe go off for a sexy weekend or start entertaining more."

"You mean be *the total woman?*"

"Half a woman. Maybe three-quarters of one." She blew a smoke ring into Rachel's face. "You said you might give a housewarming party?"

Rachel inhaled the smoke, smiling. "With all the vermin we've got running through there, we should call it a mousewarming party. I had to set one of those awful traps—you know, where the cute little mouse gets his feet caught in glue—really gross. But it's better than the racket these mousetraps make." She paused, breathing in, sighing. She glanced across the river to Virginia and thoughts of *home* and *daddy* seemed to be there, just over the water. The thought of dealing with Hugh at all made her want to crawl into bed and stay there for a week or more. *I want to scream, but not too loud.*

"Get out of yourself a little: give a party, go sky diving, join the Junior League." Sassy smirked.

"You realize you're the only friend I have in this town?"

Sassy puffed on the cigarette. "No good—you're going to have to have at least twelve friends to have a housewarming party."

Getting back up to M Street on their way home, the two women passed a storefront on the edge of Georgetown. Rachel was not aware that she had begun crying until she felt the squeeze of Sassy's hand on her elbow. "Oh, Retch," Sassy said.

"I guess my body just hasn't caught up with reality—it still thinks it's pregnant."

The store window display was of baby clothes. They were frilly and light and draped across a long blue rocking horse with painted eyelashes and a lipsticked smile.

I want to scream, she thought.

2.

On Saturday, Rachel could not get her VW Rabbit started to go to Safeway. She sat in the damn car in the alley after a frustrating few minutes of turning the key in the ignition, pumping the gas, jiggling the wheel, and praying to whatever gods were listening. The seat of the car was hot, the wheel burned her fingers, she had gotten dressed up to go to the store, and already she was fried and sweating. "You god-damn car!" she shouted, pounding the dashboard with her fist. She sat there feeling as if she were nothing but frazzled nerves covered with skin. She felt like yelling her head off, spewing out every obscenity she'd ever heard or seen written on bathroom walls in college.

She sat there a few minutes longer; a breeze actually

wafted through the open window. Her hands were shaking. She wanted to cry but was so mad at the car she didn't give it that little victory of seeing her fall apart.

Rachel looked up at her house, over the back gate, to the second floor. Hugh had come out onto the outside stairs, standing there in his paint-spattered khakis and filthy white T-shirt. When he waved to her, paint flew out from the brush he was holding. Hugh was apparently in a good mood this afternoon—when he was consumed with working on the house, planing the floor, scraping old paint off walls and spreading on a new coat, he was content. He had a way of standing there that reminded her of her father, just a certain inner calmness regardless of the turmoil going on about him.

Hugh's smile sank into a straight line, and a look of concern came across his features; his brow wrinkled. He looked like a lifeguard who had just spotted a shark fin circling a swimmer. He pointed to the left of the car. His mouth opened and he shouted something like, "Look out!"

Just as Rachel turned to her left to see what he was pointing at, something enormous and dark pushed itself into her open car window.

"Boshinus!" the thing shouted (and Rachel in the half-second of absolute terror knew it was the fat black bag woman from Winthrop Park and at the same time thought it was a monster). Her eyes were jaundiced a translucent yellow, and she stank like an unflushed toilet. Her spit sprayed across Rachel's face as she howled at the top of her lungs, "Get outta the screamin' house, lady!"

Rachel tried to scream but found she had no voice. It felt like her vocal cords had turned to solid ice. As if in a dream, she was moving in slow motion and everything around her went on in real time. She wanted to reach over and roll the window up, but her whole body seemed to have gone to sleep, and her skin crawled with a pins-and-needles sensation. All she could do was stare at the crazy woman in horror.

But *normal life* flooded back in an instant as if it had never been gone: the crazy woman moved away from the car. The back gate was opening to the alley; Hugh was running down the iron stairs to the patio.

Mrs. Deerfield came through the gate holding the garden hose, spraying it at the bag lady who ran limping down the alley. "You get out of here, you old witch, or I'll have them put you away for good this time!"

"Boshinus!" the black woman cried out as she turned the corner, her trash bags flying behind her like a cape in the wind.

3.

"It seems heartless, I know, but perhaps if I called the authorities she might have a better home at one of the hospitals." Mrs. Deerfield sat on Hugh's college chair between the rubber plant and the shedding ficus, pathetically potted in a too-small pail. Rachel leaned back on the couch, and Hugh was in the kitchen brewing tea. Hugh's framed photographs hung along the wall above the fireplace; Mrs. Deerfield studied them with some interest while she spoke. The pictures were of interesting and unusual houses, bridges, landscapes, whatever had caught his eye. One of them was of a twenty-six-year-old girl named Rachel Brennan wearing a heavy sweater on a beach in Cape Cod one autumn, trying to smile and keep her hair out of her eyes while he took the picture. Her dark hair was longer then, down over her shoulders, and what Rachel remembered about the picture the most was the way that Hugh kept laughing every time he was about to take the picture and how much love she felt for him then. In just two years, how things had changed.

"You're ever so much prettier now, with your hair cut the way you've got it, dear," Mrs. Deerfield commented. "Change is always for the better."

"Oh." Rachel felt as if Mrs. Deerfield had just read her thoughts.

It startled her a bit, but then Mrs. Deerfield returned to the subject of the crazy bag lady. "She calls herself Marty or Mattie or something, and she used to be in hospital, I think, until someone let her out. I know her well—at least I feel as if I do—she used to fling large chunks of dog feces at my window, and once she broke into this house when the two young men had just moved in. I imagine they scared her as much as she did them—they said she came into their bedroom at two in the morning waving a knife around, but evidently she didn't expect to see two naked men sharing the same bed. I suppose I would've been as shocked as she was, and she dropped the knife and ran out screaming." Mrs. Deerfield paused when Hugh brought her a cup of tea. "Mightn't you have a drop of whiskey for flavor?"

Rachel glanced at Hugh and smiled.

"I could run get some down in my flat," Mrs. Deerfield volunteered. "Oh, perhaps not, then." She sounded defeated; she began glancing about the room again, at the photographs, at the stereo, up at the hanging plants.

"If she has a knife she must be dangerous," Hugh said. He went and sat down next to his wife.

"Oh, hardly, she's all show, that one, mad as a hatter but fairly harmless, I think. She seems to imagine that her baby or something is being held hostage in this house. Perhaps she has a half dozen or more houses she does this to—I suppose it seemed cruel to hose her down like that, but you see, words and logic don't seem to get through to her. She's like a poor, dumb child, really. Oh, dear, but you shouldn't have done it." Mrs. Deerfield sipped her tea, glancing about the living room.

"What's that?" Rachel asked.

"You went and blocked that lovely fireplace. You put your telly there, and it's really a wonderfully beautiful fireplace, and I can tell you that no one could build them like that anymore, dear."

"I thought you meant I'd done something to that woman."

Ignoring her, Mrs. Deerfield went on while Hugh winked at Rachel, "I do like the paint job—ever so much more light in the room, don't you think? And the photographs are lovely, who took them?"

"Hugh did—he was big on photography in law school."

"Ever do any nude studies? When I was younger I always wished someone would've done a nude study of me before the world revolved a hundred times, and here I am today old and useless and drinking weak tea. You ought to put a drop of whiskey in your tea, dears, it adds a little sunshine to the afternoon, especially after our run-in with that creature." Mrs. Deerfield barely caught her breath when she spoke, and Hugh, sitting close to Rachel, began nudging her knee playfully with his, shooting a smile her way which she tried to ignore because she was afraid she'd laugh and hurt Mrs. Deerfield's feelings. Mrs. Deerfield seemed oblivious to this, however. She didn't look at the couple on the couch while she spoke, but scanned the room, taking in the little changes they'd made. "I've called the police on her, once or twice, but it doesn't matter, does it? The authorities around here seem to *expect* this sort of behavior. I suppose it would be easy to go crazy in this neighborhood—and this Mattie woman has been around a long time, I think. Most of this block burned out in '68, you know, when the riots were blazing. I looked out from the window and saw several men running down the alley spraying gasoline on the cars, and then an explosion as one car after another went up, and then it spread to the building behind us, and it almost came over here, too, I suppose, before the night was over, but the wind kept the fire back—thankfully. It was as if for a brief moment Hell had spilled across the park." She paused and looked away. "My Ramona is due any time now and I'm afraid she's been quite the naughty puss and run away from Nanny Deerfield—if you should find kittens in your bath-tub, you have my permission to scold her on my behalf. Sometimes," now Mrs. Deerfield was wistful, and Rachel got halfway to a smile, "sometimes, when I think of it all, kittens, this house, that insane creature," Mrs. Deerfield shook her head slowly, "it almost makes me want to scream."

It almost makes me want to scream.

Rachel looked from Mrs. Deerfield to Hugh and back again. Had she said that, had she really said that? *It almost makes me want to scream?*

"In our little sanctuary by the park," Mrs. Deerfield continued, "to be, well, *assaulted* by that pathetic woman, and where are the police to keep people like her out of our alley? Why is there no one to keep this area free of such people? But screaming would do no good, no good at all. For who would one scream to?"

4.

"What a sad little woman, in her small apartment, nothing to keep her going," Rachel said after Mrs. Deerfield had left.

"Nothing but booze." But as soon as Hugh said this, the two of them fell silent. Rachel rested her head in the crook of Hugh's elbow; she tried to match her breaths with his. The air conditioner seemed to be working better than usual, and the house with its new paint jobs and greased hinges and hanging plants seemed to be theirs at last.

After a few moments, Rachel said, "You know, your photos are good. I think that picture is my favorite one of me: I look so insecure and inexperienced and confused, and so happy. You really caught the true Rachel."

"Nose shark," he said, pinching her nose lightly between his fingers. "I love you, Scout."

"She's a good influence."

"Penny Dreadful?"

"She came up and saw our living room and she made me look at it differently. She saw it as ours. We've screwed up the fireplace, but hey, we did it *our* way."

Then Rachel and Hugh said, simultaneously: "Our home sweet home." They laughed, and Hugh cradled Rachel against him. Her body felt heavy, and his was like a soft cushion and she wished she could just sink into him and not ever rise up again.

"I must be getting old," he said. "I feel the need for a midafternoon nap."

"You are a wizened man of thirty."

"Let's just fall asleep here the way we used to in school and we'd just laze around all afternoon." He kissed her forehead, and she closed her eyes. "Let's Pretend we're in our own home, Scout, and Let's Pretend everything will be all right."

"I love you, You-Are-There-Hugh-Adair."

5.

Later they went for a walk—the evening was cool and breezy, which was unusual for the final days of July. The trees that lined the sidewalks were a pale luminescent green, offering dappled shade from the western sun. They hiked up through Kalorama Triangle, looking at the embassies and large houses. Other couples passed by, one family of four obviously sightseeing, young people walking their dogs, which Hugh would stop and pet. The gingko trees stank to high heaven (Hugh called them "vomit trees"), the blocks seemed to go on for miles—Rachel's calves ached—but she felt so happy inside she wanted to walk forever. It was as if the scare she'd had from that bag woman, following close on the heels of her car breaking down, had awakened something in her that had been sleeping. And Mrs. Deerfield, too, had unlocked something for her, some cabinet in the house, just by saying that one phrase: *it almost makes me want to scream.* So, Rachel wasn't the only human being who felt like screaming sometimes, others did, too, others like Mrs. Deerfield could admit it. Things could get to be too much for her just like they could for Rachel. *Normal life.*

Hugh grabbed her hand and swung it playfully; he twisted around her in a pretzel dance move. "Sugar pie honeybunch."

"Oh, Hugh, you're so weird," Rachel said. She grinned goofily. "Wanna play, Hugh?"

"A dangerous question."

"No, I mean like, 'come out and play.' Remember when you could call up a friend and just say, 'Do you want to come out and play?'"

"'Play' takes on a whole new meaning after the age of twelve. Why don't we go to the movies?"

"Oh, barf, let's not go to some movie theater when we finally have bearable weather. Let's go to the zoo—it's not even seven, I think we can still get in."

"And watch the chimps masturbate? Well, it's *your* day off."

"And we do what I want." They took a path beside the

parkway, walking through a wooded area just beneath the northern edge of Winthrop Park. Joggers were out in droves with blank, almost fatalistic looks on their faces as they pounded the asphalt, avoiding the couple.

"Walk on the grass!" one of them shouted as he ran by.

"Nice attitude." Hugh smirked.

"I was thinking maybe we could get away for a few days—maybe a week."

"It's a great time. We've just spent half our savings fixing up a house, I haven't worked since May . . ."

"Oh, you *are* getting to be an old man, you stick-in-the-mud. I don't mean anywhere exotic, I mean to the beach or something."

"Like I said, it's a great time."

"Well, maybe while you're unemployed we *should* do something, go somewhere. I mean, once you get a job you won't have a vacation coming for at least six months, probably longer. This might be the best time. I think my paycheck'll cover a cheap motel at Rehoboth or Dewey. And while we're gone, we can have the place de-moused and de-roached."

"Only if we take Penny Dreadful and Baby Dreadful with us."

"With the kind of work I'm doing this fall and your getting a job I really don't see how we'll get another break until sometime at the turn of the century. Except for today, the humidity sucks, the pollution is getting to me, and the last vacation we took was our *honeymoon.*"

They entered the zoo from the bike path; hundreds of tourists were milling around the exhibits and cages. They took a path along the seal exhibit, up to the otters. Rachel tried to find the otters, but couldn't see them anywhere.

"Look, if going to the beach is what you really want—" Hugh said as they continued walking. The squawks and cries of wild animals filled their ears.

"I want, I want."

"I just don't want to spend all your money—I'm beginning to feel like a kept man."

"Our money."

"The car payments and repair, your college loans, your law school loans, et cetera et cetera."

"Hey, if you're going to be in debt, do it big time."

"Okay, all right, I just feel so damned guilty. And don't think I don't see your little notes around the bathroom—it doesn't help my highly developed sense of guilt any to see the word *paycheck* etched across the bathroom mirror."

"I know, I've been a real bitch. Look, you'll get a job soon enough—I know it."

"We haven't talked about it much," Hugh whispered.

She knew what he meant. He meant: *the drinking.* Rachel was beginning to wish the conversation had not gotten so serious; she'd been enjoying herself, and forgetting about the clutter of her life.

"I know."

"You've been good about it. I know I'm slipping up some."

"Yeah, well, we all do it sometimes."

"The interviews I've been on!" He laughed, clapping his hands together. "Bufu Thompson said he'd try to 'work me in.' Work me *in?* I was practically responsible for his getting *in* to law school in the first place."

"The world is full of assholes."

"It's been kind of tense. I'll try to stay away from it." The dreaded *it.* Beer, wine, selected refined liquors. Somehow Hugh's not naming *it* specifically made her shiver. *It* must have some power over him if he could not give it a single descriptive word.

Rachel had no response to this: the past few months *had* been tense, to the point where when she was not working she'd been drifting through things, nodding her head when Hugh would say something, but trying not to turn every situation into a confrontation.

But *today.* Today had been so good. All of her anxiety seemed to have melted away, changed with the weather.

She felt happy and even *secure* with Hugh.

Hugh said, "We'll go to the beach, what, maybe Labor Day weekend?"

"Well, to be honest, the end of next week is good. I think I can get Thursday and Friday off, and the following week if I want it."

"Talk about presumptuous—how long have you been planning this little getaway, Scout?"

"I was just inspired, that's all. We could drive up Thursday morning. A couple of T-shirts, some shorts, flip-flops . . . we can get a couple of those big goofy beach towels up there, and order club sandwiches from room service."

"A cheap motel with room service?"

"Okay, we'll pick up Ding-Dongs and Ho-Ho's at the drugstore."

"Of course we have to think about your clunker car. I guess I could get it to a garage Monday morning."

"If it works by Wednesday, we're set. Or I can call Budget or something and we can rent something nice. I'll ask Mrs. Deerfield to take in the paper, you know, water the plants, turn lights on and off and stuff, and maybe we can get the roach man to come by while we're gone."

"You're just my one-woman problem solver, Scout," he said without a trace of sarcasm. His eyes were shining blue as he looked into hers; she reached up and with her fingers twirled the hair that hung across his forehead.

"Daddy always said: it all comes out in the wash."

He grinned and shook his head, his eyes never leaving her face. "If I kissed you right here—" and before she could say anything in protest, Hugh hugged her to him, and brought his lips against hers, softly, softer than she could ever remember a kiss being, cool and moist and unhurried. *I love you so much, You-Are-There-Hugh-Adair.*

Behind them, the monkeys shrieked and jangled at the bars of their cages.

FOURTEEN

FATHER-SON CHAT

1.

Ted Adair dreaded visiting his father, but the Old Man was losing it fast and Ted figured he owed him that much. For the past month and a half, Winston had been calling his oldest boy every night after midnight with bizarre stories. One about things that were after him, then something about an old bad debt. ("What, pop, can't you pay it?" Ted had asked over the phone and the Old Man replied, chillingly, "Of course, I can *pay* it, Ted, I've *always* paid off my *debts!*")

Then several weeks ago, his father had taken Ted out to lunch—to an outdoor cafe in Georgetown. Now, if you knew the Old Man, you'd know he wasn't one for dining *al fresco*. But Ted got the feeling that his father wanted to be out in the open, in the daylight, as if something waited for him, something or someone who lurked in darkness.

Winston Adair took Ted out to lunch to tell him about the dead body in the Jaguar.

"What the fuck are you talking about?" Ted almost spilled his beer.

The Old Man glanced around the cafe—the tables were filled with people, talking, eating and drinking, making such a racket he could be fairly assured of secrecy. He reached across the table to Ted, leaning forward, tugging at Ted's arm. "There's this whore," Winston whispered, and his breath was so foul that Ted wondered if the Old Man had brushed his teeth since Christmas. "She died in my car."

Then the Old Man had begun giggling.

Ted, who prided himself on being able to catch most of

114

life's curveballs, played it cool. *You watch your pop crack like an egg and you want to pretend it's business as usual.* He took a mean swig of his beer, wiped his mouth with the back of his hand and said, "I think we better clarify what we're talking about here."

The Old Man was acting spooky, his head nodding as if this were some under-the-table deal, as if this were a plea bargain or something and he just wanted it to go smoothly. Here he was in a three-piece pin-stripe suit from Brooks Brothers, a little mustard on his red tie from his pastrami sandwich, just a hint of drool at the left-hand corner of his mouth: *Pop, dad, the Old Man, Winston Fucking Adair, legal counsel to the stars and minor constellations.*

And he was losing it.

"What are we talking here, pop? Is this some kind of necrophiliac's dream? You got a dead girl in the trunk of your Jag?" Ted looked around at the other tables.

"Well," Winston Adair said, slurping up some of the spit that was running down his chin—he lapped up the slick wet trail beneath his lip with his tongue, "not anymore. You, you know, you can't keep a good corpse down. Nosiree. She up and walked away."

2.

Ted hadn't been back to the old family home in McLean since Christmas. Something had been building in the past year, and it had begun with Hugh's marrying Rachel Brennan. Ted didn't know what it was exactly, but a change had come over the Old Man, something that Ted didn't really like about his father, something that had lain hidden for years and was now emerging, coming to the surface. Of course, there was a *shitload* that Ted had *never* liked about his father—his father was a real asshole most of the time, had spent years building a reputation as someone who would as soon screw you over as look at you, but Ted took this for granted. Sometimes Ted felt he screwed people over, too, but it was tax law so *who gave a fuck, anyway?* Ted counted it a good night when he could drop off to sleep knowing he had, perhaps, screwed over one less person than he had the day before. But it was the nature of the business, and you go with the flow if you want to keep your head above water. *Now, Hughie never understood this, but that wife of his is a real catch, she knows about how things work, how the universe is put together. No flies on her. Marrying her is just about the smartest thing Hughie's ever done.*

Ted pulled his silver Mercedes SL up to the entrance of Renfield, which was the name of the Adair estate; the large Tudor-style mansion was hidden from the road, dogwood trees clustered about the drive, wysteria entangled like greedy fingers through the front gate. The burning sunlight didn't penetrate the driveway, blocked by the old giant oaks that stood guard for the half-mile drive to the house. The shade was oppressive—Ted, who was boiling from the humidity of the early afternoon, wondered if it was not possible to crack up when you lived down such a dark and lonely road.

At the front gate, a video camera pointed down at him. *Something pop must've installed since December.*

Ted rolled down his window and smiled at the camera. He raised his sunglasses up. Finally, the gate began making a humming sound, followed by a series of clicks and squeaks. The tall black gate slid open.

"Thanks, pop," Ted said, flipping the bird at the camera. He pushed his foot down hard on the accelerator and sped up the drive towards the house.

3.

Winston Adair sat behind the console and watched his television monitors. His face rippled with uncontrollable ticks, above his eyes, along the edge of his mouth. Up near his hairline, a purple vein throbbed with blood. If you could crawl inside his brain (he felt like he had done that and more, that he had crawled inside a small dark cave in his brain) *you might find that it had been carved out like a pumpkin. Yes sir, a big fat balloon filled with breath, but at least I've got that—a little breath goes a long way these days.* There were times when he did not know where he was. Right now he knew. He was safe at home, at Renfield, and his son Ted was coming up the drive. But other times he was buried alive beneath a bone-crushing fear. He was afraid that he would forget how to breathe, the way the redheaded whore in his car had forgotten.

And then something else had begun breathing *for* her.

His white button-down shirt was open to his chest and blotted with sweat; he kept rubbing his thick legs with the palms of his hands. He sat there in his shirttails and his white boxer shorts. He mumbled to himself every once in a while, *that was okay, because if you're talking you're walking, you know it, Winston. If you can wag your fat tongue then you can wag your fat ass and that means you're* breathing.

After switching the electric gate closed behind Ted, he glanced quickly from one monitor to another. Every time he looked away from one screen, he thought he just missed seeing something on it. Out of the corner of his eye he thought he saw someone, or something, move.

But it's just you, Winston. They *haven't caught up with you.* You've *caught up with you.*

"Just take what you want and leave me alone," he said to the monitors.

He rubbed the palms of his hands across his hairy, fat, white legs.

His hands still burned from the wasps.

He held his hands up to his face and kissed the center of each palm. He kissed each finger. *Kiss it and make it better.*

His hands were swollen and looked as if he'd blown them up like balloons, but lead balloons because they were heavy and he dropped them to his lap again.

And it felt, sometimes, hell, *most* of the time, like the wasps had gotten inside him and he was the wasp's nest.

4.

"Uh, pop, do you always open the door in such . . . ah, sartorial splendor?" Ted stood on the front porch of the house. His father, in the shadow of the door, looked like hell—his boxer shorts clung to his thighs, his shirt was yellowed under the arms with sweat stains. Ted thought he smelled something too awful to even wonder what it was. The Old Man's eyes were dark and sunken into brown circles, and his hands and arms were puffed up an oozing, blistering pink. "Jesus, pop, you stick your hands in a barbecue?"

The Old Man grinned. "You're just a laugh a minute, Ted. The class clown hasn't grown up any, has he?"

"Oh, fuck you, pop." Ted pushed his way past his father. As he went he smelled something that was dead, or *Near Dead. One of the Near Dead, pop, that must be you. You got the look of the grave in your eye, your skin is stretched across your fat and bones to the limit, and you've got the stench, pop, you've got the stench like nobody's business*. Ted felt an animal revulsion for his father. Ted went into the living room. The drapes on the back picture window were drawn, the furniture was covered with blankets and sheets. In a corner of the room were some pillows and a few blankets rumpled up. Next to them were jars filled with some yellowish water which Ted wanted to believe was apple juice or lemonade, but which he knew, because of the odor in the room, was piss.

The Old Man's been sleeping *and* pissing *in the living room. Maybe I should call it the Near Dead Room.*

Ted turned back to face his father, who had followed behind him. "Jesus."

"I can't offer you anything to drink, boy," Winston said. "I've drunk most of it."

"Where's your housekeeper?"

"Yolanda? Yolanda left about a month ago. She just packed her things and moved out of the guest house. I wanted to pay her, you know, she had some wages coming . . ."

"What the fuck is happening to you, pop?"

"Oh, the shit has hit the fan, boy, a big wad of the stuff, and that fan just spins and spins and where it stops nobody, not even me, knows. You see these?" He raised his hands up. "I wish I *had* barbecued them, Ted, I wish I could burn off these bumps. I tried skinning my arms. I just got a razor, boy, and started slicing through them. Just one layer of skin peeling off at a time. I was bleeding like a sonofabitch, and it hurt, but it did no good. They're still here. A man can't get rid of his insides just by peeling back the skin—that's just going to show what's *really* under there. Nosiree, it just didn't work. Because these are bug bites, but not just ordinary bug bites. These are industrial-strength wasp stings and they get buried way down deep and don't come out. They're a part of me."

Ted backed away from his father.

"What's wrong, boy? Where are you headed?"

"Look, pop, I'm just going to call your doctor. I think maybe you should see somebody about those . . ."

"DON'T YOU FUCKING CALL A DOCTOR, TED! I DON'T NEED A FUCKING DOCTOR, I NEED A FUCK-ING MIRACLE!"

When his father had calmed down, Ted drew the drapes back. Sunlight sprayed across the living room. Ted opened the sliding glass door to get some fresh air in. "Here, pop, let's sit on the back porch."

"Make sure nothing's out there."

"You think someone's on the property?"

"You've got shit for gray matter, boy. It's wasps I'm concerned about. They might be out there waiting for me."

Ted went out and looked beneath the eaves of the house. "All's clear on deck, pop."

They sat around the glass coffee table. A cool breeze spun through and dissipated all too soon—once again the smell of the Near Dead thrust up Ted's nostrils like two fingers with sharp nails.

"Pop, look, I think you need some help."

"You know I haven't been to the office for a week?" Ted had been thinking, from the condition of the house, it had been more like six weeks. "You talk to your brother?"

"Hughie's never been the most communicative brother, pop. I doubt you'll hear from him unless he needs a loan."

"I hope I'm that lucky—God, I hope you're right."

"He's a dickhead, pop. He's got a list of grudges against you and me that you could wrap around Capitol Hill."

"He's your brother, Ted."

"And he's your son."

Winston shook his head sadly. "Would a father let his son inherit what I am leaving to Hugh?"

"Is this what it's all about? Are you making yourself crazy because of Hughie's questionable lineage? I knew it—I knew it when I was four. I knew about mom and her little indiscretion. Hughie probably knows it, too. He's not completely dense. Your conscience go into overload this week? Or are you still worried about that whore who got fifty bucks from you without finishing her job?"

"She was dead. I know she was dead. I saw her die. I've seen people die before." Winston broke into a grin. "They even found her in the river later on. It was in the paper, "Prostitute Commits Suicide." She was floating, Ted, just floating. Deader than dead. But she died in my car at the Iwo Jima Memorial and she walked down Route 50 and jumped into the Potomac. She was dead, boy, but she went and drowned herself anyway."

Ted was trying to think of ways of getting the fuck out of his father's house and then calling some men in white coats with nets to come catch the Old Man. "Onward and upward, pop. I assume there's a reason you wanted me to come. We both know this isn't my favorite hangout."

"I've raised a generation of vipers."

"Good ol' pop. Maybe a martini would help. Maybe a *jug* of martinis would help. You sure you don't have a little booze in one of the cabinets?"

"I have been drunk all week, boy. I have been drunk and scared to death. I've been drunk until the hangovers started to taste good."

And pop, you sure look it.

"It's been pursuing me since I was a young man, Ted. And it's finally caught up with me."

I ain't sayin' yes and I ain't sayin' no. "You don't have something like testicular cancer do you, pop? 'Cause if you've got something like that, man, you've got a strange way of leading up to it although—heh heh—you do have balls."

"Keep the jokes coming, boy, but it won't keep what I've got away. What I have, Ted, is an accounts payable credit— that's pretty good, isn't it? I know my figures, don't I? I owe

someone, Ted, someone more powerful than a shitheel
IRS—and what I owe, I owe in blood. And this something,
this something is here, now, to collect."

"You owe the Mafia or something? Are we talking horse
heads under the sheets?"

Winston laughed. "That wit, oh, that Adair wit."

"Who the fuck do you owe?"

"It's going to sound funny, Ted. It's going to sound *really*
funny."

"Try me."

"You promise not to put me away? You swear you won't
shoot me up with tranquilizers and lay me down in a padded
cell?"

*I ain't sayin' yes and I ain't sayin' no, I'm just sayin'
maybe.*

"A bokor," the Old Man mumbled.

"A what—a 'broker'?"

"A bokor. A voodoo man—a witch doctor—a black-
magic priest—"

"Bullshit."

"I didn't believe it either, until I saw what he could do.
And still I didn't fully believe it. But now I do. Ted, I saw
him eat a woman alive—I saw him bury his teeth in—"

*Yep, pop done cracked real good this time. You can see the
fault lines erupting down the side of his face. He went and
stuck his arms up to his elbows into a wasps' nest and the
venom went all the way to his brain. Just hope his will is in
order and you find a nursing home comfortable enough for
the old guy. He's a bastard but even bastards deserve some
comfort when they crack.* "Sure, pop, calm down, let's talk,
it's okay. Where does this guy live?"

Winston licked the pink swollen flesh between his puffy
fingers. "Your guess is as good as mine." Then laughing,
tears coming to his eyes: "He's dead, and where do dead
men live, boy? Maybe all around us. Maybe they stick to one
place. Maybe they *haunt* one place. Maybe a house. Maybe
they never left the house. Maybe they're in the house waiting
for a crack, waiting for something to let them through,
something oh so perfect, something that fits the scheme of
things, boy, something or someone who would be the perfect
way *out.*"

FIFTEEN

REVELATIONS

1.

While Hugh went to the garage Wednesday afternoon to pick up the VW, Rachel sat in the turret room reading the papers Ted had given her; she had put them away three weeks ago barely glancing at them. She'd thought it better not to mention to Hugh about Ted's visit, and she was hoping that the legal ownership of the house wouldn't come up until Hugh was in a steadier frame of mind.

The turret room was still in the midst of a major overhaul: Hugh had scraped and steamed the old wallpaper off, and beneath that another layer of wallpaper that was only half removed. It was a cheap, shiny, yellowish paper that reminded Rachel of contact paper and was unpleasant to look at for any length of time. But if she sat at the cushion on the window seat she could look out over the park and read and not deal with the half-finished room. Below in the park, a group of old men sat talking on the benches, six school-children played a game of hopscotch on the sidewalk, the trees drooped heavily with the afternoon's rainfall—it had only begun to clear at five, when Rachel got out of the subway at DuPont Circle and walked up Connecticut Avenue to Winthrop Park. It had been cool and she'd felt good, good about the beach trip they'd be making in the morning, good about Hugh, good about life. She hadn't seen the crazy bag woman from the park—another good omen. Hugh had said: "It's because Penny Dreadful hosed her down—she melted like the Wicked Witch of the West."

She riffled through the white legal-sized sheets before her:

boring, boring, boring, as Hugh would say. She skimmed through the domestic instructions: *Your User-Friendly Trash Compactor, Frost-Free Refrigeration At Its Finest, Making The Most Of Your Three-Cycle Dishwasher.* Finally, towards the back of the pile she came across a diagram of the house. Page one showed the floor plan of Mrs. Deerfield's apartment: the sitting room near the front facing Hammer Street, then a brief, practically nonexistent hallway leading to the bedroom, the bathroom, back to the kitchenette, the walk-in closet, the breakfast nook—Rachel remembered *that* particular place, the Clamoring Place of Mrs. Deerfield and her weird girlfriends, the place where Rachel had all but passed out. It seemed silly to her now, and she knew that her hormones and her blood sugar were the culprits, but it had made her less anxious to go see the downstairs apartment again. There was something else, running alongside the breakfast nook—it looked to Rachel like a sketch of train tracks, and she thought it must be the back glass doors to the patio, or maybe it was something about the sewage pipes. *Or who knows? Maybe there used to be a train running through here? I am a lawyer, not an architect.*

On page two, the diagram was of the second floor of the building, or the first floor of their house. She scanned it, the living room, the kitchen, the den, the turret room, the bathroom. There was a blur of letters in a small crawl space between the BTHRM and TRRT RM. Rachel tried to make them out: VNTY. *What is VNTY?* It was a space perhaps the size of a closet, and maybe again this had to do with pipes, because there was a brief doodle of train tracks in a ray out of the VNTY. So maybe pipes behind the walls.

But there's that bricked-up window.

In the alley, between the brownstone and Draper House. Rachel had only gone through the alley on *that* side once— the first day she saw the house. It was narrow and dark and smelled of wino piss; broken bottles and tin cans sprawled across the concrete. But she had glanced up and seen the small bricked-up window, like a closed eye, and wondered when and why it had been bricked up.

And then she'd just forgotten about it, buried it in the back of her mind, *probably because I dreaded dealing with the clean-up job on that alley.*

So perhaps there was a room there, between the bathroom and the turret room.

Rachel looked over at the wall near the door.

Behind that wall is a VNTY. With a window. And train tracks.

She stood up. The yellow wallpaper-beneath-the-wallpaper was so hideous she wondered who would even spend the money on that kind of stuff. She walked over to the wall, pushing the door closed so she could imagine the whole space, the entire room behind the wall. She rapped on it, and the rap was hollow—*doesn't that mean there's a room back there?*

Oh, but this wallpaper is so ghastly to look at, and she reached up, digging with her fingernails beneath one of the greasy yellow folds, tearing off a corner of the paper. The wall was a grayish white beneath. *Okay, now we're getting somewhere.*

She scratched at some more of the paper. More wall beneath, but wall with a red Magic Marker scrawl.

This must've been some kind of nursery and some brat drew on the walls, so the mommy and daddy decided to put up cheap wallpaper in case junior went crazy with his Crayolas again.

She scraped more away, peeling back a long strip of the ugly paper.

Beneath it, a word was forming out of the red marker doodling.

Rachel pulled more of it, and the letters *HOU* were visible.

The kiddos have been writing dirty words on the walls.

She thrust her nails beneath the paper and tugged.

Rachel screamed when the nail of her index finger cracked, splitting all the way to the tender flesh. Blood rose up beneath the translucent nail. *Shit, it feels like I stuck an ice pick under there.* She sucked on her finger and then pressed down on the nail.

But the fingernail had at least done the job.

The strip of paper covering the red-markered word was hanging down below.

But the word made no sense.

Written in red marker was the word: HOUNFOUR.

2.

"Next month's rent," Mrs. Deerfield said, "August. You won't be back you said until just before the first, and I thought you might like the spare change jingling in your pocket. I hope I'm not disturbing you—I know it's late, but I heard the telly, so I knew you were still up and since you're off in the morning I didn't want to miss you, dear." She stood there at the French doors; she'd come up the patio stairs, clumping loudly and rattling the railing as if to warn them of her arrival.

It was after ten on Wednesday night, and Rachel and Hugh were playing Scrabble in front of the television.

Mrs. Deerfield was wearing her turquoise oriental robe, her hair turbaned with a pink towel: she had come right from the bath to pay her rent. She smelled like a walking ad for Yardley's English Lavender, a pleasant change from the vinegary, boozy odor.

Hugh said, "Hi," but seemed more interested in "The Honeymooners" rerun. He glanced back and forth between his wife, his tenant, and his TV show. On the TV show, Jackie Gleason and Art Carney were handcuffed together on a train.

Rachel held the door open—not quite an invitation, but she didn't want to seem rude (and yet she didn't want to invite Mrs. Deerfield in, either). "I hope the TV isn't too loud?"

Mrs. Deerfield shook her head. "No, I was actually afraid I might be making too much noise myself—I've been pickling and preserving like a madwoman, it's really my passion, don't ask me why because I couldn't tell you, and it leaves the fingers a bit sticky—I broke one of my jars and then said to myself, Penelope, slow down, you needn't do it all tonight, there's plenty of time, it can wait, now, Penelope, go take a bath and get that awful sticky-smelly-gummy stuff off your skin." Mrs. Deerfield looked in the living room. "I love a good game of Scrabble—who wins in this family?"

Hugh said, "Usually Rachel. She's got the brains."

"He's joking, he always gets the most points." Rachel took the check from Mrs. Deerfield's small, pudgy fingers. "Thanks—that's very thoughtful, but only if you're *sure* you don't mind parting with the cash this early."

"Not at all, not at all." But Mrs. Deerfield was more interested in the Scrabble board; she stepped into the living room, Rachel moving back. "Oh, goodness, there's that word."

The word HOUNFOUR was spelled out on the board.

"You know what it means? Hugh thinks it might be French, although he can't come up with it."

"After three years of high school French and a summer at the Sorbonne," Hugh said. "But that's assuming it's a real word, too."

"It was on the wall in the turret room—somebody wrote it—it was under all that horrible wallpaper."

"You're right, it *does* sound French, dear. I'd have to consult my books of mysticism, but I believe it's got religious connotations, it means an altar or a place of worship. But I'd have to look it up to be sure."

"I say Rachel can't use it in this game unless she can tell me what it is. I think it's a made-up word."

"Like I made up the secret room."

"You've got a secret room, dear? How lovely—that's one of the more enchanting things about old houses, there's always a secret room, locks with no keys, hidden staircases, old dusty tomes in dark closets."

"Well, maybe no more than a secret *closet*. I saw some drawings of the floor plan of the house, and there's something in between the turret room and the bathroom, just down the hall. It said V-N-T-Y on the sketch."

"Well, dear, that must've been the vanity, coming off the bathroom like that. Perhaps just room enough for a small dressing table. In the olden days, ladies of such wealth as the original owners of this house had to have their own powder rooms I suppose."

"That makes sense: Vanity," Hugh said, "thy name is—"

"Say it and you die, Hugh, and it doesn't make any sense at all. There's a bricked-up window in the alley. Why would somebody close that area off?"

Mrs. Deerfield nodded her head slowly. "Yes, why would someone? But this house is just a mess when it comes to rational thought. I've got that wind tunnel beneath my breakfast nook—it's always cool down there and there's no explanation for it as far as I've ever known. Although it's excellent for storing wines and canned foods. I know you two don't believe in the spirit world but I do, at times, and so I allow the irrational to connect the dots, as it were. Perhaps, after all, your vanity isn't covered up to keep anyone out, least of all you two, perhaps it's to keep something *in*."

"Oh, please, Mrs. Deerfield, between that crazy woman last weekend, the mice, and the roaches, that's the *last* thing I need to help me sleep tonight."

"Sorry, dear. Ramona's still on the lam. Any sign of her about?"

"I think I'd start sneezing if she were in the vicinity."

"Well, I have a sneaking suspicion that she's found some little nook to have her babies in already. I just hope she doesn't cause too much trouble: there's nothing prouder or more demanding than a new mother."

3.

Rachel was brushing her teeth in the upstairs bathroom, mentally reviewing the list of things she had to remember in the morning: leave the keys with Mrs. Deerfield so she could let the exterminator in, the straw beach mats, the flip-flops, the sunglasses, the suntan oil, her make-up kit, Hugh's shaving kit, a sweater, *always take a sweater to the beach, mom would say, you never know when it might get cold,* her skirts (the wrap-around skirt was always the easiest to deal with at the beach), the Solarcaine . . .

Hugh stood behind her; she saw him in the mirror, and at first it didn't look like Hugh. His face was not really a scowl, but it was quickly becoming one, lines dropping right and left. *"Our* house," he said.

He was holding up the papers that Ted had dropped off.

"Your house." His voice was not a snarl, but she wished it was. She could deal with him if he were angry, but he didn't sound angry.

He sounded defeated.

4.

She lay in bed and massaged his neck. "Don't let it bother you—it *is* our house. This is just something cheap your father did, but *he can't touch us here.*"

"Can't he? Christ, Scout, can't he? Do you know what he does to people? He chews them up. Any chink he can find in our armor, he's going to do his damnedest to explode. He's done it before to me, and he'll do it again."

"Put it out of your mind, throw it away. I love you and he can't touch our marriage."

"Really?" Hugh turned to look at her; a tense smile streaked like lightning across his face. "Really, Scout? Because he sure as fucking hell touched my *last* marriage."

5.

She closed her eyes after he told her, she closed her eyes and he fell asleep next to her, she closed her eyes and listened to him tell the story again and she felt guilty and happy and guilty *because* she was happy, because she felt freed from a larger guilt that had been gnawing at her since she'd first fallen in love with Hugh.

And it was over now, they were *home.*

Home safe.

His words spun through her head:

I never told you this—and I guess you won't blame me, Scout. When I met you I know you thought I was an asshole. One of the other guys on the Law Review *told me as much. But when I met you, I thought: God, here is a woman with whom I could really be in love.*

Not like Joanna. Never like Joanna.

Joanna was perfect. Bright, beautiful—she really wasn't *beautiful, not the way I've come to think about beauty. But* she knew how to make men think she was beautiful, the way some actresses can. She was a debutante who had never gotten over that fact, and I was her escort. You know she and I met while we were in college, but do you know how?

The Old Man arranged it.

He hired this girl in the summer to work as a gofer at the firm, and I was spending my summers doing research for them. The Old Man had set it all up: here was a girl from a good family, she had style, she had panache, she knew when to keep secrets and when not to.

I wonder if they had begun their affair before I'd even laid eyes on her? Sometimes at night I lie awake wondering, trying to imagine what kinds of conferences they must've held together, what kinds of strategies they must've worked out. How he bought her off—if she really thought she was in love with the Old Man, or if the thought of the Adair money was enough to keep her going back to him.

And I was so fucking naive.

They must've been laughing about me. All along. But every now and then I caught her off guard. She'd be looking at me, absent-mindedly, her clear blue eyes filled with some kind of joke. Joanna had the clear blue eyes of a born liar, Scout— perhaps I've got them, too, for not telling you about this. I just haven't wanted to admit what a moron I was in that marriage, how far my head was up my ass.

At times, Joanna would look at me and I thought she was adoring me. Can you imagine? Adoring me.

She was laughing at me, of course. She knew what she was putting over on me, and I suppose the plan was in another few years to divorce me, or who knows? Maybe she was content to be his mistress and sleep in my bed. God, when I think of lying in bed with her and touching her skin—my skin crawls, the way hers probably crawled whenever I touched her.

But I was a classic fool. I thought the kind of coldness I was feeling was normal to marriage—I thought that's sort of what marriage was all about, you know, and everybody played along with it. You can't blame me on that point: here's a guy whose Old Man chased everything in skirts except his wife. So my marriage to Joanna seemed like paradise. My brother Ted tried to tell me once—he's a snake, but he's got that one ounce of decency in him—maybe it was a momen-

tary lapse on his part—shit, I don't know why I never picked up on it until it slapped me in the face. Ted told me, "Watch out for her, Hughie, she means different things to different people." Something like that, and I didn't get it. I didn't know what to think, and Ted's never been much of a caring brother . . .

But, Scout, when I met you, I already knew the lie, the Let's Pretend lie, and it went like this: Let's Pretend you didn't see what you saw and the woman that you thought you saw was not your wife and the man you thought you saw was not your father. It was a big Let's Pretend, the kind that eats away at your gut until you are certifiably gutless.

I pretended for a while longer that I was happily married.

A happily married man.

A man who would soon be a father.

Hey, I'd grown up watching the Old Man lie so skillfully to my own mother and everyone knew he was lying and everyone played along with him.

So lying about my marriage was no biggie. I am my father's son, after all.

You see, five months before I even heard your name, Scout, I caught them together in his office. He had his gray slacks down around his fat ankles, his underwear stretched across his pink knees, the rolls of fat jiggling as he pushed into her, his face contorted in what looked like a grimace of pain, red as a beet, his eyes shut tight—he wasn't even looking at her while he did it to her.

And Joanna—I wasn't sure it was her, because the dress she wore was drawn over her waist, shoulders, hiding most of her face.

But I did recognize the dress. It was her Valentino, and we were due at an embassy party with friends of hers—I was wearing black tie, good for embassy parties, weddings, and funerals—and here they were all rolled up into one. Joanna had never wanted for anything, and that damn dress cost over a thousand bucks and now I knew where the money had been coming from.

Good ol' dad.

The obscenity of that moment hit me in the gut and I tried vomiting, but nothing came out.

Because I was hollow. I had been chowing down on the

Let's Pretend for breakfast, lunch, and dinner, and I knew all along, maybe not the specifics, maybe not Who Did Who, but I knew the way you know things down inside. Only I'd been hollowed out like a log—and I could float, Jesus, I could float along and be okay.

They saw me that day in his office. The Old Man and my wife saw me watching them and we all pretended I wasn't there. I stepped out quietly, not wanting to disturb them. The Old Man's secretary knew, too, and she says to me, "I always pretend it's nothing." My wife, my Old Man, and this woman, and me, too. I was thinking: Yeah, it's nothing, business as usual. You're going to float right the fuck out of here, down the hall, down the elevator, out in the street. You're hollow, you've been upchucking air, it's nothing, there's nothing inside you and there's nothing outside you.

I went out and got myself the biggest martini you've ever seen and I floated away that night and every night in law school when I wasn't studying—and this may account for my good grades.

And then I met you, Scout.

And you brought me back to earth.

But Let's Pretend wasn't through with me yet, because then I found out Joanna was pregnant. And I was still playing the game, I pretended I was the father.

I knew the chances were about fifty-fifty that the kid was mine, although in any event there'd be that Adair family resemblance.

But the Old Man, he didn't want to take that chance.

The Old Man always cleans up his messes.

Joanna told me where she was going that night, the night she died.

She was going to get an abortion.

She and her lover were going to some clinic.

But I was still floating, Scout, I was still accepting the lie, and I'd just found you. I wanted to break it off with you before the lie ate its way into you. But I was weak and I wanted you, wanted the kind of life I could have with you. I didn't want to float anymore.

And when I heard about the car wreck, the accident, I wanted to celebrate, as ghoulish as that sounds.

I had been wishing Joanna were dead for the entire year.

Twelve months—fifty-two weeks, three hundred and sixty-five days and nights. It was as if Hell had finally frozen over.

I guess that was evil of me. I guess only a monster would be happy that someone was dead.

A few days later I crashed and I wept and I mourned because as much as I hated Joanna, I knew she'd probably been manipulated by my father.

And I knew it should've been him who died in that accident.

6.

In the middle of the night, in the violet light that meant the sun was threatening to emerge somewhere beyond the city, Rachel awoke feeling her husband's face next to her cheek. He pecked her lightly; she turned to kiss him. His breath was sour and pasty with sleep; she kissed him anyway. Felt his hands crawling across her stomach (which she didn't bother sucking in).

For the first time in several weeks they made love, and fell back to sleep easily as if it had been a dream.

SIXTEEN

TED LOSES SLEEP

1.

The same night that found Hugh Adair confessing to his second wife the fraudulence of his first marriage, his older brother Ted lay in his king-sized bed at his condo in Georgetown recalling a confession he, too, had heard earlier in the week. It was all some kind of bullshit that his Old Man had come up with when the nervous breakdown came crashing down around him, but still Ted had been losing sleep over what his father had said to him.

Outside his bedroom window a street lamp shone through dark mottled trees, and a cat yowled below; occasionally a car drove by (he counted seven by two A.M.). His ceiling was the kind made of plaster waves and raised dots, a white and frozen sea, and his mind created designs among the crests and curves until he thought he could stare at the ceiling no longer without going mad.

But it's just because pop went pop! And too much caffeine —that's right, buddy, you've been hitting the Nescafé hard, and mainlining the Classic Coke and the Pepsis until your piss is brown and fizzy. You've got the jitters and your Old Man just leaked his brains like a pigeon crapping on a park bench. You put the two together and you lose a few nights' sleep and you go to work with circles under your eyes and you keep those colas coming!

Ted had had a date earlier in the evening, a woman named Holly of all things, and Holly had had just about enough of his trembling and his guzzling beers at the American Cafe. *Oh, yeah, mix some beers with the Coke, and the fear—the goddamned fear that your pop was losing it all over the place, that you could practically SEE right under his skin the lunatic blood pumping around that fat old head—the fear made you want to slap little old Hollyhocks senseless, but I will refrain, m'dear, refrain from any act of violence because I have been brought up a gentleman, and even though you needed a good stiff one, sweetheart, I will not lay a hand on you tonight. Oh, no, tonight I could not get it up even if there were three of you sucking so hard my head caved in—maybe pop went through such a transcendent experience, maybe that's what turned his brain to slush.*

Ted had dropped her off at her place on Capitol Hill. On his way back home, he took a detour. He drove his Mercedes up Connecticut Avenue, around DuPont Circle, up Columbia Road, then a left, then a right, then a left and was sitting in his car, the headlights off, alongside Winthrop Park.

The street was quiet, and he looked up at the house his brother lived in.

The upper story's lights were off; there was some dim light from the lower apartment. The house was black in the lamplight, black and featureless, and Ted shivered in his car (as hot as it was) when he remembered what his father had told him.

And when he saw the black woman sitting on the park bench not more than ten feet from where he was parked, he started the engine again and drove away, quickly.

She was fat and old and clothed in trash bags that glittered under the street-lamp light. She swayed back and forth on the bench, apparently reciting something.

She fit the Old Man's description of Madeleine Perreau.

2.

Ted, lying awake in bed that night, could not get the Old Man's words out of his mind:

I met her when I first bought the houses down there, down in Winthrop Park. I was twenty-one, I'd just come into my inheritance, and I had money to burn, boy, money to burn. The war was still raging in Europe and I had no desire like so many of my foolhardy companions to go over and fight the

Germans. War, boy, is the finest time to run domestic businesses, and property was dirt cheap. I knew if I bought that block on Hammer Street something would come of it. And something did come of it, too, something bigger than I expected.

Back then, this neighborhood was a cesspool, shit, it was a cesspool clear until 1979. I held on to it even when it was losing money because there was always something here I didn't want someone else to find. She was there, Madeleine Perreau living in a rented room in a tenement near Draper House, and you wouldn't know it to look at her, but she had something inside her, something more than looks, something sexual, something that approached the place where fucking met death—I know that now, God, I know that now. And if I had just looked before I leaped, but I believed in nothing in those days, Ted, nothing at all, nothing but myself. I screwed her whenever I had the chance, screwed her like I was masturbating against the leg of a chair, like a dog humping whatever hole was available. But I didn't know a few things about her: one, that she was in love with me, Ted, this black whore from the tenements was telling people we were going to be married, and I thought when she said it it was a joke. I saw her maybe ten times in four years, and each time we fucked, boy, just fucked, that's all it was as far as I was concerned. And one day she got pregnant and she said it was mine and I told her to get rid of it, and she threatened a lot of things, and that's when I found him, boy, the man with the magic coat hanger, the man who was making a name for himself with his seven-minute kerosene and coat-hanger jobbies. You give the girl a drink, she starts to convulse, the fetus drops a little and you twist an old wire hanger up inside her and jab that little life out. And he lived right in my own fucking building! He lived in Draper House. He ran his little outfit out of that house. He had a room all outfitted as if he were a real doctor, not just some back-alley abortionist. He was a French coon from Haiti, boy, a man who had some kind of power over the women on that block, and he and his housekeeper took care of the pregnant whores who needed to get back on the streets. It was too good to be true.

And the beauty of it, Ted, my boy, was sometimes the girls died.

But there was another side, and that was: sometimes the babies lived, sometimes the abortion didn't work and what you got instead was a pregnant old whore with a cooze that looked like a sloppy enchilada, and a mulatto baby being born nine fucking months to the day after you last put it to her. So this Perreau woman has her little baby girl and names her Nadine Adair, after the father who is at this point shelling out cold cash to keep the old bitch away from his legitimate family.

And one day I get so mad, so angry at that bitch when she asks for more money, more money for her little girl, that when we go for a walk down by Rock Creek, I decide I am going to kill the mother. I am going to kill her, but I get a hard-on, boy, a man's downfall is always his dick, the stiff prick with no conscience, so I decide I'm going to fuck her to death, boy, skewer her shishkabob style. And so we get worked up down on the muddy bank of the creek. And while I am screwing that black whore, she calls up the demons of Hell to bite me, wasps just like the ones she sent to me last week, but back then she called them out of her fucking cooze!

Ted rolled onto his stomach on the bed, clutching the pillow against his face, trying to fall asleep.

She's what they call a mambo, boy, only like I said, I didn't believe in anything, and when you believe in nothing, that's when the piano drops out of the sky on you, that's when something makes a grab for you in the dark from under your bed! But the man, he tells me he can keep that bitch out of my life for good. He's something of a voodoo expert, a priest who calls himself a bokor, and he tells me that he can make sure she never bothers me again. Man, I promise that guy, my favorite abortionist, ANYTHING just to get that whore out of my life, and he does just that, and in a way that's so ingenious that I still haven't fucking figured it out!

He makes her forget who I am, boy.

He makes her go mad.

I even saw her after that, and she didn't recognize me, and I'd just laugh at her, laugh at her and her raggedy little coffee-colored girl, now a teenager, and beautiful because she's got the Adair blue eyes, but she's filthy and stupid like her mother. That's when the man, the abortionist, quotes me his price.

You know the story about the Pied Piper, boy? How he gets the rats out of this town, and then the town won't pay him what he's asked for, so you know what he does? He takes their children, Ted, he takes their children.

But the Pied Piper at least waited until the children were born.

But this guy, my favorite abortionist, his name was Gil DuRaz, but I've done some looking into that, too, and the name was about as legitimate as the way he went about his work. Gil DuRaz was a joke name, something I guess this man knew would be found out, and let me tell you what the joke is: Gilles DuRais was a famous guy in his own way. He was also French, but we're talking France, and we're talking Joan of Arc's right-hand man who went crazy when the war was over and started poking little boys and slicing their entrails out and filling huge caldrons full of their blood before he was caught and brought to trial. And one more thing about the guy he stole his name from: he used the kids for his black-magic rituals, and he bought most of the kids from their parents.

That's part of the joke, see, because he bought an unborn child from me, actually, he bought a baby before I'd even screwed the girl.

And the girl was named Nadine Adair.

My own flesh and blood.

I did it because I owed him one.

And I enjoyed it, boy, I enjoyed every fucking minute of it.

Gil DuRaz had a ritual, and he needed that teenaged girl, my daughter by that crazy black whore, he needed her and her baby, and I stood by in a room in that house, while the riots were going on, boy, while people were shooting out windows and setting fire to entire blocks, and I stood next to Nadine's mother and she didn't recognize me. I stood there and I watched Gil DuRaz, abortionist of gutter rats, bring his face down to where that baby's heart beat inside a teenager and I saw him devour her like a hungry animal.

But, boy, that's not the best part, nosireebob, the best fucking part is yet to come. The fat lady was about to warble her chunky heart out, because they all sat down there, all except her mother Madeleine who was going into hysterics, but the kind where you just beat the walls, nothing to interfere with Gil's feeding frenzy—and he saved the baby, yes, he did. He didn't swallow that half-formed child, he held it up like it was the savior, and then they sat there and they drank that little girl's blood. They drank her blood because it was like a communion, boy, *and I thought I was going to be killed if I didn't, so I took a great big sip myself, boy.*

And son, she tasted good.

3.

Ted Adair lay in bed awake all night wondering what you do when your father has finally lost it with no hope of getting it back.

When he went to sleep, with the morning light flooding through the window, he had a dream in which he sat at the head of a great table. Before him on the tablecloth were a napkin, a knife and fork, and a plate. He was alone at the table and someone was about to come through a doorway from the kitchen, someone with a platter, someone who was going to offer him a feast.

Ted awoke before noon, screaming.

SEVENTEEN

GETTING THE HELL OUT OF DODGE

1.

Thursday morning, Rachel awoke with a smile on her face, and Hugh was already taking a shower down the hall from the bedroom. Their lovemaking had been intense, exhausting, and she felt exhilarated. She rose lazily, wondering what the weather at the beach would be like, and glanced out the window. *Cloudy.* She gathered up a towel and her make-up kit and padded barefoot downstairs, through the living room, down to the first-floor bathroom. She stood before the space separating the turret room from the bathroom, figuring the small vanity room to be about three feet across, about half the size of the bathroom. She wondered if one day Hugh would be able to tear down the wall so they could use the space.

After her shower, spotting a roach running down the pipe beneath the sink, she combed her dark hair—it squeaked as she stroked her fingers through it. In the mirror she felt she looked like Dracula's daughter, she was so pale, but perhaps a little sun would take care of that. *Bring on the crow's feet! Bring on the burn! Give me sand between my toes, between my lips, up the wazoo!* The bathing suit dilemma once again confronted her as she sucked in her gut, examining the flab that had been accumulating around her waist. She'd gained ten pounds, in spite of jogging (and she knew it was from giving up cigarettes). Her old bikini would highlight the creeping ivy of cellulite on the backs of her thighs and would gross her out even though Hugh didn't seem to notice it. Then she had a one-piece suit, naturally a gift from her mother, with a frilly edge that made her feel like she was wearing a tutu. Hugh had once given her a sexy Norma Kamali black bathing suit, but she was almost afraid to wear it because she never felt very attractive in anything that was *too* sexy. She'd seen enough women on the beach wearing sexy outfits who looked like they should be the last people on earth to wear them. Perhaps she would wear the bikini, but cover herself with a towel most of the time. Or wear a T-shirt over the top.

Thank God we're getting away for a while, just the two of us, no house, no job, no roaches, and no mice. It was already muggy at nine in the morning, but that was okay, too. It could be cloudy and humid and drippy and stagnant, just so long as they could get away.

2.

"Yes, dear, I know, the exterminator comes by at one, which is good timing because my ladies are arriving at three, and surely this man will be done spraying or whatever he's going to do by then?" Mrs. Deerfield asked. She would not open her door more than a crack—Rachel had gotten her out of bed ("But that's all right, dear, I've overslept for the third day in a row, I must get to bed earlier . . .").

Rachel passed the set of house keys through the space in the open door. Mrs. Deerfield was evidently naked—there was a flash of her thigh for a second. "Have you found Ramona yet?"

"No dear, and I am becoming slightly worried, although she's ever so self-sufficient for such a lazy feline."

"Well, you have my permission to check around upstairs while we're gone. I wouldn't want anything bad to happen."

Mrs. Deerfield pursed her lips. "If only something bad *could* happen to that wicked Ramona, as much as I adore her she's been the bane of my existence these past few days—she broke three of my best mason jars full of jelly trying to get up through that dumbwaiter. Now you have a good trip and don't lie out in the sun too long, and don't go swimming much past your knees, you know, drowning can occur so easily, so swiftly, in just a few feet of water."

And with that, Mrs. Deerfield shut the door.

3.

"I don't think we'll get caught in a rainstorm," Rachel said as she rolled open the sunroof of the car; the clouds above them seemed less threatening than they had in the early morning. Hugh rummaged in the back seat. "You packed my blue sweatshirt, right?" He was wearing a gray T-shirt with the letters *W* and *L* across the front; his dark blue shorts hung loose around his pale hairy legs.

She glanced back at him in the rearview mirror. He'd made a mess of the cooler and picnic basket, pushing them aside as he dug through the suitcase—*Am I forgetting anything? Did I pack the Solarcaine? Is there still aspirin in the glove compartment? Do we have the maps we need?* She reached into her purse for her small bottle of Keri Lotion. Down at the bottom of her purse was the one cigarette she always kept with her. *I am immune to you,* she silently told the cigarette. She rubbed the lotion across her hands. She sneezed. "Oh, great, I'm probably getting a cold, too, and it'll rain and we'll get caught in awful beach traffic."

"Scout, we'll be fine, and there's no rush anyway. You remember your allergy stuff?" Hugh got out of the back of the car, adjusted the driver's seat, and sat down, fiddling with her cassette tapes.

Rachel nodded, opening the side pocket of her purse just in case; if her allergies flared up at the beach she'd be prepared—when she and Hugh used to go up to Cape Cod or down to Virginia Beach, sometimes she would get a bad case of hives after going in the water, particularly if it was a cool day. "Me and my allergies." She waved to a neighbor who was getting into his Honda Prelude two parking places down. "I won't mind if it rains once we get there, but I hate it when it rains on the road and then all the accidents."

"There are no accidents." Hugh laughed. He drew a

tape out of its plastic case. "You mind if we listen to the Beatles?"

Rachel shrugged. "Only if it's *Revolver,* not *The White Album,* if I have to hear your rendition of 'Rocky Raccoon' again . . ."

He put the key in the ignition and pressed down on the accelerator. "I like my 'Rocky Raccoon,' and you told me you liked it, too, and to think I trusted your scout's honor. Humph."

"Don't flood the motor," she said, and then added quickly, "Just like a girl scout to give orders."

Hugh grinned. "Suddenly you're kind of tense. I like that in a girl."

"You probably think I'm crazy, but I feel strange leaving our home. I've *never* cared about any place we've lived, but I feel like it won't be the same when we get back."

"You mean it's like an old friend," Hugh said as if he were talking to a three year old.

"See, you do think I'm nuts." She was anxious to get on the road because she *was* going to miss their home, things had been peaceful and homey this week, and now *what if we go and fuck it all up at the beach?*

Hugh was talking but Rachel was only half listening—his foot pumped the gas pedal, his wrist turned, the key turned, the lights blinked on and off behind the steering wheel as Rachel thought she heard babies crying again, their voices small and apparently all around her, while Hugh twisted the key and pumped the gas. He slapped the steering wheel with the palm of his left hand; the crying sounds seemed to be coming from inside the car, inside her, and Rachel wondered if this wasn't a little like the ringing in her ears she occasionally experienced. The car made sputtering noises, backfired once, and Hugh said, "What the hell?"

She glanced over at him, trying to pretend she wasn't hearing babies. *It must be from somewhere in the alley, some woman is pushing her stroller near the back of one of the buildings, either that or I have lost my marbles. And I'm pretty sure I woke up today with everything in working order.* She briefly remembered a dream she'd had several nights before, puffing up and exploding with babies, but Hugh had said *what the hell?* and now he'd stopped turning the key in the ignition and was reaching for the car door handle to get out of the car.

She looked over the hood of the car, and coming out of the slatted vents on the top of the hood were what looked like grayish white feathers, and then she thought they might be tufts of fur, but why were tufts of fur coming out from between the openings of the hood of her car?

She got out from her side as Hugh went around and lifted the hood of the car.

"Oh, Jesus," Hugh said, and seeing her coming, "no, Scout, don't look, not now," but she looked and saw tiny masses of wet red and white fur. Then the body of a long-haired cat pushing its kittens away from the fan belt of the car, and then she saw the long-haired cat's head which had been neatly separated from its body. Its eyes gazed up at the instruments of its destruction, the fan belt, the motor. *Ramona.*

The kittens, four of them, rested on top of the battery. They mewled and cried and looked up at Rachel and Hugh with closed eyes.

EIGHTEEN

KEEPING HOUSE

1.

"Oh, dear," Mrs. Deerfield said as she went about her work in the kitchen. "Such a good mother to sacrifice herself for her babies."

Penelope Deerfield watched their car rumble through the alley—it had been another hour before the nice couple had driven off, after Penelope had taken in the kittens, her eyes full of tears. "No, you two go on, go on, I shall be fine, I will call the vet and see if we can't save Ramona's babies, I shall be fine, I insist, go on, go on, it was an accident, I shall be fine." And they'd laid dear Ramona down in a blue towel beneath the shade of the iron stairs, and now they were indeed leaving on their beach trip, and Ramona was indeed dead. Penelope Deerfield watched them go, standing over the sink in the kitchen. The sink filled to the brim with soapy dishwater, the just cleaned and shiny china cups and saucers lay glistening on a flowered hand towel that she'd stretched across her cutting board.

Penelope Deerfield kept her hands down in the water, but every few seconds one of the small white kittens floated to the top, trying to escape. "Mustn't scratch," she told each kitten as she pressed its bobbing head deeper into the dishwater.

2.

Later, after she Scotchgarded the old chair she'd recently finished upholstering, Penelope drained the sink and took the waterlogged kittens out and buried them with Ramona in the mulch pile. It was hot, and she kept swatting at her bangs which fell across her forehead every few seconds in an annoying tickle. She told Ramona's head, "I shall have to cut my hair off if I am to survive the summer."

3.

She was down in the crib when someone began ringing the doorbell like a madman. "It's too early for my friends," she said aloud, "so it must be the exterminator for upstairs." Her back was aching from lifting the trapdoor and then setting it to one side. She'd had to crouch down a bit, watch her head as she descended the four steps into the cool hold. She'd taken a deep breath of the air as she sat at the bottom step, licking her lips. "You've been a good one, today, hardly a sound," she'd told the darkness.

The only light in the crib came from Mrs. Deerfield's apartment, but even with the trapdoor completely off, there was barely enough light to see: twenty-five large mason jars filled with the memories of summers past, the preserves, the pickles, the jellies (strawberry, mint, apricot, peach, raspberry, pepper), and even a few bottles of homemade wine. It smelled of mold and dust, pickling brine and pure alcohol—the floor was made up of sandy earth. Brownish mushrooms sprouted along the corners, among the jars, and from between the clefts in the stone wall.

Another ten jars stood in a circle in the darkest corner, the part of the crib nearest the hidden steps up to the house above.

Something in the dark scraped its way between the jars, rattling them as it went.

"Be careful, dear, it won't be much longer now I think."

But then the doorbell had rung, and Penelope thought of

how much her back ached and how weary a body could get, how flesh just didn't hold up in the long run. The doorbell sounded again and again until she could no longer ignore it. "Stay here, dear, it's that exterminator for sure, come to take away all your little playmates from upstairs."

Keeping her head low so as not to strike it against the roof of the crib, Penelope Deerfield went back up the steps to her apartment.

In the dark, something behind the ten jars *not* filled with jams, jellies, pickles, and preserves let out a low moan.

Floating in the milky waters of those ten jars: human fetuses.

PART THREE

HOUSEWARMING

AUGUST

NINETEEN

HEALING WATERS

1.

Night, steamy night, a smothering pillow with the odors of rotting vegetation and carbon monoxide; the fishy swampy stink of summer curling in the dead-breeze air; the sounds of the creek running; the bright headlights on the road nearby blinding the woman who stood over the grave, beneath the bridge. The sour taste of three-week-old milk spread across her lips. Mattie Peru flicked at a crane fly with her tongue—it had crawled along the edge of her chin. Her trash bags rattled as she raised her arms up, then whipped them down through the air as if she were trying to fly away.

Who done this to you, my baby? Is he *out of Hell now? Did* he *send* his *messenger to take even your bones away from me?* "Baby!" she shouted. Sounds of footsteps on P Street Bridge above her; her voice echoed across the parkway, booming and crashing like ocean waves, but stirred up in the evening noises, the honkings, the screechings, the yowlings, the gigglings, the *shooshing* of Rock Creek, the cry diminished.

The gigglings. Somewhere in the sparse dark woods around her, somewhere in the bushes.

Mattie looked at the grave.

The grave was empty, had been dug up, a perfect oval. She had planted her only daughter here, right here where the grass sang, where the water whispered, planted her bones all those years ago, planted them in red dry earth in the spring of 1968.

The grave was filled up with water—the recent rainfall had taken over the space, had buried itself there.

Mattie flapped her arms, yipping like a pained dog.

She fell to her knees before the open grave. She bent over the water, dropping her face down to the muddy surface, cupping her hands to the water, splashing it up into her face, taking long slurping drinks of it. *Open my eyes, my baby! Open my mouth and my ears, open my heart, my little babygirl, give me your power, water of my child! Give me some power from the land of the dead, wash me in your bone water!*

And when she stopped drinking and washing her face in the water, she peeled her trash bags of invisibility from her. She stripped her raggedy clothes from her back, the old, stained men's boxer shorts she wore, the open-toed hiking boots. Naked and shining with grease, her gray hair white by moonlight, white and sparkling with the jewels of the bone water, she slipped into her daughter's grave and began washing away the clogged pores of her memory.

From under the bridge, down by the creek, among the bushes: giggling.

2.

"We found ya, nigra," the man snarled, but before Mattie saw him standing under the bridge she *smelled* him, and the smell was one from her memory, her memory which was shining and clean washed in the bone water of her baby. He was one of the men who had raped her in the springtime, up against a lamppost with his buddy, raped her and taken her bottle of Mad Dog 20/20. She could not make him out in the dark shade from beneath the bridge, but she saw what he was holding in his hands extended out from beneath the bridge: a skull, reflecting light from the moon. The one called Pete wagged it in midair, and spoke for it in a falsetto whine, *"Mama, mama, they done fucked my brains out, they fucked my brains out, and then they* et *'em, mama!"*

The other man was there, too, Willy, and he emerged from beneath P Street Bridge carrying part of a rib cage.

"You lookin' for these, bitch?" He held the ribs between his hands like an accordion, and then snapped them apart. His friend giggled, and he made Nadine's skull giggle, too. *"Oh, mama, you must be shittin' your britches, you must be pissin' your panties!"*

Mattie cried out at the noise. She remained in the grave, up to her waist in water. It dripped down her neck, in rivulets down her shoulders to her breasts, lingering across her nipples. Her body tingled with the water, with the smell of her daughter's muddy grave, with the clean feeling, the baptism she was undergoing. Down in the pit of her stomach she felt the water sloshing, her bladder filling with its warmth, her tongue moistened and smooth from drinking.

"We liked the way you went and stripped, piglet, and now you went and even fuckin' took a bath!"

The skull giggled and gibbered in midair. Pete had stuck his fingers into the empty eye sockets—he shook it like it was a rattle.

"We want a little of what you got, bitch." Willy stroked the ribs like he was plucking harp strings.

"Piglet, we been lookin' for a little nooky, and we been watchin' you for weeks, and we been seein' you come down here, we been watchin' you but we been waitin', and now no more watchin' and waitin'."

The skull roared with falsetto laughter.

Mattie felt the bone water inside and outside her skin, and her blood boiled with the cleansing that was going through it.

The power that was shooting through her.

The spirit of her daughter, rinsing her with the old power, the mind and the power and the knowledge and the *memory* of the old days, the days when she was a mambo. When she was a priestess. When she could call wasps from her womb, when she could protect the soul of the dead from the gods of evil.

"Just a little nooky," Pete said, rubbing the skull between his palms. "Seems you got plenty, and we fellers just want a slide or two."

"Sure, nigra, we done it before to ya, and you liked it, you *liked* it."

"You liked it, mama!" the skull screamed.

"Dug up my baby's grave," Mattie said, her voice a low growl. "You done stole my baby's bones."

"Shit, we just wanted to see what you got in here. You went 'n killed somebody—we gonna keep it a secret. Just the three of us if you gon' be a good girl. For such an ugly old hag you sure don't got much gratitude."

Mattie shook her head violently. Water sprayed out from her hair. "No, it's *him*, Baron Samedi make you do it."

"Crazy bitch."

"Baron Samedi, he done make you do this, and you don't know, do ya?"

"Nooky, nooky," Pete said, waggling the skull back and forth.

"Baron gets inside ya, means ya gonna *die* soon, means ya might as already be *dead.*"

Willy dropped the busted rib cage and came to the edge of the grave. He dropped to his knees, reaching down to his crotch and unzipped himself. "Nooky, nooky."

Mattie cupped her hands. She brought up a palmful of bone water. Holding her hands up to the moon, she prayed. The old prayers of her mambo days were forgotten, shut away inside her. She prayed to Nadine's spirit and the bones. *Forgive me, my babygirl, forgive your mama what she done to you, protect me from the baron, protect these old bones.*

She felt something like an eel slithering in the grave pool of water, and for a moment she was scared, afraid it was the baron here, come to drown her in her daughter's own grave.

But the water had a voice, charged with electricity, and she recognized the voice, briefly, a faint sound, the words were whispered and unintelligible, but they were her daughter's. The water around her began to roil and splash, feeling alternately hot and cold, and Mattie held her cupped hands high for the blessing.

The skull giggled.

Magic Touch, Nadine, bring me the Magic Touch.

Then she splattered the man who knelt in front of her, spraying the water across the flat small penis that flopped from his pants.

When the water hit him there, he screamed.

He screamed as if he'd been scorched with fire.

The skin of his penis bubbled and blistered in his fingers.

When she splashed water across his face, popping eruptions hissed where the water landed, his nose melting in the middle, one eye shut by its lid which had become waxen and dripped down and over to his cheekbone, his lips drooling down his chin. The screams became choked gurgles as he inadvertently swallowed some of the bone water.

The man with the skull ran to his friend's side. "You fuckin' bitch, whatchu do to my buddy?"

Mattie ducked her head down and drank in some bone water, gargling it in the back of her throat. Then she spat it out at him, and it peeled off the top layer of skin across his right arm. He dropped the skull, holding onto his buddy as they ran away through the woods.

The skull slipped into the bone water. Mattie reached down to catch it. She clutched it to her breasts. "My baby, my baby," she moaned.

3.

The dreams of the past beat their rhythms in Mattie Peru's mind as she lay across the park bench at midafternoon the next day, her trash bags thrown back away from her, her rags half falling off. A couple passed by, glancing down at the woman, upset because they could not use the bench for their lunch hour. Mattie's smell, like old dead meat in the sun, steamed from her skin and when a breeze came up, strollers in the park wrinkled their noses without quite knowing why.

She lay still as if dead, but beneath her skin, her heartbeat was rapid and fluttering, her pulse beat fast, and if a doctor were to examine her at the height of this memory dream, he might diagnose a mild coronary—and when that moment came, Mattie would move. *Chop-choppity-chop*, the ax of her blood swung into her heart. Her right arm arched and her fist tightened. Drool sluiced from between her lips.

Her eyes flickered open, then closed.

Her dreams unfolded like a closed fist, gradually opening,

the palm spreading, fingers splayed. And in the center of that hand, a small rose made of fire, a small rose opening its heart, and in its heart, the flame, and in the heart of the flame a man who called himself Gil DuRaz.

4.

Mattie Peru was on fire in her mind, but the fires raged with lust, lust for the dark man from the islands, lust for her half brother, Gil DuRaz. Gil had stood six foot five, a giant of a man, and so thin his ribs stuck out and rippled through the black cotton shirts he favored. His face was the face of a man who had seen beyond what life had to offer, who had done things that only dead men knew. It was ridged with dark knowledge, with a wild gleam in his deepset eyes, a supreme love for the dead. He looked like a god to her—he was handsome, and strong, with the sharp look of a fighter who has never lost but is always on the lookout for a worthy opponent. And his smile! Wide and thick with a forest of beautiful teeth—a gold one on the upper left side that shone when he smiled.

And she loved him because he *made* her love him.

But the man was inspired with the spirit of the dead, he knew the rotting secrets of the graveyard.

In those days, when Mattie was called Madeleine Perreau, she was the most beautiful young girl in the projects around Winthrop Park. She was tall and sturdy, but she had the smooth curves of a cello, and long, shiny black hair—she looked like a Gauguin island girl, even though she herself had never seen any island in her lifetime, not even her mother's native Haiti. But her older brother had. He was ten when Madeleine's mother, Jacqueline, had left Haiti and had come to Washington, D.C., to live with her own mother, and to bear her daughter on U.S. soil. Madeleine had been born watching her mother scrub the floors in the Bram Apartments, but the young girl soon discovered her mother's true power over the black people who lived in the enclave of Winthrop Park. And she discovered the secret of the Screaming House, the one called Draper House, the carrefour that bordered the park—the place where the petro, the spirits of evil, passed through on their way to Hell.

But then, when Mattie was a teenager, her half brother had taken her mind off such fears: he was a bokor, a high priest, a powerful man who could capture a soul in a clay jar and shatter it just as easily; he could bury a man alive and make him a zombi to do his bidding, and he could make his half sister fall in love with him, because inside him, inside his tall, lean dark body, there dwelled the mind and the spirit of the Lord of the Dead, of Baron Samedi.

Mattie's brother Gil had undergone a thousand possessions by spirits, but only at the Screaming House had the spirits stayed within him, as if now *he* were the jar, holding them.

And she learned some of the secrets of the rada and petro, of the spirits and their rhythms, and she watched as he cut the babies from the wombs of young girls, and she became possessed with the clamoring spirits of the house and she made love with her brother, with her brother and with any man he wanted her to make love with, and she became a mambo, a priestess with him.

She intended to spend her whole lifetime by his side, until he betrayed her, and betrayed her with a white woman, a woman that he emptied out and filled with another spirit, the spirit of evil that dwelt in the house.

She loved him until she saw him devouring a corpse.

She believed it had been a corpse.

Until the corpse had moved.

And Mattie knew then it was no corpse at all.

That her half brother Gil had become a cannibal, that he had developed a taste for flesh and blood, that he had perverted the Voudun religion that their mother had taught them, and had let something vile and evil into his worship. And the woman, the Housekeeper, was ensuring his corruption. When her brother finally had become Baron Samedi, the foul-breathed flesh and blood of the grave, he turned against her.

And he devoured the body of her only child, a child by a man that Gil had wanted her to love in the first place, an evil white man who had been Gil's tool for bringing the child into the world. Because the night Gil came to her like a lover, possessed by the spirits, and every night after, she did not conceive with him, no child was born.

So he wanted her child, even if it was hers by another man.

And he wanted her child's child.

And he ate her baby, and he took her baby's baby, and Mattie made him pay.

She made him pay.

And as Mattie remembered *how* she'd made Gil DuRaz pay, she heard her little girl calling something to her, something that sounded like . . .

5.

Mattie awoke, screaming. Pigeons scattered away from the bench she'd been sleeping upon. *Nadine, honey, you callin' to me, but I don't understand nothin' you sayin'.* Her breasts were heavy and she felt sharp pains along her ribs, down to her thighs. It was still hot and sunny. Late in the day, and sundown may have been five hours away, but Mattie could *feel* the night in her bones, eating away at the daylight.

Her heartbeat was like an ax chopping away at an old thick tree, pausing to swing back, and the *chop! chop! choppity-chop!* Her right hand dug beneath the trash bags, pushing aside her left breast, trying to hold her heart steady, trying to slow down its chopping. A memory of love came back to her, through a smell—it was an annoying odor, one which she could not identify, not sweat, not cologne, not food cooking, but somehow, all of these. And she saw the face of the man who was Nadine's father.

Mattie thought it was a dream as she lay there on the bench, clutching her heart, watching the two men in the car going by. One was young and handsome and she did not know him. The other was Mr. Big Man, and how he had changed on the outside, and how she could tell at a glance that on the inside he had not changed at all.

TWENTY

HE SAID, IT'S NOT EVEN HUMAN

1.

"Get me the fuck out of here!" Winston Adair shrieked. He kept his head down, his fists pounding the dashboard of his son's Mercedes. He didn't even have to look up to see the house, he knew where they were, he knew by the *tone* of Ted's voice: "We could say hello while we're here." While they'd been driving, Winston had felt calm, almost relaxed for the first time in three weeks—he had stayed inside and watched for those bugs, those crawling things, those wasps, but Ted had convinced him to come out for a drive, just for some fresh air. "It's such a goddamned beautiful day and you've been pissing in mayonnaise jars long enough, pop, it's either a drive or a loony bin, your choice." And so Winston had agreed to go, but only if the windows were kept tightly rolled up, only if the doors were locked.

But he hadn't agreed to *this*.

"Jesus, pop," Ted whisper-shouted, "the fucking world can hear you."

"Drive, fucking drive, or so help me God, Ted, so help me God!"

Ted Adair, cursing under his breath, continued driving to the end of Hammer Street, taking a left on Kalorama, heading away from Winthrop Park.

2.

They went to Ted's condo, because there was booze there. Ted needed a good stiff drink. He was trying to remember the name of the shrink his ex-wife Paula used to go to. *Steinfeld, Steenman, Steinman, something like that. Although maybe what pop needs is a whole fucking institute, maybe he needs a megashot of morphine, maybe a lobotomy.* Which reminded Ted of the phrase he used to hear in college, *I'd rather have a bottle in front of me than a frontal lobotomy.* "If I'm going to listen to this bullshit, I want to be half in the bag, pop." But his father wasn't listening.

Winston Adair glanced suspiciously around the living room, but then decided it was safe. He walked like he was already blind drunk—weaving across the parquet floor, stubbing his toes on the coffee table, then navigating uncertainly around the beige sofa, around the lamp table, along the wall, to the window that overlooked Q Street. He stayed to the left of the window. Then, spotting the dining room table and chairs, he went over, wobbling and klutzy the whole way, grabbed a chair, and dragged it back across the floor to the window. The chair made a fingernails-on-blackboard sound as it went.

Ted shook his head sadly as he watched his father. He stood in the front doorway, unsure as to whether he should stay or leave. *Why am I letting myself in for this?* "Hey, listen, let's say you're not crazy, let's say you were involved in all this voodoo bullshit, but so the fuck what? That was what, over twenty years ago? So you ate a couple of mushrooms or something, or you drank too much vino and a girl died on the operating table. You can afford therapy, and if you want my advice, I think you just might get the top psychiatrist in town and stay with him for another ten years—"

Winston sat at the window, to the side, so he could see out of it without being seen. He did not turn to face Ted. The back of his head was a large pink mound, with tufts of blue white hair spraying out. Ted watched the back of his head as if he could drill into it and find out what chemical was causing this malfunction in the Old Man's brain. "It's not just that day in 1968, son. It's the rest of it, the rest of the deal. You make a deal with the devil and your mind gets farted from a pig's rectum. When the devil makes a deal, there's always a string, there's always something within the deal, another deal, and within *that* deal, another deal."

"Jesus, you are talking in circles. You want I should make you a martini?" Without waiting for an answer, Ted went over to the bar and poked around in the freezer. "You know, you keep the gin in the freezer and it's just the right temperature. No ice, nothing. Just gets that chill. You want vodka or gin? Vodka, right?"

"Just give me the bottle."

"Will you make more sense if I do? I mean, this little outing wasn't planned out of the goodness of my heart. I wanted to make sure you were certifiable before I turned you over to the nice men in the white suits."

Winston sighed heavily. "You are some son. You are some fucking son."

"Yeah, and you're some fucking father, but let's not get into it or I might just conk you over the head with this bottle." Ted took a highball glass filled to the brim with vodka over to where his father sat. He lifted the Old Man's right hand and cupped it around the glass. "Now don't spill. *That* would definitely make me want to throw you out the window."

Winston Adair turned towards him, looking up at his oldest son with eyes that could've been empty sockets: there was nothing there, no color, no spark, no *life*. He had withdrawn somewhere inside himself the way a turtle withdraws into its shell.

Ted wanted to cry, just break down and start crying, because as much as he despised the Old Man, as much as he loathed him, it was as if his father were already dead and this were the funeral, because it seemed like there was no turning back. No cure for a man this far gone.

"It would be a relief if you did, just break my neck or

knife me while I'm sitting here." Winston lifted his glass in a toast. "Good drink, good meat, good God, let's eat, boy, now *there's* a *grace* a man can sink his teeth into. I saw him do it, too, Ted, sink his teeth into that little girl, good God, let's eat. And we all shared in the blood. My face was streaked with it—it tasted like liquid metal. That *is* insane, isn't it? Well, I was insane, and maybe I still am. But that doesn't stop it, craziness doesn't stop it. I don't know what *does.*" He was already finished with his drink; he held the glass out to be refilled. He wiped his free hand across his lips as if they were parched.

Vodka makes it easier, Ted thought as he poured out another glass. *Some good old Absolut makes the medicine go down a little smoother. Don't mind if I do.* He lifted the bottle to his lips and gulped back a shot.

"I wish I had died then." Winston fingered the rim of his glass—it made a high-pitched squealing sound. "I wish when it happened, the girl's mother had killed me the way she killed *him.* But I thought then, that by killing him, Gil DuRaz, it would put an end to it. I thought they were a bunch of crazies. I didn't really believe. When he wanted the unborn baby, not even a baby, a fetus, just a mushy wriggling pudding of flesh, I thought it was just part of his sickness, and shit, boy, I was glad to let him take it, he said, he said to me, 'It's not even human,' and that's what I thought, too, it's not even *breathing.* But then I saw it, I saw the fetus. And I knew he meant something else by that. He said, 'It's not even human,' boy, and he meant it. He was right, Ted, my boy, the thing wasn't human, it was inhuman, it had claws like razors, it had eyes like a fucking frog, it had a mouth, Jesus, its mouth was filled with warts and bumps, and it was barely formed, its spinal cord was just a knotted rope running beneath the flesh—you could practically see its heart beating, all its *veins* on the *outside* of its *skin*—and I said, 'Fucking Jesus!' and that man, Gil, said, 'Hardly fucking Jesus, Mr. Big Man. This is your son, this is your true son, the son you are meant to have, and he will be the vessel for my spirit, Mr. Big Man, he will be the possessor of my soul.' I wondered what in God's name that man had done to that girl to make her body form a baby like that, and he told me, son, he told me, get this—are you getting this? 'Cause this is important—'Don't you think it resembles you? Don't you think this is what you are *inside?*' And fuck, Ted, if that gob of flesh didn't open its disgusting perverted mouth wide and moan and twist in the negro's hands just like it was alive."

TWENTY-ONE

NORMAL LIFE

1.

"What book?" Hugh asked, cradling the phone between his chin and scrunched-up shoulder—he propped the refrigerator door open with his right leg bent at the knee, and with his hands managed to move around all the jars of pickles and jams that Mrs. Deerfield had given them.

On the other end of the line, the clerk at the bookstore said, *"Diaries of an Innocent Age* by Standish, Mr. Adair. You ordered it in June, but it was hard to locate—the company who published it has been out of business for ten years. We finally got it, though. It just took a little longer than usual."

"Oh, right," Hugh said absent-mindedly—he found what he was looking for, a half-empty Miller Lite behind the orange juice carton. "I pretty much forgot about it—I'll be down sometime today."

When he hung up the phone, he sniffed at the bottle of beer—it had gone flat. He'd opened it and put it in there the day before the trip to the beach. They'd been back a few days, so what did he expect? But he'd gone eight days without a drink of any kind, on his best behavior at the beach, for Rachel's benefit. And the beach had been trying, particularly after the accident with the car and the cat. With Rachel crying, Penny Dreadful crying, and Hugh feeling miserable and then the rain and the late start in the noontime traffic congestion; with Rachel, her eyes red, saying that they should just turn the car around and go home, wondering how Mrs. Deerfield would ever forgive them . . . Hugh had craved a drink like a pregnant woman craves pickles. Then the beach was overcast most of the time (and *still* he managed to get a painful sunburn which no amount of Solarcaine seemed to help—his nose continued to peel, and they'd been back three days), and Rachel was too listless, almost withdrawn over the cat's death, to want to go out to a restaurant. So at night they sat in the motel room and ate junk food and watched bad TV. Hugh had a terrific case of constipation the whole time, and was a Metamucil junkie by the last day—he favored the orange-flavored kind in the small easy-to-toss-away packets; it reminded him of Fizzies from his childhood, dropping the Metamucil in the glass of water and having it hiss and sputter into this utilitarian punch.

But *this* punch was even better than Fizzies *or* Metamucil. He held the bottle up and took a long, lingering drink of beer. *Flat* Miller Lite *ain't so bad.* He chugged down the rest and set the bottle on the counter. *No, better trash it. Don't need to get her upset over an old beer.* He opened the cabinet beneath the sink and tossed it out.

No sign of roaches beneath the sink. No mousedoody behind the plastic trash can.

"Scout!" he called up the stairs.

She didn't answer.

"Honey, I'm going to run down to KramerBooks for a sec. Can I pick up anything?"

2.

After Hugh left for the store, Rachel lay back on their bed. She was still exhausted from the trip, and then had plunged right back to work and it felt like jumping in the cold Atlantic that first day of the trip. The week back had passed slowly even with all the work she had to catch up on, and the weekend had taken forever to arrive. But then even Saturday was not perfect: one of her famous migraines had come on suddenly in the afternoon, so she lay on top of the covers, the shades drawn, the lights out. Her skin burned; everytime she scratched her arm, more skin flaked off on the bed. The pain and nausea were unrelenting.

But even with the pain, she smiled.

She knew it was too soon to tell, and *it's just my overactive imagination, that and this migraine, but I am never ever late like this, it's always like clockwork, always, the only time this has ever happened before was when* it *happened.*

How many times had they made love in the past ten days? Twelve? Thirteen times? *What are the chances? Oh, God, but I'm imagining things. You can't know you're pregnant until a month or two afterwards, this is just wishful thinking . . . but Scout, you knew* before, *you* knew *that somewhere inside you there was a little sphere just hopping with new life. You knew then, and you thought so immediately, and you were right. It wasn't Let's Pretend, it was real, it was Normal Life.*

"You're just being silly," she said aloud, to the walls, to the ceiling, to the drapes. Her head was throbbing, but she didn't really mind.

3.

From *Diaries of an Innocent Age*, by Verena Standish:

. . . Winthrop Park was, in those days, quite a fashionable residence, although there were still lingering traces of its bohemian beginnings: they said a woman at the Bram estate ran a blind down at the corner, mainly for coloreds and sailors, although this was all rumor and I never saw a sailor or a colored, unless that colored was a member of one of my or my neighbor's staffs . . .

Hugh sipped his beer. *Verena, you old white supremacist bastion, I'm willing to bet you were not well liked by many people. I'm willing to bet if it weren't for your daddy's money . . . Hell, just like me, Verena, you and I are part of the same class, ain't we? But I'm willing to bet that, just like me, if someone scratched your surface, you'd be as common as a whore.* Hugh skimmed the pages. Verena, in her tedious eighties while writing her life story, went on *ad nauseam* about the lost, refined qualities of *fin de siècle* society. Hugh thought: *You fucking debutante, Verena, you had everything served to you on a silver platter, you lived in one of the most fascinating times of history. You and me, Verena, you and me. For me, the best prep schools, the best college the Old Man could buy my way into, a pretty damn good law school (although not as good as the one Ted got into, and certainly not as good as the Old Man's), summers in Europe and the Caribbean.* Hugh lifted the beer in a silent toast. *Here's to the girls who do, Verena, although I guess you're one of the girls who never did.*

He finished the bottle; there were three left in the six-pack he'd picked up at the liquor store on Nineteenth Street.

Flipping pages through the thick diary.

Get to our house, lady, I don't want this shit about the glorious days before these times of Sodom and Gomorrah. I want specifics: the wallpaper, the size of the rooms.

He read:

. . . Draper House was small by the standards of my upbringing. Its narrow passages were no match for the stately halls of my father's Hudson River estate, a home which I grew to miss terribly. But my husband, Addison, was no doubt relieved to be out from under the wing of a rather demanding father-in-law, and the children seemed to enjoy the carriage rides around the park and the contact with so many other children being a daily occurrence rather than something reserved for planned weekends. Emmie and James were just reaching the point in childhood where everything seems an adventure, and if I had only had some inkling of the tragedy to come, I suppose I would have been more strict with them, I would have observed the goings-on in the house more carefully. But as I write this, for the first time, nearly fifty years later, I realize what a vain and foolish young woman I was, a woman barely thirty who believed that children should be seen and not heard, and that all matters of education and social carriage should be left in the hands of a competent governess. I have no one to blame but myself for the tragedies that befell my children, for not seeing when I should have seen and not hearing when I should have heard. But the house itself, Draper House, was as much to blame, I think, as anything.

For it was the house itself that brought about the deaths of my young children.

What gives a bad place its intention?

4.

For Rachel, the migraine came and went in a few hours. She became restless, wandering down to the living room and then to the turret room. The wallpaper was in the same shambles they'd left it in before the trip, and the room seemed washed out in the bright sunlight. That word HOUNFOUR was still up on the wall. Hugh sat over in the window seat, reading; he didn't notice her as she came in. She saw the beer beside him, and it didn't really bother her as much as it normally would have. He could have a drink now and then if he wanted to. It was no big deal. She just didn't want him drunk, because daddys shouldn't be drunk. Rachel wanted to tell him what she was thinking *(Let's Pretend, Hugh, that you're the daddy and I'm the mommy)* but Hugh seemed so involved with the book he'd bought.

"Is it any good?"

He glanced up. "Scout," he said as if waking from a nap; he made a motion to hide the bottle.

Rachel shrugged her shoulders. "Is that the Verna Standish book?"

"Verena, Scout. Yeah. It's kind of interesting. I'm just into the part about this house. Headache gone?"

"I just needed to close my eyes for a little while. See if she has anything about our walled-up vanity."

"Will do."

"I'm thinking of going out. You just going to read?"

Hugh nodded.

"Maybe I'll give Sassy a call. You think something like a housewarming party would be out of line—maybe next week or something?"

"I don't know. We've lived here what, a couple of months? Is it too late for that kind of thing? I mean, what would Miss Manners have to say?"

"Any excuse for a party. We could plan it for Labor Day weekend, unless everybody we know is going away—but I doubt it. The weather will be miserable still so people will be up for a party and it's not like we've had anybody in. Maybe we can finish this room next weekend if we work together. I have an idea for a Laura Ashley pattern I saw, but see if there's anything about the patterns in the book. Would she have something like that in there? Maybe about that vanity, too, and then my big strong husband can knock it down with his sledgehammer of the gods." Rachel went over to his tool box, stepping over scattered wrenches, to his sledgehammer. She lifted it up.

"Watch your toes, Scout. Old Verena lists everything else about her life—most of this diary's just her laundry list. If she weren't the daughter of such a famous man I doubt this would ever have been published. You see Penny Dreadful yet?"

Carefully laying the hammer flat on its side, she gave him a clownishly sad look. "Oh, Hugh, I feel so bad about her cat, I wish you'd use her real name."

"All right, all right, sorry. Penelope Deerfield."

"I'm afraid to run into her—she must hate us, and I don't know what I'd say to her at this point. The trip was fun, just what I needed, but that was like a black cloud hanging over us. I hope the kittens are okay."

5.

It was after six when Rachel met with Sassy Parker for coffee at La Fourchette in Adams-Morgan. They sat outside in front of the restaurant, and Sassy ordered appetizers.

"I am so damned starved, and I have a *ton* of things to tell you. My news first," Sassy said, "and then when the food comes I'll chow down and you can talk."

"I don't know, I haven't even told Hugh *mine* yet and I'm about to burst with keeping it in."

"All right, you go," Sassy huffed, "but this means I'll have to talk with my mouth full."

Rachel lowered her chin and raised her eyebrows. She grinned goofily, even though she was trying to be dramatic.

She took a deep breath. "I'm," and then blurted in rapid-fire succession, "pregnant—I think I'm pregnant—Shit, I don't know, but I *feel* like I think I'm pregnant."

"How long?"

"A week?" Rachel winced.

Now it was Sassy's turn to raise her eyebrows. She laughed, but then saw that Rachel didn't think this was funny. Sassy reached across the table and patted Rachel's left hand which was tearing at her napkin. "Retch, give it a couple of weeks before you feel like you think you're pregnant."

"I really *really* think I am. I haven't had my period, and I never miss, it's always on time."

"What, were you and Hugh fucking like bunnies at the beach?"

"Well, before the beach, at the beach, on the way *home* from the beach. Not that the horror stories don't abound, too, the whole time I was thinking about that poor cat. But the sex was terrific."

"And you think the rabbit bit the big one?" Something about Sassy's tone made Rachel feel like she was being mocked.

"I shouldn't have told you, it's too early, I'll jinx it, and you're probably right, I'm probably just being dumb, and maybe I'm off about my period, and I'll start gushing tonight." *You are so stupid, Rachel Brennan, to ever tell a secret before it's definite, how many times do you have to learn this in life?* Rachel stared at her coffee and watched little swirls of milk dissipate like clouds. This reminded her of a song, but she couldn't remember exactly which song, and she felt depressed that she'd ever gone and opened her big fat mouth.

"I'm not saying you're *not* pregnant. It's just a little early to start knitting booties."

"No, this is dumb and it is so typical for me to go off the deep end as soon as I get laid. And we weren't using, you know, condoms or anything, and I don't know . . . I just feel so . . . *fertile.*"

"Oh, please, what, were your eggs bubbling around or something?" Sassy laughed.

Rachel managed to smile. "Okay, let's drop it. No, really,

let's drop it. I am hoping I am pregnant and I'm being silly and you're being normal, but I don't care. We'll just drop it and then in a month you'll see I was right."

"Fair enough."

"So what's your news, now that you've stuck the pin in my balloon?"

"Well, it's your news, too. Have I got shit for you," Sassy said, "and I've been waiting for you to get your ass back from the beach."

"What's up?"

"I had to scour the archives for stuff on the DuPont Circle and Capitol Hill houses because of the upcoming house tours, and guess what I came across? No, don't even guess, let me tell you, I found reams of shit on your house."

"You're kidding."

"It has quite a spotted history, Retch. And it's just like me to forget to make copies for you. The file on your house is *fat*—I can get it to you Monday. You've *got* to read what's in it."

"A lot's been written about Draper House. I'm surprised it isn't on some house tour. Hugh just bought a book on the house, well, it has some chapters about the house, anyway. You know who Verena Standish was?"

"Chica, I *do* work for the 'Home' section of the *Her-Ex*—and she's mentioned a bit in these articles I dug up."

"What do they say?"

"Stuff like you wouldn't *believe*. You're living in some kind of haunted house."

"Oh, right, there's something about the ghost of a hooker."

"I don't know about a whore, Retch, but I do know about the weirdo drugged-out things that went on there in the sixties and seventies. Some kinky murders, and devil worshipers."

"You're making this up."

"No, it's for real."

"No, you're making this up because you know how easily I get scared by stupid things like this, just like when we were in college and you used to tell me the story about the claw, where the girl heard it scraping at the back of the car, and you had that bunny man story every time we drove over the hills and I kept thinking bunny man would jump out of the woods with his ax and smash the car up. This is going to be like the bunny man story, isn't it?"

"No, Retch, we're talking Charlie Manson meets the girl next door. You know what the papers used to call that place?"

"I give up."

"The Screaming House. Ain't it grand?"

6.

At work on Monday, Rachel glared at her desk as if she could melt it with her glance—unfortunately she could not. It was piled high with every memo known to mankind. She had three court dates in the next two weeks, and the briefs weren't even prepared. Her secretary, Carl, had come down with the flu and would be out until Friday. Gretchen, the blue-faced Slavic blonde with the sweaty palms (leaving damp fingerprints on anything she touched—including the files), was acting as both receptionist and secretary. By 10:30, Gretchen had played fifty-two-card pick-up with the summer clerk's mag cards, and Rachel would've screamed bloody murder except she *didn't really care.*

Rachel turned on the radio to listen to the local disc jockey tell crude, racist jokes; she switched it off again, and began sucking on a Rolaids. She craved a cigarette, could picture a Virginia Slims, could almost feel it between her lips. But then she remembered what Hugh had told her when they were in law school *("It's like licking out an ashtray").* She remembered the X-rays of her father's lungs, and Hugh holding her, *entering* her which she always enjoyed but which always frightened her just a little because she couldn't control his movement, *are-you-there-Hugh-Adair?*—all this curiously reminding her of the pain she'd felt in her stomach the morning of her miscarriage. Just when she was beginning to reexperience that sense of loss she'd felt (and the loss of not knowing what she was losing—*just a tiny sphere mixed with blood*), one of her lower front teeth began aching. She felt around the tooth and gum with her tongue and then decided she must be picking up radio waves because the pain vanished.

Rachel settled back down to work—or at least to *thinking* about work—when five junior associates trooped into her office to bitch about an upcoming meeting. When the other lawyers finally left ten minutes later, Rachel began separating the papers on her desk into three piles, with no rhyme or reason to their divisions other than file folders went in one stack, paper-clipped in another, and stapled in a third. She figured that if one of the partners walked into her office just then he would think she was organized when she was not. And she had no intention of becoming organized. She hadn't gone to law school for organizational skills, after all.

Sassy called at noon. "Retch?"

"Hi, Sassy," Rachel sighed into the phone, whisper-singing: "What a day this has been, what a rare mood I'm in, yes, it's almost like being in deep shit. I hate lawyers."

"It's just a job. Weren't those your exact words? 'When Hugh gets on at a firm I'm going to quit, have babies, and never diet again. It's just a job.'"

"You cold, calculating hardened woman, to turn my own words against me. Have a little sympathy: my secretary's sick."

"Some of us don't *have* secretaries. You want an ulcer or what? And here I've gone and copied all these articles for you—I stole the file from research without signing out, so I am going to be shot come sunup. And I'm going to send them over right this instant. Retch, will this ever take your mind off your work."

"Okay, send it, but I won't promise to read it, especially if it's scary."

"Chicken!" Sassy cried, hanging up on her.

7.

The messenger dropped the manila folder off at two, but Rachel didn't get to it for a week. Sassy called every other day asking if she'd read any of the articles ("You mean, *Retch, I pay through the nose to messenger them to you and you haven't touched them?"),* but Rachel allowed herself to be swamped with work and office gossip in order to make it through the week—on average, she stayed at work until seven at night. She thought about the sphere possibly growing inside her, and one evening she decided: *screw it, screw work, time to relax, get the hell away from legalese.*

It was a Wednesday evening, towards the end of August. Rachel was not sure what the weather was like outside because she was spending so much time inside her house or office, putting herself into her work more completely than she had all year while Hugh rewallpapered the turret room. She was feeling, in spite of the work, in love with life again, the way she'd been in school: the sphere inside her subdividing, Hugh being relatively productive, Hugh seeming to be happy, and work taking over whenever she began to feel the slightest twinges of melancholy. The firm was still holding an organizational meeting down the hall in the conference room, but Rachel was beginning to feel physically sick over the proceedings and went back to her office and her messy desk feeling like she would collapse across it. She looked out her window, across at the Madison Hotel; usually, if she was lucky, someone would be undressing in front of their window without noticing the offices across the street. It was a cheap form of entertainment, but she felt pretty cheap this evening.

She leaned back in her chair and turned her attentions to the news clippings from *The Washington Post,* the old *Washington Star-News, The Washingtonian Magazine,* as well as the rag Sassy worked for, *The Herald-Examiner.*

CHAMBER OF HORRORS IN NORTHWEST

Oct. 12, 1969—The bodies of seven women were found buried beneath a house in the Winthrop Park area of Northwest Washington, following an investigation into the bizarre group of individuals who had occupied the block. None of the women have yet been identified, although it is thought that they may have worked as prostitutes in the surrounding neighborhoods. Three of the women appear to have been bled to death using some kind of medical apparatus, and there are indications that the other four were buried alive in concrete . . .

SEX SLAYINGS CONNECTED TO
DEVIL WORSHIP

Oct. 23, 1969—A group calling itself the Disciples of the Last Circle have claimed responsibility for the torture and killing of seven women in the Winthrop Park area. The *Herald-Examiner* received this letter from the self-proclaimed spokesman of the group, a Mr. Swampgrass Rainbow.

Dear Pigs,
Our Lord Lucifer has arisen from his chains. We take the sacred mushroom and glorify his name. Kiss my a—, you suckers. Life is dream and dream is life, and we see the stained glass bleeding down the walls. We did not slice the entrails from the piggies, we set them free and their blood which is sacred to our Guru, the Horny One. The girls were to be His brides and the mothers of His children. The Devil is America in Nam. We drank napalm and saw it was good. You are just puppets of the pigs who run the fascist world. Imperialist running dogs crapped on the lawn of the world.
Sincerely in the Name of the Tortured,
Swampgrass Rainbow, Unholy Light Priest of the Disciples of the Last Circle
p.s. pigs
We sliced them open because they begged us to, because they wanted Him inside them, they wanted to bring it into the world.

Mr. Rainbow, whose real name is Mark Podesky of College Park, Maryland, was taken in to custody early this morning, although at press time, no charges had been formally brought against him. Mr. Rainbow was charged in 1968 with possession of drugs, and resisting arrest. One district police officer, who wishes to remain anonymous, told this reporter, "This sounds like something out of *Rosemary's Baby,* doesn't it? Except we got a half-dozen Mia Farrows cut up like the Black Dahlia, and a bunch of drug-crazed hippies walking around like zombies, and you know something? This used to be a ritzy neighborhood—all changed. It isn't just the LSD, and it isn't just all this sex going around, you know, those are just symptoms. It's the bomb, I think. The kids know the world can end and they just figure, 'If it feels good, do it.'"

EXORCIST VISITS
WINTHROP PARK "HAUNTED" HOUSE

Oct. 31, 1970—Just over a year ago, the name of a certain house in Northwest Washington became a place of nightmares. Draper House. Built by the architect Julian Marlowe in the 1800s, a man known for his bizarre architectural style known as "marlowisms," which involved numerous entries to rooms so that someone in the dining room could get to the bedroom, for example, without ever going through the kitchen or living room. Marlowe is of course most famous for the Edith Glasscock House in Newport News, Virginia, which the reclusive Miss Glasscock had him develop over a period of twenty-five years. Draper House's most famous residents were Addison and Verena Standish, from the 1880s to the turn of the century. According to Fay Randolph, the noted "exorcist" of Manhattan whose recent book of essays, *By Demons Possessed,* was published to international acclaim, Draper House's murky reputation began long before the recent tragedies of the young women's deaths.

"The house was built on swampy ground; a well, in fact, runs beneath it—a dry well. Its first occupant was a lady of the evening named Rose Draper, and it is said that in the house of ill-repute which she ran, for senators and congressmen, blackmail and knavery were the rule. She died violently, as do all original residents of such houses, and her death was similar to the famous Fatty Arbuckle case early in this century, although I believe the instrument of death in that case was a broken champagne bottle. In the case of Rose Draper, it was a rather simple kitchen utensil: an apple-coring knife. They say her ghost claps at night, the clap being her alarm to the inamorati that the place is about to be raided, and the clap also being a reference to the disease which she carried to her death.

"The illustrious Verena Standish, daughter of Horace Ashton the famous robber baron, and her husband, the less distinguished political gadfly, Addison Standish, bought the house in the late 1800s when Addison was appointed to a Washington post of no consequence. With them, they brought their two children, and a governess, and here is where the evil qualities of the house came into play. The story goes that the governess went mad and murdered the children in a most grisly fashion. Mrs. Standish herself felt much to blame, apparently because, as a popular diversion of the time, she became intrigued with spiritualism, thinking it a lark. Upon the deaths of her only children, she took an entirely different view, and believed that her playing at table-rappings and ghosts had brought something out of the house, something that was there waiting for such a moment.

"Then, for a stretch of perhaps seventy years, the house lay fallow. Families moved in and out, at one point it became three or four apartments. Then the neighborhood of Winthrop Park began to tarnish, and the less desirable elements began to occupy the neighborhood and, in time, the house. Who knows what evil has been there in the past decade? We know of these hippies who tortured and murdered girls, but who knows what may have drawn them in? Were they, after all, as their defense attorneys argued unsuccessfully just this summer, pawns of their drug habits? And if so, what showed them the way? What brought them here?"

Mrs. Randolph possesses the cherubic face of the eternal child. It is hard to believe that this soft-spoken woman wearing her fair isle sweater and kilt is the same exorcist who cast demons out of the Isaacson twins in Brooklyn two years ago. Sitting with her in her suite at the John Quincy Adams Hotel, one wonders if she enjoys spooking reporters on Halloween.

"Tonight," she says, "I will enter the house and call upon the spirits. I don't believe in the devil, not at least in person. But I do believe that evil exists, I do believe that there are places on this earth where spirits are caught outside the flesh, the same way they are caught, more often, within the flesh. And tonight at Draper House, I will find out their meaning, and if they are, as I believe, evil, I will vanquish them from the house."

FAMED EXORCIST DIES IN FIRE

Nov. 1, 1970—Fay Randolph, forty-three, author of the recent New York Times bestseller, *By Demons Possessed,* died last night in a fire in her hotel room in Washington, D.C. . . . believed to be started by the cigarette she was smoking when she fell asleep . . .

Rachel scanned the rest of the headlines:

THE "SCREAMING HOUSE"

with the subhead: *Neighbors Heard Girls' Cries Of Terror, But Did Not Find It Unusual For Winthrop Park*

MAN ARRESTED IN SEX CULT SLAYINGS

WITNESS COMES FORWARD—
ESCAPED CLUTCHES OF ALLEGED
"KNIFE RAPIST"

SUSPECT SETS SELF AFIRE

CIRCUS OF DEATH: MORE BODIES
UNCOVERED IN WINTHROP PARK

8.

Rachel groaned as she folded the photocopies in half and hurriedly stuffed them into her purse; she'd read them later when her stomach wasn't feeling so upset—much later. She wrote into her date book (without which she would never accomplish a thing):

1. *Make list for housewarming party.*
2. *Get Hugh to look at VW.*
3. *Groceries: nothing that can't be microwaved.*
4. *BANK! BANK! TAKE OUT LIFE SAVINGS!*
   (at least 200 bucks)
5. *Call to invite people: re: housewarming party: Labor Day weekend.*
6. *Set up appt. with dctr? Or wait? Re: sphere.*

9.

Waiting for her train home in the Farragut West station, Rachel felt spooked. The subway platform was deserted, although she heard footsteps from above the escalators, and the lone wind that seemed to herald the next blue line train. *It's those articles about the house.* She boarded the train, thankful that there were a handful of people on it, tired workers, some tourists probably heading back to their motels from the Smithsonian. She closed her eyes and tried to think calm thoughts, but her mind kept coming back to

177

those headlines, *Screaming House, Devil Worship, Chamber of Horrors.*

Shit, I'll have to thank Sassy personally for giving me a few more nightmares.

Keeping her eyes shut, she reached up with her fingers and kneaded her temples. *Stay away migraine, stay away migraine, migraine you do not exist, you do not have power over me. Headache, I rebuke you!*

She heard the conductor call out on the intercom, "DuPont Circle Station, this is a blue line train to Friendship Heights."

Rachel saw, sitting in front of her, staring at her, a man she thought she knew. He was tall and slender, wearing a black shirt that stuck to his ribs. He leaned forward in his seat, his hands clutching the bar above the seat in front of him. His skin was shiny and dark, and his face seemed almost reassuring as if he recognized her, also. On his head he wore a black top hat. His eyes crinkled up into small slits, and he grinned, broadly, and she knew that grin, and she felt hot and cold, chilled, when she remembered where she knew him from: the day she sat at the card table at Mrs. Deerfield's crib, when the face with the teeth came down for her, this was the face of the man from the clamoring place. He spoke without opening his mouth, and he said, "Let's pretend, Rachel, that you are the mommy."

Rachel gasped; she felt like she'd just flicked her tongue across a live wire.

But another voice came over the wire, the train's intercom, the conductor's voice again, "This is Woodley Park Station, Woodley Park," and Rachel realized that she had not opened her eyes yet, not *actually,* because the man in the black tank top was becoming a static of squiggly lines on a purplish background, and Rachel opened her eyes to normal life and a normal world in which a little boy, standing in the aisle with his mother and sister, leaned over and tugged at her sleeve, saying, "Hey lady, lady, is this the stop for the zoo?"

10.

So she had a nightmare that night.

But the nightmare wasn't about a Screaming House; wasn't concerned with a man who had materialized in her mind's eye on the Metro; she did not dream of spheres bursting from her belly.

The nightmare was about her father.

He was lying in the hospital bed—she'd never even seen him in that bed, he hadn't wanted her to see him, he hadn't allowed his favorite girl to see him once the end was just two months away. His eyes were sunken as if the fluid had been sucked out of them, his skin was pasty, his lips moved slowly with great effort. Thrust between his lips: a lit cigarette. "Old habits die hard," he said, coughing. "Took out my lungs, sweetie."

His chest was burst open as if he'd swallowed a grenade. Gray tendrils of smoke curled between his dripping ribs.

I know this is a dream flashed through her mind.

And I want this dream to end.

Now.

Her father lay in the hospital bed.

To avoid looking at the smoldering cavity beneath his neck, Rachel concentrated on his face. Skin brittle as dead leaves. Cracked at the mouth. Cigarette burning orange at the tip. Smoke exhaled through flared nostrils. Voice like gravel underfoot. "Can't have everything in this life, Rachel. You have your work, and I'm proud of what you've done, but you can't deny your body, you can't deny the destiny of every woman to bring life into this world, sweetie, it's only natural."

As he spoke, the light in the room dimmed, and she watched the smoke rise through the shadowy air, rise and curl and dissipate.

"No," Rachel said. She was surrounded by darkness.

"What?"

"This isn't you. You never said that."

"Rachel?" he asked.

"You always wanted what was best for me."

"Scout?"

Rachel awoke suddenly—she'd been sitting up in bed, leaning on her elbows.

The fan whirred in the doorway to the bedroom. Perspiration tickled the back of her neck.

"Scout?" Hugh asked again.

"Dreaming," she murmured sleepily.

"Woke up just now. With you staring at me. Like you were scared of me."

"Bad dream. About daddy. Really bad. But I don't know why."

Hugh hummed the theme from *Jaws*. "Nose shark will come and eat up all the bad dreams." He reached over to her, hugging her, kissing her nose, falling off to sleep himself. He smelled like Ivory Soap; sweat; Prell shampoo; an old T-shirt; Johnson's baby powder.

Rachel lay there in bed holding herself to her husband, shaking as if from cold.

TWENTY-TWO

BLOODMEMORY

1.

Hide me! Oh, hide me! Mattie pulled her trash bags of invisibility tight around her face. The heat was unbearable, the sound of her own breathing was like a lion's roar in her ears, the plastic of the bags was smothering.

She had drunk her last bottle of wine—she'd panhandled her ass off up in Adams-Morgan for just a couple of bucks, and then went and blew it on Thunderbird. But she needed it, and bad; the cheap wine slowed down the images fluttering in her head, the loop of film replaying the scene over and over, the scene that she'd kept so carefully hidden, even from herself, the real reason why she was afraid to go into the Screaming House. Ever again.

It was all coming back to her, all the memories, all the terrors, but most clearly: that night, that night in the spring, the night of the riots in Washington, the night her babygirl lay in a bathtub burning with fever, the night *he* tore into her. The cheap wine wasn't blurring the memory enough. The more she drank, the clearer that night became.

"My baby! Four! Death! Room! Fire!" she brayed as she set the empty bottle down by her side, but in her mind she cried out: *I remember! Hounfour! Hounfour! Oh, my baby, death in room, fire out window, stink, shit smell, death, you . . .*

181

2.

I remember!

The room smelled of death; and of new life.

The only light came from beyond the window, out where the fires of riots tore up the night. A wall of flame shot up in the projects in the back alley, the building that had housed Madeleine Perreau and her daughter, Nadine. Gunfire down the block; sirens shrieking; shouts of a city gone wild.

The window was closed to that, and what little seeped through from beneath the pane was ignored by the people in this room. A sink dripped rusty water; roaches scuttled across the cracked yellow tiles; a sound like moist chewing coming from the man who bent over the bathtub. He was naked, his legs and buttocks thrusting forward over the tub as he leaned further into it. His shoulders were skin and bone, with sinewy muscles tying them together. He kept his head ducked down into the tub, his hands moving frantically. His skin was a shiny coal black, and as he fed, Mattie could see his back muscles contract, his breaths coming short and swift with each swallow. The silk top hat he had worn earlier lay crushed beside the tub, its rim splattered with blood.

Mattie watched as her half brother, Gil, performed his operation. In his possessed state he became Baron Samedi. The muddy stink of the grave surrounded him. He was tearing into her daughter's flesh. In memory it happened slowly, excruciating seconds that stretched into hours. But that April of 1968, it had been over in a matter of minutes.

"Whatchu doin' to my babygirl?"

Mr. Big Man sat on his haunches next to the toilet, his shirtsleeves rolled up, his tie askew, his gray pants ripped at the knees from when he'd fallen down, when he'd seen Gil begin to feed. He didn't look over at Mattie, and he didn't look at the spirit-in-flesh woman either. He stared transfixed at the blood-streaked bathtub. Mr. Big Man, face white with fear, cried, "Fucking animals is what you are!" But then even his face changed, became full of beatific wonder:

something had come over him, too, something bigger than even the spirits of rada and petro.

Something in the house that screamed in madness, like a starved wild animal escaped from its cage.

Something that had nothing to do with the Voudun Mattie'd been taught by her mother, something darker, something that once loose would never be caged again.

The nameless evil that passed through the house, that drew smaller evil to it—smaller evil like her half brother—and consumed it like a fire devouring the kindling that gave it life. A battery recharging.

Mattie howled in pain as blood splashed up from the tub—Gil DuRaz turned, grinning, his wide toothy grin smeared with red, his tongue slipping out from his mouth, mopping up the string of blood that drooled beneath his chin. His eyes like twin obsidian marbles.

From those eyes, hooks flew out to catch Mattie's soul, to pull her forward, towards him. "Drink, my love, my sister, the milk of the mother." He smeared his bloodstained hands across his face.

"Baron Samedi," Mattie gasped. Her brother had crossed the line, given himself over, alive, to the spirits of death, to the guardian of graveyards. She felt a tremendous pressure push in on all sides, squeezing her brains, thumping against her eardrums; the ax in her heart going *choppity-chop!* She reeled backwards, slamming into the wall. Her breath came in quick pants, and she fouled her underwear. The stench of her own body became overwhelming—it was as if she'd opened an old grave and inhaled the fumes of an exploded corpse, and the corpse had her own face. She became aware of her flesh and its decay until the room was spinning with the smell.

She called on the old gods, the spirits, the loa, who would help her. *At your altar, I pray, you bring your vengeance down on these—*

But her thoughts were cut off, hacked at until her mind ripped in jagged cliffs and valleys within her skull. Her blood broke the dam of their blood vessels and her nose began bleeding.

Baby girl—screaming!—Mambomambomambo—guh-guhguh—

The Old One, the Spirit-In-Flesh, the one called House-keeper, half in shadows, stood above her. "You never had power, you wasp nest, you jar for jelly."

Mattie knew she had lost her magic, lost her power as a mambo priestess. Somehow it had been taken away from her, and now she was weak and spent. Mattie slid to the floor, pounding her fists against her stomach, trying to drive the evil spirits from her. She began gnashing her teeth, foaming at the mouth like a rabid dog, clawing her breasts.

Gil was done feeding. He cupped his hands into the mess of flesh and blood and brought the baby out.

It made sucking noises, and Gil held it in one hand. With the other, he poured dark blood into its grasping mouth.

Gil laughed. "This is the one, this is the vessel that shall hold my spirit."

He handed the wriggling fetus to the Housekeeper. The thing mewled like a kitten.

Mattie had no energy to move. Her mind was trickling out of her skull, her thoughts were jumbling as if she were falling down a long staircase with nothing to stop her descent.

Gil extended his hand towards Mr. Big Man. A hand that dripped with Nadine's steaming blood. "Drink."

And Mr. Big Man crawled like a supplicant on his knees before Gil. His face just beneath the offering hand. His mouth turned upwards. He lapped at the underside of Gil's hand, greedily.

When Gil pulled his hand away from the man's lips, Mr. Big Man grabbed for Gil's hands with both of his, tried to wrench them back to his face, sucking at the fingers to get the last traces of the girl's blood. Gil slapped Mr. Big Man, and Mr. Big Man let go. He sat back, sliding like a naughty child to the corner, behind the toilet, licking his lips.

"Life's milk, sister, drink and be with me, here, forever," Gil whispered. He leaned into the tub again. She heard his slurping. He turned towards her, his cheeks puffed out, his mouth full of blood.

Gil crawled on all fours across the cold wet tiles. To Mattie.

She felt as if she'd been boned like a chicken. Could not move. Had no will. No will. Mind draining down through the plumbing, into the earth. No mind, no will, no energy.

When his face was inches away from her, a dribble of blood sluiced from between his teeth.

He pressed his face to hers, kissing her, his juicy tongue shooting into her mouth, past what little resistance her lips gave. Metallic liquid burned ulcers in her mouth.

Her mouth filled with blood, Mattie saw: *her daughter's spirit standing before her, screaming in pain, screaming for release, screaming to give birth, screaming at her mother for giving her body up to this evil.*

Gil pulled back. His lips smacked.

Mattie spat the blood he'd injected into her, spat it across his already stained face. He was momentarily blinded with blood. Dropped the knife, the coring knife, the one he'd used to help open her daughter up—his teeth alone had done most of the work, but he'd used the knife to rend her small body completely. He reached up to wipe his eyes.

Knife clattering to floor. The Housekeeper cooing to the baby from the shadows. Mr. Big Man licking his fingers near the toilet. The tub with blood like a rose blooming from its basin. Gil wiping his eyes free from blood, his hands in tight fists, and in each fist a bloodrose blooming. The fire consuming empty buildings in the alley. Knife still on floor. Dull from cutting through flesh and bone, dripping red.

Slow. The memory was slow. But it was over in seconds. Over in seconds. What she'd done. What she'd done to her half brother.

"Boshinus! I give you 'boshun!"

With the shred of thought she had left in her, Mattie grasped the knife in her left hand and with her right held her half brother back. Drove it into him just below his stomach. Sliced. Twisted. Gutted. Churned.

Cored.

She screamed as the Housekeeper tore her away. The dying man choking on his own blood.

"I seen you give 'boshuns before, I seen you, I helped you,

now I give you a 'boshun the way you give 'em to my babygirl!"

And then, nothing.

Her mind gone.

Her memory gone, except for knowing the Screaming House, except for love and fear of Nadine, her child, except for dread of Baron Samedi and the stink of the grave.

TWENTY-THREE

THE NEW LEAF

1.

Hugh got his résumé over to a headhunter's office the week before the housewarming party. He'd been in particularly good spirits, and found the day-to-day work around the house occupied most of his time. But the résumé, it had to be done—*just get me some job to fill in the time, some little white-collar pigeonhole where I can at least feel like I'm less of a house-husband.* As much as he was enjoying working on the house, there were times when he thought if he didn't get out of there he would go bonkers. He began coming up with any excuse just to go down the block, and when he did he felt clumsy—as if he'd been in the damn house so long, in leaving it he was entering an alien landscape, sometimes hostile, sometimes friendly, but always *different.*

He'd notice people more on these brief excursions to the drugstore or to the hardware store, or more often than not to the liquor store *(but just beer, Scout, and only one a day sometimes, so I think I've got it under control);* he'd notice how they were dressed, the anxiety in their faces, their small daily joys, their suppressed rage. That crazy bag lady who had given Rachel such a scare a while back, he saw her in the park and she screamed at him, something unintelligible— even she seemed to be a part of the fabric of daily life. It gave Hugh a sense that somehow just being alive was good. That perhaps this house, this *home,* would work out, after all. Whenever the small voice whispered in his head, *Hugh Adair, you should be actively pursuing lawyerdom, instead of putting off the inevitable with carpentry and beer. Why the fuck did you go through those damn years of law school, anyway?* he always had an answer: *I think I went to law school to meet Rachel, I think it was some kind of destiny, I had to go through law school in order to find her.*

The week before Labor Day, he vowed to Rachel that he would turn over a new leaf.

"And not just the leaf, Scout, the whole dang tree." His spirits seemed so high that Rachel held back from mentioning what she thought (*I'm pregnant, Hugh, but maybe I'm not, but it would be okay if I were pregnant, right?*)—again she would wait until she saw a doctor. She managed to postpone this in her mind—it was superstitious, but after all, the last time she was pregnant, she'd seen a doctor and then lost the baby. *Why fuck it up again?*

"So you don't mind about this housewarming party idea."

"Nah. I just wish I had some friends to invite. I assume you'll have your usual 'This Is Your Life' contingent, Miss Former Pep Squad Leader?"

"Call Bufu up. He may be an asshole, but they're good at parties, too. And you can call up all those other Lambda Chi's. You were good enough friends with them in college."

"Yeah, so I can hear how successful my frat brothers are—no thank you. I wish I knew more losers like me."

"You're not a loser, Mr. Adair, you are my private stud and seasonal sex toy."

When she'd left for work, Hugh made a few calls, the headhunting agency, the city bar association, even Bufu Thompson. *"Yeah, a little party this weekend, just bring a friend or something, maybe a roll of toilet paper, hey, we can always use toilet paper . . ."* He waded through his small black address book, and realized that most of the people in it were either potential business contacts or Rachel's friends. He decided he'd better not use the phone much, hoping the employment agency would call back—it was times like these he wished he'd gone ahead and gotten call waiting on the phone, as obnoxious as he thought that service was.

Bored, he strolled room to room, checking lights, checking the paint jobs he'd done, checking the scuff marks on the floors, checking for upended carpet tacks. He gobbled down

BREEDER

a stale Hostess Donut that lay hidden in the breadbox, took
out the garbage, checked for mail. Too hot to lounge out on
the patio, and he didn't need to get another sunburn this
soon—that could wait for Labor Day. He put on a video of
Raiders of the Lost Ark, watching the first five minutes and
then losing interest since he'd seen the movie about fifty
times. *Ring you goddamn phone! Get me a job! Get me an
interview!* He straightened the cushions on the couch, and
the photographs he'd taken in law school—mainly of Rachel on campus, or at the beach, or walking through the
woods. He remembered where he'd left the Verena Standish
book: in the turret room, and as he went into it that
nonsensical word HOUNFOUR in streaked red on the
cheap yellow paper. *Should get someone in here and figure
out how to tear down the wall so we can open up that small
room there. Maybe just take the old sledge to it—if I could be
sure there are no pipes or intricate wiring systems back there.*

Then he heard voices, coming from the area where he'd
covered over the dumbwaiter.

Penny Dreadful and her dreadful guests.

A woman, not Mrs. Deerfield: "Well, I didn't notice
anything different about her. She seems common."

"Keep your voice down, dear, and she is quite special."

Another woman: "He chose her, after all, hon, he opened
her up to him, you saw her face that day. You *know.*"

"As if that means anything, and that was weeks ago. I
remember a time when he chose you, too, and see what's
come of it. And you weren't terribly special."

"Don't remind me."

"Now don't put those down the sink, I told you—"

"You told me, you told me."

"Yes, well, I think you might listen for once. None of that
for me, thank you, no."

"I know I'm impatient but I just wish it would happen
sooner. Then we can all rest easier."

"It's that divine justice thing he's got going, he wants her
because she's a link to the past. It's that debt. Sometimes we
must move slowly to realize the dream of, well, so much
more than just a lifetime." She said this last word with
obvious disgust.

"No, too many calories for me, right now, got to watch me

189

figger—ah, but the flesh is weak, so pass another one over, dear. Now, didn't I just tell you not to put those down there. I'll be forever cleaning them out . . ." A loud humming, a blender or some machine, cut off the voices; Hugh was almost disappointed.

Hoping he'd hear something again from his downstairs radio show, he plopped down in the window seat, gave a cursory nod to the park—its trees were becoming a drained anemic green as the summer heat continued. He picked up *Diaries of an Innocent Age,* found the dog-eared page he'd left off on—the part where Verena started to sound a little looney tunes about Draper House.

The good part.

2.

From *Diaries of an Innocent Age* by Verena Standish:

I had not looked into the background of the children's governess as thoroughly as I might have, but she'd come with good recommendations from the Preston-Finches. So good, in fact, that Walter Preston-Finch called up to tell me that he attributed his son Aaron's admission to Exeter directly to this woman's instruction, and everyone in New York society knew Katherine Preston-Finch (later to become the wife of author-adventurer Francis Earhart) to be the very model of genteel comportment at the tender age of sixteen—our governess had everything to recommend her to the post. Only after the tragedy did I learn of Miss Fields' *affair du coeur* with Walter Preston-Finch and her subsequent nervous breakdown and suicide attempt. I would not have expected it in such a well-educated woman.

I have felt, at times, betrayed by the Preston-Finch family, whose exaltation of this extremely unbalanced young woman contributed greatly to the destruction of my happiness in life. But I really blame myself, and not merely for hiring her without proper investigation of her past, but for casting a cold eye upon my own children, and, I daresay, for letting things within the house itself go unnoticed.

Emmie was just four when we moved in, and James two and a half. Miss Fields was brought in immediately, and I suppose her preoccupation with the tarot cards should have alerted me to a susceptible mind. But I thought it all a lark, then, a gay pastime, similar to my own modest interest in table-rappings. And I was so very involved in being the Washington hostess, the dinners and the parties among the political cognoscenti, trying to help my dear Addison find his way through the diplomatic maze. When I remember those times I ache with regret—how it all means nothing to me now, how it was the folly of the times, how little I truly care for the eyes and ears of the world when I now think of all I lost in the bargain.

But Miss Fields seemed such a serene presence. She was less than beautiful, always an advantage for a woman of no means and great intelligence, for she offended no employer's wife (or so it seemed to me at the time). She did not seem to care a whit for men or their opinions, except inasmuch as they applied to Latin and Greek and the questions of classical philosophy. In dress and manner she was modest, shy and deferential when in the presence of her employers; yet on more than one occasion in those first few years, I can recall her chastising Addison for his attempts to sabotage the children's early education with his outlandish stories. And I thought, at the time, well and good for her, to stand up to my husband's periodic foolishness. There was something very Quakerish about her, a tendency to plainness in speech, dress, and habit. I thought her, those four years she was with us, a sober and stabilizing presence, one that would brook no nonsense, a woman who would build character in my blessed angels. I do not remember her face, except in those last moments, and then it was much changed. But she had an emptiness of expression and a rather remarkable way of reassuring whomever she encountered with that emptiness. These were purely social reassurances—I suppose *deference* is the better term. One always had the feeling that Miss Fields was more clever than her station, but she had a way of nodding and looking down to the floor that allowed one some superiority. She struck me, upon our first meeting, as someone who had no sense of herself. With the recent popularity of Dr. Freud, we might call this a crisis of personality or identity. But Draper House solved that for her, in an unspeakable way.

She found, in the house, an identity, and perhaps even a husband, a lover—without that base connotation the word conjures in these pornographic times. A companion is perhaps a more suitable word—she found *companionship* in the house. But the house was, I believe, evil from its foundations to its roof, evil the way a guillotine is inherently evil, the way a hangman's noose is evil, the way a snake is evil.

What remained in Draper House, at any rate, was the irrational residue of evil—left perhaps by the original owner, a woman of murky reputation, or perhaps the evil grew like a fungus, from beneath the house, in the damp-encrusted walls, until finally, the entire structure was in the clutches of something beyond knowing. My religious beliefs are (and have always been) such that I allow there can be no flesh without spirit, however, there may exist spirit without flesh. And the natural law of spirit is to always seek out and invade flesh in order to carry out its benevolent, or in Miss Fields' case, malevolent plan.

When I finally was told the whole story of Miss Fields, how she had attempted to take her own life at the Preston-Finch home, suddenly I understood what this woman was looking for. Yes, on the surface, love, in particular a man to love her. How vile Walter Preston-Finch seems to me now! How he must have seduced this poor lovestruck woman and then abandoned her to the fates. And how cruel the fates had been to her! What must it take to climb a staircase and tie a length of rope to the edge of a balcony and leap off to swing by your neck until dead! And how much more cruel it must have seemed to be rescued, to still live, when all hope for the future was gone.

For, without knowing this story when Miss Fields first came to live with us, I couldn't see it in her modest demeanor. How was I to know the heart that lurked beneath the skin? She came to us without a god, without a faith, with no hope, no sense of the judgment to come, no promise of heaven when the weary toil had ended.

And in Draper House she found her god. Her savage god, a god of blood and torture and cannibalism. I do not mean to say a god exists beyond that which we call God; for this would be heresy. But as I have mentioned, there can be spirit, spirit without flesh, spirit seeking flesh, spirit hungry for flesh, hungry to corrupt and destroy flesh.

And she found it in the crib, not James' crib, but the crib beneath the house, the entrance to the back servant stairs leading to my dressing table. The hungry spirits touched her there, and through them she understood her mission.

Was she insane? This is what we have been taught to believe. But who teaches us this? Yet more Godless people. We live in a Godless age, and so we look to our empty books and we see yet more emptiness. No answers, just words. We think as a race we possess genius simply because we affirm the unknowable: we say, there is nothing, nothing but ourselves in this world. And when we die, we become part of that nothing. How easy it is to believe in nothing, to believe in empty words, and empty worlds. So what does insanity mean to us? It is just another empty word for something we can't understand, because we believe in nothing.

Miss Fields was not insane.

She was possessed.

Miss Fields murdered my children in cold blood.

But even coldblooded murderers have their reasons.

And I pray to God, every night I pray to God, that my children were dead before that woman began devouring them.

We were gone, Addison and I, on our annual month in New York. It was cool at the Hudson River estate, and I would usually take the children and governess with us. Although it seems monstrous now that I left them while they were ill, I had, of late, become overwhelmed by other, more pressing matters.

Addison and I were having our difficulties. We decided between the two of us to go up to the country without the children, at least for the first week, and try to decide what we would do. Contrary to the popular rumor of the time, divorce was never even considered. I had become a foolish and vain woman, I am afraid to admit, and had begun hearing voices in the house with my coterie of spiritualist advisers. We believed it haunted, although I now think that Draper House went beyond being merely haunted. It was a hunting ground, I think, a place of such hungry evil spirit that all forms of life were its prey. If my friend the Reverend Elijah Calhoun had told me that Hell itself bordered that house, it would not surprise me.

And if you, dear reader, witnessed the scene I beheld in August of that year, you, too, would know the insatiable hunger of that place.

We had been gone three weeks with neither a word from my children nor from their governess. I grew worried. Addison contacted the authorities in Washington, but the delay was too much. My husband and I exchanged words. In the heat of that argument, I left him, and journeyed alone to Washington. Indeed, I discovered that Miss Fields had spoken to the city police. She told them the children were taken to bed with a fever and that she had already sent word to me. In the carriage from the train station, I experienced a presentiment of what was to come: we passed an alley, stopping at a street corner, and I watched helplessly as a pack of hounds ran down a defenseless cat. Their jaws glistened with the feline's blood as they tossed its flesh and yellow fur about. And there was something inside me that warned me from this, something that made me resist entering my own house at first.

Draper House.

I rushed upstairs, expecting the worst: that my children were deathly ill, and that Miss Fields was unaware of the danger their lives were in.

But what I beheld was beyond imagining.

I will not even write here the vile, unspeakable words she wrote across the walls with their blood, and I dare not remember too clearly my angels' ravaged bodies.

Skinned, and dressed the way a brutal hunter might two felled deer, hanging as if in a meatpacking house. She had tied them up on a crossbar of bamboo, and strung them along the shuttered window in my vanity.

But Miss Fields herself, inspired with the spirit of the house, had even begun disemboweling herself. Later, although Addison tried to keep things from me, I learned that Miss Fields had choked to death on the fingers of her own left hand, which, at the moment they were thrust in the back of her throat, were no longer attached to her body.

I dare not commit to paper the shock I felt. But I did not faint, I did not give in to frailty immediately. Instead, my mind took over, shutting itself down like a machine that has become too hot. This is the way in which the medical community has explained it to me.

It was not until ten years later that I was able to live in the normal world again, ten years of Foxmeadow, a spa for genteel ladies like myself, women of culture and character who had fallen off the edge of the flat world of sanity.

I would never, of course, return to that house, or even to that city. I could not bear it. Yet the house still will not let me go. I carry it within this weak-vesseled form, and all that is that house is here with me even as I write this.

I have moments of wondering if, at every corner, I will not behold that sight once again.

3.

The telephone was ringing. Not really a ring: these new phones seemed to produce an inhuman trilling that Hugh found painful to hear. *Whatever happened to the good old-fashioned* bbrrring! *of a phone?* Hugh had just begun getting into the book, sinking into the rhythm of the prose. Finally, Verena Standish was getting interesting, if a bit ghoulish. He almost resented this new intrusive noise. *But maybe it'll be about a job.*

He sprinted to the kitchen and caught the receiver by the fourth ring, juggling it to within an inch of dropping the whole contraption on the linoleum. Hugh cleared his throat; he wanted to sound professional. His voice came out an unnaturally deep baritone. "Hello?"

But it was Penny Dreadful from downstairs. "Sorry to bother you, dear, but I'm having a bit of trouble with me garbage disposal and I was wondering what I should do—I have a plumber I can call, but I thought I should check with you first . . ."

Hugh sighed. This was the problem with being a landlord. "Oh, what's the trouble with it?"

"Ghastly noises, like someone choking on eggshells—it just spits whatever I place down its gullet back up in me face."

The cockney affectation in Mrs. Deerfield's voice was a dead giveaway as to her state of being: sauced to the gills. He was about to tell her to go ahead and call the plumber and then stick the bill in his mailbox. But curiosity about the downstairs apartment got the better of him. "I'll be down in a sec."

Mrs. Deerfield greeted him at the door in a pink silk pajamas-type outfit, smudges of sky-blue eye shadow beneath her brows, fuchsia lipstick smeared across her mouth; all framed by a sort of pink tint to her cotton-candy-white puff of hair—she'd had it curled since he last saw her. She fanned her hands in front of his face, and he caught the strong odor of beer *(makes me thirsty)*. Her fingernails were long and painted green, with what looked like small gold astrological symbols glued to them. She introduced her two lady friends quickly, slurring her syllables together. "Annie, Betty, *Hugh*. We're all a bit *legless* at the moment." Mrs. Deerfield giggled mischievously. "I was missing my Ramona, and we held a little séance and she meowed through dear old Annie. The logical thing to do was have a pint or two."

"It was embarrassing, hon," one of the women said. "I just started making these noises and I suddenly wanted to catch a mouse or something. Spirits are like that."

The third woman remained silent; she glanced down at the floor.

These must be the weird sisters Rachel had gone on about

*that first night in the house. "They're really queer, Hugh,"
she'd said, "and they kind of scared me, and you know how
easily I can spook myself without outside help. They say they
contact spirits."* Hugh sniffed the heavy air in the apartment.
The only spirits he noticed as he headed back to the kitchen
were the empty bottles of John Courage ale sitting on top of
a card table. The third woman, the blonde named Betty, was
tapping the toe of her right foot rather nervously, and he
looked beneath the table, to the area where she cast her
glance: the outline of a trapdoor.

The crib. "I just read about that." He pointed to the
trapdoor. It fit the exact dimensions of the card table above
it. *What had Verena said about it? It's a quirk of the architect,
or something? Now, Hugh, try to sound knowledgeable in
front of the weird sisters—and this might not be the right
group to tell about the governess who ate kiddos for dinner.*
"It's an architectural oddity."

"Dear?" Mrs. Deerfield was over at the sink, turning the
garbage disposal on and off rapidly.

"Oh, it's this book I've got about the house—apparently,
there's some kind of passage—stairs I guess, though there's
not much room for them—underneath there that continues
up to the second floor—next to the dumbwaiter. Although
it's kind of nutty, isn't it? I mean, why build it like that,
when you could just make it like a normal staircase? But
evidently, the guy who planned this house was into weird-
ness."

"Julian Marlowe was a madman," Mrs. Deerfield stated
unequivocally. "But everything in its place and a place for
everything, isn't that right, dear? Perhaps it was a wine
cellar of sorts, dear. It's rather cool there, even in this
weather, and it keeps me jams and pickles from boiling. But
about the disposal . . ."

"Oh, right, well, there's a trick to that—anybody got a
broom handle?"

"As a matter-a-fact—" Mrs. Deerfield went to get the
broom from behind the back door. She handed it to him as
he approached the kitchen sink.

"You just poke it around like this, sort of *spinning* the
doohickeys down there." As Hugh spoke, the women

laughed, and Hugh, when he had gotten the garbage disposal going, accepted a bottle of dark ale from them. He sipped it slowly. It was ice cold and froze the back of his throat. "I better get back upstairs."

"If you must, but it *is* nice to have a man around the house—don't you agree, ladies?" They giggled their agreement, although the one called Annie seemed to be laughing at some other joke entirely. Mrs. Deerfield said, "But you both've been avoiding me, and I want you to tell your sweet wife that it was just an accident, after all, I know you didn't *mean* to kill Ramona, accidents *do* happen. The world isn't a perfect place."

As Hugh left her apartment, he invited her to the house-warming party, and her friends, also. But there was something going through his mind as he thought about how the cat had died: *there are no accidents.* He was getting drunk. *Off one damn beer, too, but Lordy it was strong!* He almost tripped *up* the stairs, *but there are no accidents, Scout, take a lesson. Not a fucking accident from birth to death. There's a meaning and a reason for everything. Just like my good friend Verena Standish says, that coldblooded murderers have their reasons, too. Like the Old Man and my first wife—now that car wreck was no accident, it may have been a drunk driver, but the Old Man probably made good and sure they were straddling the white line, I'm willing to put some money where my mouth is,* and his mouth felt dry and scratchy. He knew that he would go out somewhere and maybe have another beer or two. *Like that cat in the car, sure, it looked like an accident, but nope, it must've been a sign—like that omen Penny Dreadful had when we moved in, the way her cat barfed hairballs—just like I'm a lawyer, it was no accident, it was real life. I had been raised to go to lawyer college,* he chuckled, *so I did as I was told until the fucking lie got to be too much, which is right now, which is,* he looked at his watch, *which is 2:30, which is Miller time.*

Hugh Adair felt in his pocket for his wallet, and then turned back down the stairs to go out into the sultry day and find himself a bar stool and knock back a couple of brewskies.

There was something, something he'd told Rachel that morning, but he couldn't quite put his finger on it, something about a leaf, and as he stepped outside to the sweltering afternoon, the front sidewalk was littered with dead leaves from a gingko tree that did not have long to live itself. *Yeah, that's it, a new leaf. Something about a new leaf.* But he continued on through the park to the shortcut to Nineteenth Street, trying to forget his unbearable thirst.

TWENTY-FOUR

CHILDREN IN THE PARK

When Rachel finally got Sassy on the line, she said, "I want to thank you personally for scaring the bejesus out of me. I have a couple of your photocopies here in my purse and I can't tell you how entertaining it is to know I live in a chamber of horrors."

Sassy snorted a laugh on the other end of the line. "I've even found another article or two. That place is some kind of magnet for lunatics. You and Hugh are just two of the recent ones. Makes much more interesting reading than most of this home shit I've got to research."

"Yeah, well, do me a favor, Sass, and don't spread that stuff around at the party."

"My lips are sealed. You all prepared?"

"Hardly, and I've got a shitload of work, I got yelled at by a client who I know for a fact is guilty and—yikes! It's four, I want to get out of here so I can get some shopping done before Larimers is swamped with yuppies."

"Can I bring anything tomorrow?"

"Your ass, now gottago. Bye."

"Bye."

Rachel had to run to the bank, which she'd forgotten to do earlier in the week. She'd barely done any shopping for the housewarming party—time seemed to be rushing by this week, between the briefs she had to prepare, and her mother calling at work to see how she was doing. ("It's just that it's been a week since you called, and that always means you're keeping something from me," mom had said, and Rachel wondered if her mother were clairvoyant: Rachel's mind, when not in gear, went to the thought of the baby she might be carrying. *But I'm not going to jinx this and blab it until we're both a ways along in gestation.*) Rachel broke down on the phone and invited her mother to the housewarming party when her mother kept needling her about seeing the house.

But the sphere *(Don't call it a baby yet, if you call it a baby, Scout, you'll lose it, it'll drop out of you and once it's out you can't put it back)* was on her mind through all of it: work, play, rushing as she was to the bank, waiting in line at the automatic teller machine. Her blouse was soaked with sweat; the back of her neck was itchy; her pantyhose was like heavy fur—*why the hell are you wearing hose in the middle of summer anyway? Do you think any of your colleagues are going to care if your legs are once again pale and knobby?* The line at the bank was long—everyone ahead of her seemed to move in slow motion, making deposits and withdrawals, not writing their checks out until they were right up to the machine, inserting their bank cards the wrong way. She dropped the cash into her purse, wrapping it with a few of the articles Sassy had messengered over earlier in the week. *I haven't thrown these out yet?* Larimers Market was already packed with shoppers. Rachel did her best to squeeze between people to get to the produce, and then there was another line at the deli counter. She glanced at her watch: 6:15.

She was just crossing Winthrop Park with her arms full of groceries when the street lamps flickered on. Children, like playful lost shadows, ran across the thin grass after one another, ducking behind the bushes, leaping over each other's backs, playing tag and hide-and-go-seek near the playground. A little girl in a pink party frock sat crying on the swing set—a street lamp spotlighted her. Rachel had seen her before, playing with a boy out in the alley one weekend day. Rachel thought she was both the most beautiful child she'd ever seen, and the saddest. Rachel's arms ached from carrying the groceries, the headache seemed to be kicking in again, and she was getting a mild, distant pain in her stomach. *You be okay, sphere, we don't want anything happening to you, we're going to do this pregnancy right.* She went over to the little girl, setting the grocery bags down in the dirt, her purse propped between them.

"Hello. What's your name?" Rachel asked, sitting down into the curve of the swing next to the girl.

The girl, who was probably no more than eight years old, eyed her suspiciously. Her eyes were red from crying. She had wispy brown hair tied back with a red velvet ribbon; her face was empty as if she were all cried out. Her eyes were pale green like lima beans. "Pudd'n'tame, ask me again and I'll tell you the same."

Rachel felt pressure on her back, and then she was swinging upwards, down again, skidding her shoes into the dirt to stop. A small boy ran out from behind her. "Ha!" he shouted. "I pushed you!"

"He's Jamie and he's my brother," the girl said. "And he's a wicked little boy, too. He made me cry."

"And he's a strong little boy, too. Jamie, is your mommy here?"

The boy, Jamie, smiled. "I stepped on a crack and broke her back." He started rummaging through her groceries.

"No you don't." Rachel caught him by the arm and pulled him backwards, lifting him up on her knee. *So light, like lifting a pillow.*

"Naughty, naughty boy," the girl said.

"Where's your home?" Rachel asked.

The boy giggled, made a snarling noise, then giggled again.

The little girl pointed across the darkening park. "The one in between."

Draper House. Mrs. Deerfield's lights were off. Their floor, the second, was brightly lit up. *Hugh's home. I hope he's got a job, oh please, just any old job.* "But that's my home. Are you friends of Mrs. Deerfield's?"

The girl shrugged. "We haven't been out to play in *forever.*"

Jamie, now sitting sturdily against Rachel's knees, kicking his feet up and down, farted. He pinched down on his nose with his right hand, fanning the air with his left. "I have this secret," he said.

"Is it a secret secret, or a telling secret?"

He giggled. "It's something you know. It's about *babies*."

The girl reached across with her right hand and gave him a resounding slap on the cheek. "You wicked boy! If you tell I will tell. On *you*."

The boy rubbed the side of his face. "I know how babies are made." He leapt from Rachel's lap, crouching down in front of her, writing with his fingers in the dirt.

"God makes them. Is your mommy somewhere here?"

"No ma'am. A man's got to fuck a woman with his prick head. In the place where she makes wee-wee."

In Rachel's head, a drumming pain, *no migraine, no migraine;* in her stomach, a spasm. She gasped as if for air. Rachel turned to the girl. "Is your mommy in the park?"

The girl shrugged her shoulders. She began swinging back and forth. The chain clanked against the swing-set bar. "He knows he's not supposed to say these things."

Jamie kept his head down, his fingers scratching in the dust. "He sticks it in and then goes to the bathroom inside her and that makes the baby."

Pain along ribs, down to stomach, side stitches. Be safe, sphere, be safe.

The little girl scowled. "Wicked boy."

"It's true! And then the baby crawls out of her cunny. Only if it's all done. If it's not all done, it has to crawl back in. What do you suppose would happen if the half-done baby couldn't find his mother's cunny again? I suppose it would find one *eventually*. Teacher says one is very much like another."

The pain was subsiding, like summer thunder, becoming more distant every few seconds. "That's very bad language for such a nice young boy to be using."

"You're not supposed to tell." The little girl stood up, pushing the swing away from her. "You're a bad wicked boy and bad wicked boys get cooked and eaten like in *Hansel and Gretel* if they don't watch out!"

"Cunny, cunny, cunny!" Jamie screamed at the top of his lungs, leaping up like a frog from the dirt and running off, out from under the street lamp, through the darkness, hooting like an owl as he went. His sister took off after him, crying, "Wicked, wicked bad boy! She'll get you, she'll get you and turn you into gingerbread!"

Rachel leaned forward in the swing, wondering if she really wanted to have children after all. *But mine will be different because they'll be* mine. She bent down, lifting the bags, sliding her purse up under her arm, expecting a hernia at any moment.

She saw what the boy had been drawing in the dirt: a clumsily sketched penis entering a hairy circle which must've represented a vagina, and beyond that, a stick figure wearing a top hat.

Beneath this crude diagram, a word:
HOUNFOUR

TWENTY-FIVE

THE THING IN THE WALLS

Hugh only caught the barest glimpse of the thing. Like watching a train heading into a tunnel, like the echo of a flashbulb, or a firefly glowing for a fraction of a second at twilight and then vanishing. Just a pure whiteness in that dark hole—then *gone.* He'd made a hole in the wall, at first just by tugging at the cheap wallpaper, and then at the paper beneath that. There was a small dent there, as if someone had poked at the wall, and he found that if he pressed there with his fingers, the plaster came off. *Bad workmanship.* He pushed a little harder. A chunk of plaster came off in his hand. The wall had been cheaply constructed. He took a screwdriver and pried some more away and peered into the dark room and saw something white.

It's 'cause I'm drunk. I am rip-roaring drunk. These were Hugh's first thoughts on seeing the thing, the white motion, the blur of movement. But he was not that drunk, he knew it. It had only been two beers; well, three. *Or maybe I drank more without realizing it? Maybe I knocked back a few six-packs, and now I just don't remember any of them beyond the first two, that would explain seeing this* thing. This *something* in the crack in the wall of the vanity, something that could not be a small animal shaved of its hair, could not just be a rat covered with white dust.

Hugh knew that in dark caves there lived creatures of transparent white jelly, blind and glowing; he knew that underground streams throbbed with life that was so differ-

ent from the daylight world as to be alien, but *this* . . . What
had lived in the shadows of this dark room and fed upon
roaches and mice, what was it that had just crawled back
into its small cave within this vanity within this house?

I must be blind fucking drunk.

A hallucination like this was what drinking was all about.
*Now, if I'd dropped acid I could label it a bad flashback and
be done with it. What should I call it?*

He shuddered. His shirt caught under his armpits, down
his back, at his chest: he was sweating. He could smell the
sourness of his own breath. His right hand held a chunk of
plaster from the vanity wall; it crumbled as his hand became
a fist. The hand even seemed alien, it seemed too white to be
his, the hair on his knuckles and the back of his hand
seemed too blond, he saw scales crossing each other like
lizard highways across his fingers. Plaster dust settled across
his fingernails. He opened and closed his fist slowly, turning
his palm upward. *Drunk, drunk, drunk.*

The house smelled differently, a subtle change, like an
odor from childhood remembered years later. Where it had
smelled like nothing to him, empty, it now smelled *inhab-
ited.*

He would probably find dead rodents behind the wall, he
would no doubt discover a nest of mice, all white, and that
would be the smell, and the mother mouse would be that
thing he'd seen.

No mouse.

God, why had its face seemed so human?

Hugh had seen its eyes before. There were eyes. It had
eyes. The white thing that drew back into the darkness had
eyes.

Hugh opened and closed his fist. It was a technique for
relaxation he'd learned to develop from a very early age. He
would pretend *(Let's Pretend, Let's Pretend, it's all pretend)*
that with each fist he was throwing away his anger, his
frustration, the way a magician makes a coin disappear, but
not up his sleeve, but out, out into the vanishing world.

The thing I saw had eyes.

He was drunk, that was enough, he could deal well with
being drunk because it meant he was under the influence.
Like Draper House itself, *influenced,* beyond the control of

natural forces, like being drunk. His fist opened and closed and opened and closed.

Pale blue eyes.

As if milky cataracts had grown over them.

Just a drunken flashback. No eyes, the white thing had no eyes, I was flashing back.

Flashback to Hugh, a child, standing before his father.

"Look me in the eyes, boy."

Hugh could barely remember a moment in his life when he had not felt this way: a child, not sure of what he'd done, waiting for punishment that could come in any form. But the worst being what his father had done to him then.

"Look me in the eyes, boy," the Old Man said, and all Hugh could see of his father were his eyes, like pools of blue-curdled milk, red lines circling the outer whiteness. "You want to play games when I have guests, perhaps you should play hide-and-seek."

Those eyes.

"But it was Ted who—" Hugh began. He stood there, barely four feet tall, his fist clenching and unclenching, making his anger vanish into thin air.

"Hide-and-seek, boy." The Old Man opened the doors to the coat closet. Why did its depths seem so scary? Nothing in it but old coats and umbrellas, scarves fluttering across Hugh's face as his father pressed him into it.

"But I didn't do anything."

The Old Man's eyes burned in his memory, in the darkness at the back of his head where Hugh shut the wild nightmare things out of his mind, where his anger went when it vanished, where it waited there, lurking. Those eyes.

"You saw something, boy."

The closet doors closed on him.

A lock clicked in place.

His fist hurt because he couldn't undo it, he couldn't flatten his hand out, he couldn't make his anger disappear.

"I only saw a lady."

His father laughed from the other side of the door. "You saw nothing, boy, nothing. And when you're ready to tell the truth, about seeing nothing, I'll let you out. Until then, you just sit there and think about making things up. Pretending is bad, boy, it hurts people."

Hugh could not open his fist; the harder he tried, the more his fingernails cut into the palm of his hand.

His father's blue eyes burning holes like twin blue-hot pokers pushing through his brain.

"Nothing, I saw nothing."

He said it for three hours in the musty darkness of the front hall closet before his father finally let him out. And when he came out his fist was unclenched and he had made his anger vanish into thin air.

"Nothing," the grown-up Hugh said to the opening to the vanity.

But the thing he'd seen there, the thing that vanished into the murk and dust, had looked like a white clenched fist with the Old Man's blue eyes buried deep in its rippling knuckles.

The vanity was itself a closed fist, and as Hugh went to get his other tools, he knew if he opened it up, whatever was inside there would no longer exist.

TWENTY-SIX

OPENING THE VANITY

1.

Rachel heard the crashing down the hall before she saw him. "My God! What's all the racket?" She plopped the grocery bags on the sideboard and rushed to the turret room.

The walled-in vanity was partially torn into—its ragged wall only came up as high as Hugh's chest.

He was covered with dust, his back to her. Wearing only his boxers, his shoulders and back muscles flexing as he tore a piece of the drywall out with a crowbar. Then he hooked the bar back into the space he'd already brought down; he pulled against the wall. Motes of dust floated along the hallway. He tossed the crowbar to the floor, picked up his sledgehammer and hefted it from his right hand to his left.

"What *is* all this?"

He turned, acknowledged her presence with a nod, and then returned his attention to the vanity, put his back into his work, slamming the hammer against the lower half of the wall that remained. It took the blow hard, crumbling and flying wildly inward. He set the hammer down, again lifting the crowbar. He began gnawing at the rubble with the bar. The floor around him was strewn with his shirt and slacks and dust and hammers and screwdrivers, bits of the wall, chips of wood. "I'm—" he grunted, "—just—opening—this—"

"I know what you're doing, but *what the fuck are you doing,* Hugh? We're entertaining tomorrow night and you're making a mess of everything?"

He dropped the crowbar, narrowly missing his toes. Its

metallic crash echoed down the hall. Sinking to the floor, he covered his head with his hands. "Thought I heard something back there, like a rat." When he glanced up from between his fingers, she could see that he'd been crying. "I was just trying to help, *Jesus,* Scout, every time I try to help I—"

He's drunk.

Beer bottles on the floor, lined up neatly just inside the turret room.

2.

"God, I need a cigarette!" She turned her purse upside down, dumping its contents out on the dining room table— combs, keys, date book, address book, spare Tampax, a half-eaten roll of Rolaids, Kleenex (both new and used), coins rolled along the table, bouncing over the edge. Finally, her wallet fell out like a brick, while tobacco bits spun around in the air—and one lone, crumbling cigarette finally dropped on top of the pile. It was the sorriest excuse for a cigarette she had ever seen. But for that moment, when she felt like her lungs were no longer responding to oxygen, when she thought of the lousy day she'd had, and the equally crappy evening she was letting herself in for, it looked like the largest cigarette in the history of the tobacco industry. Like a hungry animal, she grabbed for it and put it between her lips.

Hugh followed her out, pulling up a chair at the table. He sat down carefully. "I decided I'd had enough. Not just the room—the vanity. I was out walking around—and okay, *drinking*—but it was all boiling inside me, Scout, all this garbage inside me, always pretending that I have to do the right thing, but the right thing, well, sometimes it's *not* the right thing. So I come back, and I remember something that my old friend Verena wrote, something about this room, something that happened in here, long time ago, and I think I hear something in there, maybe a rat or something, and I start hammering at it, just hammering at the wall, and it feels good, you know, to just finally be picking something up with my own two hands and just *doing* it, not talking about doing it or studying how to do it or asking permission to do it or having the Old Man tell me I've got to do it, but just doing it. I make a crack in the wall, and then I can't stop and I take the back of the hammer and pry away, and it's a pretty weak wall, Scout, and then I get some other tools and start going at it. I can't stop. I'd had enough, you know, enough of everything, and that wall just needed to come down." Hugh's voice was barely a whisper, and she'd expected him to look away, his eyes downcast (the way she knew *she* would look if she were in his shoes), but no such luck: he looked at her steadily. He was drunk—she could smell that part of him, and he knew she knew he was drunk. He didn't seem to care about hiding that. "I'd just had . . . enough."

"You've had enough? *You've* had enough? You're so full of shit, Hugh, your eyes are turning brown." She knew him inside and out, she knew his smell, his skin, she knew his moles, for God sakes, she knew his scars, he had no mystery. That was a problem after all—she knew him too well. His eyes weren't turning brown, they remained so fucking true blue she wanted to raise her hands up like claws and scratch them out for turning her into such a witch. He was right out front like the marble blue of his eyes, they were clear lakes through which you could see right to the bottom.

"What the hell is happening here?" She almost laughed when she said that, but was afraid to because she knew she would sound like a witch and she was not going to let him turn her into one.

"I don't know," Hugh said, and seemed to mean it. He reached into the shambles of her purse and brought out a book of matches. He struck a match and lifted it up to her disintegrated cigarette. She'd forgotten about the cigarette between her lips. She plucked it out of her mouth and dropped it on the table. Hugh blew the match out. "I've been thinking about what I want to be when I grow up. Or I guess I should say when I *sober* up."

Later, Rachel would remember what she was thinking at the point when he lowered the boom, when the shit hit the fan, when the fat lady sang: she was thinking about the fact that there was cash missing from her purse, to the tune of about a hundred dollars. It was like a flash of lightning illuminating an entire landscape. She glanced away from

Hugh, looking distractedly down at the junk that had fallen from her purse. Idly, she took inventory while Hugh began talking about growing up, finally taking responsibility for his actions. Her wallet, matches, her Tampax, the bottle of Nuprin, the loose change . . .

But where were Sassy's newspaper articles she'd folded up? She was sure she'd stuck them in her usual sloppy manner into the underworld of her purse.

And the money.

She'd stuck the money inside the articles, too lazy to reach down and dig up her wallet at the very bottom of her purse. It was obvious. That horrible little boy rifling through the groceries while she turned to speak to his sister.

He had gotten into her purse and taken the money.

The money and the newspaper articles—probably just grabbed whatever paper there was and ran. How had she missed seeing it?

Rachel, feeling pale and stupid, was just about to mention getting mugged by a pre-teen when Hugh dropped the bomb.

". . . And I realized, Scout, that I never wanted to be a lawyer. And I don't intend to become one."

3.

She had to get out for some fresh air, get out for a walk, get away from him. *Not be a lawyer? But he's supposed to want to be a lawyer, it's what they'd planned for, it's what they had decided he would do!* It was dark out, but she followed the street lights down Hammer Street to Connecticut Avenue, and then turned left, towards DuPont Circle. It was crowded with young people out walking, busy, happy, productive.

Let's Pretend, Scout, that you're the mommy and I'm the daddy and we have a whole mess of kiddos, a goddamn acre of kiddos, and I'm coming home from work and you're fixing dinner, and the kiddos are fighting, and some of them are crying and one's learned to walk, and the TV's blasting "Wonder Woman" reruns, so I say, kiddos, it's time we got us a baby sitter so your mommy and daddy can have an evening out, and you throw your coat on—it's winter—and I call the

girl down the block who's free to sit for a few hours . . .
Rachel tried to block the voices from her head, all the words
he'd said to her when they would lie in his bed, before they
went and got married and fucked it all up. *Let's Pretend,
Scout, that you're the mommy and I'm the daddy and we
have a whole mess of kiddos, and we're tucking them into bed
and you're reading them the story about Daniel in the lions'
den, and I tickle their toes and the youngest begins crying
from the nursery . . .*

She passed couples walking arm in arm up Connecticut
Avenue on their ways to dinner, the movies, *normal life.*
Teenaged boys skateboarding downhill, their T-shirts
wrapped around their waists, trying to impress the young
girls who sat at the bus stop. The girls giggled and pointed
and whispered one to the other; the boys like young roosters
strutting circles around them, pretending not to be interested. Pretending.

*Let's Pretend, Hugh, that we're both in love, because we
both want to be in love really badly, we both need a little
stability in our lives, we both need family—daddy's gone off
and died on me, Hugh, and so did your first wife and your
mother and your dad's never really been there, and we can
make some kiddos between the two of us, we can have an acre
of kiddos, and we can have love, because it makes the world
go 'round, right? Not money, not work, not housing, not
surviving, but love.*

A light rain of dust swept across her face as she crossed
Connecticut Avenue at R Street. The walk signal became a
red pulsing hand, palm turned towards her, as she almost
missed the light. The drugstore was still open—it was after
8:30, but she wasn't sure of the exact time.

"Marlboro Lights," she told the man behind the counter.
Feeling just as she had when she'd smoked in the girls' room
in high school, Rachel guiltily lit the cigarette. She watched
its burning orange tip as she walked halfway down the block
at R Street and sat on some cold concrete steps. She
remembered the cigarette smell of her father, how she would
sit on his lap and smell his Camels, the bay rum cologne, the
starch of his shirts. And then, when he was dying, that smell
of tobacco clinging to his sallow skin.

But my baby, my sphere, I can't do this to you, I can't . . .

Rachel clutched her stomach—a sudden sharp pain shot through her, the muscles felt sore as if she'd been coughing. Then no pain, other than a pounding headache raging behind her eyes. The baby-sphere inside her had become such a secret that she was afraid to tell too many people about it because they might convince her it wasn't there. Even Hugh would try to convince her of that.

A man said, "You all right, miss?" She looked up to see a young man walking with his boyfriend, their hands interlocked.

She nodded. "Yes . . . thank you."

The couple walked on.

Let's Pretend, Hugh, let's fucking *pretend that love is something real that lasts, that doesn't miscarry before the term is up.*

Rachel stubbed the cigarette out onto the steps. She said aloud: "Thank God for you, sphere, thank God I've got you." She patted her stomach, wondering if she would be gaining as much weight as she'd begun to the last time she was pregnant.

After a few moments, she got up and walked back towards the drugstore, to the phones outside it. She scavenged through her purse for loose change.

Over the phone, she told Sassy, "So I just walked out. I was livid. And I'm still livid. I feel like everything he's told me has been a lie, and on top of that some damn kid picked my pocket. I'd almost be happy if he was having an affair or something normal, but no, he's got to go have a fucking identity crisis the same day he tells me he's going to get his act in gear. Hell of a day, Sassy, hell of a day. It's my house and I left it, but Jesus, that man's driving me crazy. And I was even going to tell him, too, about the, you know, the baby."

"Retch—you've seen your doctor?"

"No, but I *know.*" Rachel was on the verge of sobbing; she hiccuped her tears back. She was not going to break down at the corner of R and Connecticut with all these happy goddamn couples roaming the streets with their adolescent displays of affection. "I don't know why I love him, I really don't."

Silence on the line. *Come on, Sassy, say something to make me feel better.*

"Kick him out."

"Huh?"

"Kick him out. It *is* your house and you don't want him there. So go ahead and throw the bum out."

"That's cold. I didn't say I didn't *want* him—I couldn't do that. He needs me. He wouldn't know what to do—"

"He doesn't need you, Retch. Have you ever considered that maybe he would land on his own two feet if you weren't there to catch him every time he fell?"

Rachel covered the receiver with the palm of her hand. She glared incredulously at the phone. She let her gaze wander, to the etched graffiti on the wall (For a good time call . . .), to the people lining up for the 9:30 movie at the KB-Janus, to the Red Top cab which had pulled over and parked beside the drugstore. The cab driver was reading a magazine. Rachel heard the static and squeal of voices from his radio.

Sassy said nothing.

Rachel uncovered the receiver. "Well, listen, I better go."

"Retch, come on. I'm just playing devil's advocate here. I've known Hugh just about as long as you have, maybe not as well, but I know one thing about him. He can be a good team player, but not when he has to outperform someone else. He shrivels. And you ever notice that when you talk about the two of you, you always say 'I'm doing this' or 'he's doing this,' but never *'we're* doing this'? You're like separate entities. Not a team. Don't get mad at me for saying this, Retch, because if you weren't my best friend I wouldn't risk telling you. But you asked, and I've got to be honest."

"Thank you, Dr. Joyce Brothers," Rachel said, sniffing.

"Yeah, well, you're just plain wrong. Hugh and I—*we*—don't compete. Jesus, I've been a fucking *earth* mother for him and—"

"You're supposed to be lawyers, but *you're* the one who passes the bar, *you're* the one with the big job, *you're* the one with the direction and the drive—"

"—And we don't even compete, either, not really, as it turns out, because he's not even interested in law, so *there*, and God I need a cigarette! And what kind of supportive friend are you, anyway? If this were reversed, believe you me, the last thing I'd do is tell you what I really think, no way. What I'd tell you is that everything's going to be okay, it all comes out in the wash. I don't need friends who kick me when I'm down."

"Okay, Retch, you win. Everything's going to be okay. It all comes out in the wash."

"Fuck you. Everything I'm hearing today is such complete bullshit."

But Sassy had hung up before Rachel had the "fuck you" out of her mouth. *God, Mrs. Adair, you've got the maturity of a two year old—what kind of mother are you going to make?*

She redialed Sassy's number. It rang nine times. "Pick up the phone, pick up the phone, pick up the phone," Rachel chanted under her breath. She sighed with frustration, hanging up.

She recycled the quarter into the phone slot, trying to remember Ted's number (*last digits 46 or 48, well, here goes nothing*), then dialed it.

"'Lo?" The voice was so much like Hugh's that Rachel almost thought she'd misdialed and gotten her own home.

"Ted? This is Rachel."

"Rach—where are you? I hear strange noises."

"Traffic. I'm out and about. Is this a bad time to call?"

"As good as any. What's up?"

"Well, we're finally throwing that housewarming party this weekend. I was wondering—I know it's just tomorrow night—but if you—I'd like you to come."

"Why do I get the feeling that my better half isn't in on this?"

"Oh, Ted, please come." She didn't mean to, but somehow the sadness she was feeling inside slipped out in her voice. Sadness and desperation.

"I don't know if I should, but not for the reason you're probably thinking. The Old Man's told me some weird stuff about your house."

Was he joking? She couldn't tell. His voice was slightly jittery.

"Oh, not you, too, Ted. I've gotten a dose of that—ghosts and goblins and bumps in the night."

"Something along those lines. You all right? You sound . . ."

"Just a little winded. Been jogging." *God, you're a terrific liar, Scout.* "The party's seven-thirtyish. Saturday. You'll come? Please?"

"I shouldn't."

"Because of Hugh."

"One reason among many."

"Tell you what: don't make up your mind this instant. I'm inviting you last minute, so, well, you can decide to come last minute, too."

"Oh. Well. Listen, I better go. I've been sort of caring for the Old Man, and I think I hear him breaking things in the bathroom."

"He's there? Is something wr— Is he all right?"

"Well as can be expected. But we'll talk."

"Saturday night?"

"I ain't sayin' yes, and I ain't sayin' no, I'm just sayin' maybe. Take care," he said, hanging up the phone.

Walking back home, drained of emotion, wondering what she would say to Hugh when she went to bed (hoping he was asleep), Rachel made a mental list:

People I have alienated from my life by age 28:
1) My husband
2) My best friend
3) Probably the lady downstairs for killing her cat

Oh, daddy, you'd know what to tell me, you always had good advice, you could put things right.

Something twisted in her gut, like a case of diarrhea coming on. She hurried up Connecticut Avenue; as she went she told the sphere that must be growing inside her that everything was going to come out in the wash.

TWENTY-SEVEN

THE OLD MAN TAKES A SHOWER

When he hung up the phone, Ted hurried down the hall to the bathroom where he'd heard the smashing of glass. The bathroom door was locked; he pounded on it. "Open the door—pop? Open the damn door!"

"Give me five minutes, son."

"What's all that noise?"

"Accident. Just a little accident."

The sound of glass crunching underfoot.

Ted could hear his own heartbeat.

Through the door, his father said, "Just a few minutes, son, it's all I need."

"Open this door before I break it down."

"Do what you will, boy, do what you will."

Then a moan of pain.

Ted shook his head. "Jeez, pop." He brought a dime out of his pocket and fit it into the keyhole and twisted—the doors were cheap in this condo. When he heard the click of the lock, Ted turned the knob, swinging the door wide.

The first thing he saw was the broken mirror. It looked like it had been punched in the center, sending rays of broken glass outward. Four shards were missing. On the floor were three of them, slightly chipped. Bloody footsteps led Ted to the shower, its curtain drawn.

Ted held his breath as he went over. *No, pop, don't have done this, don't have gone and sliced yourself open.*

He pulled the shower curtain over all the way back, tearing it from the rod.

His father was hunkered down in the shower. His hands were cut and bleeding. He held a fat slice of broken mirror between the fingers of both hands. It was triangular; he was pressing one end of it against his throat,

Winston Adair looked up at his son and said, "Just a few minutes and I'll be done. Then you'll believe me, boy, then you'll see it's true."

But he was not slicing into his throat. He sat there immobile, the sharp mirror fragment beneath his wattled chin. Ted squatted down beside him, reaching over. This kind of thing was becoming a normal occurrence—although the Old Man was getting more creative with the instruments. He'd gone from a kitchen knife to a screwdriver to a pair of scissors, and now mirrors. "Jesus, pop." Ted grasped his father's hand between his. "Drop it! Drop *it!*"

The Old Man's hand opened, silver glass clattering against tile. He looked up at Ted, his eyes staring dully, his face devoid of expression. "I wouldn't have done it, boy, I wouldn't have done it. I'm as scared of what comes after life right now as I am of life itself. I wouldn't have done it."

"I know, pop."

Sometimes I just wish you would go ahead and do it.

Like a cat cleaning itself, Winston Adair began licking the blood from his fingers, rubbing his damp hands across his face.

TWENTY-EIGHT

BEFORE THE PARTY

Rachel felt like she'd never even gone to sleep. *But the party, good Lord the party's tonight*—it came to her like that when she awoke in the morning. Just lying there on the sofa staring at the ceiling, a ceiling she had memorized through the night. When Hugh had made his grand announcement she'd had nothing to say: what do you say to a man in whom you've believed, whom you've looked up to, whom you would've dented the corners and edges of your life to accommodate, when he tells you such a thing? Rachel had never felt completely tongue-tied before—she'd always been his pleasing machine, somebody who could smooth out the rough spots, fill in the potholes, but now how could she possibly say or do anything that would make him comfortable with his new decision?

At least she'd resisted that cigarette, for her baby's sake, for her sphere's sake—although the sphere may just have been Let's Pretend, *Let's Pretend I'm going to have a baby, Hugh,* but she hadn't even made an appointment to see her doctor, because what if she were wrong? And Hugh, looking so different last night, looking like a stranger, like a stranger who *almost* looked like her husband, but not quite.

Was he the same man she'd married at all? Had she really known him as well as she thought she had? Was it all *Let's Pretend?* She'd come in last night to a dark house; Hugh had already gone to bed. She thought of calling her mother about this new development—she imagined the conversation they'd have: *"Rachel, if you just don't take this phase too seriously—and that's all it is, a phase, your father went through something similar—if you just don't make too big an issue of it, this too shall pass. He's probably depressed from being unemployed, and men are notorious for making sweeping and regrettable statements like that . . ."*

And there, she'd been all prepared to tell him her little secret, about the sphere inside her, what she *thought* was a sphere inside her, *but don't call it a baby just yet because then you'll lose it, just like you lost your last little sphere by thinking of it as a baby when it was still just a tiny subdivision.* She wanted to tell him, and he'd gone and topped it, he'd gone and told her something that made her think this was the worst possible time for a sphere, unless there was some magical way of keeping the sphere from subdividing all the way to babyhood.

So when Rachel awoke in the morning, remembering the party, remembering Normal Life, she tried to put it out of her mind. Put *him* out of her mind. She was lying there, staring at the ceiling, and the light through the French doors was still purple and hazy—it must be just dawn, and it had been years since she'd been up this early. Usually, she woke up about half an hour before she was due at work, and then on weekends, slept till nine or ten.

But it was the baby crying that awoke her, and she had not even been aware of it—she'd opened her eyes with the sound, but she'd been dreaming of her sphere, and the transition to wakefulness had been so smooth it hadn't seemed unusual to hear the baby—*her* baby crying. Dreams were like that.

But now consciousness seeped through her like a transfusion, and she sat up on the couch, wondering where the crying was coming from.

She went to the French doors, unlocked and opened them—it was actually chilly, and she hugged herself as she stepped out onto the narrow balcony. But the crying was not outside—dogs barked, the sound of trucks going across Connecticut Avenue, a helicopter going overhead, and silence slicing through these early morning noises. But no babies, no bawling.

The doctors all said you'd be hearing babies every time you ran amok emotionally, but Jesus, could it please end?

Rachel went back inside, shivering from the startling coolness of the August morning.

And she heard the crying baby, and followed the sound down the corridor, to the torn walls of the vanity—and heard a scuttling sound like . . .

Rats.

There better not be rats coming up from down below.

But there were no rats, at least she didn't see anything—just the rubble that had been there last night, the bricks half built up into a wall as if the person building it was interrupted before finishing the project. A small metal washtub still lay overturned, and she wondered if maybe there were rats beneath *it.* She tapped on the edge.

It thumped like a hollow drum. *The only rat here is lying upstairs, snoring.*

The baby—wherever he was—was whimpering, and the sound seemed to be coming from down the stairs. Rachel gingerly stepped around the shards of broken glass, over the fallen bricks, leaving footprints in the white dust. The floor was cold, the room itself was cold, colder than it had been outside.

The baby seemed to be crying down those dark stone steps—where did they lead? To Mrs. Deerfield's crib? Rachel shivered, remembering her experience over that spot in the lower apartment. The man with the teeth that seemed to be coming for her.

Something was scratching on the stairs, like an animal raking its claws across the stones.

Rachel felt fear trickle down her spine. She was suddenly overcome with dread. She remembered what Mrs. Deerfield had told her, about the crib being a place where spirits cross on their journeys, and the articles Sassy had given her that she had barely scanned—the house now *did* seem evil, and Rachel knew that if it were anything other than just before sunrise she would not be so terrified, more rational thoughts would take over, she would be part of Normal Life, but this was becoming too much like *Let's Pretend,* and her imagination was running wild.

She backed away from the steps leading down into darkness, knocking into and almost tripping over the washtub. She kicked it away and it went clanging against the entry to the bathroom. She didn't realize until she was out of the vanity that the baby had stopped crying, that she herself was sobbing, that her feet were finely cut with bits of glass.

That her breasts had begun leaking milk.

TWENTY-NINE

THE OFFERING

1.

"Retch?" Sassy called up the stairs, pushing the door open wide. It squealed conspicuously, slamming against the wall. She sensed (without knowing for sure) that the downstairs tenant was spying on her from the fisheye peephole of her door. Sassy repressed the urge to turn and stare at it.

She stood in the downstairs hallway of Draper House. She'd been so upset the night before, after she'd gotten off the phone with Rachel, that she'd actually gone back into work at ten o'clock at night and worked on next week's "Home" section articles—*and Sassy Parker never works a week ahead of time, particularly over a holiday weekend.* She'd done some work, but she mainly stayed up writing nasty things about Rachel Adair on her computer screen, getting upset, erasing the bad things and typing in: *You're my best friend, I was only trying to help.* But Rachel *had* been the one who'd asked for her advice, *had* been the one who said, "Fuck you," *had* been in the wrong. *But it doesn't matter, you don't let your best friend down when she's that upset, you don't tell her off.* So Sassy had felt guilty when she'd finally hit the sack at two A.M., got up at noon, went out and bought a peace offering—the flowers she picked up at her neighborhood florist in Mount Pleasant, wrapped up in tissue paper—and thought she'd surprise Retch.

This'll teach you to always call first. A note on the door: Scout, Ran out to pick up dry cleaning—also, cleaning stuff at drgstre—Swept up most of vnty mess—Hugh.

But he must have run out in a hurry, because both the

outside and the inside doors to their house were unlocked and slightly ajar.

Sassy called out again from the bottom step (she'd moved up one giant step without asking mother-may-I). "This is your good friend Sassy Parker! Halloo! Retch?"

She heard floorboards creak from behind the downstairs tenant's door.

Water from the flower stems soaked through the tissue and into her yellow cotton blouse—it felt gross, and she held the flowers away from her body. "Shit."

A noise. Upstairs.

One more giant step up the stairs. "Mother-may-I," she said.

Why do I feel like I'm breaking and entering when this is my closest friend's home and nobody's going to get mad if I am caught sneaking up these stairs?

A loud smashing sound, and then scraping. Thumping across the floor. Scraping. A sound like a sponge being squeezed out. Slurping. More heavy objects falling.

"Retch?"

Up more stairs, to the first floor.

A baby began bawling its head off after the last crash, and Sassy, worried, ran down the hallway towards the sound, wondering what in hell was going on at the end of the hall.

2.

When it was over, when the woman had stopped struggling, Penelope Deerfield saw the crumpled piece of paper in the dirt. She disentangled her small pudgy fingers from the woman's scalp—a handful of blood-matted hair was caught like a cat's cradle between her hands. She shook it out. Penelope knelt down and picked up the piece of paper. Too dark to see what it had written on it, although she could almost make out a photograph. "Slipping notes behind teacher's back, are we?" She stuffed the paper in her apron pocket. The palms of her hands were spotty with calluses and blisters—the gardening had taken its toll this year, between that and her ward. "My little fleshling," she called it.

The dead woman lay among the broken jars, her hands streaked red from razor cuts. Her heart was no longer beating. The fleshling was sated and had crawled back behind its brothers—they floated lifelessly, eternally staring out of their watery graves, their bodies barely formed. And none of them chosen, none of them like the baby, the fleshling. None of them inspired with the breath of death, with the spirit of Gil DuRaz, with the spirits of the house. None of them *special*.

Penelope had to coax him into his jar. He crawled like a slug across the corpse, his tiny bumpy fingers clawing into the earth to propel himself along, then scraping through the tangle of skin and bloodied cloth of the dead woman. The jar was tall and wide, the smell of alcohol stung the air like a tragic memory. Bits of translucent tissue hung suspended in the fluid. "Must stay moist, dear, or we shall never be born." She was exhausted, but this intrigued her—this piece of paper. She knelt down, jostling mason jars—they clinked together like bells with their clappers muted. A rat ran across the dead woman's right foot, which with its shoe, a Papagallo espadrille, lay disembodied alongside an irregular growth of luminescent white mushroom just beneath the stairs to the main house, far above the woman's head.

The shoe, and the foot, remained where the woman had stepped down the last step.

When the fleshling had descended upon her.

Hungry.

She would have to make sure that no one came down there snooping again.

"But children are always hungry," Penelope Deerfield said to the thing that treaded water in the jar. Large blue eyes staring out at her; wart-filled mouth opening and closing, breathing in the solution; crisscrossed string of veins gorged and throbbing; small raisin heart pumping furiously; the tiny body red with exertion and fresh blood.

Penelope pressed her cheek to the side of the jar and felt its coldness before setting it down among the others. She turned and went back up through her trapdoor.

Sitting on the patio at her small table, Mrs. Deerfield brought the crumpled paper out from her apron pocket. "So many years ago, so many lives gone by," she said, shaking her head with memories. "And the children, oh dear, all the children I have loved, all the life I delivered then." She scanned the paper: a photocopy of a newspaper article, the contents of which she knew well.

From *The Washington Herald-Examiner,* January 17, 1967:

MISSING WOMAN FOUND DEAD IN NW
Identified as "Deadly Baby Sitter" of Baltimore

A woman's body was found early this morning in the Winthrop Park section of Northwest Washington. Cause of death is as yet unknown. She has been identified as Nora Garrett, aged sixty-one, A.K.A. Winifred Stanhope, Sarah Masterson, and Mary Devine. Under this last name, she made headlines in Baltimore in late 1966 as the Deadly Baby Sitter. Working in the household of the Marrow family of Baltimore, she was held responsible in the deaths of the two Marrow children, Laura and Philip, and with the discovery of the children's deaths came a string of other similar murders, seven in all, of former employers' children. But by then the so-called Deadly Baby Sitter had disappeared without a trace. Authorities know very little about this woman, other than she was an illegal alien born in London, England, and that she had managed to elude them for the four years she conducted her murderous activities.

Below this article, two photographs of the woman:
One, in death. She lay sprawled across fragments of brick and concrete, her face upward, a raincoat laid over her body, and yet the face was clear, her mouth slightly open, eyes closed.

The other photo, taken some years earlier, with a fifties look to the make-up and hairstyle. A small round face. Dull mousy hair, small eyes, nose almost indistinguishable from the rest of the face. Plain. Thin lips. Eyes slightly downcast, a tightness to the face as if she didn't enjoy having her picture taken.

And there was no doubt who the woman was, through the maze of aliases and the nondescript quality of her features.

"So long ago," Penelope Deerfield said to herself, "as if in another life." It was nice to relax on a summer afternoon in the shade, nice to lean back and have a martini, a martini because her body needed it, a martini because alcohol kept her going these days—nice to just rest her bones and have a drink and reminisce about the good old days.

When she'd had choices.

When she'd been alive.

THIRTY

HOUSEWARMING PARTY

1.

Two hours before the party, while Hugh was running around on last-minute errands for cocktail napkins and fresh pineapple for the piña coladas, Rachel answered the door in her bathrobe, her hair greased up and back with conditioner. "Mom," was all she could say—she'd been expecting Hugh, or perhaps Sassy, and when the doorbell rang, she looked out the kitchen window to try and see who it was, but the view was blocked with the heavy wisteria vine that was strangling the lantern just above the porch. She'd seen the bag lady in the park again—the crazy one, although Rachel was herself beginning to think that *she* was the crazy one in this neighborhood. Whenever she noticed the bag lady, Rachel wondered if it really was a person or just a collection of trash bags, like an urban scarecrow. *But I'd hate to think what she's scaring away from Winthrop Park.*

"I thought it might be Sassy—we were supposed to go jogging, and I've tried calling her to cancel . . ." *Rachel Adair, you are getting really good at the Let's Pretend lies.*

Her mother asked almost sweetly, "Don't you think that girls who have miscarriages shouldn't jog?"

Afraid my uterus is going to drop on the sidewalk? But Rachel merely smiled pleasantly. "You're early."

"Invite your mother in to see this townhouse of yours," her mother said. She was dressed in a beige skirt and lavender blouse, her light brown hair, fresh from the hairdresser, only slightly frazzled with the humidity. She looked mildly beautiful, as mom always did.

They went upstairs, and Rachel gave her a brief tour of the first floor.

"Lovely, lovely," her mother said as she followed Rachel room to room, but there were obviously other things on her mother's mind.

Finally, Rachel said, "I'm glad you came by, but you're here for a reason, I guess."

"No reason. It was a pretty afternoon, I had my hair appointment, I was dressed, I knew your soiree would be starting up soon, so I thought I'd give you a little warning about tonight. Rachel, I am bringing a date tonight and I am scared—shit, I'm terrified."

The shock of hearing her mother use bad language was not as great as the shock from that word *date*. *Moms don't date, even if moms have been widows for two years. Moms stay moms eternally.*

"Fantastic," was all Rachel could muster. "Who?"

As if waiting days for someone to ask her, her mother blurted, "Well, he's a very nice man, and I hope you don't mind my bringing him tonight."

"And? . . ."

"He's just a nice man. He seems like a nice man. I didn't want to come alone, and Kelly and her husband can't make it."

"Give me more scenario. How do you know this guy?"

"If I asked you all these questions when you were dating, you would've claimed the Fifth."

"Mom."

"All right, you know him already, anyway. Mr. Martin. David Martin."

"As in Mr. Martin the man who lives in the cul-de-sac who dad couldn't stand because he said he was a lout?"

"You asked. It's just a date. He's a nice man."

"He asked you out?"

"Well . . . we went out last Sunday, just to the movies. Don't look so judgmental, Rachel, that's a very unattractive quality in a young woman, and it's my life anyway."

"Mr. Martin who used to yell at us for cutting through his yard?"

"Well, I see you've grown up some in the past twenty years. You were trespassing, you tomboys all ruined his garden, and Rachel, it's just a date. Everyone else at this party will have a date. It's not one of these modern dates like your generation, where the word *date* is just a euphemism for sexual relations, it's a *date*. And I am glad I dropped by after all, because I don't want you insulting him or being rude just out of some misguided effort to preserve your father's memory and keep me a lonely old widow in the suburbs. No one *ever* asks me out places, not you kids, and not my old girlfriends. David Martin asked me out, and now I am asking him out for tonight. He's a nice man and it's either go out with him tonight to your party or stay at home and try to outguess the people on 'Wheel of Fortune.' So be good."

After her mother left, Rachel tried Sassy's number again, but there was no answer.

2.

The guests began arriving at quarter to eight, but the pains in Rachel's sides continued unabated as the evening wore on—and her craving for a cigarette—especially since Connie and Dan Stewart, from her office, were smoking up a storm on the patio and every time she went out there both the pains in her back and stomach grew worse and her need of a cigarette became unbearable. All the smokers stayed on the patio, in fact, so Rachel did what she could to avoid going outside. Her mother arrived the earliest, with Mr. David Martin, and on the outside, Rachel said, "I'm so happy you could come. Hugh, sweetheart, see if you can't get mom a 7-Up, and I think Mr. Martin—David—mentioned a gin and tonic." But on the inside she was screaming: *Daddy's rolling in his grave! How could you, mom, how could you bring a man who daddy disliked so much!*

In fact, she felt as if on the outside she was being witty and cordial and polite, and on the inside she was a volcano waiting to erupt. *Hugh, don't you think you've had enough martinis for one night? Why doesn't Sassy show up and rescue me from all this? Damn it, my stomach hurts—damn I need a cigarette, damn this dress is tight.* But she managed to smile—she was sure it was a pained smile right now as she led her mother and Mr. Martin over to the bar with Hugh there mixing drinks, actually telling jokes with that asshole Bufu Thompson who should've been convincing Hugh to get ready for the legal bar rather than the cocktail bar.

Nina Mcleod, one of Rachel's girlfriends from college, was arguing with the man she'd brought and introduced as her "lover," a term which Rachel felt not only told too much about their relationship *(You're lovers? So basically you fuck)* but also was particularly ironic at this moment. The harsh words were spoken *sotto voce,* and Rachel admired their nerve but not their timing—she was almost jealous of this display of hostile communication, in which they were both equal partners. Whenever Rachel argued with Hugh, he always caved in, leaving her feeling like the Wicked Witch. Both Nina and her lover seemed equal in their nasty comments to each other. "I saw that look you gave the waitress tonight," Nina whispered, and her lover replied, "I don't know how you could see anything with your head so far up your ass."

Rachel even smiled genuinely, and she felt suddenly like a hostess—*I'm not the only one in the world with problems, and at least Hugh and I can be discreet.*

Tom and Jill Fulcher complimented Hugh on his photographs, but Hugh shrugged his shoulders and started telling jokes. Tom had been one of Hugh's closest childhood friends, but Hugh had had a tendency all his life to drop old friends and move on. It had been at Rachel's insistence that he invite them, and Chris Shreeve, his roommate from college. Noticeably missing were most of their law school friends, but that was where Rachel had been a bit sensitive to Hugh—she knew he would feel humiliated if they all came. They would all have good jobs, and here he was, a failure in their eyes.

Ted Adair arrived just after nine, just after Hugh was beginning to slur his speech, just after Rachel's mother and Mr. Martin left because they hadn't yet had dinner and he knew a place nearby. It was a relief to see Ted.

"Thank God, someone normal," Rachel said, grabbing his hand and leading him upstairs to the party.

"I wasn't sure if I should come," he said.

"Well, I'm glad you did. I wish your father had come, too."

"I'm afraid he's not doing too well."

"I'm sorry to hear it."

"Yeah, well, you know, you get to be that age . . ."

She took him to the buffet. "Ham and turkey, but stay away from the goat's cheese, my cousin Larry brought it and it tastes worse than it smells. But try the ranch dip, and the lady downstairs made this apple pie—she's here somewhere, too."

Mrs. Deerfield was, in fact, on the back porch among the smokers, coughing and drinking, and reading palms.

"Oh, my big brother!" Hugh yelled from the bar.

"Hughie," Ted said, "you're sailing three sheets to the wind."

"You an emissary of his majesty the Old Man?"

"Not tonight."

"Good, good. You know Bufu, don't you? Boof, this is my big bro, Tedward Adair."

"Rachel," Ted said, "could you and I talk?"

Rachel nodded, but Hugh grabbed her arm. "Let go," she said softly.

"Scout," Hugh warned.

But Rachel pulled herself away from him. "Don't you think you've had enough?"

Hugh lifted his glass up. "Never enough, Scout."

"Bartender," Bufu said, whistling, "what's the name of the game?"

"Thumper!" Hugh said, slamming his glass down on the bar. Gin splattered across his shirt. He chugged down what was left in the glass.

"Why are you doing this?" Rachel asked quietly.

He would not meet her gaze.

Instead he glanced over at Ted. "Listen, you sonofabitch, I want you and the Old Man to keep your claws out of my wife."

Ted, pretending that nothing had been said, nodded, smiling. An aside, to Rachel: "Look, we can talk tomorrow, but we should talk soon."

"You're not leaving?"

"I think maybe I better. No point causing a scene, and Hughie and I are famous for causing scenes."

"I don't blame you. But I'm sorry, Ted."

"It's okay, there's some business I need to attend to anyway." As she walked him down the stairs to the front door, he turned and kissed her on her forehead. "A girl like you shouldn't get such a raw deal."

She stood there in the open doorway. Ted walked out onto the sidewalk without looking back.

Damn you, Hugh, damn you and your goddamn drinking! I knew I should've gotten you into AA last year. I knew I shouldn't have just pretended it was going to go away. And now you're going to drive anyone decent, even your own family, out of your life. She leaned against the door frame. Ted turned once, at his car which was parked at the end of the block. He stood still. His hands holding the keys to his car. Looking back at her.

He's waiting for me.

Why? Does he feel sorry for me? Or is he the joker that Hugh says he is?

Somewhere in the distance, the sound of faint thunder.

You're not going to do it, Hugh, you're not going to do it to me, and you're not going to do it to your brother.

Slamming the front door behind her, leaving her own party, Rachel stepped out onto the street.

Ted came to her.

3.

"What'll you do?" Bufu asked drowsily.

"Don't know, no idea," Hugh said. "Always been good with my hands, maybe I'll do some carpentry. Ha."

"You fucked *this* house up," Bufu said.

The two men laughed.

"Boof, she's gone."

"No, not Rachel."

"Yeah, my Scout is gone. Without her, I don't know where I'm going."

"What's the name of the game, Hughbert?"

"Damn it to hell, Boof, it's no game."

"You got to stop calling me Bufu, my associates wouldn't think it was all that funny."

"No game at all."

4.

They walked without talking, almost touching, almost arm in arm. Rachel was glad to be out of the smoke and noise and liquor smell. As they passed the small restaurants on the way down Connecticut Avenue towards DuPont Circle, she glanced through the glass windows and watched the young couples enjoying their evening out. "My God," she said pausing at a Greek restaurant.

"What is it?"

"That's my mother."

"So it is. Should we say hi?"

"No, God, no. She's on a date with a despicable man, someone daddy hated."

"And you're out with your husband's brother, who your husband loathes."

"Not the same. Hugh is not a sacred cow. Now *daddy* is a sacred cow."

"Moo."

"Silly."

"Now you've got me thinking about dairy products, how does an ice cream cone sound? Haagen Daz's still looks open."

"So does Steve's, and I like Steve's Ice Cream better."

"That's the trouble with life, too many choices and nobody agrees on any one of them."

"So this is where Hugh got his dime store philosophy from."

"I can see why he fell in love with you." Ted put his arm around her waist.

"No, um . . ." Rachel stepped away, pretending to watch for a break in traffic so they could jaywalk. "I better not have ice cream anyway—I'm getting too fat."

"Women always think they're too fat."

"Look, let's go back—now I feel bad for leaving. Hugh's

probably passed out and our friends are probably already gossiping."

"I've got to tell you something."

"Oh, right, we're supposed to be talking."

"I don't know how you're going to take this."

"Shoot."

"Our father—Hugh's and mine—has gone crazy. Whew! I haven't told anyone, you're the first, and it's that easy."

Rachel continued walking.

"I mean really nutso, off the deep end with no hope of coming back. And he wants me to deliver this message. And it's crazy, but he said if I tell you this, he will agree to see whatever doctor I bring on. So, even though this sounds nutty, I've got to tell you, and then you can call him or write the Old Man a letter and tell him that I told you."

"Sounds weird but fair."

"Perfect analysis. He wants me to tell you to get out of the house, both you and Hugh, but if Hugh won't go, then *you,* especially."

"What—I don't get it, do you mean he wants the house back or something? Can he do that?"

"He doesn't want the house back. In fact, he'd like to burn it down but I think he's too scared to go near it. He thinks you're in some kind of danger. Look, here's what he wrote." Ted handed Rachel a letter.

She opened it up.

Rachel,

In name of everything holy get the fuck out of the house. Its baby needs a mother, don't you hear it crying? It's real, it's real and nobody can stop it, but if you get out maybe you can be safe—the Housekeeper has to do it, and you're the one. Deal I made only I didn't know what deal when I made it. Ted will explain rest. Not blessing on marriage, Rachel, but curse. Please forgive me.

Winston Adair

Ted said, "He's really lost it."

"Is he all right, Ted? I mean, shouldn't you tell Hugh about this?"

Ted grinned, avoiding her. "Look, let's get you back, you can call the Old Man up in the morning, and then I can bring in a psychiatrist. He's hurt himself a bit, got stung by some wasps, but he's physically okay—he's living like Howard Hughes in his last days—even growing his fingernails long."

"It says you'll explain the rest."

"He's cracked, Rachel, my pop has cracked." Ted said this matter-of-factly, but she could see sadness in his eyes.

"Oh, Ted, I'm sorry."

"Yeah, well, I promised him I'd tell you, I can do that. All the bullshit he's been going on about the house, about it being haunted or something, he called it 'the screaming house,' he's really off—"

"But I just read about that, *the screaming house.* In some old news clippings, Ted, there were some murders in the house. It spooked me at first, but I figured they happened so long ago, maybe twenty years. There were some cultists and hippies in the house."

"You're kidding—maybe pop dropped a little acid back then—"

"The way you and Hugh go on about that poor man—oh, I'm sorry. I know he's done some horrible things, at least to Hugh, in the past . . ."

"Poor dear Joanna, right, well, Hugh was a fool not to see that, everyone else who knew her knew she was after the Old Man's money and not Hugh. I tried telling him, but he can be pretty stubborn sometimes."

"I've noticed."

"But pop's put his boys through the wringer all right. And I guess he's paying for it now."

"Ted, now I know it's crazy for me to ask, but did your father tell you why the house screams?"

"You're right—it does sound crazy, but not half as crazy as the answer. He says the house screams because it's in labor, Rachel; you know, *giving birth.*"

THIRTY-ONE

AFTER THE PARTY

1.

The party was over when Rachel returned home, having to drag herself through the front door, up the stairs. Her stomach pains were returning and she thought again about the possibility of being pregnant, and wondered if the pains were bad or good. She laid her hand across her lower stomach and the pain went away momentarily. *On Monday, I'll call Dr. Langford. Shit, on Monday I'll probably be filing for divorce.*

Hugh was sitting on his college chair, his head in his hands. The room smelled of cigarettes, perfume, and beer.

"Oh, Hugh," she sighed.

"Scout," he said, looking up. "I thought you were gone for good."

"I guess you were wrong."

"I'm sorry."

"I just don't think 'sorry' cuts it."

She stepped out of her heels. Her feet were sore, and it almost tickled her toes to step down on the soft oriental rug. She walked across it and stood in front of him. He leaned over, embracing her hips, resting his head against her stomach. She felt warm inside when he touched her. She reached down and combed her fingers through his hair. She could smell his sweat, and it was like river water and she wanted to dive in.

She disentangled herself from him, holding his hands. Crouched down in front of him, she kissed him just beneath his left ear. Kissed him on his lightly bearded neck—it had grown out like microscopic blades of grass since he'd shaved that morning. Her lips found his—they were rough and dry and stank of gin. But they were warm, and she needed warmth, and as if in a dream she saw herself kissing him, drinking him. Felt his arms go around her back as they both fell to the oriental rug, losing themselves in the swirling patterns, undoing the back of her dress and slipping out of it. Her back ached and the sharp pain pinched her just along her ribs, but he was kissing her, he was rubbing his fingers across her just-freed nipples, and she wrapped her legs around his waist, ripping her dress, but who cared. He was warm and she needed warmth, she'd been cold for too long, cold and in the heat but never warm, never this. Her skin tingled with his warmth.

His tongue was like a scaly lizard in her mouth. Her own breath went bad with his. Under ordinary circumstances this would've been all wrong and she would've been turned off, but as she closed her eyes she thought it was Ted even when she knew it was Hugh, and not just Hugh, but Hugh and Ted and Ted and Hugh and all of them licking her and stroking her and entering her. And whatever pain she'd been feeling was gone with the rhythm they were creating, all her senses were concentrated in that one area, and her mind was a dark closet of sensation and movement. She had no control, and could tell by his raspy breathing that *he* had no control, that together they were out of control. She heard her baby inside her crying, and he was licking her breasts as he shuddered inside her, licking her breasts which dripped with liquid warmth.

And when it was over, and she lay there in his arms, and the baby inside her had stopped crying, and the unpleasantness of post-coitus had come back (the body smell, the muscle soreness, the wet spots, the need to urinate, the vulnerable nakedness), she realized what the pain in her sides and back had been.

There, faintly shiny between her legs, and partly on him, too, and even on the rug, was a dark brownish smudge, a red carnelian stain.

Menstrual blood.

Rachel did not know when she began crying, was not sure when she pushed Hugh away from her, but sunlight burned its way through the French door glass, creeping across the living room, eclipsing the dark emptiness of night, when her sobbing finally ended.

2.

Penelope Deerfield held the thing to her breast. "Soon, very soon, my love, you will be born again. We who have waited will wait no more."

It cried for its mother.

PART FOUR

COME LABOR DAY

THIRTY-TWO

RISE AND SHINE

1.

If you were to pass by the alcove in the wall at the DuPont Circle Metro stop, you would think someone had left their trash bags piled up, perhaps waiting for the city sanitation trucks to come by and take them. But if you were to watch the bags for several minutes, you'd notice that they'd rise and fall in barely perceptible ripples.

And sometimes they'd gasp.

All night Mattie prayed, and in the morning none of her prayers were answered. She lay on the cold, dusty floor of the subway station, in the shadows. The filthy wind brushed the tunnels, fluttering across her dark, shiny form. Trash bags of invisibility cloaked her, but she knew they would not protect her from what was to come, what was in the daylight world above her.

What waited in the house.

Come and get me, Baron Samedi! Take these old bones and tear them apart!

Mattie Peru slept uneasily in the subway, afraid that at any moment the baron would find her through the darkness. He could go anywhere as spirit, he could travel any distance. She prayed he would come for her, come for her while she slept so it would be over and done with. Her power was coming back along with her memory, but slowly, and it made her sleepy, sluggish. She wished she could throw the power away: it was of no use against the greater power that remained in the Screaming House. She was afraid of him, the baron, but not as terrified as she was of the other one.

The spirit of Nadine.

Forgive me, daughter! Forgive me for letting him get to you, you and your baby!

When the subway gates slid open in the morning, Mattie rode the escalator up. Mr. Big Men and Mrs. Big Women in their suits, lugging their briefcases, dodging her as if she were a hole in the fabric of the world; if they touched her they might fall out of their comfortable hammocks of existence and land butt first on the ground. But the *down,* the subway, was the land of the dead: these people were dead, their eyes were dead, no life in them despite the fact that they continued to move, to glance at their watches, to whistle for taxis. They had no *spirit.* The whole world seemed dead to her. She didn't have the urge to panhandle for breakfast; she had no appetite, no thirst. Mattie had abandoned her shopping cart days ago—left it in an alley on Newport Place. All her possessions were in it, all that she had in the world. She felt the power surging through her, the power of Voudun, the religion of her mother, the power that came from the spirits, and she knew the house was stronger than even the gods of her youth. The Screaming House was like a furnace that consumed spirits to fuel its evil. And even with her power returning after so many years, she felt weak and useless. How could she even *think* about trying to stop what was going to happen in that house? Why should she even care? A Mr. and Mrs. Big Man lived there now, and when had a Mr. Big Man ever tried to help old Mattie Peru?

Screamin' House gonna make 'em scream, but so? My babygirl scream loud and nobody heard, I scream louder, nobody come runnin'! Mr. Big Man, he drink her blood like it was whiskey, so let 'em scream, let 'em scream. She beat her fists into her stomach. From her mouth came the words, "Let 'em scream!"

She began walking faster, her fists beating her hips like she was trying to fly; and she flew, her trash bags floating in the morning breeze behind her, her open-toed hiking boots barely touching down on the pavement; she felt light as she ran. *Let 'em scream! Let 'em scream!* The ax in her heart going *choppity-chop-chop!* She brushed people at the bus stop. They laughed and gasped and swore at her. *Let 'em scream all they want, it's out of my hands, can't go back into the Screaming House!* The chopping of her heart slowed her. She heaved, gasping for breath, leaning against a brick wall. There, on the other side of a gas station, was the bridge, and beneath it, the place where Nadine's grave had been.

When Mattie caught her breath, she trudged towards the bridge.

And my baby, forgive me. Forgive me for letting 'em do it to you. I didn't know, my baby, I didn't know. He said he was just going to make you better. I didn't know.

2.

Ted watched: Rachel spread-eagled on the bed, ripping her dress off with her bare hands. Pocketbooks and sports coats lay between her skin and the bedspread. Beneath this bedroom, down in the living room, the housewarming party continued, the laughing, the stereo blaring "Tuxedo Junction." Ted could even make out the sound of Hugh's voice booming over the rest, "What's the name of the game?"

Ted dove into Rachel, sliding across her tummy, catching her by her breasts, folding into her like a scrambled egg, into her skin, into her moist warm body. And she cried out, but he slapped a hand over her mouth, and she bit down, drawing blood. And for Ted it was ecstasy like he'd never felt, like he was shooting himself into a mystery—

Other voices invaded his erotic dream.

One, the clock radio. The alarm was set for nine and had apparently gone off. A DJ said, ". . . And it's ten o'clock on an oldies fave Labor Day weekend with yours truly, the slime ball of the airwaves, Sludgeman, and I'm gonna lick out your inner ear with this blast from the past, the Monkees, and 'Daydream Believer' . . ."

The other sound, his father's voice.

"You're not taking me to any hospital," Winston Adair said.

Ted awoke slowly. First thoughts: *What time is it? What was I dreaming? Who's standing over me?* The dream left a sticky residue in his underwear; it was the first wet dream he'd had in years. The apartment smelled like crap, thanks to the Old Man's messiness coupled with his unwillingness to open any of the windows. When Ted had come in the previous night the Old Man had gone so far as to try and nail the windows shut. Ted, too tired to argue, told him, "After this weekend, pop, we go in for an exam, okay?" Then it had been off to erotic dreamland with his brother's wife.

While the Monkees sang on the radio, his father stood beside the bed looking down at him. Ted rubbed his eyes, coughing. "Pop? What's—"

His father stood beside the bed, holding something in his hand.

The object in his father's left hand was a hammer. Ted was not used to seeing it—he never used it himself. Ted avoided manual labor as often as possible. He usually kept the hammer in a drawer in the kitchen, along with a plastic case full of nails and some screwdrivers. For a moment he wondered if his father was still nailing down windows to keep the wasps out.

Winston Adair was naked. His bloated pink flesh gave him the appearance of a skinned animal—he had been losing so much weight that folds of skin, deprived of their usual fat, hung like pancakes down his sides, under his arms, along his neck. He looked like a walking cadaver whose innards had been sucked out. With his right hand he was playing with his balls; with his left he took swipes at the air with the hammer. "Buzzing, buzzing, all around us," his father said, grinning. "You heard of the lord of the flies? Well the old black whore, she's queen of the wasps, she is, and you know what they're telling me, those wasps? All the buzzing in this old brain? Son, they're telling me I got no choice but to high-tail it over to the Screaming House and set that house on fire, send them all back to Hell where they come from!"

His bloodshot eyes fixed on the hammer. As if every bit of energy the Old Man possessed was concentrated on holding it steady as it hit the air.

And still his hands trembled; the hammer wobbled; folds of skin shivered.

"Put it down, pop," Ted commanded, trying to sound in control. He sat farther up in bed, kicking the sheets off his legs.

"You hear them buzzing?" His father was sweating. "No

doctor, no hospital, boy, they're gonna buzz right in between the sheets. But I *can't* go back there, Ted, and no hospital's gonna keep them from getting to me."

"Give me the hammer, pop." Ted sat up, kneeling. He extended the palm of his hand.

On the radio: "Wasn't that a sweet tune, all you virgins of the world? But the world isn't really like that, is it? It's a nasty, naughty place, and Sludge had himself a tough night last night. Sludgeman knows what goes on out there while you're listening, I know about your *kind*, yeah, Sludgeman likes it when you talk dirty to him, so give me a call right now, kick your boyfriends and girlfriends out of bed, and ring me up at . . ."

His father's voice steamed. "You don't believe me, Ted, but all I've told you is true. They're trying to buzz me right over to that place. I have given up Hugh and Rachel to that house, to what is in that house. But I'm not dumb enough to go there. Do you have any idea what the housekeeper is going to do?"

"It's okay, pop, it's cool, just give me the hammer."

"She was drawn to Draper House, you know, and she died there, but something evil, another waiting spirit, invaded her flesh, and she now belongs to the house. She's the Housekeeper, boy, and she's the wet nurse to that . . . *abomination.*"

"The hammer."

"She's the one renting that apartment, Ted, calls herself Deerfield. But she is as old as the house, her *spirit* is as old as the house and what it contains. And do you know what she's going to do, Ted? Any fucking idea?"

"Pop."

"She's got the aborted fetus from my daughter Nadine, my daughter and one of my long line of girlfriends. And the housekeeper's going to bring him back, bring Gil DuRaz back in the flesh, but not just him, boy, but every breath of evil in that house, in the flesh, brought into our world. As some kind of Messiah of the damned. I saw its face, son. It was part me and part that little girl, but mostly something else, something scrawled across its bloody chewing flesh that looked like the inside of somebody's festering wound. You think I'm insane, but so the fuck what? If it happens, if that monster is born, insanity's going to be nothing compared with what happens. Insanity will be a goddamn *blessing!* But what do I care? I'll be dead soon enough. I'm old, I'm dying, I can hear the buzzing in the walls. Let the world go to hell, let it burn, let it buzz. I'll be dead, boy. Let the bomb drop right on top of my grave, let it mushroom over this sky like a rainbow, spray the fucking wasps with Raid, let it all die when I die! But son, a baby needs a mother, even a fucking monster fetus, and they got one, I've *given* them one. And the Housekeeper is going to stuff the new mother with that creature from Hell, is going to use her as an incubator, and when it's ready, when it's ready to be fully born, *Ted my boy,* it will use her body like a host and eat its way out of her."

From the radio, "And Sludge is now gonna spin three in a row from the BeeGees, so disco down, babies . . ."

"Pop, please, the hammer."

"You don't believe me, but screw belief! Nobody believes in nothing, but I tell you, son, if you'd been there, the night of the riots, the night we all drank that girl's blood, if you'd seen what I saw, you'd *believe.*"

3.

The grave had filled with mud. Mattie bent over it, imprinting her face against it. The mud was cool, like a reassuring touch on her cheek, on her forehead. She began digging with her bare hands through the soft dirt, water squeezing against her fingers, digging, tossing mud back over her shoulders, burrowing beneath the mud until she found it.

Nadine's skull.

It was covered with slick wet strands of grass and dirt. Mattie carried it down to the creek, dipping it into the water as if in baptism. Gradually the skull came clean. The lower jaw was gone. It was a small skull, and she closed her eyes, feeling along the top, the sides, the ridges of bone that rose up and fell, and she imagined that she was bathing her daughter, washing her hair, wiping her face with cool water. She kept her eyes closed, imagining that Nadine was there, with her, and not off in the world of the dead. Mattie kissed

her forehead, cradling her daughter's upturned face, rocking
back and forth on her knees, singing a lullaby.

Then her daughter spoke to her.

Through the skull.

It was faint, as if from some great distance, and then it
was in her ear, buzzing.

And as Mattie listened, she knew what she would have to
do.

She knew it was time.

4.

The music on the radio continued.

Ted said, "The hammer, come on, now."

"None of it should matter, boy, we all have to die
sometime, it's the way of all flesh, we're born to die, so what
the hell? Let the monster be born, let it disembowel her
when it's delivered, let the demons of Hell rejoice!"

Winston Adair swung the hammer down. Ted slid to the
far side of the bed quickly. The hammer thudded against his
pillow.

"Shit, pop!" Ted leapt out of bed.

"We're all gonna die anyway, boy," Winston giggled,
foam dribbling from his mouth, "it don't make no never-
mind! It's getting closer, gonna buzz around and around and
around until it stings you. Between you and me, I'd rather
get ripped to shreds by the talons of the demon than stung to
death by the wasps out of that black whore's cooze. And
when you got wasps after you, you better sure as shit have a
fly swatter. What's it gonna take to make you believe, boy?"
Winston twirled the hammer around, swinging it down
between his own legs, smashing his testicles. He dropped to
his knees. "This?" he coughed, *"this?"*

"Pop!" Ted rushed over to him.

Winston held the hammer up to warn Ted away. He
swung it through the air in front of him.

Ted stumbled back. The hammer just missed his knees.

Winston pounded the hammer right above his own eyes,
whispering, *"This?"* as it smushed into his forehead.

Ted heard the crack of bone, but it might as well have been a crack in the universe, a rip down the side of reality.

He had no voice to scream.

Winston continued smashing his own head in until it caved in, a bloody pulp, a swirling nest made of gray paper and pomegranate juice.

Ted thought he heard it, the buzzing sound.

His father's mouth went slack, sagging open.

Blood obscured his teeth, his tongue.

And then the wasps flew out from the red, gaping chasm of the Old Man's mouth, and Ted tried hard to get his vocal cords to flex in just the right sequence, just the perfect arrangement for a scream. But Ted had never had to scream before, and to scream the right way you've got to practice just like with anything else. Maybe if Ted had screamed then a neighbor would come running. He had neighbors. He knew he had neighbors and if he screamed loud enough they'd be pounding at the door. But Ted had no screams in him. He rasped instead, he hissed, he moaned.

On the radio, "Staying Alive" was playing.

The Old Man grinned a river of blood. "Now you believe, boy, *now?*"

5.

"Mr. Big Man's gone, Baron Samedi got him now," Mattie said to her daughter's skull. She twisted some of her plastic cloak through the empty eye sockets, wrapping the skull up into it. "You send wasp to take his spirit home, take him away from the baron. But you and me, Nadine, you and me'll stop that house from screamin'."

And then Mattie stopped in her tracks.

She was speaking aloud; she knew she was speaking aloud, the vibrations were humming up her throat, her teeth were clicking together, the sounds were coming out clearly, completely.

But the voice was her daughter's.

THIRTY-THREE

DREAMLAND TEA

1.

I'm not pregnant.

It was Rachel's first thought upon waking. She was aware of a smell in the room, heat, and stale air. Sweat on her back, on her neck. Sheets twisting about her legs.

Hugh?

Her eyes were sore from crying, her head ached from wringing out the tears. She'd cried all day Sunday—but was Sunday already gone? Was it really Monday morning? Or was this Sunday morning, still? Sunday night? She had the vaguest memory of swallowing at least one of the antidepressants she had kept in a shoe box beneath the bathroom sink. Just one pill. Or had it been two? No more than two. She had to consider her sphere—*wait, there* is *no sphere. Never was a little subdividing ovum. I was just late. I was just imagining it.*

She stretched her arm lazily across the bed; Hugh's pillow was hard and flat, no indentation where his head would've sunk down into it.

"Hugh?"

Rachel somehow expected him not to be there.

But why?

"Hugh?" She heard her own voice as if she'd thrown it, and now it came back to her. How could she expect him to be there—down the hall, in the bathroom shaving, whistling, putting the tea kettle on the stove. *But, God, did I really throw him out of the house?*

Had she done that or merely dreamed it? If this really was

Monday morning, where was he? Why wouldn't he have come back home? Didn't he know how much she needed him?

A sharp pain like an icicle thrust between the hemispheres of her brain momentarily blotted out the thought of Hugh. Like a hangover, but with a sweet edge. Her father, as he lay dying and coughing in his hospital bed, told her, "Pain's never bad, sweetheart, it's just part of the transformation. It's resisting the pain that hurts, but if you just give it its due, well, it's just another way of feeling is all." *Smoke rose up above her father's head, from his flared nostrils, up to the ceiling, circling around itself, and the smoke became bubbles drifting out the hospital window, popping as it met the heat and the stale air.* Rachel was losing consciousness again, she was drifting downward into her pillow. *Back to sleep, oh, thank you Nanny Deerfield for sleep and for that wonderful dreamland tea you make special for boys and girls, thank you. Antidepressants and dreamland tea from dear Nanny Dreadful.* She was sleeping and dreaming of an entire field full of running deer, all of them leaping over the yellow grass, the young bucks butting their heads, and the fawn nursing from the young doe.

And Rachel dreamed that she awoke sometime later and Mrs. Deerfield stood at the foot of the bed, beyond the grasp of the writhing sheets. But it was daddy standing there, not Mrs. Deerfield, and daddy said, "Nothing wrong after all, she's sleeping, and sleep will take care of it." And Rachel felt good in her dream, and then the haze descended again and she met blackness with her sweet dreams.

2.

Mrs. Deerfield had heard Rachel breaking the china and had come up the back way, from the crib up through the vanity, through the rubble that was the vanity. Rachel had been frightened when she'd heard the footsteps coming from that end of the house, but it was only Mrs. Deerfield after all.

"I was afraid you might hurt yourself, dear," Mrs. Deerfield said. She wore a green kimono and looked like she hadn't slept a wink the way Rachel also had not slept a wink.

"I'm just breaking dishes," Rachel said, not even pretend-ing to make sense.

"I've made some tea, dear, to help you sleep." Mrs. Deerfield offered her a cup and it tasted like raspberries and cream. Rachel was beginning to feel calm again. "It's full of veetamins," she said as Rachel drank up, "and those sorts of horrendous ingredients that go into healthful solutions. A touch of brandy, too. I call it dreamland tea."

"I don't drink," Rachel told her as she finished the last drop in her cup. "I don't really drink, but I want to scream."

Mrs. Deerfield said nothing. Rachel caught something in the older woman's face: a smile? Not a smile. A grimace. For a second she thought Mrs. Deerfield was in pain. Pain is our friend. It's resisting the pain that hurts. If you just give it its due . . .

"You've been so sweet, thank you so much," Rachel said as Mrs. Deerfield walked her upstairs to her bed.

"It's me should thank you, dear."

"I thought I was going to be a mommy. An acre of kiddos. All screaming."

"You'll make a wonderful mommy."

"I don't know about that, I just don't know about that." Rachel felt goofy as she lay across the sheets while Mrs. Deerfield closed the curtains. White noise of the fan—Hugh would like that, but Rachel didn't give a fuck what Hugh would like. Hugh would not like the way she'd destroyed the Havilland china, their wedding present from her mother.

"Two birds with one stone," Rachel murmured, still tasting dreamland tea in the back of her throat.

Mrs. Deerfield smiled that beautiful gap-toothed grimace. "Yes, dear, two birds with one stone."

Rachel awoke tasting something sour. A small red stain on the pillow next to her head. *Did I cough that up?*

She felt queasy standing up, getting off the bed. The sunlight through the bedroom curtains was too bright for such an early hour. She didn't want to look outside to see that the world was going on all around her in a pale imitation of normal life.

There was no note from Hugh on the dressing table. All husbands should leave notes for their wives on the dressing table even when the wives kick them out of the house. Hugh always left notes for her whenever he went out. Rachel left notes, too, but hers were Post-it Notes and messages scrawled on steamed bathroom mirrors.

"Let's Pretend!" she had shouted at him, covering her face, kicking her legs out to push him away. They had just made love on the rug in the living room after the housewarming party. "Let's fucking not pretend anymore, let's just get down to the real thing."

Rachel sat back down on the bed. The mattress was hard. Her back was achy; she'd been sleeping on her back and stomach all wrong. She leaned back into the pillow. *Falling through the pillow.* She coiled around Hugh's pillow, sank into her pillow, rubbed his pillow between her knees and kept it there. Comfortable. Sleepy.

3.

"Did I just do something?" he asked. Hugh had that face—he looked like a little boy who didn't know when he'd been naughty.

She didn't mention the blood, or the fact that the blood meant there was no sphere. Maybe there had been one, maybe she'd had a mini-miscarriage. Nature, at any rate, had once again taken care of it. Nature in all her brutal perfection had cut her womb open and had let it bleed.

She didn't say anything to him, but wouldn't let him come near her while she cried.

The world was quiet on Sunday morning after the party.

She began smoking cigarettes—there was that pack of Marlboro Lights in her purse, and she chain-smoked them one after another until they were all gone.

"I know I've—" he began. Hugh was always beginning things he couldn't finish: law, the vanity, fatherhood. So very Hugh.

"Let's Pretend!" she shouted.

After he was gone she realized she was having a migraine headache and hadn't even noticed. Rachel felt then that she would never again let a migraine headache bother her because things like this could block it out. Things like wanting to scream but not being able to, not loud enough, not the way she could dream of screaming.

Then she began breaking the china, one dish at a time, against the walls. She thought of her mother on her date with Mr. Martin—David, and Hugh, and the lost spheres of the free world, and daddy puffing on his cigarettes dying like that just because she hadn't been as good a girl as he would've liked her to be. But just give pain its due. Pain is our friend.

Of all the things that could've been on her mind, she did not think of the baby she heard bawling from downstairs because it had become a constant for her, like her migraine, and she was beyond all that, beyond pain, beyond caring.

4.

"Getoutgetoutgetout." But Rachel didn't scream. She was holding that scream in. The scream she had in her was special. She had one good scream to give and she was saving it.

Rachel felt as if she were watching herself sleep. She floated above her own body, looking down at herself: greasy hair, make-up wiped clean with drained emotion, cracked lips. Her arms were curled around her knees; her legs were pale white. Hugh's pillow was tucked up between her knees.

"Enough," Hugh said and went out the French doors to the patio, through the back gate.

The phone was ringing. It tickled her ear, and Rachel watched herself roll farther into the sheets, away from the sound.

She watched Hugh walk down the alley, and for a moment she thought he looked back. But then she realized it was just Let's Pretend because she knew that he would never look back to see her again. She was beyond that. She would hurl her wedding-gift china at the walls and she would put it all in the broken past.

Hugh?

Scraping in the room. Her eyes were sealed shut with crusty sleep. The feeling of being watched. In the back of her throat she tasted the bitterness of dreamland tea. Things moving in the room. She could barely lift her eyelids wide enough to see through them. Hugh must be back, Hugh must be back and maybe he would be begging her forgiveness, or maybe he wouldn't but she would overlook what he'd done to her. What had he done to her? Something, she knew he'd done something. *No, it was what he* hasn't *done.*

She tried to focus on whatever was there on the bed next to her. A shoe? A glove? A children's toy? A small baby shaking a rattle? Her sphere, with its tiny hands clutching a noisy rattle, shaking, shaking, shaking.

She was too tired to even lift her head, too tired to move. Her arms and legs felt like stones.

The taste of raspberries and cream and cigarettes on her lips.

A rat the size of her fist sat up next to her face in bed and in its jaws it carried a small dead mouse. The rat shook the mouse violently, and the mouse let out a high-pitched squeak that could only have been a scream.

But Rachel watched all this from above her bed, and could not awaken her body which lay awake and asleep and staring and listening to the sound of the mouse screaming.

THIRTY-FOUR

IF I HAD A HAMMER

1.

On the clock radio in Ted Adair's condo, the Sludgeman said, "Looks like another hellacious day, my little Sludgettes, truly hellacious . . ."

The bedroom smelled like overflow from a sewer, like a butcher's shop on a hot afternoon. Ted's chest was covered with some of his father's blood and Ted's own dribbling spit as he rocked back and forth on his knees as if praying to the Old Man, crouched before him.

"Shit, boy, that bastard won't let me die, that goddamn voodoo abortionist won't let me rest." Winston Adair's voice whistled through the ridge of broken front teeth as he continued hammering away at his face.

Ted didn't want to look at the Old Man. He wanted to crawl inside himself. He wanted to wake up from what he hoped was a nightmare. A spray of blood shot out of the Old Man's nose, speckling his throat. Blood spurted from the open wound of red pulp just above his father's eyes. The nose was completely gone. The Old Man's jaws sagged into his jowls—a few good hits with the hammer had separated the lower jaw from the rest of his skull. His pale skin was dripping like an ice cream cone in the sun. *Here comes the blood.* Ted had watched while his father hammered off each of his toes, all ten of them, and then slammed the hammer into his ankles.

From the clock radio, the DJ droned on. "It looks like it's gonna be a hellacious ninety-five degrees today and even hotter come Labor Day, yes, boys and girls, another lovely

Washington day of smelling your favorite armpits, and for those of you who love to sweat and sweat to love, I've got a tune coming up from . . ."

The wasps that had flown from the Old Man's mouth spun around his head, alighting across the matted red scalp before floating off like scraps of burnt paper towards the window. Their tiny blood-encrusted bodies smudged red prints on the glass until the lower half of the window seemed to be stained dark crimson.

Ted knelt in front of his father, his mouth open, staring. He had no scream in him, *and, anyway, if I did my neighbors would be pissed at me for ruining their Labor Day weekend.* "Oh, pop, pop, pop, God, pop, juh-juh-juh-just puh-puh-put—" Ted felt his mind was sluicing out from his skull just like the Old Man's brains were: *Make it stop, make him die, make him die. He's supposed to die. Can't live with your skull half off and your testicles shot like twin golf balls splat against the goddamn walk-in closet doors, can't keep talking when your teeth are somewhere down your esophagus and your tongue looks like you been chewing on razor blades. Cheese Whiz, Daddio, didn't anyone ever tell you the rules? Don't you know you're supposed to die when your body's doing the Mashed Potato from the inside out?*

Ted tried catching the hammer in his fingers as the Old Man swung it down to shatter his own left kneecap. The hammer swung wide and missed.

The Old Man grinned toothlessly, jabbing the hammer's claw into his right ear, its thick tines scraping away most of the lobe; still he pried further into his brain like he was opening up a boiled lobster. "You believe now, boy? I told you that voodoo priest had a hold over me, and I guess he won't let go. He's gonna use Rachel to get into the flesh again, and he's bringing with him every perversion that house has to offer, boy, and he'll be born like a fucking monster."

Ted leapt up, knocking his father backwards. As the Old Man fell, Ted heard a sickening crack like the crack of a crisp breadstick. *But,* Ted reasoned, *it's only one more cracking bone among the multitude of those already smashed up.* The hammer flew from his father's hand and thudded against the wall, just beneath the window. Wasps murmured angrily as they tapped their way around the window ledge, searching for a way out.

"Oh, son, Gil DuRaz will not let me die, I partook, boy, I partook of the girl, I et her and she tasted so damn sweet and now they want me for leftovers. They've got their mother now, they've got the fetus, how the fuck much more do I owe that bokor?" The Old Man leaned against his son. Ted clasped the broken, torn body to his. Dampness seeped from his father's flesh to his. The Old Man stopped babbling. Stopped moving.

I am crazy, I am insane, and I am imagining this. I am hallucinating. The Old Man is alive, shit, maybe I hallucinated this whole damn morning, maybe I'm still curled up in bed dreaming about Rachel, and this is just some subconscious guilt drama playing out in my head and I'm going to wake up in another hour or two. Maybe another ten minutes and it will be Sunday morning and even the damn clock radio alarm won't have sounded.

On the radio, the Sludgeman said, "I'm gonna be calling your house sometime in the next hour and if you can tell me who your fave-o-rave of the airwaves is, you win a dinner for two at . . ."

Ted hefted his father's body up into his arms. The Old Man was ridiculously light, like a toy with the stuffing coming out. Ted's arms had never felt so weak, so shaky, and yet the Old Man was no burden at all. He laid his father down on his bed, but could not bring himself to look down at the ravaged face.

The hammer lay where it had fallen on the carpet. Stray wisps of blood-dyed hair were caught in the claw.

Did I do it? Am I as far gone as I thought the Old Man was? Was it me who just bludgeoned him? Shit. Ted rubbed his eyes, tears stinging behind the lids. *Got to get clean, clean it off, all that blood. Who'd think a man has that much blood to go around? Get clean, a shower, a shower and a shave and maybe a cup of coffee and then maybe I'll be sane again, yeah, that oughta do the job.*

The DJ said, "You're worthless, you cud-chewing scuzzhound, we play only the best on—"

On his way out of his bedroom, Ted picked up the hammer and smashed it down on his clock radio.

2.

He was in the shower so long his skin began to wrinkle. The water went from boiling hot to ice cold. But the steam had felt good on his skin, and he had that smell of deodorant soap on him and the blood was gone and he had stopped shivering. Ted took his time shaving; combed his hair, sliding some gel into it to keep it neat; brushed each of his thirty-two teeth and flossed. He only looked directly in the bathroom mirror when he drew blood from flossing.

His face was worn and gray and almost as tired as the Old Man's had been.

And then he knew.

Something had knifed right through the skin of the world.

My God. It really happened. He killed himself. The Old Man killed himself, and he still couldn't die.

That voodoo abortionist he was babbling about, yeah, that's who got him. Came for him and wouldn't let him die. Always keep an open mind, you never know what's going to want to crawl in there and start gnawing away. An open mind and closed eyes. The Old Man wants me to believe? Well, I ain't sayin' yes and I ain't sayin' no, I'm just sayin' maybe.

He stepped out of the bathroom counting the number of parquet tiles on the floor until he came to the hall carpet (thirty-six squares of tile).

I ain't sayin' yes.

In the bedroom would be a corpse who was not yet allowed to give up the spirit. *Feel it in my bones, in my blood, way down in my gut with last night's supper just about to go up or down or sideways.*

"He won't let me die."

His father's words echoed in his mind.

When Ted entered his bedroom he avoided looking at the bed and the body on the bed. He looked above the bed, to the white wall above the headboard.

In blood, the Old Man had written: HELPRACHEL.

Wasps danced frantically around the windowpane.

Ted, calmly, went over to the window, brushing the wasps away. They stung his hands, but he paid them no mind.

With his numb fingers, he cracked the window open. "Ain't sayin' no."

The wasps darted out into the shimmering air. Down below the building, a middle-aged woman was out walking her Shar-Pei. The dog urinated on Ted's Mercedes. The woman wore curlers and congratulated her pet for doing his business; she swatted at wasps that flew around her.

Ted shut the window.

The words were burned into his mind.

HELPRACHEL.

"Just sayin' maybe," he said before turning around to make sure the Old Man was really and truly and finally dead.

THIRTY-FIVE

HELPRACHEL

1.

Ted lifted the phone receiver. His hands trembled so much he tossed it out of his hand. The high-pitched *pips* started up a few seconds later. Ted gazed down at the fallen phone and said, "Hi, Rachel? Just thought you ought to know the Old Man's duh-duh-dead." He laughed, slapping his chest. *Get real, Ted, my boy, let's have a trifle more coordination between mind and tongue.* "Get Hughie and get out of the house, Rachel. Don't ask me why, I don't fucking know, but it's something that the Old Man set in motion years ago and if I sound crazy, well, then I guess I am, but just get out for a while, get as far the fuck away from Draper House as you possibly can."

Sounds sensible enough, Ted, my boy, now all's you got to do is pick up the phone and call her and then maybe it'll be copacetic. "I ain't sayin' no." He barely recognized the whispery voice that came from his throat.

He left the phone where it was.

Nope, can't really call her up with this kind of news. Call the cops? Not a great idea with a dead body in my bedroom. Particularly one this far hammered away. Cops might not be too sympathetic to my plight.

He wandered back out to the living room feeling as if a grenade had rolled right into his condo and blown up in his face—*yeah, that's right, I got shards of the Old Man's insanity in my skull.*

In the freezer, he found a half-full gallon of vodka.

When Ted decided what he would do, where he would go, he took the bottle with him.

Driving was easiest for Ted when he was drunk. With a little medicine in him he didn't have to worry too much about where he was headed. He'd dressed quickly, almost forgetting his shoes in his eagerness to get out of his place *(don't go back in that bedroom again, Ted, m'boy, you don't need to double-check to see what's dripping all over the white carpet).*

In blood: HELPRACHEL.

Uncharacteristic of the Old Man even in death, even *after* death.

Hell, Ted thought as he dropped his car keys on the sidewalk for the sixth time, *who'd the Old Man ever help in his life?*

The hard part about being drunk so early in the day was getting the keys in the door of the car. *Damn it, they make these things too small and slippery.*

The vodka had made it all go down easier, just like it had when the Old Man had cracked. *Cracked, but not yet* hammered. It was all crazy, but vodka helped Ted over the rough spots of credibility: *I ain't sayin' yes and I ain't sayin' no, I'm just sayin' maybe.* Finally he managed to unlock the car door without dropping the keys; he opened the door wide and checked under the seats for wasps before sliding in behind the wheel.

His eyes blurred with tears. He tried turning on the windshield wipers to slash his tears away. *You are drunk, son, you sure you didn't hammer your own head in?*

He started the car, swerving to avoid a boy riding by on his bike. *HELPRACHEL. Hallucination—that's what this whole damn thing is. You didn't see the Old Man dent himself silly and then keep yapping away like a manic schnauzer, you been walking in your sleep, Tedward, you been drinking too much of the Russian poison and dry humping your pillow, lusting after your brother's wife. You just* want *Rachel to need your help, you want her the way you want every toy you've ever had and now you feel guilty 'cause it's your asshole brother's wife and you're a sinner and now guilt's going into overdrive on the fuel of Absolut—ain't sayin' yes.* He pressed his foot down on the accelerator as the light at the corner of Q Street and Connecticut turned yellow; his silver car swerved, screeching as he turned up Connecticut Avenue, pedestrians scattering, shouting curses. Ted barely noticed them. *The wasps? Well, bugs always get in places in the summer. That's it. They just squeezed through a crack last night and the Old Man swallowed them while he was snoring. I ain't sayin' no.* He waited at the light on Columbia Road, tapping his fingers on the steering wheel. He glanced over at a girl in a VW Bug that had pulled up next to him.

He could still smile, that was good. *See? I haven't cracked, I can be a regular guy.*

The girl, a pretty redhead, wrinkled her nose and quickly looked the other way. Like he was the most repulsive thing on the face of the earth.

Fuck you, too, sweetheart. Ted brought his gaze up to the rearview mirror. All he saw were his eyes: bloodshot.

And in those eyes a certain wildness. The girl must've seen that insanity there in the baby blues.

The eyes of someone out of control.

A madman.

Just sayin' maybe.

The light turned green.

At Hammer Street, on the edge of the park, Ted spun the wheel into the curb, going up onto it and then down to the road again. He parked his Mercedes with a ridiculous amount of care for someone who had stopped giving a fuck.

I won't pretend to know what's going on. Maybe they'll put me away like I should've put the Old Man away weeks ago, before his madness started rubbing off on me.

But I'll get Rachel out of there and then show her what's in my apartment. And if the Old Man is back there laughing his head off at the clever trick he played on me, then they can give me some more booze and I'll go off and be a bona fide alcoholic for the rest of my natural-born days.

But if I take her home and there's a corpse and blood on the walls, then she can have me put away and she will be safe.

2.

Rachel, in bed, dreaming. In her dream someone was at the door. Knocking. Calling her name. Was it Hugh? She went to the door in her dream and opened it. It was not Hugh standing behind the dream door but a black man in a dark shirt and pants, a top hat on his head. When he opened his mouth to speak to her she felt as if she were being sucked into the mouth, and the mouth became a dark cave whose monstrous teeth became rows and rows of babies, their clicking talons raised to her, their mouths like balloon lips, opening and closing to drink her milk.

3.

Ted smashed his vodka bottle against the front door of Draper House. "Rachel! It's Ted! Open up!" The stone balustrades on either side of the steps seemed to have grown around him, fattening each time he shouted for her. He was standing in a cold, shadowed spot, there at the entrance, and the sunlight reached everywhere on the street and in the park, everywhere except this front porch and these steps and this door.

When the door finally drew open, its wood squeaking against the floor of the lower hallway, it was not Rachel Adair standing behind it, but someone who invited him in nonetheless.

THIRTY-SIX

THE MAGIC TOUCH

1.

Hugh passed out drunk on a bench in DuPont Circle; he covered his face with the front section of the Sunday *Post*. He had spent the morning and early part of the day wandering, just ambling drunkenly from sidewalk to sidewalk. It was a holiday weekend and not many people were out early. The city seemed dead. He liked it that way because he felt dead on the inside like an eggshell with the yolk sucked out. He had clutched his stomach in pain when he felt the need to throw up—*don't want to be sick, just want to die.* At around ten in the morning he passed a shop window and saw a man staring back at him. The man's sandy blond hair stuck out from his head like he'd slept on it wrong. His face was gray and pasty; his shoulders slumped forward. He was shaking, shivering. His eyes were smudged with sleeplessness, his lips cracked dry like water-starved earth. Hugh couldn't look directly into the man's eyes because he knew *the man is me.*

Let's Pretend, Hugh, that you're not a loser, that she'll forgive you and take you back, that it's going to work out.

Then a conflicting thought shuttled its thread through his mind: *To hell with her! She wants you to be something you're not, screw it, maybe you're better off a single man living as you please.*

He felt in his drunkenness that there might as well have been a cartoon angel on his right shoulder and a devil on his left.

He tried calling Rachel from a pay phone, letting it ring

ten times, but there was no answer. A family walking by him, all dressed up for church, eyed him suspiciously. *I guess I look pretty scary, but fuck you, too.* A man standing with him at a crosswalk handed him a dollar. "Don't spend it on liquor," the man said. "My advice to you is get a job, buddy, it don't get no better." Hugh watched the pudgy hand fold the dollar and put it into Hugh's hand. He couldn't bring himself to look the man in the face.

Oh, well, at least I'm a dollar richer.

But most of all he just wanted to die, to lay down and give up the ghost.

He stretched out across the bench in the park at DuPont Circle hoping that death would come to him. Before he lay the newspaper across his face, he saw the clouds gathering in the sky and thought: *Even God's going to piss on me.*

2.

He awoke suddenly. "Rachel?" Something had touched him. Something or someone. It had grown dark—clouds hanging low in the sky coupled with the sun pressing westward. Someone had grabbed his ankle, and before he sat up he instinctively felt for his wallet. It was there, in his hip pocket. The newspapers had dropped from his face and now lay crumpled beneath his head forming a makeshift pillow. He had drooled on them—newsprint ran together in a black smudge. His tongue felt like salted meat. What he tasted in his mouth—the product of not having brushed his teeth as well as the unique mixture of drinks from the housewarming party—well, his mouth tasted like he'd kissed the wrong end of a dead cat.

"I'm talkin' to you," a woman said as he sat up. "You the man that lives in the Screamin' House. I seen you there."

He didn't recognize her at first: just another bag lady. She was fat and dark and dirty. He heard thunder and thought it might be the rumbling in her throat, but it was just thunder. Rain was on its way.

"You been sleepin' too long," she said.

The crazy woman. He remembered her—when Rachel

had tried to start her car, this woman shouting in their back alley.

"You been sleepin', mister, but the house don't sleep, it just screams 'n' screams, and now, mister, now your woman gonna scream, too."

From in between one of the folds of her rippling trash bags he saw what looked like a human skull.

And from the empty eye socket of that skull: a wasp. It crawled along the orbital ridge, a finely-cut blue sapphire. And then it flew towards him.

Jesus, you meet all kinds of creeps when you sleep in the park.

Then he felt the bite on the back of his neck.

He slapped at the wasp. *Gotcha, you sonofabitch.*

Feeling that needle-prick pain shoot into him, he saw *in blood: HELPRACHEL, written on a white wall.*

He heard voices whispering, indistinct.

He thought he was passing out again, everything faded to black as if the light bulb of the universe had finally died. But still, he *felt* consciousness. He was in a dark cold place, and he knew where he was: *the crib, below Draper House, the place he'd thought he'd seen that* thing *with my father's eyes, that delirium tremens hallucination, that inhuman jellyfish pulling itself further down into darkness, almost human, the bluest of eyes, almost the way a baby might look if it had been born about five months too early. A baby not born of a human mother.*

Hugh saw before him *a fetus floating in a jar. It opened its eyes, screaming with the Old Man's voice, "You saw it, Hugh, you weren't just drunk, you were* enlightened, *the house is unclean, it's the asshole of the universe, son. Verena Standish lost her children to it, and now you'll lose Rachel. They're gonna make her the mother of it, of that monster child, it's gonna eat its way into her, that abomination from Hell!"*

3.

"Rachel," Hugh gasped. *It's the hangover, the Queen Mother of hangovers, the place where hangovers are conceived, born and die right here in my head—must've slaughtered a few million brain cells this time out.* He was looking at the dead wasp in his hand. He had smushed it after all. But the insect began wriggling again, getting up on its small legs. It stretched its wings out and took off from the palm of his hand. The insect flew up into the darkening sky.

It seemed to him that all the sounds of the earth had stopped, that someone had thrust the tip of a pencil in both his ears, because he was no longer aware of the crunch of the grass underfoot or the chatter of teenagers crossing the Circle or the traffic or the cries of birds or the growling thunder.

I'm really drunk and so hungover it's like someone's hammering my brains to oatmeal.

Let's Pretend I'm a drunken sot whose wife has finally given him the boot, who finally is going to get what he wants . . .

What do I want?

Sleep. Just sleep.

HELPRACHEL.

Do I want to die?

He was afraid to look back at the bag lady. His hands were shaking, and to try and calm them he pretended that none of it was real, all of it was Let's Pretend: the park, the crazy woman, Rachel, too, all of it. He tried to turn his hands to fists and then unfold them again, but they just shook. He could not keep his hands from shaking. *I want . . .*

"What you want ain't important, mister," the bag lady said, "just like what I want ain't no big deal. What we gotta *do*, what we gotta *do* is stop that house from screamin'." She put her hand to her breast as if in pain. "And I can't do it alone."

4.

Mattie kept one hand on her daughter's skull, hiding it beneath her trash bags of invisibility, and her right hand under her heart. The ax was in her heart again, chopping at it. *Help me, Nadine, just keep me goin' long enough to do this one thing, this one righteous thing. Gotta stop it, gotta stop the house.* The beating of her heart calmed, the chopping grew more faint.

You with me, Nadine?

Mattie thought she heard an answer.

The Mr. Big Man who sat there on the bench was staring at his fingers. *You gotta give him the Magic Touch, Mattie, you gotta make him* see.

She reached over with her right hand and touched his left, the one that held the wasp.

The man flinched, his hand shivering.

Magic Touch, Magic Touch, you gotta work, you gotta make him believe, 'cause Mattie's only got enough fight in her left for the Housekeeper, so I'm gonna need help, gonna need to make him understand.

Mattie felt a tickling in her finger; she was afraid the man would pull away from her—she could smell fear in him, fear and doubt and *even a touch of belief.* Just a slice of believing would be enough, just a rusty kind of believing. She knew he had seen Nadine's unborn child, and that was where the believing in his soul had come from. With her Magic Touch she could tell that he wasn't like the other Mr. Big Men. He was more, but he'd buried it all down, buried himself alive in disbelief. As she held his hand, she heard the words *Let's Pretend* in her mind. He had it in him, *yassir, he does, he got it in there, but way down where you gotta get a shovel and just start diggin'* away.

Through her fingers, she spoke to him: *"You got alotta problems, mister, but you got life and that's better than what the Housekeeper's got—crawlin' with death in that place— you got life and a body to get you places. You gonna run and hide or you gonna fight? You got to get her outta the*

Screamin' House, mister. Things gotta be done, spirit laid to rest. I got the bugs in me. I gottem to help with the Housekeeper, but you gotta get that girl before Baron Samedi gets inside her."

5.

The words hit Hugh in the gut, and he felt the sour vomit of day-old-drunk gin threatening to come up; he wanted the crazy woman not to touch him like that, not on his hand because she seemed to be connected to an electric current. The current stung him and hit nerves in his arm, racing up to his head, to his brain, and then in his brain it felt like doors sliding open, lights flicking on, and behind the doors in the rooms:

bloodstained sheets, the Old Man's battered spirit fighting to remain inside a fragmented, flesh-torn body, using the tips of his blood-spurting fingers like they were fountain pens, scratching letters across the white wall: HELPRACHEL.

Hugh recoiled from touching Mattie's hand as if he'd stuck his fingers into a light socket.

Suddenly, the evening was normal again, all sounds returned, cars honking around the Circle, screeching brakes, men shouting to each other, women scolding children, and children running around the fountain, radios blaring. Hugh felt like he'd been diving down for miles and then was swiftly pulled up, his eyes popping, bursting, and then breaking the surface: Normal Life.

"Look, whoever the hell you are, get away from me," he said. *God, I feel sick, like I'm dead. Oh, Scout, forgive me, please, I love you.* Balancing himself against the peeling green back of the bench, Hugh managed to stand without keeling over.

6.

Mattie Peru watched the man walk off. "I'm gonna make you see, mister."

Holding her daughter's skull with both hands beneath the folds of her trash bags, she felt a wave wash through her:

a walking dead man building a wall of bricks at the crib.

and in her apartment, the Housekeeper holding a sucking half-formed baby, the one that had been taken from Nadine's mutilated womb. The Housekeeper held it up to another woman's wrist. Ragged vertical slices up and down the wrist. The baby was sucking blood from the woman's wrist like milk.

Too late, am I too late?

But the woman nursing the child on her blood wasn't the woman they had chosen as the mother, this woman was older and the Housekeeper said to her, "Betty Kellogg, you'll spoil him."

A vision of the woman upstairs, the one called Rachel, sleeping the sleep of one who has been given the baron's sleeping juice, her bloodstream already turning to ice.

They were preparing her.

Am I too late?

As Mattie came out of her trance, she heard the *choppity-chop-chop* in her heart and felt stabbing pains between her ribs. She held her breath until the ache went away. *Gotta keep goin', Mattie, gotta keep the spirit in this old bag of skin and bones. No more girls gonna die in the house for no Baron Samedi. If I gotta do it alone, I'm gonna. If her man don't care enough for her—it gotta be done.*

She felt warm drops of rain spattering down on her scalp, tapping along the edges of her trash bags. She raised the bags around her neck up over her head like a hood.

Mattie Peru began shivering, but not from cold. Her bags rattled, and she felt her bones chafe against her tired flesh. The taste in the back of her throat was warm and sour, like her daughter's blood.

Mattie knew what waited for her in the house. She knew if she stepped over its threshold, it would mean death. She could stand in the rain and scream at the house and let it do its worst. She would be safe on the outside.

You could just get Mr. Big Man to go in and stop it and you could live, but as this voice tunneled through her brain, she swatted at it. "Nadine," she said aloud, "how am I to do this thing? I am weak, I am nothin' against *that.*"

Nadine, I will die *in there.*

Mattie wiped rain across her face with fear and memory.

But I will die nowhere else. And I will take the screaming with me. And Mr. Big Man would help her.

THIRTY-SEVEN

SLEEPWALKING

1.

"Okay, okay," Rachel slurred her words slightly as she tumbled out of bed, grabbing Hugh's terry cloth bathrobe, "I'm coming, I'm coming." She squinted at the clock on the dresser: 7:00 P.M.

Have I been asleep all day long? Her arms were sore; she thought she must've been sleeping on them all wrong; her back ached, and a muscle spasmed along her lower ribs. Her legs were still asleep—she steadied herself against a bedpost as she slipped her other arm into the sleeve of the bathrobe. An aftertaste from dreamland tea on her tongue: *raspberries? More like drippy licorice and almonds, not cream, not anything sweet.* She combed her fingers through her clotted hair, untangling the greasy strands. She avoided looking in the full-length mirror as she passed, wobbling and stiff legged, the bedroom door. She could barely keep her eyes open and someone was still banging at the front door. *Should never have taken the antidepressant, it must've been that and the brandy that Nanny Dreadful gave me.* Whoever was knocking at the door had been doing it for at least the past hour; she'd been dreaming of things banging.

The hallway was dark; she felt for the light switch when she got to the stairs. She flicked the switch up, and then brought her hand back to her waist. Rachel pressed her fingers against her stomach to stop the dull ache that throbbed there. Her skin was ice cold. She tied the bathrobe together. "Hugh?" Her voice was still groggy from sleep. The brilliance of the hall light hurt her eyes. She covered them as she switched off the light. *Not dark enough to worry about tripping down the stairs.* But her feet weren't working quite right, she had to *think* carefully with each step, feeling around the edge of the stair to make sure she didn't slip. Her legs now seemed rubbery, reminding her of an experiment they used to teach in elementary school where she'd soak a chicken bone overnight in vinegar and it would bend like a plastic straw. She clutched the bannister. *Scout, you are a klutz.* "Hugh?" *Am I still dreaming?*

As she came down into the living room the floor seemed warm, like the heat was on. Where she'd been cold a few minutes before, now she was sweating from heat. She wiped at her forehead. *Fever.*

Whoever had been banging at the front door was now banging on the wall, or a door, or a window, down by the turret room. *Was Hugh back and in one of his rages, tearing down more wall, mad at himself because he wasn't a better husband?*

Only in my dreams.

As she drew closer to the room, she realized the noise wasn't banging at all but scraping and a kind of soft patting. Remembering the morning when she thought she heard a rat *(or babies? Am I off my rocker enough to believe there are babies down that tiny staircase?)*, Rachel approached the end of the hall with caution.

Something was coming up, just a shape emerging from the narrow staircase half hidden in the torn vanity.

Rachel knew that sometimes, when she blinked, she saw things for a fraction of a second—things that weren't there. Something was hanging from the ceiling in the vanity. Had Hugh hung his shirts up along the molding? But not shirts—no, they looked more like—*sacks?*

But as she drew closer, the objects hanging in the vanity became clear to her:

The little boy and girl she'd seen in the park, naked and dressed the way she knew a hunter would dress his kill. They hung upside down, a long wooden pole running through their ankles. The boy, Jamie, opened his mouth and said, "I know how babies are made."

Rachel stood still and waited for this image to disappear. *Fever, antidepressants, brandy, dreamland tea.*

The girl swung around on her pole and reached over and thrust her small hand into her brother's mouth to shut him up, and told him, "You're not supposed to tell her*, you little fool, she'll find out soon enough." Her small white arm was ragged with festering sores. Her hand disappeared up to the wrist into Jamie's mouth. He began making choking noises, his eyes bugging out, as his sister kept pushing her hand further down his throat.*

But then Rachel saw nothing hanging from the molding in the vanity. *Fever dream.* She rubbed her eyes.

She was almost relieved, too tired to worry about her sanity, reassured that it was just a hallucination. *And now, here's another one.* A man, naked from the waist up, sweat glistening across his chest, his hands and arms dusted with gray plaster. Coming up from below. *Is he really here?*

"Oh, Ted," Rachel said, her knees about to give out, a headache thumping gently in her temples, the bitter licorice aftertaste of dreamland tea in her mouth.

Ted smiled. She was sure it was a smile, but her fever twisted his smile into something carnivorous. He was slightly hunched over, too tall for the miniature passage. His hands were soaked with gray mud; he wiped them on his khakis.

"Ted, what are you—I mean, thank God you're here, I'm not feeling too . . ." Rachel stammered.

"Some things have been happening." He was smiling, it was a smile, she was *sure* it was a smile. He came towards her, his palms outward to show how well he'd wiped them clean, as if that mattered, and she could tell by the way he kept looking everywhere but at her that there *was* something dreadfully wrong, something he was afraid to admit to her. "It's in this house, Rachel, something happening here, something to do with the Old Man, and Hugh, and with you."

Am I dreaming? Rachel leaned back against the doorjamb. No children hanging from rods. She felt hungry and weak and sleepy. Mrs. Deerfield's words of admonishment came back to her: *"Must watch what we put in our tummies, dear."*

Ted came up beside her, still unable to look her in the eye. His arms snaked around her, catching her as she fell. *Am I falling?* "Here," he whispered, "let's get you to the window seat." She closed her eyes as the room spun around her.

Opening her eyes again, she was sitting up by the window. In the park, no one played, the swing sets were empty. "Hugh and I had a fight," she said. She pressed her fingers against her robe, down by her stomach. "My tummy's upset."

"I gathered, about the fight." Ted was sitting beside her, his left hand on her right knee.

His right hand on the place where her stomach hurt. *Is he putting his arm around me?*

But it felt good, she needed someone's arm around her, she needed a good strong hug.

"Rachel, I think you should know what happened."

"Mmm?" She was so dizzy; she would get him to help her get back into bed. The thought of bed made her feel good. The thought of drifting down into sleep. The back of her head rested against the windowpane. The glass was warm, molten, curving around her ice-cold head.

"Something's happened, Rachel, and it's this house. Hugh was raving."

"Hugh? When did you talk to—did he say—about house?"

"Raving. What it was doing to the two of you, what the Old Man had done by giving it to you, how it was evil."

"Hugh?"

"Rachel, he went crazy, Rachel, he went off the deep end, Rachel."

"Hugh? Crazy." She let the word sink in, and she nodded dreamily.

"The Old Man died."

She let Ted talk because she was feeling a little nauseated, just in the pit of her stomach.

"He was drunk, Rachel. Hugh was stone dead drunk and he had this hammer."

The bones in her legs began aching, and she would've liked to massage her thighs to get the circulation going again but Ted's snaking arm was in her way. The bones in her legs felt like they were trying to break free from her skin. Like they were ripping through her skin right then. But her bones stayed put. Bones didn't rip through skin. They always stayed put. But they ached so much, they seemed so sore pressed up against her skin.

"Rachel, he broke the door down at my place, he was roaring—"

"Hammer?"

"He killed my father, Rachel. I tried to stop him but he swung out at me with the hammer and I went and called the cops. But by that time the Old Man was dead, and Hugh was screaming at me to leave you alone because he said I was as bad as the Old Man, Rachel. Then he said he was going to come get you, get his wife if he had to take you kicking and screaming out of this house forever. He said it was his responsibility."

"Not Hugh." Rachel shook the thought out of her head; Ted was being so silly. "I know Hugh."

The annoying chirp of the telephone came from down the hall.

"The police," Ted said. "I gave them your number. I should get it."

Rachel sucked air into her lungs. Shock was awakening her; her legs were so sore, but she managed to get up on her feet, leaning on Ted for support. "No," she said, "I'll get it."

She felt as if she were walking on air; her feet making the motions, but not quite touching the ground; Ted's arms holding her up. But she made it to the phone. *Not Hugh, I know Hugh inside and out, I know what he laughs about, I know what can make him cry, I know what his goddamn socks smell like, he's all there in the blue of his eyes, he's all up front, on the surface.*

But the booze. The depression. The fight. Kicking him out. Telling him to go to hell. That night, before the party, seeing the frustration and rage in his face as he took the sledgehammer and crowbar to the vanity wall.

"I know Hugh," she said, lifting the receiver. "Hello?"

No sound. Rachel was about to hang up.

Then, Hugh's voice came on the line. "Scout?"

Rachel covered the receiver with the palm of her hand. Ted said, *"It's him?"*

She nodded.

"Dangerous," he whispered in her ear and his breath was cool.

I know Hugh backwards and forwards.

"Scout?"

"I'm here."

"I want to come home, Scout, I want to come get you."

Ted's whisper was like a fly crawling in her ear. *"He did it, Rachel, and he wants you next. I saw him."*

"Hugh? Where are you?"

"P Street—Rachel, listen, I don't know what, but there's something there, in the house, and I don't want you there alone."

Ted whispered, *"Tell him you're going out."*

Again she covered the receiver. "I can't *lie* to him. He sounds like he's been through hell."

"He wants to drag you there, too. I saw him hammer the Old Man just like he was a fucking nail. Say you're going out."

She gasped into the phone, "Hugh? I'm going . . . out."

"Say it's going to all come out in the wash."

"It's going to all come out in the wash, Hugh, I'll be fine."

Hugh hesitated before speaking again. "Is someone with you?"

"No."

"Look, I'll come get you. I love you, Scout. I'm so damn sorry about the way I've been all summer. Jesus, this whole year. I didn't mean to hurt you."

Rachel shivered, remembering the wild look in his eyes when he'd torn the vanity wall down. It had stung more than if he'd actually hit her. Just that look in his eyes. *Madness.*

"Tell him you'll meet him someplace."

"I'll meet you. Hugh, I'll meet you down at—" *Oh, Christ, what's the name of the bookstore he likes so much?*

"Scout? I'm just ten minutes' walk. I'll come get you."

"No—Hugh—KramerBooks, I'll be at KramerBooks, I'm practically out the door now."

"You sure?"

"Yes. Hugh . . ."

"Scout?"

"Nothing." She hung up the phone.

Ted squeezed his arm around her waist.

She drew away from him instinctively. There was something about Ted as he stood there, something about his *smell*. He'd been drinking, she'd noticed before when he'd brought her into the turret room. But after what he'd apparently been through, anybody might knock back a shot or two. But there was something besides liquor on his breath.

"You're a terrific little liar, Rachel," Ted said, winking at her as she tried to push him away. But his arms kept snaking around her, *inside* the robe, cold and damp on her skin. She had no energy, her limbs felt like jelly. His hands sliding up along her ribs, his thumbs twisting beneath her breasts as he poked and probed them, pinching her armpits, squeezing her. She felt the scream rise in her throat, but all that came out finally was a moan of fear. Ted reached up with one hand, still *scraping* her side, holding her to him, covering her mouth with the palm of his slimy hand. It tasted like *mortar? Is this a dream?*

"Those who clamor," he told her, "we've been listening to you for a while, Rachel." Then in a high-pitched voice he said, *"Howsaboutamousefuck?"*

She struggled against his arms, her robe falling open. Just as she was about to kick him in the groin, her rubbery legs moving in too slow a motion, she saw a large rat poke its head through the zipper in his khakis. It leapt from between his legs and scampered off across the floor. Rachel reached up to Ted's face as he brought his lips down to meet hers; she brought her fingers up to his eyes. Already her vision was going out of focus and sleep seemed to be drawing her back into its dark embrace.

She felt her fingers slide into the soft pudding of his eyes, and when she looked again at his face, working hard to keep her own eyes open, she saw his eyes hanging like gummy strands of runny eggs from the tips of her fingers.

2.

Am I dreaming? She lay in the darkness of sleep.

Can't be happening, can't be happening. Are-you-there-Hugh Adair?

A woman's voice drawing her up through sleep almost to consciousness. "I knew the dose should've been stronger."

Mrs. Deerfield's voice. "You silly cow, if it had been any *stronger* she'd be dead now and where would that leave us?"

Dark purples swirled in Rachel's mind, dancing with dots like mosquitoes, and she wondered where the dream had begun—*down the hallway to the vanity, she was walking, it was a dream after all. A dream because babies surrounded her, dozens of babies, spheres with arms and legs. Their mouths opening upwards to her. At the end of the hall, at the vanity, hanging up to dry: the children from the park. Skin ripped open from their stomachs to their chins, torn and hollow. Jamie kept talking even with his sister's fist in his mouth. "It's where babies come from. But if it's not all done it has to crawl back in. What do you suppose would happen if the half-done baby couldn't find its mother's cunny again?"*

Purple haze of sleep again, as if she were rising out of the dream, about to open her eyes.

Mrs. Deerfield said, "And you, you stupid fool, you're here for one purpose and one purpose only, to guard the wall, your sleazy hands all over her, she can't be damaged, twit, if she's to carry the child."

That's right, Rachel nodded in her dream, keeping her eyes closed, tasting the licorice and almonds in her mouth, *can't be damaged if I'm going to carry the little sphere.*

Falling downward into sleep.

3.

Rachel's lips were parched, her throat dry. Pins and needles poked at her toes, along the soles of her feet, around her calves. A hand tenderly pressed against the back of her head, raising it slightly. She opened her eyes.

To see.

Mrs. Deerfield's face. Dim and flickering like candlelight. The old woman's face was flat and empty, a pie crust of a face, but kind and colorless, with her translucent eyes looking right into Rachel, right *through* Rachel. "Don't talk now, dear, just take another sip and you'll be fine." Mrs. Deerfield held a cup to Rachel's lips.

"Bone china," someone giggled from a corner.

Rachel murmured, "More dreamland tea?"

"It's full of veetameens," Mrs. Deerfield said, "some herbs and even a lizard's gland or two. An old recipe passed down through generations."

"You're . . . so . . . funny . . . and . . . I'm sleepy."

"Well, you've been having some bad dreams, dear. You're here in my flat."

"Oh? Oh. Is Hugh here?"

"Honey," a woman said from somewhere nearby, "we are so proud of you." It sounded to Rachel like one of the weird sisters—was it Annie Ralph? But then, *it must be daddy, that's what daddy would say, "We are so proud of you."*

"Daddy?"

Laughter, women's laughter like pattering rain on a rooftop.

Rachel tried lifting her head on her own to look around, but her skull seemed heavy beneath her skin, her neck was pure liquid. She was lying flat somewhere. On the cold tile floor. The opening to the crib nearby, and flickering candlelight from down there, down below. Rachel's whole body was jelly and jam. *"Jellies in those jars,"* Mrs. Deerfield had once said. *"Jams and preserves. Whatever'll keep. Most things* do *keep."*

"Daddy?"

Someone said, "You'd think she'd say 'mommy'—it's not fair, I don't see anything so special about her."

Mrs. Deerfield turned her face away from Rachel. The woman's yellow hair fell across her cheek as she turned. Mrs. Deerfield said, "She's open to the influence, which is more than I can say for some people, Elizabeth Kellogg. Now, one of you get over here and loosen these scarves— you'd think you were tying the Gordian knot here and not just a simple Boy Scout slipknot—yes, right now, do you think she's going to jump up and bite you?"

Scout? Hugh? Rachel's thoughts blended in half sleep. "Did something bite me?" She had no energy, and when she looked at the bone china cup that Mrs. Deerfield held near her chin it didn't look like a cup at all. It was a shallow saucer, a yellowed *bone* saucer with jagged edges around the rim as if it had been sawed from something. *Bone.* "Am I sick, Nanny Deerfield?" Rising into consciousness and nausea.

Mrs. Deerfield returned her gaze down to Rachel. "Bit of fever, dearest, but Nanny Deerfield will make it all better."

"Dream," Rachel murmured, her lips moistened by dreamland tea. Something twisting at her wrists—like copper wire wound around them—and then just a distant throbbing pain. She turned her head to her left and saw Annie Ralph standing there.

"Hi, honey." Annie nodded; she was doing something with Rachel's hand. "Sorry if they were too tight." Annie's face blinked on and off with flickering yellow light. Every inch of the floor was covered with votive candles.

"Dreamland," Rachel sighed.

"Yes, dear."

"Ted—and the children, Jamie, I saw them, I saw them, hanging in—" But even these words made no sense to Rachel, even she didn't know what she was trying to say. More flickering candlelight poured up from the open crib. The clamoring place. The dark hole full of jams and jellies and pickles and preserves and whatever will keep.

Mrs. Deerfield was stroking her forehead with a damp cloth. It felt like ice across her face. "I knew you were sensitive. Would Baron Samedi bring us the right flesh without the right spirit?"

Rachel's throat felt like it was burning, but pleasantly, warm. She wanted to wake up now, but she felt so damn good and pleasant and the weird sisters were being so lovely and sweet she just let this dream continue. *A while longer and then I'll wake up. Hugh? Are-you-there?*

"She's closed her eyes again," Betty Kellogg said.

Annie whispered, "She seems heavier now."

283

Rising up and then falling back, falling into sleep, falling through the floor, falling down into the earth to sleep.

"Be careful putting her in," Mrs. Deerfield said. "Watch your toes there, and be mindful of the candles."

Put me in? Where? "Nanny?" Rachel asked dreamily.

"Yes, dear."

They were carrying her but she didn't have the energy to open her eyes. *They're putting me to bed, that's what she meant.* "Where are we going?"

"I don't like lying, dear, so you should know. I've given you a drug, dear, powerful medicine from an extremely deadly plant, but in a small dose. We're going to put you down in the crib."

"Nice," Rachel replied, "you'll take care of me."

Falling down into sleep, down where the babies play in their nurseries, crying for their mommies.

"Yes, dear, I care about you more than life itself. You and *him.* He's our god, dear, not yet born, once a man, a man of spirit, named Gil DuRaz. He inhabits my sweet fleshling and when he's allowed to grow in your womb, he will be fully born with greater power than, well, either you or I can imagine. He shall be a devourer of human flesh and the spirits of this house shall be released from their cage."

Nice, nice and sleepy, nice and cool and soft down here, darkness like an arm around my waist, like Hugh against my back at night, and candlelight between the eyes of darkness.

Words sinking from Mrs. Deerfield, bobbing and floating like a balloon half filled with helium. "Do not be afraid, my dear, your friend Miss Parker is here to keep you company. Motherhood is a natural part of life, and a part that has been denied you much too long."

A sound like the *clack!* of a mousetrap snapping shut.

4.

In the darkness of sleep she heard voices around her:

Mrs. Deerfield said, "Volunteers?"

"Me first, honey." It was Annie Ralph.

Then Betty. "Well, I've never really disemboweled *anyone before."*

"*Honey, it's like carving a turkey. And if you don't do it now, I'll do it myself.*"

In her dream of absolute darkness, Rachel heard a sound like wet rubber splitting, tearing, and heard a series of thumps, a groan.

"*Dear old Annie, such a trouper. Now dear, by your own hand. Rules are rules, Betty, after all, can't have any living witnesses. Time to join the house with the others.*"

Betty Kellogg said, "*I can't.*"

"*The flesh is weak, yes?*"

"*No, don't—I can do it.*"

"*He wants you to go over, dear. Now.*"

"*I can do it. It's just that it looks awful. All over my hands—Annie's—all over me. The knife.*"

"*It's an apple-coring knife, but it's served other purposes in the past. A little pressure might help, dear.*"

"*Please, don't—it—it hurts, it hurts so much—not like—when you push, don't* push *it against my skin—it hurts—I can—please, it hurts so damn* much, *my stomach, please, no, it's not—*"

"*Pain is brief, dear, but if you think of what the pain is for, well, then. We're born, we live, we die. That's it. Mustn't get sentimental.*"

"*Please, I can do it myself—it's the blade, feels so cold, so damned cold on my stomach, no, don't, I'm not ready, not yet—not yet—God—not—*"

In the dream of candle-lit darkness that Rachel was having, the sound of wet rubber tearing, the sound of boots treading in the mud, the suction of pulling a boot out of the mud, and a whine, almost a scream, coming from beside her and then she thought she heard her little sphere, the one she'd lost last year, weeping in the corner because it was still trying to be born.

THIRTY-EIGHT

BELIEF

Hugh waited in KramerBooks for Rachel for over an hour. Rain splattered across the sidewalks outside, sheets of rain hammering down the darkness beyond the wide windows of the bookstore. He stared out into the rain. The store was packed with people milling around the stacks of trade paperbacks, customers flirting with each other, couples sitting over in the cafe section. Hugh stood alone, staring out through the blurred glass.

Watching.

Hugh knew that Rachel would not be coming. It had been in her voice on the phone. She sounded as if his calling her had repulsed her.

The world is a crazy place.

The bag lady standing in the rain, watching him, only seemed to confirm this opinion.

My God, that crazy woman is patient.

But what if Rachel is in some kind of trouble?

The thought seemed to buzz around his ear, and for a second he thought it was another damn wasp.

Let's Pretend, Hugh, that there's something going on here. You saw the words in blood: HELPRACHEL. Is it some subconscious thing? Do you really think she needs your help? Shit, she's the most self-sufficient person in the world, right? She needs you about as much as she needs a hole in the head.

The bag lady stared through the window at him, unblinking. Hugh felt he'd spent the past hour trying to erase her from the street landscape, trying to see through her, trying to turn her invisible. His head throbbed from a hangover.

But she communicated *with me, somehow, don't know how, but it was as if she refocused my eyes. HELPRACHEL. Scout? You in trouble?*

The bag lady began to look urgent; she stomped her feet in the puddles, sending water splashing up against the storefront.

I'll wait her out. If I have to wait here another hour, I'll do it.

But the woman turned away and began hurrying up Connecticut Avenue in the rain.

Go ahead, wherever the hell you're headed.

But she's headed to my home.

What if there's—Let's Pretend. Rachel is in some kind of danger. You asshole, Hugh, just standing here, you should be home, you should be there with her. She did *sound funny on the phone. Funny and scared the way she was when she lost her baby, why the* fuck *haven't you gone home yet?*

Hugh made his way through the crowd of people at the entrance of KramerBooks; he felt like he was drowning. When he was on the street in the blinding rain, he ran after the bag woman, towards home.

Halfway up the hill he caught up with her. "Wait!"

She turned and glared at him. "You seen the signs! You know you seen the signs! They gonna do it tonight. Ain't no more girls gonna die, and if I gotta do it myself I will, Mr. Big Man, but I can't help your woman if I'm fighting the other one. I ain't God, just old Mattie Peru, flesh and blood and I can only fight one battle at a time!" Her anger seemed to dissolve with the rain, and Hugh realized the woman was crying. "I know what waits for me up to the Screamin' House, and I ain't afraid for *me*. I know the hell I'm headin' for. I know my *crime."* She drew the skull from between the folds of her bags. "This here's my babygirl that those in the house killed, mister, and it was a Mr. Big Man just like you that gave me the seed for my girl and gave my girl the seed for her baby, and now they gonna bring something into the world that don't belong here."

She tossed the skull to him and he instinctively caught it the way he would catch basketballs in college. When he looked back at Mattie, as he held the skull, he saw:

The Old Man, battered, rain washing blood from the jungle of cuts and open wounds. His upper jaw opened and closed mechanically, the lower jaw just hung slack in a pocket of skin. "Hugh! Fuck everything, and get up to that house now! It's too late for me, and they got Ted, they killed him and they filled his body with one of their own, but Rachel! For all the love you have for her, get the fuck up there!"

Hugh glanced down at the skull: it glowed in the slashing rain like a lantern.

And he believed.

He believed the way a man believes when it is four in the morning and the rational world doesn't tell him otherwise. He believed the way a man wakes up when he remembers a smell, wakes up and realizes he has been sleeping, and the smell is fire, and his house is burning. He believed the way a man believes in something when there is nothing else to believe in.

"Rachel," he said.

And he knew it was true. It cut through every ounce of intellect in him, but he knew these visions were real, oh, but God, what if he'd waited too long?

But when have I ever been right before? It's all been delusions, this could be just another one.

And then he thought: *fuck* that.

Knifing through all his thoughts: *Scout, you be safe, I'll come get you.*

"We gotta go *now*." Mattie grabbed his arm. The touch of her hand was like an electric shock, a current ran between them. He heard her voice in his head: *"I am Mattie Peru, and the spirits of this house are evil, and of them, the most powerful and malevolent is called Gil DuRaz, Baron Samedi, the guardian of the dead. He has been both man and demon, and he murdered my daughter."* Interwoven with the sound of her voice, Hugh saw *a fetus with the translucent blue eyes of his own father, the creature he'd seen in the shadows of the vanity.*

"God," Hugh gasped.

Mattie let go of him, and the vision evaporated. "They been waitin' for a long time, and now they got their chance, mister, but we gotta get up there, we just gotta."

THIRTY-NINE

HOUSECLEANING

1.

Rachel awoke because she was having difficulty breathing.
The air was thick with incense: the candles, all around her
like tiny eyes. Mrs. Deerfield was at her legs, massaging
them, but Rachel couldn't feel anyone touching her. Some
kind of shiny grease in Mrs. Deerfield's hands, pressing
down on her legs. Rachel's robe was open. Rachel came in
and out of consciousness, feeling like a tired swimmer,
drowning, going down for the first time, second, third. Her
shoulders were sore, her neck ached. She was in a dark cave
surrounded by candles, a dark cave with Mrs. Deerfield
massaging her legs. Rachel felt her own bones chafing
beneath her breasts, down to her womb. Above her, mushrooms grew from the stone ceiling. *The crib.* The candlelight
cast animated yellow shadows across the etched stone.
Things seemed to move inside there with them. There were
others, faces Rachel could barely make out. Two women
watched Mrs. Deerfield grease Rachel's legs. Annie Ralph
and Betty Kellogg, their faces unmoving, their eyes open
wide. They sat up in the dirt behind Mrs. Deerfield. Rachel
clutched the earth under her fingers; it was moist. Her
fingers clawed at the earth. Hurt, every muscle hurt. Annie
and Betty watched her, unblinking. Shadows danced across
their faces, giving them a semblance of movement, but they
were still.

"Am I dreaming?" Rachel asked Mrs. Deerfield. She
didn't want to look over Mrs. Deerfield's shoulder at Annie,

because just beneath Annie's chin there was an opening into her throat, a jagged but precise cut as if someone had taken a knife . . . *"It's an apple-coring knife . . ."* and the slit began beneath Annie's chin and ran down farther, but Rachel couldn't look, she just couldn't and anyway it would be a dream.

Mrs. Deerfield glanced up from her work. She was wearing her work apron over her jeans and a blue work shirt. She had various gardening tools stuck in the pockets of her apron. "Well, you're up and about, how unexpected of you, dear, and yet not something to fight."

"Is this a dream?"

"Life is but a dream, dear, you just go back to sleep and think of England if you must."

"I've had the worst nightmares." Rachel's fingers in the damp earth floor of the crib, fingers curling into tight claws. She tried to move her legs, to pull back from Mrs. Deerfield, but her legs did not budge. Sleep tugged at her; her mind hurt from being so weary and wanting to fight the tiredness, too.

"About children, dear?"

"Oh, God, about everything, what are you doing?"

"Preparing you, it's a simple procedure, age-old."

Her mind fighting the sleep, retasting dreamland tea in the back of her throat, her throat which felt scarred and numb as if healing from an operation. She wanted to scream, but she had lost her voice, all she could do was whisper. "You poisoned me."

Mrs. Deerfield shook her head. "No, no dear, it's just what I called it, dreamland tea, and it'll make it so you won't hurt. Pain is nothing to be afraid of, really, but you're a weak vessel and the trauma it might cause . . ."

Rachel's head ached from having lifted it. "Are you going to kill me?"

Rachel was standing over her father's hospital bed. Smoke puffed rhythmically from his burst chest, yellow and gray smoke, tickling around Rachel's face. Her father was smoking a Camel, his eyes milky white with cataracts. "We all die, dear, we all must go, but the thing of it is, sweetheart, what's it all for? Is it just to go to dust like all the rest, or did we do it for something? Something bigger than us? Something that we can't even fathom, but we know, dear heart, we know it's for the best? Now that's what I call a sacrifice."

He reached up to her, through the smoke, touched her breasts, and his fingers were wet.

Rachel opened her mouth to scream, but when the smoke cleared, she saw a slender plain woman in a floor-length dress at the end of a long hallway brushing the long golden hair of the little girl from the park, and the girl screamed so that Rachel would not have to, screamed because the woman was brushing her hair too hard, screamed because the woman had a small jagged knife in her other hand and brought it beneath the girl's throat. The boy ran past where Rachel lay, and Rachel tried to call out to him, to tell him it was too late, to not help his sister. "Emmie!" the boy cried, and the woman at the end of the hall turned smiling to him as he ran to her.

"Rachel? Retch?" It was Sassy, leaning over, her hand coming down softly onto Rachel's forehead. "Man, you have got a temperature to beat all. Why didn't you call your old best friend up?"

Rachel said weakly, "Sassy?"

"I got something in my purse for that, you know me, Retch, I always have got something in my purse for these things." And as Sassy turned around to reach into her purse, Rachel began crying because she was so happy that she'd just been sick, that it had all been a dream, and then Sassy turned towards her again and Rachel was more afraid than she'd ever been in her life, because the light was flickering candles, and she held damp earth in her hands, and above her mushrooms grew like stalactites from the cold stone roof of the crib. And when Sassy turned around again, it wasn't the same face, even though it was still Sassy. But Sassy's face was streaked with dried blood, her hair matted down with an enormous gash across her scalp, her eye sockets small and empty.

"This'll do the trick," Sassy said. Her teeth cracked as she smiled, and in her hands was something that looked like a small, small baby.

A small mutilated baby, a baby that was barely more than a sphere.

And it gripped Sassy's fingers and ripped into them.

* * *

"Hush, dear." Mrs. Deerfield wiped her forehead.

Rachel felt like someone was punching her in her eyes with their fists. "Please, please," she whimpered.

"It's what you want," Mrs. Deerfield said. "Nanny Deerfield will take care of it, she'll make it all better." Mrs. Deerfield helped her sit up. "It's a simple procedure, dear, and it's not as unnatural as it may seem, why, doctors do this all the time. We're just vessels for spirit, dear heart, like clay. You are blessed to be the strong vessel that you are. We are all just jars, all jars waiting to be filled, waiting for inspiration." She held Rachel's head up, letting her rest in the crook of her arm. "Just like these little ones, in their jars."

And Rachel saw what appeared to be a dozen or more gallon jars in a circle around her, and in each jar some small fish swimming. *But not fish, not anything as simple as fish, but what in God's name?*

"The legion of unborn, our lord Baron Samedi took them from the fruitful womb and saved them from human decay. And of these he chose one, one child yet to be born, a child taken from a ripe womb. A child conceived in such perversion and corruption, conceived upstairs at the altar of the dark gods. Conceived and torn from its mother——"

Rachel lay in an enormous steel tub, and all around her was screaming, and out the bathroom window was a yellow and red night, burning. Hugh's father gibbered madly in a corner. "You fucking animals, get this over with now!" His pale blue eyes wild and angry. "Right now, you hear me? I am an important man, I have more important things to worry about than this piece of trash."

Mrs. Deerfield held up a small curved blade.

It's an apple-coring knife.

The man with the teeth leaned into the tub towards her, rubbing her stomach. "Flesh always dies, we die so that others will be born. You die for your child."

And his teeth came down for her, and Mrs. Deerfield handed him the blade—coring knife—

And when his face came back from her stomach, it dripped with blood and slivers of skin. He handed the coring knife back to Mrs. Deerfield, and then with both hands brought up the small wriggling creature, so much like a rat whose skin had been ripped off, its veins pulsing on the outside of its body, its small catlike claws snapping at the air, its nose and mouth wart-studded indentations, and its eyes.

Blue eyes.

Blue human eyes.

Large blue human eyes. Something in them so sad, so pitiful, and so hungry.

It opened its eyes and mewled, "Mama."

2.

Hugh put his shoulder against the front door of Draper House. The key turned in the lock, but the door still didn't budge. It was as if some *force* were on the other side, and the more he pressed against it, the more it held its ground. Finally it gave, and he pushed it open, crying out, "Rachel!"

Mattie came in behind him; he rushed up the stairs to their living quarters. Mattie went to the downstairs apartment. The door was ajar. Her trash bags of invisibility rustled as she went quickly over to the crib, but her heart was going *choppity-chop,* and she had to stop and hold herself just beneath her left breast, the pain was so fierce. The apartment was filled with candles, and she tripped over them as she made her way, but the crib was sealed shut with dry plaster. Mattie nestled Nadine's skull in the folds of her trash bags. She got down on her hands and knees and scratched at the solid lid. *Magic Touch is sure to open this, open all things.*

She was about to call upon her powers to open this place, when she heard the man, Hugh, screaming from upstairs. *Help him, and through him, enter the clamoring place. Make the house stop its screamin'.* She pushed herself up from the stone floor and headed back in the direction of the scream.

3.

Hugh cried out when he saw his brother, and although he never enjoyed seeing Ted, it was the fact that his brother did not seem to have any eyes in his sockets that made Hugh scream.

"Hughie!" Ted waved. He stood in front of the back stairs at the vanity. "How's it hanging, baby brother?"

Ted hefted a sledgehammer from one hand to the other. "You really got into this carpentry kick, Hughie, all these tools and junk—the happy homeowner. I just wish you'd been here this morning. Jesus, the Housekeeper is a stern taskmaster. She made me build a wall down there with your stash of bricks and mortar from out back. And then the bitch *killed* me when I was done. Ain't it just like a woman?" Besides the fact that Ted Adair had no eyes, there were other things wrong with the way he looked. His scalp was half torn off so that his hair looked like a toupee hanging down over his right ear, a toupee with a fleshy underside. And all the dried blood running from his chin down across his chest, which had been flayed so that the skin was peeled back above his stomach. As he spoke he bashed the sledgehammer into the remaining drywall of the vanity, on the bathroom side, knocking a hole the size of a man's fist through it. "Stay away, Hughie, or I'll come take care of you the way a big brother should. Like father like son, you know, the Old Man went and hammered himself just like he was a fucking nail, a fucking nail, bro."

"Oh, God, what have you done with *Rachel?* Where is she?"

"I ain't sayin' yes and I ain't sayin' no, I'm just sayin' maybe."

"What the hell are—"

"I ain't sayin' yes."

"She's down there, let me—"

"And I ain't sayin' no."

"What *are* you?"

"You know how blood coagulates? Well, I just sort of coagulated here in this house, baby brother Hughie, it just all came together for me here." The sledgehammer whistled through the air. "What do you think a skull looks like when you knock it back with one of these babies?" Ted stood above Hugh, bringing the sledgehammer above his head. Both hands gripping the handle.

Hugh grabbed one of the loose bricks and pitched it up at Ted. He shut his eyes for a second, terrified to look. He rolled over to avoid the hammer coming down. A sound like rotten fruit *smushing*. He glanced up. The brick caught Ted across the teeth—they were broken, Ted's mouth now a ripped, open sore. The hammer slammed into the floor, splintering boards. Getting to his feet, Hugh grabbed the crowbar from amongst the rubble. He brandished it like a sword as he retreated into the turret room, drawing Ted with him.

"I guess you need some taking care of," Ted said, picking the sledgehammer back up, swinging it back as he stepped forward. "This is a sacred place, Hughie. Can't have you desecrating it like you want to—"

"What have you done to Rachel you bastard?" Hugh sliced the crowbar across Ted's face—scraps of skin and blood sprayed from the wound, spattering Hugh's face and hands.

"Nothing you wouldn't do, although maybe you wouldn't. We're just giving her what she wants, we're giving her a baby, a baby among babies, something you're maybe just not *man* enough to give her."

The sledgehammer barely missed Hugh's skull. He was almost to the huge convex window, his knees buckling as the backs of his legs met the window seat. The whole house was vibrating now, shivering as Ted swung the sledgehammer against Hugh's right elbow.

"Shit!" Hugh cried out with pain, clutching his arm as he dropped the crowbar. It rolled beyond his reach.

Ted leered, his face bloody and empty of human life. "I win. Come on, baby brother, let's see what you're made of."

Ted raised the sledgehammer, swinging it in a clean arc, and Hugh was sure it would come down square on his head.

4.

"Can't breathe," Rachel whispered, her voice growing weak.

"It's the candles," Mrs. Deerfield said matter-of-factly. "They'll take the oxygen and then go out one by one. But before that happens, dear, you'll faint, which is good. It serves no purpose for you to see what we are about to do. That's when I will perform the insertion. The unborn child needs to crawl back inside its new mother, with a little help from Nanny Deerfield and her tools of the trade." She held up the coring knife. Its curved blade caught the flickering light. "And then, deprived of air, you will die here in the darkness. But we will keep your flesh and blood alive. We need your womb, for within it the fruit shall ripen. Like my mulch pile, dear, your flesh will be ever so much more useful here in the crib with us than it would be if you just die the way all other flesh does."

Rachel heard the low mewling of the *thing*, the unborn child. She glanced in the direction of the sound. It had furrowed its way into the opening of skin just beneath Annie Ralph's left breast and was devouring what looked like a heart. Rachel's own heart was racing within her, and she wondered if the chill that had suddenly descended within her was a sign of shock. *It's all a nightmare, wake up, for God's sake, somebody wake me up! Please Hugh, wake me up now, let it all never have happened, let it be dreamland tea, let it not be so real!* "Please," she whispered.

Mrs. Deerfield sat back on her haunches. "And when he is ready to come into the world of death and pain, fully formed, he will devour flesh and avenge the wrongs done to those who clamor here in their cages yearning to be free." She sighed, rubbing Rachel's knees. "Yes, well, a place for everything and everything in its place."

The fetuses within the mason jars began bobbing frantically to the surface, their formless heads poking upwards as their paws pressed frantically against the curved glass.

Rachel was not sure if she dreamed or actually heard the voice screaming, but it sounded like Hugh, and it sounded nearby.

5.

Hugh thought, *This is it, old boy, when he swings that hammer down again there won't be another chance.* The pain in his right arm was enormous, and he knew the sledgehammer had shattered his bones. *You just gonna sit here and let him break you bone by bone?*

Ted was grinning his empty-mouthed grin, the skin around his eye sockets crinkling as if he were squinting to see better. "I'm really gonna enjoy this, Hughie, I really am, because I'm gonna go slow, first your right arm, well, next, maybe your left legs, smasherooni, then your left arm, then zigzag back to your right leg. I'd like to start the really delicate operations next, maybe that crowbar you lost, maybe prying your ribs back one at a time." The sledgehammer went up again; Ted's fingers cracked as he clutched it tightly. He held it up and to his right like he was about to swing a baseball bat. "Batter-batter-batter—suh-*wing!*" he shouted, bringing the hammer down. As the mallet hit the window seat, Hugh rolled to the floor, grabbing for Ted's leg.

Ted dropped to his knees, off balance. He dropped to the floor, bringing the sledgehammer down in a smooth line into his own left hip. Hugh was up quickly, grabbing the hammer from his brother's hand.

Ted stared down at his fragmented and useless hip. "I ain't sayin' yes."

Hugh closed his eyes, fighting back tears, and smashed the sledgehammer against the side of Ted's skull.

Even then the battered corpse tried to move, tried to crawl after Hugh as he ran back towards the vanity and the stairway.

"Rachel," Hugh gasped, pain shooting through his right arm; in his left, he swung the sledgehammer.

Just as he reached the stairs, something grabbed him on the right arm, and he saw white flashes as pain shot through him. He screamed, turning around.

Hundreds of wasps formed a burning tower, humming and chewing, climbing one over the other, as if forming a long nest, and then the wasps widened and flattened. A streak of flame ran down the center of the wasp column, and they burned away.

Standing before him, emerging from what had been wasps, was Mattie, holding her daughter's skull up before her, triumphant. "This is the *hounfour*, but beneath it, down *there*, is the cage of the dark spirits. The Housekeeper has sealed herself in with Rachel, and the unborn creature." Overlaid on Mattie's face was another, one Hugh didn't recognize. It was the face of a young girl, gaunt and feverish, with large pale eyes and coffee skin.

"We will stop my child from being born," the girl said.

6.

RACHEL!

Was the voice in her mind? It sounded like Hugh. *God, where are you, Hugh? Are you there? Hugh?*

But all she could see through her watery eyes was the shining of the curved blade in Mrs. Deerfield's hand, and she knew what Mrs. Deerfield would do with the knife. Rachel tried to lift herself up farther on her elbows, but her legs were paralyzed from the drug, and her arms ached with the effort. Mrs. Deerfield was speaking in some language she could not understand, going into some kind of trance.

"Hugh," Rachel mouthed, but no sound came from her throat.

Something pounded against one wall of the crib.

7.

When Hugh and Mattie had rushed through the vanity, down the steps to the crib, they were met with a brick wall. *Sealed her in. Buried her alive, Jesus.* Hugh swung the sledgehammer back and smashed it against the bricks. The whole house seemed to shake with the impact. "Rachel!" he shouted, the numbing pain shooting up his arms, the pain and something else, something that emanated from Mattie as she touched his shoulder, something like liquid fire flowing through his arms and into the hammer. A strength he had never had before. The sledgehammer glowed with a yellow green light, and when it smashed into the bricks, the wall began to crumble.

"We will fight spirit with spirit," Mattie growled.

As his hammer broke through the bricks, arms began jutting out to fill the gaps in the wall, long pale white arms, their hands grasping at the hammer.

Hugh drew back as a hand reached for his shirt, tearing it.

"They are the caged, they must be destroyed." Mattie grabbed the sledgehammer from Hugh, and brought it down on one of the outstretched hands. It burst like a blood-engorged mosquito. Then she whacked at another, and the arm went flying. Hugh grabbed one of the arms and twisted it around as if it were in a shoulder socket, and then pulled with all his might; the arm broke off from the brick wall with a sickening crack and fell lifeless to the floor.

8.

Mrs. Deerfield turned back to look in the direction of the crumbling wall. "We'll just have to hurry this along. I guess you won't have time to die peacefully, my dear, and I do apologize."

Rachel used every ounce of strength that was left in her, lifting herself up on her elbows. The jars of fetuses glowed nearby, and she stretched her arm out to grab at one, knocking it over. The alcohol spilled out, and the fetus fell to the ground, flapping its useless arms.

A dream. A nightmare. Can't be happening.

Mrs. Deerfield screeched, "What are you doing? My dear sweet babies!" She leaned forward and slapped Rachel hard on the side of the face, and Rachel felt herself passing out.

Don't lose it, not now, Scout, Hugh is almost here, don't go off to dreamland. Let's Pretend you're strong. Let's Pretend you can beat this thing, that you can do something to keep her and that thing *away from you. All right, you can't move your legs, but your arms still work, maybe if you lean forward, maybe you can at least get the knife.* She tried to sit up farther but could not. Mrs. Deerfield turned towards

Annie Ralph's corpse. The creature with the blue eyes was still sucking on the dead woman's internal organs.

"My sweet, my darling," Mrs. Deerfield said, plucking the thing out of the chest cavity. The fetus was soaked with dark blood, its small pink tongue slurping noisily as if trying to nurse.

Rachel felt across to the fallen mason jar. The fetus had stopped floundering in the earth, and Rachel touched the jar. A weapon. *No strength, oh, God, I'll never be able to do it. But I won't die, I won't die here like this, not like this, not in this nightmare.* She felt as if she were having a heart attack as she tried to lift the jar but couldn't. It was too much. *I'm going to die. No, I won't.* A fragment of broken glass at the jar's edge. She cut her finger across it, but barely felt the pain. *Only weapon, the only weapon, broken glass.*

She clutched the shard of glass in her hand.

Mrs. Deerfield turned back to Rachel. In her hands was the creature, its mitts sprouting claws that clacked together as if it were eager to crawl inside its new mother. The thing was small, barely larger than a fist, but it was so unspeakably perverted with its blue eyes and its wart-filled mouth with a small ridge of spiky teeth just beneath its tongue, its veins on the outside of its sallow body pulsing with just-drunk blood. Mrs. Deerfield brought it close up to Rachel's face, and the thing said to Rachel with her father's voice, *"I'm so fucking proud of you, Scout."*

Like a streak of lightning, adrenaline pumped through her as she smelled the creature's foul breath, and she brought her fist up, opening it, jabbing down into the soft flesh at the creature's head. It cried out like a baby in pain. The fetus scrambled out of Mrs. Deerfield's arms and landed on Rachel's neck, snapping its mouth open and closed while it bawled, trying to reach up with its claws to pull the glass out.

So you can be hurt. *Good, at least I can die knowing I hurt you.* Rachel closed her eyes, all energy drained. *Let me die now, let me die, let me out of this body.*

The creature slid like gelatin off her neck, crawling around to her ear. "You'll burn for this, you fucking cunt." Now it spoke with Ted's voice, and Rachel opened her eyes again. She felt its razor claws on the side of her face. "I'm gonna get

inside you and eat my way out, and you're gonna be alive for
it, too, you're gonna feel it, mother, you're gonna *feel* it."

Mrs. Deerfield lifted the knife above Rachel's stomach
and said, "You *bitch*, what kind of mother *are* you, anyway?"
A shaft of light cut through the flickering darkness.

9.

The arms and hands had fallen to the ground at Hugh's feet;
when he looked at them again, they were the rotted bodies of
rats with hundreds of roaches chewing at their festering
wounds.
"Quick," Mattie said, pressing forward.
Hugh pulled at the remaining loose bricks in the wall,
making a space just large enough to squeeze through.

10.

Mattie felt the *chop-chop-chop* of her heart as she crouched
low, following the man into the crib. *Nadine, be with me,
child, make me live long enough to stop the house from
screamin'.* She could taste a blood memory in the back of
her throat, her own child's blood which she'd tasted that
night so many years ago.

11.

As if the light that flooded the crib carried with it some
source of power, Rachel felt the needle prick of *feeling*
coursing through her arms, and even slightly in her legs. An
almost welcome soreness soaked through her, and she began
coughing. *It's air, there's air in here now, I can* breathe.
Above her, Mrs. Deerfield plunged the coring knife down
to open her stomach up; but Rachel rolled to the left, and
the knife sank into the damp earth. Mrs. Deerfield, off
balance, fell to her side, shrieking, knocking candles over.

The creature scampered over Rachel's belly; she felt its razor claws raking across her; but then it landed in the dirt and scuffled around making mewling noises.

Then she saw it move back towards her, to her face.

Rachel was looking directly into the eyes of the fetus. Its blue eyes scowled at her, and she almost felt sorry for it with the piece of glass still protruding from its scalp. Rachel crawled backwards, farther into a dark corner, away from the creature and Mrs. Deerfield.

Mrs. Deerfield ignored her, turning in the direction of the shaft of light. And in the light, two blue shadows.

"Now," the creature growled at Rachel, its head shivering. "Now, mother, I will open you up."

Rachel gasped when she saw what was in its small claws.

The coring knife that Mrs. Deerfield had dropped in the dirt.

12.

What Hugh saw when he bent down to go into the crib:

First, a circle of jars and a hundred or more candles. And in each jar, a fetus moving in slow motion through a watery solution.

But then each fetus began to grow, stretching out to the full size of the jars, and then the jars cracked as the fetuses grew larger, forming like clay into human flesh. On one side of him stood two children, a boy and a girl, which he could not possibly know were James and Emmie Standish. Their skin fell from their faces, their bodies ragged with scars. "Please help us find our mother," the girl said. She reached out imploringly to Hugh. Another fetus had grown tall and wide, and was the Old Man. "Hugh," he said, "you fucking son-of-a-whore, why don't you just let us have her, she was unfaithful to you, she fucked your brother."

And Ted was there, too, his head smashed in. "Yeah, Hughie, she seduced me, man, she was so damn hot for me I couldn't resist, although, you know, I tried to. I really tried. So let 'em fuck with her, she's nothing but a cunt."

"Just a cooze like your black whore friend," the Old Man wheezed.

303

Mattie stepped out from behind Hugh. "Nadine," she said through clenched teeth. She reached into her trash bags and withdrew her daughter's skull. She held it in front of her, and dropped it at the children's feet. An invisible wind lifted the skull up.

For a second, Hugh saw Mattie's daughter standing there, naked, and then it was no girl at all, but a column of wasps forming a young woman's body. It stepped towards the children, knocking over more candles. A column of fire tore up the wasp legs, and the whole body glowed with a blue yellow flame. The little boy backed away from the wasps, but the wasp arm reached out and flicked some of the burning insects onto his scalp. The fire spread from his hair down around his face and he screamed; his sister tried to put them out with her hands. The Old Man stepped forward and grabbed the sledgehammer from Hugh's fingers, but Hugh tugged it back and swung it around against the Old Man's chest.

From behind the burning children, Mrs. Deerfield emerged.

13.

"Mambo whore, you are too weak, your heart," Mrs. Deerfield said, lifting her hand to her own breast.

Mattie felt the *choppity-chop* of the ax in her heart, and the pain was hot like the growing fire that surrounded them. She tried to call the wasps up, tried to call up the Magic Touch, but her energy was dissipating. Hugh was swinging his sledgehammer across the burning line of apparitions. Mattie knew she would die here. *One last prayer, Nadine, one last prayer.*

"Your heart is breaking down, whore. I will slice it with my fingernail and swallow it while it still beats." Mrs. Deerfield reached over and grabbed beneath Mattie's trashbags, for the place where her heart beat.

Getting weaker.

She reached up with all her strength, bringing her trash bags down around Mrs. Deerfield's face.

Mrs. Deerfield laughed. "Can I die twice, then? Three

times? Do you think that this flesh matters? I am the Housekeeper. I am here with those who clamor."

Mattie felt the woman's fingers pressing into her skin, *under* her skin, along her ribs.

One last prayer, Nadine.

Choppity-chop-chop-chop.

I will join you, daughter. I will be with you, but one . . . last . . .

"Die *now*, whore," Mrs. Deerfield said through the smothering trash bags that Mattie kept hooked around her head.

Mrs. Deerfield plucked the beating heart from Mattie's body and with her fingers squeezed it until it burst like ripe fruit.

14.

The fetus jabbed the coring knife into Rachel's shoulder. "I'll find a way to get inside you, mother, and then we will be together for a long time, another four months should do the trick."

Rachel shrieked as the searing pain went through her.

The creature lifted the knife again with both its mitts. She reached up and grabbed it even while it sliced her hand.

To her left she saw a wall of cool blue flame, and beyond it, shadows flickering.

15.

Mattie, dying, dropped her arms from around Mrs. Deerfield's face, and the trash bags fell to the ground which writhed with flames.

Mrs. Deerfield brought the dripping heart up to her mouth. She bit down on it.

Mattie Peru's corpse stood, quivering, staring.

From Mattie's mouth came Nadine's voice.

"Spirit cannot exist without flesh. It is your cage and I will free you, Housekeeper."

The heart in Mrs. Deerfield's mouth burst again with life,

becoming a nest of burning wasps, and they dropped down her throat, stinging and biting as they went chewing into her skin. Mrs. Deerfield's cry of rage sounded like that of a tortured animal as the wasps ate through her.

Within a few seconds, the insects had left nothing but smoldering bones.

16.

Rachel struggled with the creature. The coring knife flew out of her hand as she pulled it from the monster's grasp. The creature began crawling down her breasts, towards her stomach. It felt cold and wet as it trailed down her body.

"Rachel!" Hugh's voice cut through the fire.

"Mother." The creature turned back to her. Its blue eyes were rimmed with red tears. *Tears of blood.* Rachel's back was sore as if she'd been run over by a truck, but she pulled herself up and brought her hands down on the creature, wringing its neck. Its claws dug into her hands, but the thing was crying out like a baby, *"Mama! Mama!"*

"No!" she keened.

For just a moment, Rachel was lying in bed, holding her baby, a fully-developed sphere in her arms, and she was humming a lullaby to it, but it was crying and she didn't know how to stop it from crying.

"Rachel." Hugh was leaning over her. He put his arms beneath her back, lifting her slightly.

"Hugh?" She looked down at her hands. The *thing* had gotten away. Her hands were streaked with her own blood where it had cut her. "Oh, God, it's still here, Hugh, it's still . . ."

But he was lifting her up, covering her with her own robe as he took her through the crib, dashing back through the wall of flame, and then out of that accursed place.

She did not turn to see if the fetus with the blue eyes followed, but she thought she heard it crying in a corner as tongues of fire shot out of the crib, almost touching her.

THE ANSWERED PRAYER

1.

Hugh carried Rachel up through the house, and then back through the French doors to the patio. He kept her wrapped in her robe; his arms blistered with burns, but were blessedly numb with pain. He knew once the shock wore off he would be clenching his teeth in agony, remembering the sledgehammer slamming into his right arm. But there were worse things than physical pain. He took her through the back gate, leaning her up against the car. Where would they go? What would they run to? But in his mind, just one thought, those words, *help rachel*. It was all he wanted to do. He unlocked her door and opening it, maneuvered her around and in. She held onto him, still feverish, still fighting to stay conscious. Then he went around to his side of the car and got in. He stuck the key into the ignition and turned it hard. Nothing. The car would not start.

Rachel clutched his arm. "Hugh, look—" She pointed up to the second-story window. But there was nothing there. "I thought I saw something, I thought I saw that *thing.*"

Hugh kissed her tear-streaked face. "It's gone, we're safe."

"Let's get out of here, please," she murmured.

"Won't start." Hugh turned the key once, twice, cursing.

"I know I saw it," she said, *"look."*

Hugh glanced up to where she pointed, the French doors. For just a second he thought he saw a flash of movement, but it was red and yellow, and he realized the fire had spread to the upper story.

"Our house," Rachel gasped, but sounded like she was recoiling from the thought.

Hugh finally got the car started, putting it in reverse. "Let it burn, let it just burn."

He backed quickly out of the alley.

Rachel said, "Where are we——"

"I want to get you to an emergency room first. Then . . ." But he didn't know what to say next. He didn't know what would come next.

"Everything hurts, God, my arms, my legs."

"The burns aren't bad."

"The house, the spirits in the house, wanted me, wanted to put that *thing . . .*"

"They're destroyed, Scout, no more fears."

"It was . . ." Rachel tried to find the word, but there was no word.

"It was hell. Plain hell." Hugh turned the car onto Connecticut Avenue. He would drive until they were at the hospital and he would carry her inside and he would do whatever he could to stop Rachel from hurting ever again.

2.

The fire in Draper House died of its own accord. It *had* spread to the second floor, riding the narrow staircase up from the crib through the vanity, and then consuming the wallpaper down the hallway and the drapes, until it finally came to the living room. The photographs that Hugh had taken years ago, of scenery and of a younger Rachel, were consumed in the spreading fire, along with the furniture, the plants. The walls blackened but did not fall. And there it had died as if the air outside the crib was not fine enough to keep it burning. Neighbors had called the fire department, who came and put out what was left of the flames.

One fireman swore to his buddies that a dozen or more rats swarmed up from the downstairs, out into the alley, the lamplight shining on their backs. And what he saw one rat carrying between its jaws terrified him, for it looked like a tiny child, or a skinless animal that lived in the dark, a pink creature with blue eyes, its mouth opened in a scream while the rat shook it between its jaws.

But the man had seen this through smoke and shadows and when he told his friends, they laughed at his imagination.

3.

Almost a year later, in the suburbs of northern Virginia, in a house that had been built in the 1970s and had no history of malevolence other than the rumor that the last owner had perhaps drunk just one beer too many at the local barbecues, Rachel would lie awake at night thinking she heard Mrs. Deerfield singing lullabies to the *thing*. And she would scream, because it still frightened her and she knew it would for a long time to come.

"Scout?" Hugh reached over and hugged her close to him.

"Sorry."

"It's all right. Was it bad?"

"Same old same old."

"Let's Pretend, Scout, that we banished them, banished them forever. We sent them back to their cages, we threw the key away. We vanquished the foe."

"I'm still afraid."

"It comes and goes."

"I love you."

"Well, that's news to me."

"What if we went back? Hugh?"

"Never."

"Good. I never want to, either. I know it's just a house. But there's still the chance . . . *it's* still there."

"No, it's gone. And no one will ever live in that place again."

"I just wish my dreams weren't so bad."

"Well, I can tell you a bedtime story, Scout. You and the lumpkin." She felt his hand patting her stomach which had grown slightly in the past month. She knew that her baby would be healthy, that what was growing inside her was untouched by the abomination in Draper House. It just felt right. If she was sensitive at all to things, if she had any sixth sense about what was right and what was wrong, she knew her baby was *right*.

"So let's hear it." She put her hand over his as he rubbed her stomach gently.

And his stories all began the same, which is why she liked them, and sometimes they made her cry because his stories were so much sweeter than the way the world could ever be again. He would say, "Let's Pretend," and his voice would be soft and his story would be hopeful. Then she would drift off into a peaceful sleep of sweet dreams for at least that night.

4.

From *Diaries of an Innocent Age* by Verena Standish:

. . . One can never put such an event completely behind oneself. I carry the horror and the sadness within me even as I put pen to paper. But life takes over and years pass, and memories become less vivid. Their power to disturb loses some of its hold.

Draper House exists still at the border of Winthrop Park in Washington. It remains as cold and hard as the stone from which it is made. It is my fervent prayer that this cursed house of evil shall stand cold and hard and empty until the day of judgement when it shall be cast into the flames . . .